No Ordinary Vengeance

Looking Beyond the Ordinary

Book Two

Janee Thompson

First paperback edition October 2021

Book design by Benedicta Buatsie

Edited by Megan Joseph at Joseph Editorial Services

ISBN: 978-1-7345264-2-4 (paperback)
ISBN: 978-1-7345264-3-1 (ebook)

Find out more at www.booksbyjanee.com

Author Note/Trigger Warning

This novel explores topics around family, teen sex, physical and sexual abuse, mental health crisis, and healing. **Due to content (strong language and mature subject matter), this upper young adult novel is strongly recommended for ages sixteen and older.**

Acknowledgements

First and foremost, thank you to my husband Michael for listening to me read this out loud to you and for always being my thought partner. Mom, thank you for being my critical eye and honest critique. Thank you to Shania and Ahyanna, two of my students, for inspiring me to publish this series and your excitement about the first and second installments. Shout out to Audra Russell who has supported me in every way on social media and just being an amazing friend. Huge thanks to my editor Megan for your candidness and vulnerability, helping me to appreciate this book more than I ever have. Thank you to all who have purchased a copy and supported book one. Family members, friends, coworkers, beta readers, and social media supporters and finally, my indie social media friends, thank you. This second book was not possible without any of you.

Chapter One

Point of View: Jade Williams

RECAP

*Just breathe. Breathe, Jade. We won't die here. We **can't** die here. Not unless we fight.*

"Aye!" a jarring voice called from the backseat above, rattling my teeth. "Say one word, and I'll shoot both of y'all. Now when we leave this mothafucka, you don't move, you don't look out this window. We got a long ride."

Mmm. Just when I thought I couldn't tremble any harder, his voice echoed off the truck windows, and then silence stole the show other than our occasional breathing in this sliver of space. A new guest, a shotgun, crept between the headrests and pointed right at our skulls.

"Put your head down! Don't look at me, either!" he screamed.

The cool metal of the gun's barrel pushed my temple, forcing me to follow his command. Unfortunately, it was there to stay.

"We good to go y'all. Let's move!"

Without another word, the SUV sped away in a screeching flurry. My chin settled on my chest as far as it could go. Fingers wiggled, but no sensation as my wrists settled behind me. The truck smacked potholes every chance it got, causing my butt to jump and pound back down on the trunk floor. So much so, I was afraid the gun would fire.

This was the kind of shit you only see on crime shows or read about on Twitter. Stories about how young girls go missing after they messed around with the wrong guys and end up getting pushed through sex trafficking operations. Or how girls randomly got snatched off the sidewalks from men in scary white vans and never heard from again while their "Have you seen me?" faces sat taped on boards at Walmart or on street poles of busy cities.

As we sped off, I whimpered. My face could *not* be labeled as *missing*.

"Didn't I tell you to shut the hell up?" the faceless guy roared and shoved the gun at my head again, this time, much rougher than the last.

I sniffed, sucking in the only air left back here and held it in my chest.

How the hell did I get here? Me? Jade Williams? I was once the teen celebrity dance phenom, flyest girl at school, fashion guru, two-time cheerleading captain, and the bitch everyone respected all up and through Crenshaw's hallways! Being flashy, arrogant, popular, rich, and self-serving without consequence was what many girls deeply envied me for. They wanted that privilege. That clout. And I flaunted it any chance I got. So never in a million years did I ever think I'd be held hostage with Crenshaw High's biggest, most bullied outcast: *Jarell Hendricks*!

But this was reality. Jarell Hendricks was my *boyfriend.* And everyone hated it.

As the pain trickled from my neck and shoulders down to my mid back from sitting so rigid with that pocket of air still lodged in my chest, I glared at the only thing I could see, which had fallen from my pocket just minutes ago: Jarell's latest gift he endowed to me. An original origami masterpiece created with his skilled hands and sightless eyes of my silhouette that represented the real me. The true beauty I felt inside, unlike the fake ass image I created and forced everyone else to internalize over the last four high school years.

But none of that mattered. Jarell's last question to me lingered in my mind… pressed on my heart more than anything. He had asked, *"Was it worth it? Was being with me worth all this trouble?"*

We weren't being treated this way because everyone hated us being together… was it? Two grown eighteen-year-olds minding their own business? Why would anyone care about us being together this much to the point of such extreme measures?

And… was Jarell worth it?

I almost drowned three days ago trying to save him after some asshole Sophomore pushed him in a pool in gym class to be funny, resulting in days at the hospital. All loyal ties with my former school crew D-Block, an exclusive group of bullying juniors and seniors, had been severed after two brutal fights Jarell won against two of its popular members, Marcus and Martell. Particularly when I defended his actions in public, a move that guaranteed ex-communication from the friend group. My man hoe ex-boyfriend Mike Harrison wasn't gonna look my way either after Jarell put him in his place. I lost a bond with my mom, who hated me for dating Jarell, and she had harassed him, and pushed him to the brink of a suicide attempt. All this within six months. And ultimately, I somehow still felt like Jarell was everything to me and if he died, I'd die with him on this journey to wherever we were going.

Damn man. This *couldn't* be because of us being together. This had to be karma for being a D-Block bully and such a bitch to everyone before Jarell came through and changed me for the better. Someone had to be coming for my neck. If so, I just prayed vengeance came for our abductors the way it had come for me. Hopefully, without Jarell being an unintended target the way he was an unintended target in everyone else's bullshit his entire life. If that wasn't it, then … why?

Chapter Two

Point of View: Jade Williams

How did Jarell *ever* get accustomed to the presence of a gun?

I never had a gun pointed at me before today, but he did. Almost every day at one point in his life. Its authority alone scorched my skin in a slow burn, so there was no way in hell I would ever want to experience its blast.

Just don't look up, Jade. Don't. Look. Up…

"Get the fuck on the ground! Get down! Don't move or I'll cap your ass!"

Screaming like someone ripped my limbs apart, I fell to my knees with shaky hands as a huge guy in a full black mask pointed a long gun at my chest.

Two more masked guys rushed out of a black truck ahead with what looked like Uzis and pointed them at Jarell.

"Please don't shoot!" I shrieked, ducking my head and taking cover with my arms. "What do you want from us?"

"Shut up." Without warning, one of the guys gripped my hair with a relentless fist, pulling me up from the ground. Yelping, my hands shot up in reflex, digging my nails into him in hopes of him letting go.

He pried my hands away and forced them behind my back, tying them with brutal tightness and threw me into the trunk.

"Jarell! Please don't hurt him! Please!"

I kept crying out for them to not do anything to him, but the two guys in the masks circled around Jarell with their guns pointed at him.

"If you try to run, I swear I'm going to blow your fucking head off!"

I stifled another cry. I prayed for this scenario to stop replaying for however long we were gonna be here, but I was betrayed. When my mind wasn't screwing me with flashbacks, it ran sprints about who. Who could've found us this late at night in such a secluded area of the park? Were we followed or watched the whole time?

The guessing was for naught. I just wanted to know...

Was doing all of this that serious?

Over time, I built enough courage to stop trembling like I was in somebody's tundra to look at Jarell whose chin still sat on his chest while his eyes remained closed. Like, sleep shut. *NAH*... he couldn't be sleep when all this was going down! We had to get out of here! Now!

I bumped my leg against his without alerting Sir Shotgun, but Jarell didn't budge. This time, I pretended to stretch, bumping him in the process again, but no response. No movement, no head raise, no nothing. *Was he ignoring me? Did he even realize I was trying to get his attention?*

More and more time passed driving and now, my bladder was ready to explode. The further we got from LA, the more the tears poured and the more effort I had to put in to make sure my cries were without sound. No one had any way to track and find us since right before we left, they had ransacked our pockets, and one of them took my phone and smashed it with a bat next to our picnic blanket.

We never stopped either, except for one time, but I couldn't even look out to see what for because the gun never left our presence. Like Sir Shotgun had waited his whole life to do this one task right to prove his worth of existing. Stupid ass.

"A'ight we here. Get 'em inside," one of the guys blurted when the truck came to another complete stop.

Shuffling from the front seats took over until three doors opened and then shut. When the trunk flew open, two other men from a second SUV ahead stormed to us, still dressed in their black masks. The smaller of the two snatched me by the hair, and the larger guy grabbed Jarell's leg and dragged him out, causing his head to slam against the edge of the trunk.

"Oh my God, Jarell!" I sobbed.

"Shut up!" Sir Hair Snatcher growled and thrust a pistol at my temple. My mouth snapped shut as my lip quivered.

Flickering the blur from my tears away to survey the scene, a boarded up, abandoned building encased by the woods was the only view. The air blew different than the balmy night winds of LA, but it was too dark to get a good sense of our true location. The only light provided was the moon reflecting off broken glass bottles scattered in the gravel walkway.

"Get a fuckin' move on, pussy ass nigga! Let's go!" Sir Shotgun shouted as multiple men pushed a woozy Jarell and me towards the building as we stumbled over our feet. The larger guys had Jarell's forearms vise gripped with no sign of easing up, and a third guy pointed an Uzi at his back. Sir Hair Snatcher, who escorted me, squeezed my neck so tight, I might bleed.

Jarell and I reached the destination, and the biggest guy of them all opened the building. Our escorts pushed us inside and to the ground like we were rotten trash.

"Where the hell you think you going?" Sir Hair Snatcher asked the second he noticed me scooting away from impending harm and dragged me back. "Get yo' ass over here."

"Let me go!" I screamed, aiming my heel boot for his balls, but to no avail. Instead, his hand met the side of my face with a vicious blow like he released all his frustrations. My life lights dimmed as I twisted to the ground, cheek planting on the wooden floor.

"Who the hell are y'all, anyway? Don't touch me!"

When my head stopped spinning, three of the guys wrestled with Jarell to tame him while Jarell shouted obscenities. He was putting up a pretty good fight too with just his feet alone until Sir Shotgun pistol whipped him right in the gut. Jarell yelped out and sunk into a partial fetal position.

My God.

"Get him and her crybaby ass downstairs. Tie 'em up to the wooden chairs. Tight. Move it!"

It was like clockwork. A drill sergeant activity. Jarell's respective men lugged him away as Sir Hair Snatcher took hold of my locks again without mercy and forced me towards the steps of the cellar. Didn't know men could be such pussies by grabbing hair all the time.

"Let me go! I'm not going!" I shrieked, twisting and writhing, jerking and digging my boot heels in as they screeched across the floor. What I look like being found dead in someone's dungeon because of someone else's problem with us that didn't need to exist?

"Shut up and stand still!" Hair Snatcher roared, yanking my head back and forth, giving me whiplash.

"Bro, you can't handle that sissy bitch on your own? Weak ass." One of them laughed after straining to stand Jarell straight with the help of two others after he refused to walk down the steps by sinking to his knees.

Hair Snatcher smacked his lips and pointed at Jarell. "Man shut up. Three of y'all can't even get that punk to move!"

"We are right now," he responded and pushed Jarell's back with his gun.

Jesus, my scalp felt like it was lit by a match. I didn't even have the energy to fight back at this point, so down we went. The deeper we got, the stench of sewerage, mildew, and a sack of assholes attacked my nose. I held my breath while just ahead of me, Jarell gagged. I struggled to blink the sight of Jarell getting thrashed by the men away as the taste of bitter iron seeped onto my tongue.

Someone turned the lights on. Brown water stains decorated the walls, and the floor was a grungy cement. No windows were found, and a combination of rust and chipped paint covered the pipes as a slew of mice and cockroaches scattered into the cracks of the walls. My eyes stung. This couldn't be real...

Hair Snatcher tied me up tight to a small wooden chair as two others did the same for Jarell with their guns raised. He grunted and sought to dig his feet into the ground in a last-ditch effort, but he failed. Instead, his head hung, struggling to catch his breath after being jumped. Once tied, everyone moved out the way and to the side while one of the five guys ambled over to Jarell with a long, metal bat in his hand.

My heart sunk to my toes. *Please don't hurt Jarell or beat him with that bat... Not in front of me...*

The other four guys stood nearby with their arms crossed, watching everything unfold like it was some stage play. Instead of keeping my eye on Jarell and awaiting his demise, I observed the four like a hawk, taking note each of their size, demeanor, body language, and skin tones from what I could see through the eye holes of their masks. Best believe they weren't getting away with this alive once I figured out who they were. I swear to God.

The first guy? Hair Snatcher. He looked to be of Asian descent based on general stereotypes and my limited view of his eyes, but I wasn't sure; I ain't wanna make no sweeping assumptions. But what was apparent was his stocky build with an overbearing aura. Like he was trying way too hard to prove something. Short man syndrome. Little bitch.

The second guy was taller and thinner than Hair Snatcher. From the slight drop of honey in his tone around the eyes, he looked to be mixed. He held a tight grip on his pistol as if waiting for a signal to shoot while he stared at Jarell – like he'd been wanting to do it all night and was getting restless.

A tall, burly White guy was next. His piercing blue eyes held a gaze so menacing; he could've drilled a hole in Earth's core with it. His presence was the most domineering from the bunch, and it wasn't some fluke. I damn near cowered at him, and he had barely come in contact with either of us. If I stared long enough, I might become the devil. I shivered and moved on to the last guy.

Sir Shotgun. A tall dark-skinned Black man with thick, protruding muscles where his veins popped out further when he crossed his arms. His gun laid against the brick wall behind him as he looked on with a twinkle in his eyes like he was the proudest father for watching this go down. Easily could've been related to some of the assholes at school.

All of these men were sick. Fuckin' sick. And yet, I still had no clue who they were. Not an ounce.

"I heard you been clowning at school on mothafuckas, Jarell. Pulling knives out on cats in the hallway. Putting people in neck braces after fights and shit. Chokin' niggas out. Ain't that right?" asked the fifth and final guy standing over him as he pointed the bat at Jarell's nose.

This guy was average sized. Not too big and not too little, yet he had the frame of someone much stronger than he looked. Kind of like Jarell. I couldn't see his face since his back faced me, but just by the inflection of his voice, he was Black for sure. Maybe someone we knew, considering he was talking about school.

"I also heard you been messing around with a girl you ain't got no business talking to," he continued.

"The fuck is you talking about?" Jarell huffed.

"Oh, so you just gone play dumb? You gone sit in my face and act like you not out here thinking you some hard ass nigga and that you ain't tryna holla at the bitch sitting right across from you? I oughta bust a cap in your skull right now for acting like some clueless punk," he growled.

"I wouldn't have to beat up niggas if—"

"Shut the fuck up! Didn't nobody tell you to speak!" Sir Shotgun bellowed at Jarell from against the wall.

"Yeah, and if you say something outta turn again, it won't be just you that comes up missing. Believe that," the mixed guy threatened, his finger still shaking on the trigger.

Jarell rolled his eyes and shook his head but wouldn't dare say anything else. Instead, his lips tightened into a mini ball while his nose flared.

"And you… Jade," the fifth guy turned towards me, still gripping on to the handle of the bat.

I swallowed.

"What made you think it was cool to even go running off with a nigga like this? You're outta this mothafucka's league, and because you doing the things you doing with him, you done caused a whole lot a hurt for people."

My eyes squinted. Despite my chest quaking, I couldn't hold my sharp tongue on this one.

"What's this supposed to be about? Last time I checked, none of y'all are my daddy. So, whoever y'all supposed to be and whoever sent y'all dirty asses to get us can take y'all right back."

"Man, see that bitch got a smart mouth. She lucky we ain't here because she's da—" whispered Hair Snatcher, but the mixed guy gave a subtle, yet swift elbow to his ribs.

"Shhh! Talk too much!" mixed guy snarled.

What was that about?

Before I could process, Sir Batman walked up close to me and kneeled to my level. His deep-set, brown eyes held a world of trouble. Without a word, he pointed the bat at my mouth and shoved my head back. The dirt and metal taste leaked right between my lips, giving me a nasty sample I hurried up and spit out.

"You talkin' real, real bold for some little dainty ass female who ain't got a drop of balls to even defend yourself. You better watch your mouth before you become the number one target in this mothafucka."

My upper lip curled the moment the bat left my face. Then, he stood and regathered himself.

"Anyway. Listen. There's a whole lot of payback to be had up in here," Batman started and turned towards Jarell, "and it starts and ends with you. You ain't getting away with everything you pulled at school over the last couple weeks. Got this girl out here drowning for you, you fighting and putting niggas in the hospital over some stupid shit. Ain't no way you ain't making it out without paying the price. So now? Your time is up…"

With a slight jerk of his head, Batman signaled the other four men, they all left the wall and surrounded Jarell, cracking their knuckles.

I damn near soiled myself. If it weren't for my Kegels, I would've. I couldn't even talk. Couldn't even scream. My mouth dropped to do so, but only a soundless squeak had come out. I was not… I could not… watch Jarell suffer anymore. I couldn't even register or think about how these men knew any of what had happened over the last two weeks to try and connect the dots of who they could've been.

"Any last words, punk ass nigga?" Batman asked Jarell.

I couldn't see him at all to get a sense of how scared he felt, but the silence had said enough. You could hear a pin drop down here. And then, a faint sound.

Bzzzz….. Bzzz…. Bzzz….. Bzzz…. Bzzz….. Bzzzz….

"What's that sound?" one of them asked.

"What sound?"

"Shh. Listen."

Bzzzz….. Bzzz…. Bzzz….. Bzzz…. Bzzz….. Bzzzz….

"Sounds like a phone vibrating!" big burly White guy yelled.

"I thought we took care of all that!" Hair Snatcher cried, throwing his arms in the air.

"We did!" the mixed guy whined, defending his partner.

"Shut up." Sir Shotgun pushed Hair Snatcher's face with an open palm. "Dumb asses can never do anything right! You had one job!"

"Where's it coming from?" asked Batman.

"His ankle!" yelled out mixed guy, lifting up Jarell's jeans. "Damn! It's a GPS tracker or monitor!"

I gasped. *Oh God! How could I forget Jarell was on suicide watch and put on GPS alert?*

"SHIT!" they all bellowed in unison.

"How long has it been going off?" asked Batman. "How would that thing even have service or a GPS signal down here?"

"I don't know and don't care, but we gotta get the fuck outta here. Somebody's on their way," Sir Shotgun said and gave direct eye contact with the big, White, burly guy. White guy nodded, and then Sir Shotgun rushed over to the wall to grab his gun.

"Real shit. Let's go," Batman said and each of them sprinted towards the stairs. The only one to stay for a second was Sir Shotgun.

"Don't think this is over... Jarell," he mumbled, and kicked Jarell's chair so hard, he flew towards the wall and fell over. Then, he disappeared up the stairs with the rest, leaving us down here alone.

I let out a rugged cry as the waterworks came on in full effect. Jarell sighed a long one with his forehead planted on the cement floor in defeat. All the while, his ankle brace continued buzzing.

Neither of us said a single word as I wept until my head banged like the loudest trap 808.

Jarell and I had been through too much. For no damn reason.

How much more of this could I take? All of this for just being together? No way. Enough was enough. But I for sure, wasn't gonna give up on finding out who did this. Even if it was the last thing I did in my life.

If we ever got out.

Chapter Three

Point of View: Jade Williams

BANG! BANG! BANG!!!

BANG! BANG! BANG! BANG! BANG! BANG!!!

"Police!! We have a search warrant! Open up!!"

I jumped clean out of my skin as I woke up from a semi slumber to obnoxious pounding on the door from upstairs, right in sync with my excruciating headache. All the tears and hair pulling did a number on me. I worked to regain consciousness before my eyes landed on Jarell who still laid on the floor. But this time, a new small pool of blood surrounded his head underneath him, mixing in with the corroding cement floor.

"Oh my God Jarell. Are you okay?" I asked. His sightless, shaded eyes roamed around the basement.

"I will be when I can get off this floor."

"No, seriously. Are you okay? You know you're bleeding, right?"

"Yeah, but it don't hurt," Jarell said in the blandest voice. I shook my head.

The amount of pain this man could withstand blew my mind. It wasn't normal at all, but never mind that. We had help upstairs, and we needed them down here and fast. They continued banging on the door, all while my heart raced.

"Jarell, how are they gonna get down here? That door is locked, and we're deep in this disgusting place. We're pretty far from the stairs."

"We better start screaming and yelling," Jarell responded. "HEY! DOWN HERE! HELP US!"

Woah. *Jarell could get that loud?* Wait. No time to perseverate in that. I followed suit and pulled an ear shattering scream from my gut. It had to have traveled through the cracks of this nasty place because it resulted in a raw throat, likely to be the only time I screamed like that.

A loud crash and splintering wood suddenly happened as multiple stomping boots roamed all over the top floor with unwavering authority.

"DOWN HERE!" Jarell yelled. "We're down here!"

After a few minutes, the door to the basement thrashed open.

"We're here! Down here!" I screamed this time.

Their steel toed boots boomed down the steps like thunder, and once they turned the corner, four officers dressed in all black with thick, heavy gear, guns, and helmets appeared, searching the area in a hurry.

"It fuckin' stinks down... holy shit," one of them griped under their breath the instant he saw us.

"Anyone else down here?" shouted one of the officers.

"No, it's just us. Please help us," I whined as the water show burst again from my eyes. A mix of joy and angst. "Get us outta here. Please!"

"Alright, ma'am. Alright. It's gonna be okay. We got you," one of them said as he rushed to untie me from the chair.

Two other officers investigated the basement together with their guns drawn as the fourth and final officer tended to Jarell, untying him and helping him to stand. Jarell expressed his gratitude as the officer put what looked to be some tissue or gauze against the side of Jarell's eye. As he did that, more boots trudged upstairs, hollering and probing around the building.

"Ma'am, are you okay? Are you hurt?" The officer who helped me held on to my shoulders and analyzed my body for potential injury.

Hyperventilating, I attempted to answer, but I ended up being a blubbering, stuttering mess.

"Breathe… take a deep breath," the officer coaxed. "Try to breathe for me, okay?"

I took a long inhale, breathing in the stench of the space and coughed it back out. Still, it had helped me enough to speak.

"We just got kidnapped!"

"Are you hurt? Do you know who did it?"

I shook my head. If I was, I didn't feel it. Adrenaline was something serious.

"Alright, well let's get you both upstairs and into a more comfortable space. You're going to be taken to the nearest police station, okay? Detectives will interrogate you there, and then we'll have you call someone to pick you up to take you home. We will stay here and continue investigating the building, okay?"

I nodded, and both officers assisted Jarell and I up the stairs and outside. A few police sedans parked right out in the small lot with their blatant red and blue lights flashing in the dark night. I turned my head so they wouldn't blind me as we were led to another car that wasn't a part of the raiding pack. On the side of the vehicle, it read Fresno County underneath the big sheriff letters. *Fresno County?* Why the hell were we that damn far from Los Angeles?

"Are you two alright?" the sheriff asked, standing outside the car, gazing with concern.

Jarell shrugged as the sheriff helped him into the vehicle. In response to his question, I shook my lowered head as my shoulders sunk towards the ground. If those assholes thought they were getting away with this shit…

"Okay. Let's get you outta here so we can figure out what exactly happened," he said. "I know you both have to be freaking out right now. I'm sorry this is happening."

Neither of us said anything as the sheriff took us to the nearest station. Once inside, he had given Jarell and me a small snack, strawberry PopTarts, and then told us we'd be going to separate rooms with a detective. Why the hell did we have to go separate ways? At this point, I just wanted to go home. How we were gonna get there was something I didn't even have brain space to consider.

Now, I sat across from a detective in this small ass room you could hardly breathe in. If nonchalant had a photo, this person would be it. The detective's eyes were close to not even being open as they slouched back in the chair, chewing sluggishly on a piece of gum. They might as well have their leg upon the table with a blunt and some lean.

"Okay, Jade. Tell me what happened. Start from the beginning."

I did. I told them everything. I started by explaining all the instances of relentless bullying Jarell had endured for the last six months to explaining the pool incident. I moved to his suicide attempt at the hospital after my mother's shenanigans, and finally, to how Jarell was put on an ankle monitoring device after becoming an in-patient on suicide watch. I ended by sharing how I took him to the park to get his mind off everything. That was the point at which we had gotten kidnapped.

Whole time? They just nodded, barely even writing anything in their notepad, popping their gum and watching me with lethargic eyes. No questions were asked. Didn't even respond, nothing.

As their lack of effort persisted, I just stormed out and sobbed. *No one seemed to care about either of us.* At first, I was gonna sit in the lobby and sulk in misery alone, but much to my dismay, Jarell was already done and sitting out there. He didn't need to say a word to me. I didn't even want to look at him.

Once Jarell realized it was me bawling, he stood and attempted to approach me, but I turned and dashed to the public bathroom. Punching the door open, I paced back and forth up the aisle with balled fists and heat blowing from my nose until I was calm enough to breathe and lean against the wall.

"Ma'am, are you alright?" In walked a short, rotund White lady with teased hair. A person who worked here.

I gave her a look she buckled at. "No, I'm not okay! Your detective, Jamie Newhouse or whatever their name is, didn't even seem to give a flying fuck about what happened to my boyfriend and me. We got kidnapped for fucks sake. Tied up in a basement with guns pointing at us. Someone needs to act like they care!" I screamed.

"Ma'am, I need you to calm down," she said with her hands out in front of her in caution, but I interrupted.

"No, I don't! I need to be supported by someone who needs to be doing their damn job!"

She stumbled back. "How about we get you a different detective you can speak with, okay? Would that help?"

"As long as they act like they give a damn, I don't care."

"Okay. Hang tight, okay? We'll get another detective, and they'll call you in. In the meantime, try to get yourself together and sit in the lobby, okay? We can't call you in from the bathroom, and they can't interview you when you're riled up like this."

"I'll be out in a second," I mumbled.

She rushed out and I went to the sink. I didn't even wanna look at myself in the mirror. Instead, I ran my hands under cold water and splashed it onto my face. By the time I dried it and walked out, they were already calling my name into a different room with a different detective.

This one was much better. He asked me a ton of helpful questions such as the color and style of the SUV, potential license plate (which I couldn't get), descriptions of the guys, the types of guns, the park we were at, what they had wanted and said, and everything. His questioning was thorough while he took notes and generally seemed interested in doing the job he was paid to do.

Afterwards, he revealed that Jarell's mom was the one to call the police in Los Angeles, suspecting a kidnapping or potential suicide, which prompted the Fresno police department to get involved due to the location of Jarell's monitoring device. He promised he'd follow up with Jarell's mom about any updates since neither Jarell nor myself had phones.

I couldn't thank him enough for his work on this. At least we had somebody doing their part on our behalf. Regardless, I was gonna do my own investigation. If I had flaunted about how I was no one to fuck with over the last four years in the halls of Crenshaw High, they were about to find out now, for sure. Even with just a month left of school. Just wait.

"How are you two getting home? Los Angeles is three hours from here. Is there anyone you know who could come pick you up?" Detective Ryan asked as I leaned back in exhaustion in his chair across from him.

Hmph. No way in hell was I calling Janet Robinson. I could've called my best friend Laurie or my boss Alise, but I honestly didn't want anybody in my business right now who wasn't family. But then, I thought of my stepfather, Corey.

He was the perfect person to pick us up. I always had the softest spot in his heart; I could do no wrong in his eyes. He never pressed on anything that wasn't his business, he wasn't manipulative or vindictive, he was supportive, caring, loyal... all the above. I hated he and my mom's relationship ended, which I still never knew why. One day, I was gonna ask him.

"You can call my stepdad Corey," I said.

"His number?"

I gave the detective his number, and when he picked up, the detective gave Corey information about where we were, why, and that it was an active investigation of which he couldn't divulge much information. Finally, he told Corey he needed to take us home. It was just enough to get Corey worried to drive up here yet keep him from flipping out.

Thank goodness Detective Ryan did that for me. So, once that was taken care of, I went out to the lobby as the sun glimmered unapologetically through the large glass windows, but that didn't stop me from going straight to sleep next to Jarell. It was short-lived though because by the time I got settled, what felt like about an hour, the front door of the station busted open.

"Jade!" Corey rushed to me in panic. Standing up and trying to rub the sleep from my eyes, his towering body encased mine as he hugged me close. The moment I felt his warmth and love, I broke down and sobbed into his stomach. "Talk to me sweetheart. You a'ight?"

I shook my head and angled my head to watch his tawny skin turn beet red.

"What happened? Tell me now. I'll fuck somebody up, real talk. Wass' really up, Jade? You wanna talk about it?" he asked.

Again, I shook my head and put my hands up in a gesture to get him to stop talking.

"Dad, it's okay. They got this handled. I think I'm okay."

He sighed and ran a hand down his bald head.

"I'm so sorry, baby girl. I'm glad you good. Did you talk to your mom about this? Does she have any idea of what's going on? Last time I heard from her, you were at the hospital after nearly drowning. I heard it's going up over what's going on at Crenshaw, and now this. What the hell is going on?"

"I don't wanna talk about it right now. Ma don't know about this whole thing, and I don't want her to know either. Please don't tell her."

"Why? Jade this is something she should know…" he warned.

"Please. I'm begging you not to tell her. There's a huge reason for this. I will tell her, okay? I'll tell her on my own."

He hesitated, throwing me a long side eye.

"Alright. I'll trust you'll do that. What you need *me* to do right now? How can I help?" he asked. "Please tell me something. You got me scared."

"I just need you to take me and my boyfriend to his mom's house," I muttered, pointing to Jarell. "That's all I need right now."

Corey turned his head, and his eyes followed my finger.

"Oh yeah, I remember him. You brought him to your Chris Brown performance in December." He nodded.

"Yeah."

"Everything going okay with you two? I don't have to drop his ass because he ain't treating you right, do I? Does he have anything to do with this situation?" he asked, squinting as his voice got deeper.

"Dad, Jarell's the last person you need to be worrying about." I waved him off. "Can you take us?"

"As long as you're safe and you're alive, I'll do anything," he said, hugging me again.

"Thanks, Dad. Jarell, come on. We're leaving," I called out as I walked towards the exit door.

Without a word, Jarell slogged towards the direction of my voice, maneuvering through the waiting chairs that sometimes got in his way as he ran into a couple of them. Corey frowned, watching Jarell like he was on drugs.

"What's wrong with him?" Corey whispered in my ear.

Pointing at my eyes and shaking my head, I mouthed, "Blind."

"Ohhh. Didn't know you had a blind boyfriend."

"You would've never guessed it either, had I not said anything," I replied.

Once Jarell reached us, he took a deep breath and stuffed his hands in his jean pockets. "Ready."

"A'ight, cool. Your name is?" Corey asked.

"Jarell. You must be her stepdad, Corey."

"That I am." Corey nodded.

"It's nice to meet you," Jarell said and stuck his hand out for Corey to shake. He gladly accepted the gesture.

"Likewise, man. You alright?"

Jarell shrugged. "For now."

"I understand," Corey said and began walking towards his truck. Jarell tailed behind with his head dipped low.

"Dad, I'm gonna crash while we're riding back home. I promise I'll call to update you later, but we both just need rest, okay?" I interjected.

"I'll be looking forward to that call," he said. Ooh. I knew that voice. He wasn't playing.

Once Jarell and I got in the car, Corey turned on some soothing jazz. Gosh, I loved him. He was the best. With that tone set, there was no other option for both Jarell and myself but to fall into somewhat of a peaceful slumber, even though the flashbacks of what happened interfered in the mix. At least for me. But still. It was enough to rest and prepare for the next challenge this day would bring.

Chapter Four

Point of View: Jade Williams

By the time we got to Jarell's mom's house, it was already noon. Even though the three-hour nap was sufficient, I still missed my huge, plush bed over at Janet's place. Ugh. Just the thought of her name damn near made me puke the PopTarts I had eaten at the police station.

I'd seek rest later though. The main objective was getting Jarell home safe because there was no doubt in my mind his mom was going crazy right now.

And so was I. Jarell's suicide attempt happened just a couple days before this kidnapping, and because these idiots tried to kill us, the seriousness of Jarell's mental health situation wouldn't get the level of attention it deserved. It was likely going to get swept aside while we focused on trying to stay safe. Thinking of my role in both situations sank me to an energy level that would need weeks of personal restoration.

We rolled up to Jarell's stucco home, and both of us thanked Corey before we got out the truck. Sure enough, before we could take two steps forward, Jarell's five-year-old sister Kylah came barging out of the front door like she always did when she saw her brother come home.

She gave the biggest smiles. The most exuberant excitement. The warmest hugs. And the most innocent kisses. The sweetest thing. If she wasn't eager to see her brother, I was the second one in line.

"Relly! Relly!!!" Kylah screamed and giggled, hopping up and down in front of him on the sidewalk and patted his legs to be picked up.

"Ahh... baby sis." He swung her up high with a smile and tickled her belly while in his arms.

She squealed and laughed as he hugged her close. Wrapping her arms around his neck, she returned the love.

Jesus.

What would this girl's life be like if Jarell succeeded in taking his own life? If those men had succeeded in killing him?

"Jade!!"

She finally noticed me as she wriggled out of Jarell's hold and ran over to me, hugging my legs. I ruffled her wild, sandy brown hair and squeezed her cheeks with one hand.

"Hey honeybun!" I kneeled to her.

"Where were you? I was waiting all last night and all morning for you and Relly!"

With a guilty look, I shrugged. "We'll talk about that later, okay?"

"Okay."

Kylah put her hand in Jarell's and led him to the door, telling him where to step and what to watch out for. The entire time, Jarell's mom Rachel stood on the porch, bawling her eyes out. Her tattered clothes hung off her increasingly thin body, and her hair was the most unkempt I had ever seen it. I turned away. I couldn't bear it.

The closer Jarell and Kylah got, the more restless she became until she finally broke and rushed to hug him, nearly knocking him over. She was frantic and couldn't even speak.

A hushed sob escaped my lips.

As Ms. Rachel swarmed over him, he stood emotionless and still without a single ounce of care, concern, reassurance, nothing.

"Baby, look at your eye!" Her hands felt all over his face, examining any other potential wound. With a scowl, he gently swiped her hand away. "What happened, Jarell? You do realize you were all the way in Fresno, right? Three hours away! My GPS alert goes off after you guys were at the park around midnight, and then the further away you moved from the city. You both scared the hell outta me! I had to call the police, so start explaining."

Then, her eyes cut towards me. Fuck. How was I supposed to explain this?

"Ma, I don't wanna talk about it right now. I'll update you later," Jarell uttered and tried to walk by her, but she stopped him. I grabbed Kylah and pulled her from the middle of the two and picked up her bike that laid on the lawn nearby.

"Here, ride your bike on the sidewalk, Kylah, okay?" I convinced her, and she accepted with no pushback. She didn't need to be seeing this, anyway. As she rode, practicing her training wheels on the sidewalk and away from the drama, I stood close to keep my eye out on this showdown. It was like I had become invisible to them.

"Oh, hell no, Jarell, you aren't just gonna walk away from me again," his mom threatened, yet Jarell had already scooted around her and made it inside.

Ms. Rachel was right on his heels and slammed the screen door shut. Feeling safe to move, I sat on the porch to listen in.

"You have a whole bandage on your eye that wasn't there yesterday. What the fuck am I supposed to think? I didn't get an ounce of sleep! I had to call the police because after I paid for an Uber and stopped at the park you were at with Jade, your sunglasses, a blanket, and Jade's purse were left behind. I called Jade and her phone goes straight to voicemail, then I saw it got smashed next to the blanket. I knew something wasn't right. Now when the police called me this morning, the only thing they told me was that you're alive and that this 'case' is under active investigation. What case? What happened?"

"Ma, I told you I don't wanna talk about this right now!" Jarell hollered.

"Alright, I'm gonna go ask Jade then."

"Don't try and bring Jade in this! She's tired and I'm tired! Leave us both alone, man."

"Don't yell at me!" she cried. "As a matter of fact, yo' ass need to go to the hospital. Not for one second did I forget you were in the psych ward because you tried to kill yourself. You're going back until we know you're ready to be released!"

"I ain't going nowhere!" Jarell shouted.

"Jarell... I know you better stop yelling at me. Who you think you talkin' to? You need to go back. I don't know who I need to call or who I need to drag yo' ass there, but I'll do it if I have to!"

"I'm eighteen, so it don't even matter. You can't make me do anything. I'm not going back there. End of discussion."

Jarell's room door shut with a boom, and then a loud silence followed. As expected, and before I could even process anything, Jarell's mom stormed out onto the porch. I stood in haste, dusting the dirt off my pants.

"What. Happened." She gazed at me with a rising rage I wanted nothing to do with. "You're all dirty and your hair is a mess, so I know something happened. Don't you fuckin' lie, or else this will be the last time you're on my porch."

Woah. Gulping, I spilled without filter.

"We got kidnapped. I don't know by who, but there were five men. They threatened both of us at the park with a bunch of guns, threw us in the trunk tied up, and took us to some abandoned warehouse. I'm gonna find out who did it, and the police are looking too, but that's all I know."

"Oh my God..." She rubbed her temple. "Are you okay? What did they want?"

"Yeah, I'm okay. My scalp hurts from my hair being pulled so much. I don't know what they wanted. They tried to say it's because of the fights Jarell got into and because they don't like us dating, but I don't believe them. It's gotta be much more. The police came and raided the place, but they weren't able to catch them in time."

She sighed, leaning up against the house, her eyes becoming even redder with tears. I didn't think they could get any redder than they already were.

"But we're okay," I continued. "I'm sorry for taking him to the park. I didn't know that would happen, but I agree with you that Jarell does need to go back to the hospital. Between everything at school, my mom harassing him, and now this situation… this is getting too heavy. For both of us."

She nodded.

"I get it. This is all getting way out of hand. I'm sorry you're getting dragged in this. You've been there for my son when no one else would. I don't know how else to repay you or how else he could repay you."

"There's no need to repay, Ms. Rachel. But listen. I agree with everything you've been saying to Jarell. You think if I talk to him about going back to the hospital, he'll listen?"

She gave me a knowing gaze.

"Jade, you really asking a question like that? It's you. Of course, he'll listen. Or at least he'll hear you out more than he will ever listen to me. That's just the way it is with you kids," she replied.

I took huge inhale. "Alright. I'll shoot my shot. Just give me a second, okay?"

She nodded again with pressed lips. "Thank you. And thank you for watching my baby while I was inside."

"No worries."

I moved past his mom, inside the tiny home, and to Jarell's room. With a hand on the knob, I rested my forehead on his door. What the hell was I gonna do and say? Jarell and I couldn't keep living and operating this way, feeling unsafe and attacked by everyone who disliked our situation. Something had to give.

After giving myself a quick pep talk, I knocked on his door. I was met with silence from the other side. Well. I invited myself in anyway and walked inside his origami wonderland of flowers, birds, animals, and nature. Despite the beauty of his room, he sat on the bed fuming to himself as he faced the door.

"Jarell..." I whispered and stood underneath one of my favorite pieces he created of a stunning, red bird.

He didn't respond. Just turned his head and closed me out. The way he always used to. Hmph. There was no way in hell I was going to take fifty steps back with him. Not after all the hard work I put in to break all those barriers down for him to even just acknowledge me.

"I heard you arguing with your mom," I admitted, wiping my hands down my jeans.

He paused.

"And?" he mocked.

"And..." Oh, the nerves strumming my chest. "I think she's right, Jarell."

"Right about what?"

"About going back to the hospital. I don't think you being out without some sort of high-level monitoring is good for you right now. Not after everything that's happened. I just want you to be safe."

His teeth clenched and his jawbone flared. One thing I vowed to be with Jarell was honest, no matter how difficult. He deserved that.

"All of this... everything happening with us is getting to be too much. You know you can admit to that. From you fighting Martell and Marcus, to me saving you from drowning, from my mom attacking you at the hospital with your suicide attempt to follow, and now this kidnapping... it's a lot. You need to get help, and I need time to just process everything. This is more than I've ever had to carry in my life."

His eyes became slits as he sent a long glare my direction. Ooh. That calmness in his demeanor before the storm was classic Jarell. One of the first things I had learned about him. I braced myself for it.

"Why are you even talking to me about this? You act like that shit's gonna help! Going to the hospital or the psych ward is not gonna erase anything that's happened, so it's a waste of time. You know that! It's better to fuckin' deal with it like I do with everything else and move on. Next topic."

"Just hear me out, Jarell!" I raised my voice too, putting both hands up to get him to calm down. "To be honest, I don't think you've dealt with anything. You're hurting, Jarell. You are. And guess what? What you're going through is affecting me just as much as it's affecting you! I don't want to ever see you the way you were in that hospital again. You gotta get the help you need. As soon as possible. I mean..."

A pall hit the room. When it was quiet for too long while the rest of my sentence blended with the air, my tears dropped onto his carpet with a quiet splash. The more I wiped them away, they came back twice fold. I held my breath, trying not to sniff.

"S-So... so you want me to be locked up in some fuckin' mental institution?" Jarell finally asked in a painful whisper. "Is that what you're asking for me to do? I don't wanna go there, Jade... I don't. It just feels like you and Ma want to just send me away and not even deal with me anymore. It's like ... I feel like you both are calling me insane."

The look he gave. The pleading... the despair... all of it was packed in one lump sum in those damn eyes. I had to turn away before I broke to my knees. As much as I wanted Jarell to be free, out with me, and for us to try and forget all the shit we've faced for the last six months and just try to move on happily ever after, it just...

The last thing I wanted to be in Jarell's life was *someone else* who left him hanging because I couldn't be there for him in the way he needed me to be or because I didn't have the tools necessary to support him. I didn't want to be the next person to do that to him. At all.

"You're not insane or crazy. But please understand. It's not your fault. None of this is. I just don't want to continue being in harm's way because I don't deserve that either," I said and sat down next to him with a hand on his thigh.

"What harm are you experiencing, Jade? What harm are you even talking about?" he asked with his lip curled up.

"The harm of you not listening to me or your mom's advice. Eventually, it's gonna affect our relationship, and we won't be healthy people for each other. Hell, all of this has put me through the ringer in ways you have no clue."

"Give me a clue, then!" he said in a snark tone.

"No because that's not the point of all of this."

"Then, what you tryna say, Jade?"

After he asked, my eyes shifted towards the ground as I let out a huge belly of air, thinking of ways to be concise about how I felt in a way he could digest.

"I mean… I don't know what I'm trying to say other than the fact that everything we've been going through is hurting me, and it's definitely hurting you more. This isn't about me, to be honest. You have to go back to the hospital, Jarell no matter how you feel about it. It's what's best for you."

He turned his head and laughed with scathing sarcasm as he ran a hand through his fade. Once he turned his head towards me again, his entire expression was void of anything close to funny. His face had actually hardened.

"If I go to the psych ward, that means I go away for a while without us seeing each other. And if we're gonna be together, it's either now or never for me, Jade," Jarell said, crossing his arms.

My mouth dropped. "Huh? What's that supposed to mean?" I demanded. I hoped he wasn't referring to what I thought he was talking about. But his silence told me everything.

"Hello?"

And yet, he remained mute.

"See? This is what I mean, Jarell. How in the hell can we be together if the first thought in your mind is to end your life? How are you gonna make room for me when you don't even want to be alive?" I asked as my eyes flooded. "You realize the only reason we were saved was because of that ankle bracelet, right? I want you to listen to your mom and me and go back to the hospital. Or, damn it, at least *go to therapy*."

Jarell blinked, giving me a look like I had told him the sky wasn't blue.

"Are you serious? You're asking me to either go to the hospital or go to therapy?"

I shrugged. "That's what I'm begging you to do because I care about you, and I care about where you end up. Just try it out and s—"

Mid-sentence, Jarell rose up from his bed and stormed towards his bedroom door. I was right on his tail to go after him, but his mom stood dead at the door. Jarell ran right into her, not realizing that she'd be there. I didn't think she'd be there either.

"Ouch," his mother winced as her elbow hit the wall when Jarell's body smacked into her.

"What the..." Jarell started. "Ma?"

With guilt swimming in her eyes, she opened her mouth, stuttering over a few incomprehensible words.

Jarell squinted and asked, "You were eavesdropping?"

"Jarell." Her voice quivered.

"Why would you do that?" he roared, rattling the walls and off in the distance, Kylah began to cry. "Why would you think it's cool to eavesdrop? Why don't you ever respect my damn privacy?"

My heart shot to my throat the moment his mom cringed. She looked like a helpless ragdoll right now, and there was no way I was gonna let Jarell instill fear in her like this.

So, I stepped right in his face.

"Jarell! You need to stop!" I screamed and pushed him in the chest to back off. "This ain't cool!"

Shortly after, Kylah made her way down the bedroom hallway and hugged Ms. Rachel.

"Mommy why is everyone yelling?" she wept.

Rachel bent down to whisper to her that everything would be fine. After running a quick hand through her wispy curls, she kissed Kylah's forehead and told her to go play in her room. A different emotion rose in Jarell's eyes as Kylah cried. It weighed on him to the point of turning his back and pressing his forehead against the wall.

Once Kylah walked away with hesitation after giving a long, concerned glare at Jarell, his mom spoke.

"Jarell, I'm not sorry. This is my house! We just want you to get better. We want you to be alive and well, baby. Not just for us, but for yourself. Please listen. Please go to therapy," she pleaded.

"Yeah, and I don't like this tag team crap between you two..." he uttered.

I exploded.

"Jarell, cut the crap! Here we are standing here, almost on hands and knees, pleading you to do something that'll help keep you alive, and you're concerned about us 'tag-teaming' you? You for real right now? You got your sister crying, and had you succeeded in killing yourself, she would be the most affected. Please, Jarell. Please just do the right thing!" I shouted and pushed him again. "And while I'm in your life, you're not gonna intimidate your mom. I'm not going for that."

The entire house went quiet other than Kylah's soft sobbing in the back. Then, Rachel shifted her weight, holding onto her elbow.

"Thank you Jade," she spoke. "I'll talk to him from here. Can you check on Kylah for me real quick?"

"Sure thing," I answered, still giving Jarell a death glare I hoped he could feel. Turning on my heels and huffing, I brushed past him, bumping him out of the way and went to Kylah to calm her down.

"Is Relly mad at Mommy?" she asked, as her beautiful, bright grey eyes pierced into mine. She was so beautiful. Poor girl.

"Well… Relly is mad about a lot of things right now, sweetie." I shifted to sit on my knees.

"Why? Relly never gets mad."

"Everyone gets mad sometimes."

"Are you mad at Relly?" she asked.

I nodded.

"Yeah. Yeah, I am, but it's a lot that you won't understand right now, honeybun. Don't worry about it though, okay? Everyone is alright. Sometimes when people get angry, we yell. And that's not how we should talk. So, when you get mad, you promise me you won't yell?" I asked, wrapping a small blanket around her tiny body.

She nodded and smiled a sad one.

"Okay, Jade."

"Don't look so down. I promise. Everyone is going to be okay. Now can I get a hug?"

Stepping forward, Kylah wrapped her arms around my neck and hugged me.

"Can you stay here with me?" Kylah asked once she let me go.

"Sure. What would you like to do?" I asked, moving from my knees to sitting pretzel style.

"Can we play with my Barbies?"

"Of course, we can. Whatever you wanna do."

"Really?" Her face lit up.

"Sky's the limit."

"What does that mean?" she asked with a finger on her chin.

I laughed. "It means that your ideas can be as big or as much as the sky outside. And whatever you pick, I'll do it."

"My ideas aren't *that* much, silly," she said with a hand on her hip.

I giggled again and grabbed a doll from her toy box.

"Alright, I got my Barbie. What are we up to?" I asked.

"Okay! Today, we are going to the mall to get our hair done and buy clothes. And do our nails. Then we're going to drive to Ken's house because he has a birthday party, and you want to kiss him. Deal?"

I paused, throwing her a side eye. Kiss Ken? This girl and her imagination were something else!

"I'm not kissing Ken, Kylah. I have to get to know him first."

"Okay. Well, we go to the birthday party, and we take Ken to the beach because you want to know him."

"Okay. Deal."

Kylah and I went to her makeshift mall set up in a tight corner of her room with a bunch of scattered Barbie clothes. We shopped together, and we were in the middle of brushing our dolls' hair when suddenly, a body appeared in Kylah's doorway. Hesitating, I looked up, and it was Jarell glaring towards us. His shoulders had relaxed, and his face was void of any wrinkles between the eyes. Still. I wasn't buying it.

"Relly, we're playing Barbies! Girls only! Get out!" Kylah yelled.

"Hey," I whispered and interrupted. "Remember we talked about yelling, right? That we're not supposed to do that?"

"Oh yeah... I forgot," she said as her features drooped. "Sorry Relly."

"It's okay baby sis," Jarell said with humor in his eyes. "Can I borrow Jade for a second?"

"Okay. As long as she can come back."

"She will," Jarell said with a laugh.

"Okay. Jade, I'll be doing her hair."

Nodding, I got up and went over to Jarell who led me just outside the hall. Crossing my arms, I took a step back from him. He sighed, obviously feeling my cold disposition.

"I..." He paused looking towards the ceiling. Then, his shoulders fell, and he closed his eyes. "I'm sorry, Jade. What you saw ain't me. I don't want you to ever think I'm hurting my mom, bullying her, or manhandling her."

"Okay?"

"And... and..."

"And?"

"And I'ma go to therapy. For real. I'm gonna go twice a week. Tuesdays and Thursdays. Like Ma had planned out a couple weeks ago."

A smile lifted on the left side of my mouth.

"I can't lie to you. I don't want you out of my life because I'm not doing something to keep you around. You don't understand how much I need you. So, I'll go. Not just for you, but for me, too. I believe in us. I'm sorry, Jade. I know this is gonna help me and everything but... I'm just scared," he confessed and stretched his arms out.

Wow.

As stubborn as I knew Jarell to be... as much as it was like pulling teeth to get him to feel outward remorse about anything, this was the first time since I've known him to ever, ever deliver such an extensive apology to me.

Nonetheless, I fell into his arms, taking in his natural scent, absent of the smell of his old, oversized hoodie he used to wear every single day. Grateful he was alive and breathing. His muscles were a little tense, but once I refused to let him go, Jarell softened and hugged me back.

"This is the best news ever," I purred.

"But." He pulled away and gave a somber glare. "There is a big but. I'm not lettin' that shit go of us being kidnapped. Therapy or not, I'ma find out who did this, and I swear to God…" Jarell promised.

"No." I shook my head. "I need you to focus on getting better. Okay? I will handle figuring that out. Can you trust me with that?"

Jarell leaned his head to the side and peered. I took his hands into mine just to reassure him.

"Jade, let a man handle this, alright? This might be too dangerous for you to be taking on."

"Yeah, I know, but everything will be okay. Allow me to take this on, Jarell. There are no better investigators than women. I promise, if I get any leads or any updates, I'll share it with you. I won't leave you in the dark about it. Deal?"

I didn't wanna go there by asking him how the hell he was gonna figure out who did it, considering his disability, but saying anything of the sort would emasculate him. This time, his head fell back as if it took everything in him to relinquish this stronghold and entrust it with me. I squeezed his hand, urging him to agree. He rolled his eyes and smacked his lips.

"Fine."

"Thank you. Trust me," I whispered, ducking my head low towards his face. "Just as much as you want revenge?" I squinted. "So do I. Believe that."

Chapter Five

Point of View: Jade Williams

It was noon the next day. Time to check out of this hotel. Back to reality.

A new reality.

I couldn't hide forever. Staying for free at a hotel Jarell's mom worked at overnight and away from everyone else was the best decision I could've made, although sleep evaded me all night, dreaming about the ruthless Sir Shotgun and Hair Snatcher gripping my hair like a lifeline.

Now that it was time to leave, I didn't know where to start or where to go to integrate into the chaos of my personal world outside of Jarell and all this drama. A part of me wished I could go a little longer in hiding and watch the world happen on my phone, even though my social media presence was fleeting. Living on Instagram, SnapChat or any social media wasn't my thing. I only used it for the convenience of following other people who knew all the tea to keep eyes out about what was going on and who was talking about who whenever I wanted.

Right now, it was gonna be hella necessary if I was gonna get any information about our abductors. Especially since my "popularity" card got revoked in real life.

After returning my hotel room key, I decided Hip Hop Emporium, the dance studio, would be the place to start my "reentry" process back into daily life and routine. Nothing pulled at my stomach more than the chance to dance again.

It had been three days since I last checked in with my girl Alise Marie, my partner in crime and co-choreographer, but also, her intern. Celebrity dancers don't take days off, so I wasn't about to be the one who did.

But first, I had to get some new clothes, get my car back, get new debit cards, a new phone, all that shit. Thank God my car keys had been in my pocket the entire kidnapping. None of the men took those away. Wearing these same clothes, especially being in that nasty ass basement, was disgusting so it was priority to get this done ASAP.

I called a taxi from the hotel to take me back to the park and surprisingly, my car was still where I parked it. The area where Jarell and I sat before we were ambushed had been cleared just as I suspected. Either our things had been stolen or seized by authorities. I tried not to dwell on it because the last thing I wanted to do was go searching there and get snatched up again. Who the hell knew where they were at this point, being still on the loose? So, I hurried up, got into my little red convertible slug bug and left.

First stop was the bank. Which took forever to make sure my funds were okay after I canceled my cards to get new ones. Thank God my savings were still intact and spending funds were still looking good. Real good. Then the next stop was Fox Hills Mall. The official new name is Westfield, but everybody still calls it Fox Hills. I needed to buy a new phone – the latest iPhone – and new clothes.

Before I hopped out the car, I donned my oversized shades and looked in the mirror. My lip curled. I still looked like Hell in human form. I reached to at least fix the atrocity that was my hair, but a searing pain shot right through my scalp and radiated to my neck as soon as I tried taking out my ponytail.

"Ssss ahh!" I hissed as my hand snatched away.

Still too tender. Instead, I took a magenta scarf and wrapped it around my head, almost like a hijab, which then, exposed more of my dirty shirt. I sighed, that familiar burn at my nose and lump in my throat creeped its way through.

Let's make this shit quick.

I ran in that bitch fast to buy something cheap and simple – a floppy summer hat, t-shirt, flip flops, and new jeans plus some workout clothes from JC Penney's. I changed right in the mall bathroom and threw my old clothes in the trash along with my heel boots.

Still not feeling adequately dressed enough, I maneuvered through the mall to T-Mobile to buy my new phone. All the while, I prayed I saw no one I knew, even though I was pretty inconspicuous. I wasn't ready for the questions, the pity about me being in the hospital, or anything else related to what was going on. Or most of all, be caught with these cheap ass new clothes.

But low and behold…

My ex. Mike Harrison.

With some bitch sitting on his lap keekee-ing and haha-ing like his jokes were earth shattering funny as he kissed her hand right outside of Cinnabon. Yuck. She wasn't even cute with her fire red hair and trashy tattoos in comparison to his blemish free, honey skin and hazel green eyes.

It was Wednesday afternoon. Weren't they supposed to be at school?

The more I watched, the more nauseas I felt. Mike always had someone new ever since he and I officially went our separate ways after he damn near raped me in the back seat of his uncle's car Homecoming night. Looked like he was showing a whole lot more affection to these other thotiannas than when we were together.

Every single fiber in me wanted to go up, cause a scene, bust that shit up, and tell the girl that he was a cheating, inconsiderate ass hoe who didn't deserve her but…

I thought of the kidnapping.

If Mike had any role in it … he wouldn't be at the mall, right? He'd want to keep a low-profile, wouldn't he? Did he know anything? If he saw me, would he make any phone calls? Scurry away? Act weird?

Taking a deep breath, adjusting my glasses, and shifting my sunhat down, I erased all considerations of confronting them. I walked by, managing to not be seen and went into T-Mobile. At first, I was gonna set everything up on my new phone at the store, but I didn't wanna push my luck any longer with the potential of being spied on in public with these damn kidnapping suspects at large. Nor did I want to watch my ex-boyfriend love on someone else when he had showed no ounce of loving me. Even when I begged him to.

Chapter Six

Point of View: Jade Williams

I managed to make it to Hip Hop Emporium after forcing myself to not think about Mike and even better? I was the only one there. After setting up my phone in the car, I went straight to the studio office and sat at my desk, which was as spic and span as I left it a week ago before I got admitted to the hospital. Once I got settled, I stared at the blank screen of my new phone, hand trembling as my thumb swiped to wake it up. Did I want to know what had been put out there on either in the media or on social media about our kidnapping or about the near drowning at school?

Come on, Jade. You can't hide forever. Especially if you're seeking revenge.

First place I went was Google. I typed in "two teens kidnapped in Los Angeles," but nothing popped up except old cases that happened years ago. So instead, I typed in "Crenshaw High students."

The search results were:

HEADLINE: Crenshaw High School under fire for bullying incident, lawsuit filed by mother of victim

HEADLINE: Crenshaw High's principal RESIGNS after social media outrage, community backlash about bullying and lack of student behavior control

HEADLINE: Crenshaw High student arrested for pushing student with disability in swimming pool (VIDEO)

<u>HEADLINE</u>: Los Angeles Public Schools Superintendent Robert Morey issues statement following community outrage over swimming pool incident at Crenshaw High

Holy shit. Our school was on the spotlight like *this*? As I skimmed each article and learned about what was going down between parents, the community, and the administration of the district, no doubt about it. There wasn't gonna be such a thing called D-Block ever again. Not after the courts get involved.

I didn't even know Ms. Rachel filed a lawsuit. Good for her. They deserved all the money for physical, emotional, and psychological damages so many people bestowed upon Jarell from that school. Not to mention Jarell already had impending court dates for his fight a couple weeks ago, brutalizing Martell nearly to death. And who knew? He might've had charges for choking out Marcus, too. But I had no doubt in my mind those charges against him would be dropped after this.

Wow. This shit was getting crazy. I had so many questions.

Let me check Instagram and see what they talkin' 'bout. It was one thing for the media to say something, but what was being said on the ground directly from the folks who went to our school was most important. Or even check the D-Block GroupMe that I never used.

I hit up the GroupMe first, but it no longer appeared as a list of chats I was a part of.

"Fuck," I whispered. They were serious as about ex-communicating me. Time to try somewhere else.

There wouldn't be anything on SnapChat three days after the pool thing. Tik Tok? Maybe. This kinda drama wasn't Tik Tok worthy. Instagram might have had something from somebody. Ain't no way everybody would be close mouthed about this; somebody had to have done a live about it. Once I logged in, I checked every page of the people on D-Block. Erica. Laurie. Mike. Martell. Tazz. Marcus. Ro'Shae. Arianna. And a few others. One by one, I typed their names in my "Following" list.

@hoopstar_mike14 *Username not found*

@forever_ericaaaaa *Username not found*

@datniggatazz *Username not found*

@_prettygirlariiii *Username not found*

@da1nonlymarc *Username not found*

@_shae.shae *Username not found*

@lauriebae *Username not found*

What the fuck! All of them *blocked* me? Even my best friend since damn near diapers, Laurie!? They hated I was with Jarell that much, they'd go outta their way just to block me on the 'gram and all other social media? I was too through. Especially with Laurie. She was just at my hospital bed a couple days ago with a card and flowers, telling me to get well.

Hell naw. Something wasn't right. Now, my stomach bubbled. Were these assholes up to this kidnapping all along? I had more questions than I had before.

"Jade! Girl! Where the fuck you been at?"

Startled, my phone tumbled out of my hands. I swiveled my chair towards the direction of the familiar voice, and there she was. Alise Marie stood in the door frame.

Giving her a quick onceover, she was beautiful today; not that she wasn't fly any other time. Wearing a fitted cheetah jacket with gold accessories, black dance leggings, and matching cheetah heels, sis was always top notch. I thought I was "miss high fashion," but I looked up to her more often than myself on how to show bitches up at school with my dress.

"Hey!" I ran towards her, giving her a near-tackle embrace. She held firm, accepting it with no fight.

Alise, even though she was just five years older than me, had always felt so motherlike. She had every characteristic I wanted in my mom – loving mentorship, guidance, care, and she was a bad bitch! She was the only person separated from the drama other than Corey.

"Sis, it's so good to see you! I heard you got released from the hospital two days ago, and I haven't heard from you since I visited to check on you. Why didn't you call me or come home? Where were you?" she prodded.

"Girl… it's a long story."

"Did you go to your mom's and stay there or something?"

I scoffed.

"Um, no. I don't fuck with her. Why you think I got kicked outta there and had to come live with you?"

She gave me a long, indignant look.

"Come on, Jade. That's your mom. Chill."

"So?"

She rolled eyes and shook her head. "Anyway. Seriously. You heard all this buzz about Crenshaw with the principal resigning and all this shit about bullies and the adults having no control of the school? Where did you end up going after getting out the hospital? We been missing you here at the studio," she harassed, moving towards her desk in the office we shared and set down her phone and keys.

"Somebody's warehouse basement," I said, shifting my eyes away from her with instant regret for letting that spill.

Her head snapped towards me so fast, I actually heard the movement.

"What? What you talkin' about?"

I let out a long breath in exhaustion. "I'ma tell you, but you can't say a word about it. It's an ongoing investigation and they say any info about it is embargoed. But, I got kidnapped the day I got released from the hospital. I don't know who did it or why. I was at a park chillin' around midnight, and two SUVs came rollin' up. These men in masks came out with guns, tied me up, and threw me in the trunk. They took me to Fresno in an abandoned warehouse basement in the middle of nowhere. Then threatened me about a whole lot of shit. Hot ass mess."

The more I spoke, the wider her eyes got and the further her mouth fell open.

"Wow. Are you okay? How'd you get out? When did you get back? Wait. Girl. What? I don't understand. What the hell were you doing at a park by yourself at midnight? I have so many questions about this. I need more detail than you're giving me…"

"It don't matter. I'm good now," I said. Telling half-truths to her was as far as I would go. Alise knew nothing about Jarell and me, and I intended to keep it that way. Explaining our blossoming relationship and Jarell's mental health or his suicide attempt was none of her business and nothing she'd understand. She didn't even know he was blind. She'd have too many questions about why Jarell would wear an ankle monitor – the cause of us escaping. I wasn't finna go there.

"Girl, this is crazy." Alise glared at me with a quiet sense of foreboding. "Everything you've been involved in lately from being hospitalized after nearly drowning to being kidnapped is some weird shit. Do the police know? Please tell me they know… Are you hurt?"

"Yeah, I just told you they're investigating," I said. "But Lise, I promise. You don't have to worry about it. I'm good. But here's what I do wanna say."

"What?"

"I don't wanna go back to that school. I don't give a damn about graduating anymore. Can I just move my start date earlier as the Youth Choreographer?"

Yes. I had been hired for career employment before graduation with a nice ass salary working full time at Hip Hop Emporium. I had a certain start date, but with the way things were going? I hoped it could be changed to earlier. She was already shaking her head with her eyes closed and arms crossed. I continued, putting two pleading hands together.

"Hear me out. There's only a month and some change left of school. I'm not going to college and you know that. There's no use in finishing, and I don't care to deal with the drama there after everything that has happened. Just please, let me start my job early."

"No, Jade. I know everything going on is weighing on you, but I'm not allowing anybody eighteen or older to work up in here that don't at least have a high school diploma. As your mentor sis, I wouldn't want to do that to you or encourage you to not graduate. What if you decide you don't wanna dance again? Then what?"

I looked her upside her head.

"Girl what? You know dancing is my life. You think I'm finna give up celebrity status and stop dancing when it's bringing me the kinda bank even grown adults don't get? Are you crazy?"

"Nah, I'm just saying, Jade. You never know what could happen, and if dancing happens to not be a reality for you down the line, I want you to be able to move on to something else and at least have a diploma under your belt. College is a different conversation, but high school is an absolute must, sis."

I let out a loud, grumbling sigh.

"Seriously, Alise?"

"Dead ass. You can start the position the day after graduation. No earlier. Besides. Don't you wanna go to prom and graduate with some of your homies?"

"I ain't got no 'homies' anymore," I pouted, and the tears stung my eyes.

"What you mean? What about that White girl Laurie? What about Mike?"

I shook my head. I forgot I hadn't told her how and why Mike and I fell apart. Nor did I feel like talking with her about Laurie. Even though Laurie hadn't done anything wrong over the last few weeks, she still didn't like Jarell. And she fucking blocked me off social media! I couldn't trust her.

"Again. It's a long story..." I started, but she interrupted.

"Speaking of Jarell, I'm at his head for leaving the dance studio on me when you brought him here. He was so rude, but I don't care because he was so dope! You need to bring him back. Convince him. Something," she chided.

"I'll try, but I'm not focused on that. I don't wanna go back to school."

Alise paused, and then she shrugged.

"Well, it don't matter what you want Jade if you want to keep your role as the Youth Choreographer or to continue working here with me in general. I know you can do without me and continue getting gigs on your own with different artists because you're that talented. But I'm putting my foot down. Matter fact, if you don't get your diploma, I'm not letting you stay at my crib anymore, and you'll have to go with your mom again or your stepdad. Getting your diploma is too important to me over any routine or concert we have to prepare for. Please listen to me, if you listen to no one else. You know I got your best interest at heart."

I rolled my eyes. Even though I didn't wanna hear shit she was talking about, she was right. She did want what was best for me. Unlike my mom.

"Fine, Alise Marie," I sulked. She rolled her eyes at that. "I'll go back. I'm just nervous because I don't know who the mastermind behind the kidnapping could've been. Any one of them ugly ass kids could've set me up."

Giving me an understanding gaze, she walked around her desk and stood in front of me.

"Come here."

With reluctance, I stood and let her bring me close.

"Please don't let all of this get in the way of what you have going on. You have a lot on the line here at the studio, a lot going on as an up-and-coming celebrity, and I chose you to lead for a reason. Let the police and investigators handle this. They got this covered. I just need you to focus on the studio and bettering yourself, okay? Leave all this high school drama shit at Crenshaw," she said as she held onto my cheeks with both hands in a loving, motherly way.

I sighed.

"Alright. Fine."

"Nothing's gonna happen. Not unless I'm around and got my eye on you. Now get dressed so we can dance since you ain't hurt. Five days off? I know you're rusty, so it's time to get back in the groove. Hurry up. I'm boss lady on you today. No mercy. I got a phone call last week and it was Cardi asking us to be in her new video, so I need you to be on your shit, real talk."

With that, she walked out of our office and into the main studio. I dipped my head with both hands on my hips, trying to figure out my next move. I understood what Alise was saying, but something was fishy. I had no choice but to go back to school now that Alise forced me to if I wanted to keep my job, I suppose it made sense to start searching for answers. Publicly. Whether I was welcomed back on D-Block or not.

But before that? The first place I was gonna start was with my toxic mom. Because if everybody else had me blocked… even Laurie, Momma had to know something. She was best friends with Laurie's parents, so I had a good feeling. A good, yet dreadful feeling.

Chapter Seven

Point of View: Jarell Hendricks

Jade laid the ultimatum on a nigga.

She was serious, too. Not that I thought she wouldn't be. I just ain't realize how much us being in a relationship, and the baggage it came with, weighed on her as much as it has. A part of me wished I coulda just told her from jump that being together was a bad idea because of my shit.

Now, we were in too deep to walk away from everything we've shared together. Well... I guess for her, it would've been easy had I not agreed to go to therapy.

I sighed. *I ain't worth a damn.*

Jade loved me through everything. Through action and words, and even when she expressed it to me, I just left her on silent like an idiot. I remembered the exact moment. She confessed her love as I sat in that dumb hospital room in the psych ward. I couldn't even tell her I loved her back. Yet, she still showed up.

I shook my head. *I ain't shit.*

Sitting in my bed, I wrestled with a piece of paper in my hands, trying to get it to fold how I wanted it. I had to create a new origami piece of Jade since my original one got lost during our kidnapping. The feeling of paper between my fingers as my hands manipulated every fold and shape brought a rare sense of control. Flexibility, fragile, lightweight, yet durable were my favorite qualities working with paper. The crackle crumple sound of it, the woody smell, and the smooth, sandpapery feel were bonuses.

What I loved most? My favorite qualities about paper were a few of my favorite qualities about Jade.

When I got my final fold right and felt around the edges of the piece to confirm I had done it the correct way, I smacked my lips and put the project down to be finished up later.

I should probably check in with Ma. I couldn't sit in my room alone anymore, letting everything that happened sit on my heart and having this cloud over the house.

Swinging my legs over my bed, I walked outta my room.

"Ma," I called out.

"In here," she responded.

The sound filtered through my left ear more than the right. Living room. I followed her voice towards the front. On the way there, a sharp edge of a small object sunk right into my foot.

"Ahh fuck," I hissed. "Kylah!!"

"Yeah?"

"Come pick up your toys!"

"Sorry, Relly!" Her little footsteps pounded the floor until she made her grand entrance to the hall and rushed to move the toys out the way.

"Hey." I kneeled before she ran back to her room and spoke gently. "Remember I can't see, okay? I can't know where your toys are all the time. So, when you're done playing, can you take them to the room?"

"Yes, Relly." She dipped her head as her voice inflected towards the floor. "I'm sorry."

"It's okay. Thanks."

Wrapping her little arms around my neck, she pulled me in for a hug and kissed my cheek before running back to her room to play.

I proceeded until I leaned against the wall where the living room and kitchen connected. I didn't quite know where Ma was, so I waited for her to speak to get a better idea of which direction to stand.

"What is it?" she asked. "You need something?"

Shifting my body to face her more, my back met the wall again.

"Nah. Just checkin' in. You good?" I wiped my moist hands against my white t-shirt, biting my top lip.

"I'm fine," she said, but her voice was flat and unconcerned.

"You sure?"

"Yep. You never did tell me what happened in Fresno," she mumbled.

"I thought Jade told you…"

"She did, but I wanna hear it from you. What the hell happened?"

"Ma, I don't know. Everything Jade told you is what I know. I don't have any additional info."

"Yeah… okay. I don't believe you, but I'ma keep asking until I get your side of the story and your involvement with this. I'll leave it alone now, but best believe you ain't seen a pest yet until you watch me. Trust me on that."

I nodded and pursed my lips, moving my eyes around, trying to figure out a better way to stop talking about this. "What day of the week is it again?"

"Wednesday."

"Oh well, I missed school this week." I scratched my head and threw a long look in her direction. "I ain't going back there, Ma. I know you been pushing me to stick with it, but I can't." I shook my head. "I'm not graduating, and I don't care."

"I figured." I heard the shrug in her voice. "I hope you didn't think I would expect you to go back after all this mess."

"I didn't, but—"

"You don't know this, so I'm gonna tell you now. I filed a lawsuit against the school."

My eyes bucked and neck jutted forward. Aww hell, wait. *She did what?*

"Wait, wait, Ma. Why you ain't tell me? Is that even a good idea? Who gon' pay for that? We don't have money. Plus, I got my own court date about that fight with Martell. I'm only here because I got bailed out by Jade. We're trying to keep a low profile, so doing this will—"

"Jarell," she interrupted, "just stop. This is why I don't tell you anything. You always tryna stick your nose in matters you don't need to worry about. I said I filed the lawsuit, so let's leave it there. You should already know I've thought about the money piece."

"Okay, but what about the … you know who… piece?" My breathing quickened and my heart raced until my throat nearly closed. "We're already in an investigation for this kidnapping mess, which will probably become super public because of who Jade is. Tryna sue the school will draw attention to us in ways you know we both don't want. I don't want him to find us and …"

I was talking about my mom's ex-boyfriend. Her abusive ex-boyfriend we endured for a ruthless two years before we fled and went into hiding after he nearly killed us five years ago. Fled miles and miles away from where we had stayed, and we've kept a very low profile ever since. That piece of nasty shit. I couldn't even say his fucking name. Never wanted to, and I never wanted to even bring him to the front of my mind. Every time I did, I felt like I was suffocating.

"I've thought about that too," she replied as if saying "so what?"

I smacked my lips. "Ma, but—"

"I don't care about that mothafucka, Jarell nor am I worried. I want justice for you. You deserve justice after everything that school put you through. I've kept quiet because I didn't want to draw attention to myself or our family for the same reason you're concerned about, but this was the last straw. Enough is enough.

After that boy pushed you in the pool, Jade's mom going crazy at the hospital, and I watched you break down to the point of wanting to take your life…" her voice cracked.

"Ma, ple—"

"Let me finish, Jarell. Please. I watched the worst thing a mother could ever see happen to you. I got free legal help as of now, and they're hooking up some payment plans as we move forward. They think it's a case we will definitely win anyway, so that's why they're doing it at this cost right now. And if the payments are above what we can handle right now, I'll just have to work overtime."

"But—"

"I need to do this. I need to fight for you more than I ever have. Let me do this," she cried.

Whoa. That was the first time she ever, ever admitted anything like that. I ain't know if I should say about damn time, thank you, or what. My eyes moved around, trying to think of the right way to respond with my mouth slightly opened, but couldn't come up with anything.

"Anything else you wanna talk about?" she asked. "Because quite frankly, I'm done with this discussion."

I swallowed. She wanted to be done, but I had a whole lot more to bring up. Taking a deep breath in as my chest rose, I closed my eyes and swiped a hand down my face.

"I… I'm sorry for scaring you and yelling at you the other day," I drew out. "I shouldn't have done that. My fault."

"And I shouldn't have been eavesdropping on y'all. But listen here. I'm still your mom. You don't disrespect me in front of your girlfriend. I won't tolerate that. Because then, you're acting just like Nathan," she said, and I cringed, my lips tensing into what I imagined to be a thin line. I fucking *hated* hearing his name. "Jarell… you have to know. I'm trying."

"I'm glad you tryna be better, but I think you just need to listen to me and stop shutting me down all the time. Every time I try to talk to you, you treat me like I'm some unimportant kid." She smacked her lips. "I tried to talk at least five times during this conversation, and I can't even get a word out. Then you wonder why I rarely talk to you or come out my room or why I don't talk to nobody. I'm a grown man now, so treat me like one."

She huffed, shifting with aggression where she sat.

"Lord have mercy, Jarell, what is it that you have to say now? Huh? What is it? Because regardless of what you have to share, the lawsuit is happening. Besides. You don't need to be doing much talking anyway. You need to go back to the hospital and get the help you need. Suicide is serious, Jarell. You can't mess around with this shit anymore," she retorted.

"I already agreed to that. I agreed to therapy, but I'm not going back to the hospital. You can take that ankle monitor back."

"Okay, so whatever you're so pressed to talk about, you can address it in therapy." She brushed me off.

I shook my head. "Nah. To be honest, the first person I need to address about all this shit I been feeling inside, especially about suicide, is *you*."

There. I said it. For the longest, I had been wanting to express that, and just didn't know how. Everything that had happened with our lives and her role in it up until this point hurt, sliced, and cut way too deep for me to replay or relive it to even bring it up, so I just remained quiet. For years.

As the silence grew, I clenched my teeth, waiting for the storm I knew was about to come.

"Me?" she asked with this breathy, surprised tone. "You need to address me?"

"Yes. *You*."

"I thought you said everything you wanted to say to me about my 'bad parenting' in the hospital already. You got even more?"

"Ma, that was scratching the surface. Barely that," I said, and the moment it came out, I squeezed my eyes shut. Fuck. That didn't come out right.

"Oh really?" she responded, full of grand sarcasm. "Not even scratching the surface, huh? Bullshit. I'm not a bad parent, Jarell. What more negative shit do you have to say? Or did Nathan do something else to you?"

"I didn't mean it like that. It's less about him and more about your deci—"

"My decisions?" she countered before I could even finish. I could tell she was holding a hand to her chest. "Jarell, stop making me the fucking problem. Nathan is the real issue. And you need to go to counseling to deal with everything he's done and stop putting that on me. That's what all of this comes down to. That's the truth."

"Nah, it's not just about th—"

"Yes, it is! Jarell, how long have I been trying to get you to go to therapy? Come on now. There ain't nobody else in the hood whose Momma is telling their kid to go to therapy the way I been tryna get you to go. Don't play with me. And now, all of a sudden, you're wanting to address and blame me? Why?"

"Ma," I warned.

"I'm not the one to blame, Jarell. Trust me, I ain't the one. I won't let you do that shit to me!" she said, raising her voice as I heard her stand up from the couch.

"Can you just list—"

"No, Jarell. I can't listen to that bullshit. I know I haven't always made the best decisions. I know that! But you aren't gonna make me feel guilty about it for the rest of my life, and right now, the issue isn't me. You play a role in how you need to better yourself, too. I don't know what it will take for you to give a fuck about your health!"

"But—"

"I've been begging you to get the help you need, and you've continuously said you wouldn't go!" she yelled.

"Can you ju—"

"No! I won't 'just' anything! You ain't finna use me as an excuse for issues *you* don't wanna solve on your own! I don't wanna hear it!"

"Would you just shut up and listen to me for a second?!" I finally roared.

"What? What do you have to say Jarell?"

At that point, she broke down. I smacked my lips and turned my head. There was nothing I hated more than hearing Ma cry. The rage once brewing in my stomach turned into a hollow pit of misery. I couldn't keep doing this, but I tried to get through to her once more.

"Ma, just listen to me. I been wanting to say so much to you, but I been keeping it in. I wanna tell you so we can move on. Every time I try to talk to you about something you don't wanna hear, you act like I'm some little ass kid who don't deserve to be heard. I ain't ten years old anymore."

"That's not true," she sobbed. "That's not fucking true at all."

"So, you calling me a liar? Even when I bring up how I don't want the school lawsuit to bring attention to us because it'll give him another way to trace us, you shut me down. I can't get a word in. Then you say you don't care. That you're not worried. You do realize that's exactly what you said to your ex-boyfriend before he threw that bleach in my face to blind me before taking advantage of you right next to me on the floor, right? Don't you realize that? So why don't you care? Why don't you ever listen to me? Why won't you just apologize for not listening?"

Suddenly, something whizzed past my ear and crashed against the wall just to the left of my shoulder. I nearly ducked to the floor to avoid anything else that might've been thrown at me the way I used to as a kid trying to avoid any wrath that piece of shit brought whenever he was raging, but my knees managed not to buckle. Then, she exploded, her shriek shattering my eardrums.

"How dare you, Jarell! You're not gonna throw that shit or that day in my face. A fucking low blow... Get the fuck out! Right now! Go!"

Her frantic cries came closer until she got in my face and punched my chest as hard as she could. "You aren't gonna do this to me. You ain't finna keep blaming me. Get. OUT! Get outta here!"

"Ma... that wasn't meant to blame you for anything that happened that day, I swear," I backpedaled, my voice shaking, yet trying to diffuse the situation with a soothing voice. Shit didn't matter; she pushed me, scratched me, and slapped me where she could. I stiff armed her from what I could feel to keep my distance, but it didn't help. Damn it, I done messed up. Ma never, *ever* went crazy on me like this.

"Get out! What you waitin' on?" she screamed. "Why you just standing there?"

Ma spoke through audible and harsh breathing between sniffs as she cried. Again, in the back, Kylah sobbed, too.

"And go where?" I asked, feeling every bit of energy float from my body.

"Out of here."

"After I just got kidnapped? And knowing I'm blind..." This shit blew me.

"Being blind ain't stopped you any other time from going wherever you wanted to go while I worried about you, so don't try to act like it's some barrier now. You a grown ass man, right? I just need you to go. You better call Jade, if you can figure out how."

My shoulders sank. Wow.

Biting my lip, knowing she didn't have her own space in the house to escape since she didn't have a room, the next best thing for her was to get rid of me. So, I went.

I grabbed the origami piece, my new OrCam glasses Jade bought me for Christmas from my bedroom, threw on my shoes, and walked right out the door and sat on the porch. Maybe she just needed a minute to cool down.

"Hell naw. Get the fuck off my porch, too. Get. Out!"

"Ma!" I yelled, damn near pleading. "Are you serious? I didn't mean—"

"GET OUT Jarell!" she hollered to the top of her lungs, and in the back, Kylah screamed and begged us to stop. "You're eighteen now, so you can do whatever you want right? Get the *entire* fuck out! Now!"

Shaking my head, I marched off her porch and just went... I didn't know where. I paced as fast as I could down the road, dragging my feet to feel cracks in the sidewalk and to locate the edge of curbs. I tried regulating myself multiple times before I tore this fucking city apart, but it just didn't help. I could barely walk or concentrate on the environment around me as the camera on my glasses spoke to me, informing me of my surroundings.

As I made it further and further away from the house, a part of me wanted to just rush out into the middle of a busy street and let someone take my ass out by a hit and run.

But I didn't.

So, I settled for sitting on the edge of a street curb and let my body shake as rage filled my lungs with nowhere for it to go. And I sat that way for hours and hours until I was suffocating.

Until I felt numb.

Chapter Eight

Point of View: Jade Williams

Today was hard in every single way.

Emotionally, physically, and mentally.

Alise was serious; she wasn't playing around with me on the dance floor while teaching me the new routine for Cardi's new video for her newest single. We were gonna teach our crew the routine early next week just for our dance class, but she and I were gonna be the only ones in her video. Alise didn't care if I was out for five days or that I was in the hospital. Sis was all over me like we weren't co-choreographers and partners. Any little step I missed, any little move that looked lazy, she ripped into my ass like a bitch off the street. I lowkey had a crazy urge to talk back and come at her head, but I knew it was because the turnaround time of which this had to be done. Cardi wanted us with her next Friday and it was already Thursday tomorrow, so Lise was just trying to get the best out of me.

But that didn't make it hurt any less.

By the time we were done, around seven at night, Alise and I went our separate ways without much verbal exchange to our cars. Once she was clear out of the parking lot and down the road, my forehead rested against the steering wheel, and the tears poured as the weight of the last six months crushed my chest.

After how rehearsal went today and the conversation be-tween Alise and I earlier, how the hell was I gonna be able to focus on dance, my upcoming career as a Youth Choreographer, and fo-cus on my relationship with Jarell all while figuring out who kidnapped us? So much had happened in such a short amount of time. How much more could I take? Not to mention, I still had to confront Janet tonight, so that had warped my mind while dancing too, leaving me hella distracted.

With index and middle fingers, I pressed and circled my temples for relief.

What the hell was I gonna do?

When the tears stopped on their own, I took the long way home in a silent car. No music, no nothing. I made it safe, managed to walk inside unseen by Alise, and went straight to the bathroom to take a shower and wash the emotions and sweat away in ice-cold water. As the water hissed from the shower head waiting for my entrance, I stripped down and stood in the full-length mirror in her high-end bathroom and luxury apartment.

I gazed from head to toe. Took in every inch of my bare, naked body in its natural form. I moved from my defined, square shoulders to my B-cup breasts which bore a few tiger stripes, dark brown areolas, and perky nipples. Down to my tummy, which had a four pack, but didn't quite complete the rest of the six for my lower belly. I sighed. I gotta work on that.

I glanced over the outline of my shape. I had always wished I was a little more hourglass-like, but I was content with my slender body type and slightly wide hips. I moved to the center of me. Which needed to be shaved again soon; the shit was getting too bushy. Then, my legs. My favorite part of me. They were long, slightly thick, and strong. I had a dancer's legs for sure. The strongest, most durable and reliable part of me.

I turned to the side. Whew, my God, I had no booty. I was gonna have to do some squats.

I turned back to the front, examining my face. My eyes had new, dark circles that weren't there before. My thick lips and cute, curled nose still were the highlight of my face along with huge, dark brown eyes.

Finally? My sloppy ponytail I had yet to change since my time in that basement. A sad smile crept at the corners of my mouth. I didn't look like myself, even though my physical features remained the same. I had a completely different disposition. I wasn't that confident girl anymore who used the halls of Crenshaw as my personal runway and talked down to anyone who came my way. Who *was* I? Who *am* I?

As I reached up to my head to cut the ponytail holder off instead of pulling it out, a thick bunch of my locks had fallen with the ponytail holder.

Jesus. My hair had been pulled out.

Burying my head in my hands, I bawled.

I was going out sad as hell. I was about a month away from being done with school, so what was I gonna do? When graduation was all said and done and I never had shit to do with Crenshaw again, who did I want to be? Who was I gonna be?

Wiping my tears away and pulling out the rest of my loose hair that had been snatched out, my hair was broken in so many different areas. Fuck this shit.

I shut the shower water off. Taking the same pair of scissors I utilized to cut the ponytail holder, I went crazy, chopping out thick chunks of hair section by section until it was even with the broken sections. Now, it was only earlobe length. However, for the first time, my face was free as the draft of the air conditioner whipped over my neck and through my scalp.

Taking out Alise's electric clippers she saved for her boyfriend whenever he came over, I began shaving it into a pixie cut. I had no idea what the hell I was doing, nor did I have any expertise whatsoever in styling, but at this point, if I fucked it up, oh well.

I kept working the clippers, watching what was left of my hair fall to the floor. When I was finished, I looked in the mirror. Oof. Yeah, it was hideous for sure, but I hadn't cut it down enough to where it wasn't salvageable for a stylist to take care of it. Alise knew a million of them in town, and some of them even came by the house to do her sew-ins and U-part wigs from time to time. Matter fact, she was getting her hair done tonight. Ol' girl might've already been here.

I took a shower and hopped out, dressing into something simple, and went out to the living room. Right on time. Her stylist, my favorite, Kim, had already come in and set up her station to take care of Alise. She had the most vibrant personality, and even though I wasn't particularly in the mood for the over-the-top foolishness today, it might've been what I needed.

The moment my appearance was in their direct line of sight, they both balked like they had seen a donkey with a lion's head poof in the space.

"Jade, what the fuck…" Alise called out with her jaw damn near touching her titties.

"Girl…" Kim said. With the look she gave, she might as well reach her hand out to slap me. "All that beautiful, bra-strap length hair you had… the fuck is you on, girl? Looking like a bald Powerpuff Girl."

"I know." I rolled my eyes and shifted my gaze away. "I need help rather than y'all admiring the problem. I cut it for a reason."

"Um. Yeah. A'ight. I don't even wanna know why, Miss Thang. Have a seat then. I'm sorry Lise. Jade's going first today. Up, up," Kim said, rushing her out of the chair, gesturing a shoo motion.

"Bet. It'll give me time to make dinner anyway. You want something?" Lise asked me.

"I'll eat whatever you make."

"Kay. I'll be back in a minute. Work your magic girl. She needs it," Alise said as she walked out of the living room.

"Don't worry honey. I love a challenge." Kim laughed and then ran her fingers through my short hair and examined it. "Hmm. Actually? You didn't do too bad now that I'm looking at where you were going with this. A pixie cut?"

"Yup."

"Okay, okay." She nodded with a smirk. "I ain't at yo' head no more. Let me just perfect it and make it look good. Girl you gon' be looking like a caramel-skinned version of Kehlani by the time I finish this. Vintage Nia Long!"

"Do ya thing then." I encouraged her with a smile.

As Kim went silent and concentrated on my hair, Alise came out of the kitchen with a bowl of what smelled to be some sort of pasta. She sat across from me, watching Kim do my hair like a TV show with a pensive frown. More so, she just shook her head for a long, long time the more my hair dropped to the floor. I tried pretending like I didn't notice because I didn't wanna hear her fuckin' mouth. Especially after how our dance practice went today.

"Jade, for real, girl. I feel like you holding a whole lot from me. Your dancing was absolute shit today, and I know *something* is cutting you deep. I'll say this again. Whatever you got going on is affecting what's important and you need to cut it out of your life," she spoke at last.

"You made dinner pretty fast," I said, scrolling through my phone. "What is it?"

Alise froze and stopped chewing, giving me that "don't play with me" look.

I scoffed. "Alright, listen, this ain't your business. None of it. I told you what I wanted to tell you earlier so now just leave it alone," I griped. "Or at least let's talk about this later."

"Nah, that's not how this is gonna go. You don't get to dismiss me. Now's the perfect time to talk. Trust me, Kim don't care enough about any shit regarding high school to be running off telling folks your business."

"I told you to leave it alone..."

"I don't care what you're telling me because at the end of the day, I'm the only one you can trust right now. I'm your friend, and I also just so happen to be the person employing you. Who is this about, Jade? Because I ain't never, ever seen you acting so withdrawn. You don't even wanna graduate from school and you got six weeks left."

"It's not about a certain person..." I mumbled.

"Is it Mike? Hell, is it Jarell even? The cat you saw dancing out somewhere one night that you were so excited to show off to me?" She raised an eyebrow, disregarding my previous statement.

"It's definitely a nigga," Kim chimed in with her unwanted ass opinion. "Girl, just by her whole attitude, I can tell it's some boy who got her in some shit. We all been there, sweetie. Just be real with yourself. It's okay."

If she wasn't cutting my hair, I would've cussed her out. Only reason I didn't was because I didn't want her shaving me bald.

"Girl, which one is it? Last time I heard you be real with me about anything boy related was when you told me about how Mike dissed you at a party with a bunch of other girls. Does he have something to do with whatever is going on with you?" Alise asked.

I picked at my nails. "Mike and I are a done deal."

"So then is it Jarell?" Her neck poked out. "The nigga who wouldn't shake my hand and was just flat out disrespectful in my studio when you brought him?"

I growled low enough to where they couldn't hear. Alise wasn't gonna let this shit go. I don't ever remember her being so persistent and such a nag, but apparently, this was the first time my "behavior" affected my ability to dance. So now, it actually had something to do with her.

"Fine. Since you won't let up. Me and Jarell are dating, alright? It's a long and complicated story that I don't want to share, and you need to respect that. Happy?"

Her eyes bucked, her bowl of pasta almost landing on her chest. "You're dating him? Why? Didn't you just meet him when you saw him dancing? You don't even know him. I ain't think it was like *that*."

"Um, no." I sneered as Kim pushed my head down to cut the back of my head more precisely. "He's no random, and I know him well. He goes to Crenshaw."

"Well... no wonder yo' ass was thirsty to show him off to me. Y'all got a thing goin' on. Hell, even though he can dance his ass off and I'd love to have him with us at the studio, he's rude and stand-offish. Why would you wanna have anything to do with that? He isn't even anywhere near Mike's looks. So wassup?"

"First of all, it's not about looks, and even if it was? You haven't seen Jarell outside of his hoodie and sunglasses. He's more attractive than Mike. Anyway…"

I sighed and rubbed my temples.

"Jarell is facing a lot of different things right now and he's suffering, Alise. He's suffering from years of neglect and abuse. Yet, no one knows what his life is like except for me. He has no one in his corner, he doesn't have friends, and everyone bullies him. His mom is the reason he's struggling, and he's trying to keep all that inside. He needs someone. So yes, I've been standing up for him. I saved him from drowning in a pool when someone pushed him in. That's why I went to the hospital. I'm there for him when no one else will be. That's the truth. Any other questions?"

"So, what I'm hearing you say is that Jarell is also a part of the reason for what happened the other night, right? I'm just trying to connect the dots here," Alise said.

"I'm not divulging anything about that." I shrugged. "All you need to know is that I'm safe and that Jarell and I are together."

"Whoever this Jarell dude is, his personal drama and trauma is not your responsibility to carry, Jade," Kim said, the most serious she has sounded all night. "You don't need to play hero for him."

"Right. And even if you are there for him, do you need to be *dating*? Why can't you just be friends to do that? Listen. You need to end that relationship girl. ASAP. It's messing with your whole life right now," Alise said. A bombshell.

"Mmm hmm," Kim co-signed with sass. Lord if I could cut her a look…

"I can't do that to him, Alise," I whispered, giving her a pleading gaze in the mirror.

"Why? Girl, please. Let's be real. If it was the other way around and it was that nigga carrying your baggage, he would leave you in a hot second or cheat on you because he doesn't wanna deal with it. All niggas do that. Us women always have to bear the brunt of a nigga trying to get himself together in the name of loyalty when they wouldn't do it for us. And when they do get their shit together, they go find some other bitch who ain't Black, and she reaps the benefits of his new and improved self," she said as she stuffed another forkful of pasta in her mouth.

"Period, sis," Kim again cosigned.

Damn they were relentless…

"Jarell isn't like that…" I countered.

"That's because he's the one trying to get his shit together. Like I said. Let this be the other way around. Jarell wouldn't stick around and deal with that. These niggas ain't shit."

"Yeah, but I'm the one that told Jarell I wanted a relationship. I can't just end it because of something he can't control, especially when I was the person who wanted to be with him. It would crush him if I left him to be on this island alone."

Kim and Alise looked at each other, and then they both cackled like hens in a barn. I smacked my lips. Alise must've had a cup of wine or two. We were talking about someone I loved here. I didn't have time for the jokes.

"This isn't funny…" I whispered.

Alise ignored me after catching her breath. "Girl, he can control it! He can control whether he goes to counseling. He can learn how to control his rudeness. He can control whether he wants to keep dragging you down. He can control talking to his momma about his problems. He has more control than you think. Girl, you have your whole life ahead of you. All three of us do, and you don't need a nigga holding you back while he figures out his trauma. Tell him you made a mistake to date him and move on."

"I'm not telling him that. I don't know why y'all tryna put these thoughts in my head to leave him when he needs me most. He's making the decision to go to therapy because he wants to be better and wants to keep me around. So, knowing that, the last thing I want to do is break up with him," I said as a lump developed in my throat.

"It's less about Jarell, Jade, and more about you. There's a reason why he wants to keep you around – he wants a crutch for his own selfish reasons. Listen. It's okay for women to be selfish and look after themselves. You're *eighteen*. Trying to graduate from school. You have these dance routines and music videos to worry about that will pay your future bills in your new apartment I'm just now finding out you applied for because I got something in the mail about it. You have to focus on your new career as a Youth Choreographer. You have so much shit on your plate. Trying to also carry his baggage ain't it."

"You sound like my mom…"

"Well…" Kim and Alise grumbled together as if withholding additional thoughts.

"Look… I don't know what else you want me to tell you but breaking up with him won't be wise. He will harm himself if I do that," I concluded, crossing my arms underneath the salon coat.

"And that's the problem. That's the toxic shit, Jade. You don't want to be in a relationship with someone who will hurt themselves if they can't have you. That's not something that should weigh on your heart. Now that I know all this information, it's beginning to explain everything. Everything as to why you've not been as sharp at the studio lately. You got this shit on your mind. Let it go, Jade. You and Jarell can still be friends, but once you add relationship perks and sex in the mix, it gets to be too much. Did you have sex with him? Seriously, be honest with me."

"You know she fucked that nigga. Otherwise, she wouldn't be riding this hard for him," Kim said with a laugh.

"Shut up, Kim," I finally said. "It's about time you mind yours."

"You just mad I can read your ass from a mile away," she said, and I heard the smugness in her voice. "Shit is so predictable."

"Well, Jade… that's just… you have to stop while you're ahead. No more dating and having sex with him. I'm warning you. I'm gonna need your undivided attention on the studio in the coming weeks. It's going to be a lot of work, and I need someone with focus. I would hate to have to choose someone else, so you need to decide what your priorities are. Your downfall with Jarell, or your promising career with dance," Alise said as Kim put a mirror in front of my face, showing the results of my new cut.

I ignored whatever Alise said and studied what I saw in the reflection.

Yassss.

I absolutely *loved* my new look. It was so bad ass. I didn't look like a teen girl with a teen attitude anymore. I looked like I was becoming a young woman who kept her youth yet carried her edgy characteristics to a new chapter.

And with that, I knew exactly the type of woman I needed to be tonight when I visited Janet. My mission to find out who, what, and why about this kidnapping situation wasn't going anywhere any time soon, and this whole conversation about Jarell was just gonna have to sit on the backburner for now. So let me go on ahead and end this right now.

"Thank you for cutting my hair, Kim," I said and rose from the chair. "Look. I'm not just gonna bow down and do what you want me to do about me and Jarell's situation. Let me sleep on it, okay? I'll take what you're saying into account later tonight, and I'll make my own decision. Whatever decision I make, you will need to respect that and respect my privacy. Alright? I'm out. I'm gonna go pay my mom a visit."

Without another word, I grabbed my keys and left the house. I couldn't listen to any of their unsolicited advice anymore. What I needed was a clear mind and heart to deal with Janet... the ultimate vibe killer that neither of those two ladies could come close to matching. So, I definitely took the scenic route to her place to clear my mental slate.

I had a feeling Janet had some answers about who may have been involved that night.

Chapter Nine

Point of View: Jade Williams

By the time I pulled up to Janet's mini mansion, it was already nine o'clock at night. I was smart to clear my head because if I was in a sour mood now, it would be ten times worse once I left her. Talking to Janet was begging to be angry for the rest of the week.

But it didn't matter.

If she didn't have anything useful to say, it would be my last day even engaging with her anyway. After the shit she pulled at the hospital? There was no way I would ever be able to look her in the eye or respect her ever again after what she said and had done to Jarell as he sat in my room, waiting for me to return to consciousness. Name calling, throwing drinks and shoes at someone who she knew was not only blind, but was straight up innocent was the most wrong thing I've seen a human being do. Jarell had done nothing to her. I will *never* get over that, so if she had anything to do with our abduction, she was gonna be cancelled. And jailed.

When I walked inside the house since I still had the key, which was going to be returned, she was already sitting and reading a fashion magazine with a glass of wine in her hand. As usual. Her face was fully beat, and her hair was slicked back into a tight bun that sat at the top of her back. For once, her outfit was simple – a long tunic and leggings with red bottom heels. She looked up briefly in concern to see who had walked into her home this late, and when she realized it was me, she raised a surprised eyebrow as the magazine slid off her lap and onto her infamous white couch.

"Oh... wow." She blinked. "You get released from the hospital and decide to become a whole new girl, huh? You got yourself a whole different look. A pixie cut. When has that ever been you?" She huffed.

See. Already. She was already criticizing me. Sucking in the air of the house through my nostrils, I held it in for a moment. *Calm yourself, Jade. You know that's how she is. Let her get it out. Don't let her upset you when you've only been here thirty seconds.*

"Ma'am." I rolled my eyes, knowing her wanna-be-young ass hated being called that. "Just say you don't like it and be done."

"I don't like it," she jeered.

"And I don't care at all about what you think. Now that that's out the way..."

"Look who's crawling back home? Jarell's love, care, and stability wasn't enough for you?" she asked with a smug smile, taking a sip of the wine.

"Look. I'm not here for your crap so let's make this visit quick. I'm here to return my key, since I won't ever need it again and second, to ask you something. What did you do?" I seethed, delivering her a suspicious glare and standing as far away from her as possible.

"What the hell are you talking about, Jade?" she asked with a scowl. "What do you mean 'what did I do?'"

I clenched my teeth. "You know what I'm talking about!"

"I don't know anything, so you better get to explaining what you mean. Or else you can go back to whatever rock you're living under and get outta my house."

"You got me and Jarell caught up with some crazy mess that threatened our lives. I'm talking about being threatened at gunpoint. You could tell it was planned..."

"What? Girl..." She waved me off and grabbed her wine glass. "You don't look like someone who's been caught up with anything to me. Regardless, it sounds ridiculous."

"What you mean you don't believe it? It doesn't matter what I look like. It happened the night before last. I got a feeling you had something to do with it because you don't like me being with him. Just be honest for once in your life!" I bellowed.

"Don't be coming up in my house demanding answers like you pay bills up in here. You're nothing but a little spoiled girl who won't listen to her mom. That's all you are, and that's all you'll ever be at the rate you're going if you don't woman up and grow up. Stop playing these little games with that bum and get you a real man. Then you wouldn't have to worry about being threatened at gunpoint or whatever the hell."

"Really, Momma? If we gon' be real, you shouldn't be giving me advice about any man when you couldn't even keep the ones you dealt with. They left you. You can't tell me anything about anyone I'm dealing with, period," I said, swiping my hand under my chin.

Her eyes got so big that I thought they might explode. Like they were set off by TNT.

"Now you done lost your mothafucking mind, Jade Anastasia!" she screamed, and stood up as the wine spilled all over the front of her clothes. "I will slap the hell outta you for trying to disrespect me."

I smiled. She should've known she can't match my tongue talking all that nonsense to me. She was gon' learn today what a grown woman's clap backs could be like, since that's what she wanted me to be so bad.

"Only thing I care about right now is the truth, which you just can't ever seem to embody. Did you or did you not set me and Jarell up?" I asked again.

The room, with its tall, vaulted ceilings had fallen dead silent. I could even hear the air coming out the vents as the air of the fan above whipped around and circulated it. My eyes widened and my heart sunk.

"Jade." She sighed, shaking her head. "You doing all of this? You would rather destroy our relationship all for that dirty scum of the Earth? I swear that boy gonna leave your ass high and dry one of these days... He's gotten you into so much crap in a short period of time, and you're that desperate that you would ruin our relationship?"

"Did you do it or not?!" I rumbled.

"I don't have to answer anything. I owe you nothing, and I honestly don't care what you're talking about." She shrugged, sat back down on the very edge of the couch, and took her final sip of wine that hadn't already spilled on her. "You can move around now."

"So, no detectives or anybody contacted you to ask you about anything?"

No disclosure. Only thing she served was blank stare I couldn't read at all. It was so void of any human emotion that I just pursed my lips.

"Alright." I threw my hands up.

Finally, a smidgen of emotion surfaced as she scrutinized me from head to toe.

"Who are you?" she whispered.

I smacked my lips and sneered.

"What? Please." I huffed, looking away from her.

"No. Who. Are. You? I didn't raise the girl standing before me. You're nothing like yourself. Still got a smart-ass mouth, but that's about it. Your hair. Your attitude. Even your body language is different. All because of that damn low-budget ass boy. I promise you; this was my biggest fear for you growing up. And now, you just... slipped through my fingers. You waited until your senior fucking year to act a complete monkey doodle fool. What's wrong with you? Tell me. What is so special about this kid that you would rather throw our bond and our relationship away for someone like that?"

The entire time she spoke, surprisingly, tears had welled in her eyes, and then fell onto her lap without restraint.

Aww man.

I wasn't expecting this, nor did I want to put my guard down, but I couldn't help feeling *some* remorse. Before Jarell, it was true. Momma and I were tight, but then, as time went on, through her actions, I peeped more and more how awful she was. She was too manipulative for me to fall into a trap I couldn't wiggle my way out of with her. It was just rare to see her cry or show *any* sign of weakness.

"Momma... don't try and pull this whole 'you changed' mess on me. If you were present for even just a little bit in my life, by first, being around and at home, and second, by not bossing me around about everything, you would understand me a little better. Don't think I forgot you left me by myself on Christmas! I can handle my own life. I'm here for you to tell me the truth about your role in setting up me and Jarell to potentially be killed. And if you did, I'm here to burn this bridge you call a bond."

She leaned back onto the couch and rested her arm along the back. "If it makes you feel better Jade, I don't know what the hell you're talking about with this whole threatened at gunpoint thing. Yes, I did speak with detectives, but I didn't know what they were talking about. If that's what you were looking for me to say, cool. There. I said it."

"It's not about what I *want* you to say! Did you do it, yes or no?" I screamed.

"I just want my daughter back." She ignored me. "The one I raised. I don't know what I have to do or what I have to say for you to understand that I don't give a flying fuck about this Jarell kid. You're asking for your life to be ruined. I can't believe this. I can't believe the daughter I raised would do such a thing. What do I have to do, Jade? Tell me what I have to do to get my old daughter back?"

At this point, my inner temp was on broil as I imagined my fingers around her neck. I stepped back, close to the foyer so I wouldn't do anything I'd regret. Taking a deep breath, I proceeded.

"Why do you hate Jarell other than the fact that he has a disability, and he doesn't have a ton of money? You don't know him.

He's the sweetest person. He treats me with respect. You wanna know something?"

She glared at me, waiting for me to continue.

"For the longest, since Freshman year, you've been pushing me to be with Mike. You wanna know what happened on Homecoming night? His sorry butt almost took my virginity by forcing himself on me in the backseat of his uncle's truck. Nearly raped me. That's the kinda man you want me to be with? Simply because he 'looks good on paper?' Jarell never treats me that way when I'm with him!"

"Wait, so you done messed around and slept with this boy?" Her eyes shot right out of their sockets. Wait. *Did she hear anything I just said?*

Now, she was hysterical, too. It was so bad… borderline second-hand embarrassment. This woman struggled big time accepting that I made my own choices without her input, and which also included my love life. And now, apparently, my sex life. It was sad as hell watching her lose herself because she no longer had power over me.

"Jade, I'm begging you. Do not let that walking filth ruin your life. Please. I've been there. I let it happen to me."

"Momma, cut the theatrics. If you've raised such a daughter who has a good head on her shoulders like you always brag about to everybody, you would know I'm too ambitious to just throw my life away to take care of another man. I will still have my career. I will still run my own business. Get over yourself." I rolled my eyes and looked away.

"You know what?" She stood up, wiping at her eyes and then pointed at me. "Fine. I can't control you, but like I said the first time I kicked your ass out. You better not come back crying and asking to move in because of some trouble he's gotten you into. I can't believe you would deal with someone like that. You're so naïve Jade, it's sick!"

"Don't worry. I won't be coming back here. Trust me on that."

It hurt me to no end that she would even tell me not to, knowing what happened to her when she was young and had gotten pregnant with me. You'd think that she'd learn not to leave her child high and dry the way her parents left her, but I guessed it was true; for some people, the apple doesn't fall too far from the tree. That didn't apply to me, though. Might as well leave her with this final dagger before my grand exit. Just for fun.

I walked towards the door as she ranted off at me in her screeching, crying voice, trying to get her last words in. But I heard none of them. They went through one ear and out the other.

"You still doing all that talking and yet, you ain't saying nothing. Bet you'll be even more pissed to know that I'm pregnant, too. With Jarell's baby. So, if that's the way you feel, I won't be coming back with your grandchild either. Good riddance."

And for the one second I stuck around to watch her reaction before I opened the front door and slammed it in her face, life had drained from her body. It was priceless. I laughed as I sauntered to my car with my head held high.

Who cares? This relationship was over.

As far as her level of involvement with the kidnapping? I couldn't be so sure. She did give all the signs that suggested she played a role. Did I have proof? No.

I didn't know what to think.

I needed answers from a few more people.

Chapter Ten

Point of View: Jade Williams

The next day. Thursday morning. I was met with the sun beaming through Alise's spare bedroom window bright and early at five-thirty in the morning. My phone alarm screamed it was time to go to school. I groaned, hitting the snooze button and stared at the ceiling. Not like I needed to snooze anything; I was already fully awake and didn't sleep at all last night.

Considering all my options just so I wouldn't have to go back to school didn't sound like a bad idea at this point. I swear.

Typically, I didn't get up this early to go to school anyway. Regardless of Alise and Kim's warnings about Jarell and Alise's ultimatum regarding school, I had one thing left to do before I made my grand, rare appearance to first period class: go drop Jarell off at his first therapy session, which started at seven o'clock am before school started at seven thirty. A smile rose like the sun. This was going to be the best thing ever. Feeling proud of him for taking this next step was an understatement.

However, the truth of where we stood and will stand still lingered.

Last night's discussion with Kim and Alise stole my sleep for the night. If the shoe was on the other foot, and I was in Jarell's position, would Jarell stay with me? Would Jarell ride for me the way I did for him?

I just didn't know. I didn't know him well enough yet.

And even if I did. Was I truly ready to take the risk of giving my new role at the studio half-assed attention because I was so preoccupied with my relationship with him? Which one was the long-term benefit – the relationship or the career? Which one meant more to me? Which one would foster my personal growth? Which one was sustainable? Was there any possible room for both? Could I strike a balance between the two? What boundaries would need to be set? Which one, if I chose one or the other, would I regret? And most of all…

Would I truly die with Jarell?

Those were the questions.

And I answered every one of them before dawn.

Rolling out of bed, I dressed in a killer lavender and blue romper that showed off my long legs and defined shoulders. Ultimately, the outfit accentuated my neck, bringing full attention to my fire ass haircut.

Finishing my look off with studded earrings, a flashy gold watch, and sparkly gold sandals, I grabbed all my necessities for school and left after giving Alise a quick farewell, who was sitting at her breakfast bar drinking tea. When I rolled up to Jarell's mom's house, he was already outside and sitting on the curb with his arms settled on his knees and his new glasses on that I bought him. His head was down as if deep in thought. Hmm. Strange. Any other time, he sat on the porch to wait, but nonetheless, he looked ready to go. I think.

Taking care not to run his feet over, I pulled next to the curb.

"Hey! My name is Jade, and I'm looking for someone named Jarell. He's got cocoa brown skin, juicy lips, and a smile to die for. Is that you?" I called out, laughing at my own corny joke.

When he heard my voice, he stood and pulled my door opened. He didn't smile, flirt, or anything the way he always would when he got in. Matter of fact, his body was stiff and tense. I was about to give him a quick pick-me-up, but his energy weighed the atmosphere so heavy, surprisingly, the tires didn't go flat.

Okay. This was a side of him I hadn't seen since the first day I had given him a ride home from school. Back when he had hated my guts. He didn't look my way, acknowledge me, or even greet me using any body language or gesture.

Did I do something? Say something? I had left his place on good terms after he agreed to go to therapy, even after our argument. We had hugged and kissed since then. So, what now?

Drilling a hole into the side of his temple with my stare, a long scowl that remained strained the muscles in my face. Jarell no longer owned his favorite oversized hoodie he used to wear every single day to hide his feelings or insecurities by pulling his hood up when he felt discomfort. His mother had torn that apart while trying to save him from harming himself. The most sacred thing he cherished.

Now that he couldn't hide in plain sight, he showed every inch of what he would've been concealing: a look of resignation. What the hell was going on?

My eyes moved over the rest of his body and landed on something that made the hairs on the back of my neck shoot right out of my skin. Three small, open wounds ran down the length of one of his forearms. They were thin and subtle, but noticeable. They didn't look old either, like they had been done just hours ago. I swallowed.

"Jarell, are you okay?" I finally asked.

My eyes met his face again. This time, his head leaned against the window with closed eyes.

He shut me out.

Sighing, I tried not to make a big deal out of this. Things were gonna get worse before they got better. That's why he was going to therapy. But now, his mood complicated how I was going to break this news to him. Maybe this was better than him being in a good mood. I don't know. It was hard to tell with Jarell.

The ride was nothing but the whoosh of other cars passing by with no muffler, and the bass of those who blasted their music until I pulled up to the small therapy building and stopped. His head remained turned towards his window. No matter what, I couldn't let this deter me. I had to do this. For us.

"Hey, before you go in, I need to talk to you about something, and I don't know when else to do it," I started with a voice like silk, cutting into the thick silence. "So, can you please give me your attention?"

He didn't respond, but he opened his eyes. I took a deep breath.

"I don't know how to say this, but… I'll just start from the beginning."

Without a word, he just blinked. Letting out a long exhale, I continued.

"Alise and I had a long conversation yesterday afternoon and last night. Long story short, she gave me an ultimatum."

Now, my breathing was shallow.

"The first part of the ultimatum was that she won't give me a job at the studio or a place to stay if I don't finish up at Crenshaw, even though I've already been applying to apartments anyway. But the second is that she needs my focus on the studio at a time where a lot of things are growing and changing there. Basically, she left me to think about where my priorities need to be. So, I ultimately… I… I…"

"You what?" he mumbled.

"I …think maybe it's best that we… just go our separate ways right now, Jarell. It's best for me, and it's best for you."

Without a second wasted, he shut his eyes and slammed his head into the car's headrest. I tried to not let that distract me.

"I'm gonna have so much responsibility coming up over at the studio, Jarell. I'm shooting for Cardi's new music video on Friday on short notice; Alise doesn't care about all this other shit going on around us, and she expects me to be as sharp as I can be. In just over a month, I'll be running half the studio, and she expects me to be fully present. I'm trying to get through these last few weeks at school and get caught up on missing work. I can't juggle all of this. You should put your energy on getting better and coming to terms with everything. As much as I care about you, and even love you, I just can't throw away my dreams. I've worked so hard for this."

As I spoke, Jarell's eyes remained closed, but a single tear fell from his left one. With aggression, he swiped it away.

"Jarell..." My voice cracked.

He put a hand up and shook his head. I kept speaking, desperate for him to understand.

"I want us to remain friends. I do. Let's keep in touch, let's dance together sometime, let's hike and walk and do the things that make us happy. I promise I'll keep you posted if I find out anything with the kidnapping situation, but as far as having a relationship... we just need to slow down and let all the shit around us settle. I think we might've just been moving too fast. I'm sorry. You don't understand how hard this is to tell you..."

Jarell looked at me, the tears puddled in the bottom of his shaded eyes as he clenched his fists. Yet, the restrained violence in his body language was the complete opposite of how he responded with words.

"I understand, Jade," he whispered. "I don't wanna hold you back from anything. I never expected you to carry the burden of me. That's not what I wanted. Trust me."

"Really?" I huffed with surprise and a grateful smile. "I mean... I don't see you as a burden, though. Are you a lot to support during your healing journey? Yes. But you're not a burden."

"Yeah. I get it." He nodded as if he believed nothing I said. "It don't matter though. You deserve all the happiness, including your dance career and whatever else you got planned. You don't deserve to be held back by me." After that, he opened the car door and slipped a leg out.

"Wait—"

"I'll talk to you later, Jade. I got a lot on my mind right now, so I'll just catch up with you later, whenever you feel like you wanna remain *friends*."

Pulling something out of his pocket, he threw it in my direction, and it landed in my lap.

A new, fresh origami piece of me. Even better than the last one he created. My heart sank. Damn.

"Jarell... wait..." I blinked.

"Later, Jade."

With that, Jarell walked towards the building. I stared at his back, shook. Woah. What the hell just happened? *What the fuck did I just do?* I sobbed as I stared at his origami masterpiece before clutching it to my chest. I had to cherish it because I didn't know if Jarell would ever speak to me after this. Fuck!

In the back of my mind were those new scars on his forearms. They were so *fresh*. I considered running after him to ask about them, but I stayed put as I watched him walk inside. I wiped my eyes and took a deep breath. I just didn't want to see him hurting anymore.

Looking away from the door and putting my car into drive, I pursed my lips. Time to head to Crenshaw, not knowing at all what to expect. I was looking good, had on a cute outfit today, so that aspect about me was nothing that new. I just didn't know how people were gonna receive me, and now, I didn't have Jarell to protect me either. I had to be prepared for the worst. Mentally and emotionally.

Chapter Eleven

Point of View: Jarell Hendricks

It is what it fuckin' is.

That's what I kept convincing myself as I checked in for my therapist appointment. Jade and her so-called breakup with me couldn't be at the center of my mind right now. Too many things fogged my mind for her to be the lightning that made the cloud pour. Not this time.

I sat in the waiting room, scratching at my stinging arms while the familiar feeling of scabs formed when cuts or wounds healed.

Of all people I'd expect to hurt me, I ain't think Ma would be one of them.

I leaned back with a long, irritated exhale. Thinking about Ma wouldn't be wise either. Damn I wished there was a memory vacuum you could just turn on and suck away the bullshit. Not only for my sake, but for theirs. So, I wouldn't have to feel like I should retaliate.

"Jarell? Jarell Hendricks?"

Damn, that was quick, but my awe wasn't with the timeliness more than with the person who called me. She had one thick ass drawl. Like she came straight outta Arkansas. Ain't like I ever been there, but when I was still going to Crenshaw, back Sophomore year working with Ms. Jenson and learning about regions of the United States, she used to play recordings of different dialects to help me remember different areas of the country. Never thought that shit would come in handy until now.

A small grin played at the corner of my mouth as I stood and walked towards her voice. It was rare for someone of the south to take on an overwhelming city like Los Angeles, but here she was. Just by her voice, an image twisted and morphed from nothing to create a complete, live picture of the person who was now going to be a part of my life for the next eight weeks right in front of me.

Her image was so *real*. Down to the body language.

She was short and round with thick thighs, a chubby belly, and a big butt. Her skin donned the color of tree bark and her black, jaw length hair laid pressed straight with a slight curl on the ends. And finally? A motherly "I don't play that shit" kinda scowl, yet her dark brown eyes held the warmth of LA beaches.

She could be my granny fasho. Too bad I never had the fortune of meeting my real ones on Ma nor Dad's side of the family. Either way, it was rare when a visualization of a person happened so quick like this with their voice being the only guide. A part of my heart melted for her.

I sucked in the air. Nah. I had to shake this feeling.

Whatever her name was, probably Hattie Mae or Missy or some shit, was just gonna make me talk about my problems and then make me leave. Like she would even give a fuck. I'm sure ol' lady had enough of her own problems to be buried with mine, even if it was her job to help me. Because with my life? Niggas would need a shot or two of the strongest, top shelf shit before dealing with all the baggage I came with. Hell, Jade couldn't even make it a week as my girlfriend.

"Come on back," she said.

I waited for an added "darling" at the end of that, but it never came. I just lowered my head and followed the sound of her shuffling feet. When we made it to our destination, burning incense wafted through the air, causing my nose to wrinkle. Never liked those things.

"Alright, Mr. Hendricks. There are a couple of sofas in here, all very comfortable. Allow me to guide you to one," she offered.

"I can find it. Thanks," I rejected. I wasn't no helpless vegetable, and she wasn't about to get the satisfaction or even the premature thought to treat me like I was.

In my quest to find the perfect spot, I trudged through the room, my feet sinking into the semi-thick, lush carpet. Various objects in the room had become obstacles at the tips of my toes as I accidentally ran into them while making myself familiar with the space. Instead of getting frustrated, I took the opportunity to reach my hand out to discover its properties.

After a full-on investigation and self-tour, I painted a complete picture of the fairly large room: A round table in the middle was the main attraction while a couple feet away, a desk sat near a window with a bookshelf behind it. That's where the incense burned. A yoga mat hung up next to the entrance door. Two sofas sat on opposite sides of the east and west wall, one leather and one a smooth, velvety feel. I chose to sit on the velvet. I deserved it.

Whole time?

Hattie Mae Missy, whatever her name was, remained silent. She was probably taking notes somewhere or something, watching me like I was an alien.

"You settled in?" she spoke once I felt myself sink deep into the couch to the point of almost dozing off. I forgot I had gotten zero sleep overnight.

I nodded in response.

"Alrighty. Let's start with introductions, but first, I'd like to ask. How are you today?"

Staring out into space, I blinked.

"I don't know," I replied.

"Okay. Well, thank you for being honest. I'll go ahead and introduce myself. Is that okay?"

I shrugged.

"Mmkayy. My name is Trisha Hawthorne. I'm excited you're here with me. It's gonna be a good, helpful, and practical experience. This will be an eight-week program on Tuesdays and

Thursdays for two hours, and hopefully you will leave at the end of the program feeling ready and equipped to handle future challenges that come your way. Any questions so far?"

I shook my head.

"Okay. Based on your profile, I know you've been through a lot. The goal of our sessions together isn't to 'fix you' or 'change' how you feel about anything that has ever happened to you. The goal is to help you build strong coping strategies, exercises you can use and do to help you when you think of these traumatic experiences, and second, to help you seek people you trust when you're having a hard time. The last thing we want to do is re-traumatize you or damage you in these sessions. And sometimes, I will rely on you if you are able to tell me when things get to be too much. Or of course, if I see you are visibly displaying a level of stress or emotion that shows we should stop for the day. How does that sound?"

Again, I nodded, but the more she talked, the more my body quaked. I didn't know if I could do this.

"Okay. Are you sure you don't have any other questions?" she asked.

I shook my head.

"Well, let's not waste any more time and begin for today," she said as the page turned in her notepad. "First request I have. Let me get to know you. Tell me about yourself, Jarell."

I blinked and tilted my head before giving her a gesture that suggested I ain't give a damn about telling her anything. What kinda question was that?

"W-What do you want to know?"

"Anything you'd like me to know. Or anything you'd like anyone to know about you when they first meet you. What would you tell them?"

"Um..." I started as my eyes shifted around the room. "I ... I don't know."

"Anything. It's up to you. You can define who you are in this moment instead of saying things other people would say that don't necessarily reflect you and who you are."

"I said, I don't know," I replied. "Final answer."

"Well… if you're not going to say anything on your own, I will have to use what others say. I will confess that I've read a lot about you." The smile in her voice broke through.

"From who and where?"

"Your profile. Your mom set it up for you before our first appointment. You seem to be a special and very unique person."

"What she say?"

"For starters, you love basketball, you love to dance, and you love making origami. Are you able to tell me more about these things?"

Damn. Basketball. Hadn't thought about that in a while. Surprised Ma even remembered that.

But in response, I just shrugged again. I wasn't tryna talk to her. Not only was I not in the mood, but I just didn't trust her. She wasn't gonna stick around and stick with me through all of this. She didn't care – she was here to get a check and go home. I wasn't telling her shit.

"Are you just going to shrug your way through our time together, Jarell?" Trisha asked. I could even hear the eyebrow raise in her voice.

"Maybe." I shrugged again.

"You know that isn't going to be helpful, right?"

With another lift of my shoulder, I said, "It wasn't going to be helpful to begin with."

Silence then followed before she sighed. Her chair slid back as she rose, and then the couch dipped a little bit next to me. I scooted as far to the end of the couch as possible to keep my distance and scrunched up against the arm rest of the sofa.

"Jarell, I'm not going to hurt you," she replied with a gentle tone.

I didn't care. I had already felt violated for some reason or another. I couldn't help it, but both of my hands met each other as I began to fidget.

"I know you've been through a lot, okay? I'm not going to pretend that I know you because I don't. I don't want to be arrogant, or some know it all and tell you everything about your life and how to fix you or how to even tell you how you should feel. I'm here to help. Okay? I know that it will be hard, but the main thing I am here to do is listen. To listen to you because I am quite sure not many people have. Let me be your sounding board. At least use me for that. You don't have to trust me right now, okay? Or quite frankly, ever. But what you say here will stay here. I can guarantee you that from our time together."

Still, I didn't look her way or even relax. For some reason, I didn't feel like I had the option to. This was already way too much. Kinda overbearing. Or maybe she was overbearing. Or maybe I was just too much of a closed-off person to even let a harmless old lady in to talk about things in my life I could talk to no one else about.

For real. Was I intimidated by someone who I felt like could be my grandma the second she opened her mouth to call my name? Damn. Was I that messed up? Silence led the way for a few minutes before Trisha spoke again.

"You can share whenever you'd like, or we can end our session for today and start fresh next time. It's up to you. I just wanted to introduce myself to you, give you an overview of what to expect during therapy, and give you an opportunity to tell me a little more about yourself, just so that we start on a fresh footing. I understand your distrust, Jarell. I do," she added.

"...Nah, s'cool. I'll share," I replied, biting my lip without giving her eye contact.

"Okay. You can talk about origami, dance, or basketball. Or something else of your choosing. Whatever it is, I'm sure you'll expose just how unique you are."

"Well… I loved basketball a lot before I went blind. I'm assuming you can already guess that I can't see. I used to play with my friends back home all the time. One of the only things I cared about back then when I was in elementary and middle school."

"Interesting. Say more."

"I mean…" I tilted my head, still reluctant to speak. "I can't play anymore, so I avoid having anything to do with it now because it reminds me of what I can't do. I also do like to dance, but I didn't always care about it the way I do now. But the one I love the most is origami. I just like … doing things with my hands and making things of the world I can't see anymore. Especially because I like being outside and doing things outside in nature."

Trisha scribbled fervently in her notepad.

"Very good! I see when you spoke about basketball, you smiled. The light in your eyes just twinkled. Tell me more about that. What makes basketball so special?"

Damn, I was smiling? Shit I ain't even realize it. I had to wipe it off before she got too excited. I dipped my head before I answered.

"It's special because it was a huge part of my old life. When life was good, and I didn't have many worries. Back in Chicago."

"Oh! Chicago, huh? Didn't know you lived there before. How long have you lived there previously?"

"Mmm… about eleven years."

"Okay. Is basketball in Chicago something you'd like to relive and share?" she asked. "I'd love to know that part of you as we continue our time together. And it will definitely be a great thing to use as we talk about strategies and healing."

Damn. Chicago. Where would I even begin? There was so much there I left behind. So many things I wished I could've brought with to my new life here. Yet, it was also a special place. A happy place for many years until it all came crashing down. I closed my eyes and searched my vault of memories for the perfect one to tell. After a few minutes, the memory began to play back like an old film.

"Well," I finally spoke, "this ain't just about basketball itself, but it happened on the apartment courts, which was my favorite place. I remember when..."

Chicago, Illinois – May, 2009

Already two in the afternoon and I'm late.

Way late.

Everyone probably asking about me, wondering where I am. Everybody in the hood my age comes outside by at least ten in the morning on Saturdays, so I know they're thinking I bitched out of this dare I said I was gonna do. That's what happens when you be out with your mom in the mornings on her errand runs. Or should I say **marathons**. *And I know I'm not the only one who feels like this because me and my bruhs talk about it all the time. How moms never seem to care that you got your own plans while they force you to be a part of theirs on Saturdays. And don't even think about letting them know your plans, either. They'll ruin it and take even longer.*

I'm eleven now, but Mommy still won't leave me in the house alone or let me go outside and take care of myself while she takes care of her Saturday business. I keep telling her I can make my own grilled cheese sandwiches, and can even pop in a mean frozen pizza, but she still thinks I'll burn the house down. How could that happen if I set a timer?

I also tell her I won't get into any trouble outside on the blacktops either because her friends, like Alex's mom, are watching me, too. She don't care though. That's the thing about Mommy. She calls me super responsible and helpful but won't let me be responsible on my own. Moms don't ever make sense, I swear.

One leg in my basketball shorts and the other one out, I hop around in a rush, looking for my outside shoes. Dang, where are they? I got places to go, people to see! I can't waste another minute in here when I saw how fun it looked outside when me and Mommy rode past on our way home from the grocery store. Either way, I can't find the stupid things. I pause and growl.

Wow, my room looks like a tornado came through. Mommy would kill me if she saw me even think about going outside with my room like this. Quickly, I shove my clean and dirty clothes combined under the bed and in the closet to be sorted out later. She'll never know. I just gotta hurry up.

I find my shoes in a corner near my dresser. I stuff a couple of important things in my shorts pocket I'm gonna use later outside. I put on my shoes without untying them, heels not even fully in them and rush to the front door.

"Aht, aht! Jarell!"

Got darn it! I sigh and dip my head. My hand was literally on the doorknob. So close!

"Yeah, Mommy?"

"Get in here," she growls.

I thrust my head back and roll my eyes. Slowly, I drag my feet to the kitchen where she is.

"Yes, Mommy?"

"Before you go outside, I need you to help me put away the groceries, wash these dishes and sweep the floor. I'll clean everywhere else. Your friends ain't going nowhere."

"Are you serious?"

This can't be the day. This is the absolute worst day she could do this. I had a whole plan with my friends outside today that I've been anxious about all day! **Please don't do this to me.**

"Mommy," I start to stomp and whine, "it's already two-thirty!"

"Jarell, don't you start with me. You were supposed to do this two days ago, and I let you go outside until eight p.m. both nights after school. You're not getting away with it this time," she says, crossing her arms.

"But I was with you all day!"

"I don't care if we were together twenty-four-seven for a week. You have responsibilities at home, Jarell. You ain't missing nothing outside."

"I am, though!"

"No, you're not. Trust me, I been there before. And if you missing something, your friends will tell you all about it at school Monday."

"By the time I get done with all this, it'll be like five o'clock."

"Then so be it. I don't care about your little friends out there. You got stuff you need to do, and they mamas need to make sure their kids doing what they need to do as well."

I know that voice. That sharp voice with a little bass that says she ain't arguing anymore. I ain't winning this one today. I smack my lips and take off my shoes with reluctance in the middle of the kitchen.

"See look, you dirtying up the kitchen even more by putting those shoes you been playing in the dirt with up in here. Next thing you're going to do is mop, since you acting all crazy right now. And your damn feet weren't in the shoes all the way anyway; I know I ain't raise you to dress like that!"

I huff at the thought of extra chores, ignoring the critique about how I put the shoes on.

"You're just trying to hang out with me," I mumble. She thinks I'm talking crap. I know it, just by the way the air tenses up.

"What was that?" she asks, and gets close to me, her ear in my face. If I'm not careful, I might get popped. "What was that you just said?"

"I said, you're just trying to hang out with me, or you want me around, but you're saying that I have to do all these chores instead of just saying you wanna hang out," I say louder.

She pauses for a second to take in what I said, and my stomach kinda jumps a bit because I know I'm in trouble for talking back this time. Her frustrated mom look turns into a smile, and then laughter. I sigh in relief. She gives me that look that she always does when she can't stay mad at me. It's like this twinkle in her eyes that shows just how much she loves me.

Of course, I love Mommy, too. But you know, sometimes, I gotta do my own thing with my friends. She doesn't get it sometimes and be cramping my whole style. I'm like her best friend. She's mine too, but I ain't as clingy. Next thing I know, she'll be telling all my friends I still call her Mommy to isolate me so she can have me all to herself. I hope that never happens. Me calling her Mommy is an "us" thing.

"Boy," she says, putting me in a playful lock hold and digs her knuckles in the top of my head.

"Ow, ow stop, stop!" I scream and giggle, she and looks at me again like I'm her most prized possession.

"Get to them dishes before I put a hurting on you."

She grabs my head and shakes it. I smile. I look around, and there are a lot of groceries, which I'm thankful for. It's been so long since we've had a full house. Man. I guess that's the least I can do. Help her out with that, since it looks like a big task to do on her own.

I help her with everything she asks me to do. The groceries and the sweeping. She's actually serious about me mopping, which I didn't expect, so I go and get the bucket, filling it up with hot water. I try my hardest not to look at the clock. I guess it's just one of those days I don't get to hang out. I'll have to do the big thing I had planned to do today another time.

"Jarell, how's school? You never talk about it much. I know it's because I'm at work all the time but tell me. What's going on there?" she asks me as she wipes down the counters.

"School is school," I say with a shrug, starting up the dish water.

"Seriously, Jarell. What are you learning? If you're learning anything at all? What's the social life like?"

"We're learning about … um… I don't know. I think we're learning long division in math. In reading, we're learning about grammar. In science, we're learning about bugs. And social studies, we're learning about map skills."

"You think you're learning that stuff? Maybe you should stop socializing and flirting so much so that you will know what you're learning," she says. She has a smirk on her face.

"I'm not flirting."

"How's your friends?" she asks and gives me this weird side eye.

I shift. I look around the kitchen with a frown and say, "They're okay."

"That's all? You sure were pressed to go outside today for them to just be okay," she says, smiling. Alright. Now, she's being strange.

"What am I supposed to say about them?"

"I found a note in your jeans from doing laundry a couple days ago. You got something to share with me?"

"I don't know what you're talking about, Mommy."

"You like a new girl, now?" she asks and raises her eyebrows.

Oh. Now, I understand. My heart drops, and so do my shoulders. The note is in my shorts pocket right now, and now, it seems like it burns my leg. She smiles even wider at my reaction because she knows I'm caught. I forgot I left that note in my good pants pocket before the laundry.

The note she's talking about is when I'd ask Isabella out. I've crushed on her since kindergarten. We're in fifth grade now, so we're grown up. And she just gets prettier and prettier. Especially her long, black hair. My friends who know about it keep daring me to ask her out, but I've been scared. I stupidly accepted a new dare yesterday at school and told them I'd do it and give her the note to-day in front of them when we go outside. It's kind of a whole letter, not a note. I just hope Mommy didn't read it. I'm okay with her knowing I like someone, just not knowing what I've written.

"Yeah, Mommy. I like Isabella."

"Awww," she squeals. I roll my eyes.

"You didn't read it, did you?" I ask turning my back.

"Of course I did, honey. I thought it was thoughtful and sweet," she replies. "It just confirmed I'm raising a gentleman."

"*Can I have any privacy?*" *I say while she laughs.*

"*You can. It just fell out of your pocket, so I couldn't resist.*"

"*Yeah, yeah.*"

"*Isabella is a nice girl. Her mom is nice too. Good choice, son. Did you ask her already?*"

"*Well, no because that was the plan before you told me to come in here and do chores,*" *I mumble and begin to scrub an iron skillet.*

"*Oh, so that was the big rush!*" *She nods her head.*

"*Yes, Mommy. That was the plan. Alex, Rob, and Jon dared me to ask her today.*"

I can feel her staring at the back of my head while I wash these dishes. I turn around, and she's looking at me all dreamy eyed. Maybe not dreamy eyed, but a look like she feels my pain. Or understands at least. Finally, she sighs with her hands up.

"*Alright, fine. Listen. Finish the dish you're doing and go on outside. I'll mop the floor and put your laundry in your room,*" *she says.* "*You're coming back to finish the rest of the dishes though. You're not going to bed until you do.*"

"*Yes! Thank you, Mommy,*" *I say, and kiss her on the cheek. I put my shoes on halfway again and then sprint out the door, so she doesn't find something else for me to do. I know she laughs at me.*

~ ~ ~

All my friends are in the same spot they were in when Mommy and I drove past, playing around on the black top of the basketball courts when I arrive. Thank goodness. I didn't even check the clock when I left the house, but it doesn't matter now. I'm here.

I see my homies Alex, Robert, and Jonathan are playing a game of twenty-one when they're closer to my view. They're not paying the girls any attention on the other half of the court who are talking, jump roping, dancing, and doing each other's hair. Girls can be so boring sometimes. Who does hair for fun?

I scan around, and once I see Isabella is one of the girls who is in the crowd, I blank out everyone else. My heart starts beating fast.

The note starts burning my leg again along with the fifteen dollars I stole from my mom for this dare. Today is the day.

She's with her friends in a circle talking, and I take a deep breath as I approach the courts. Jonathan sees me first and brings all the attention to me.

"Hey, look who's finally here! Rell, Rell! What took you so long?" he asks, holding the ball to pause the game.

"My mom," I say.

"Oh. You got in trouble or somethin'?"

"No, she just wanted me to go to the store with her and do some chores. That's all."

"Oh alright." He nods, glaring at me like I'm supposed to say something else. I turn away so I don't have to meet his eye.

"Hey, you should hop in this game," says Robert. "We been waiting on you all day!"

"No. Forget the game for a second. He has a plan, ain't that right, Rell? We ain't forget what you supposed to do," Alex says, and gives me a dark look with a smile.

I smirk and give him a side eye like I don't know what he's talking about. He knew about this dare before anyone did, since he's my best friend. So, he definitely isn't letting this slide.

"Oh yeah!" Robert says, smiling all bright. "That's right!"

"There she go over there," says Jonathan.

We all turn towards Isabella, and she doesn't even notice we're all staring at her. Good. I need a bit more time to build up some confidence. I've asked girls out before, but they were never like Isabella. And I never liked them the way I liked her. Secretly, the whole time I've dated other girls, I liked Isabella more.

"So, you gonna do it or what?" asks Alex.

"You might as well get that five dollars ready. All of you," I say, but inside, I'm feeling like Jell-O.

"Man, whatever. You scary, I ain't losing my five dollars. You been liking her since kindergarten, and you never asked her. What makes today so different?" asks Robert.

"I don't know." I shrug.

"He ain't gonna do it," says Jonathan. "He won't even ask her out, so I know he won't give her that letter he wrote. Did you bring it?"

I nod.

"Alright. Double the cost if you ask her out and give her the letter," says Alex.

"Triple the cost if you kiss her," says Robert.

They all look at each other with satisfaction.

"Yeaahhh," they all say in unison.

Man, see they always had to take it too far. Kiss her? What if she doesn't want to be kissed? I'd hate to get slapped in front of everyone. My mom always taught me to ask a girl how she feels first before making any move.

Again, I look over at her. She's smiling this time, showing her pretty teeth. I can't let myself and my friends down. I'll show them. I may be the shyest one out the group, but I never backed down from a challenge.

"It's a deal," I say, looking each of them in the eye.

They all burst into laughter.

"Yeah right. Go do it, then."

"Alright." I shrug like it's no big deal, but my palms get sweaty the moment the word comes out of my mouth.

One last huge breath, and I am walking over to her and her friends. My homies follow behind, making fun of me. I hate them for the moment. They need to root me on, not make me more nervous!

When I reach the circle, Isabella and her friends look at us like we don't belong on their half of the court. Like it was reserved for all girls only. I stop in front of Isabella and give her a smile.

"Um... hey Jarell." She waves.

"Hey," I say, and I know I sounded like a cat. Immediately, my friends cackle behind me. I turn around to them and whisper, "Shut up!"

"What's up? What are you guys doing over here?" she asks.

I look back at them again, and they all have their eyebrows raised. I sigh and turn towards her.

"Izzy, I have something to give you," I say, and I feel myself blushing. I wish I wouldn't.

"What is it?"

"Well..." I look at my friends again, and they're still snickering. "Before I give it to you, I want you to know that they didn't put me up to this. This is something I feel, so please don't think it's something that has to do with them."

"What are you talking about?" she asks.

"I want to tell you something."

"What is it, Jarell? You're scaring me."

"It's nothing to be scared about. I just... I want to tell you how pretty you are, and I've liked you since Kindergarten."

"Ooooh!" My friends mock me, but I force myself to ignore them. Isabella just stares at me with wide eyes. She's so beautiful, I barely even remember what I'm supposed to say.

"And... I'm wondering if you'd like to go out with me?" I finally ask, swallowing.

It's dead silent right now, and the anticipation is killing me. I pray she doesn't reject me in front of everyone. That will suck, not only because my friends are around, but because I like her. My friends are kind of relentless in that way, too. They will never let me live it down if she does.

"That's sweet, Jarell," she says, and her friends are also behind her, giggling. "I wish I could, but I'm moving away tomorrow. I'm going to a new school."

"What? A new school? Tomorrow? Why?"

I feel everything inside of me crush. She can't be moving away!

"Yeah. My mom said something about people tearing down our apartment and doing construction. She said our building is going to change and the cost is going to go way up. So, we have to go somewhere else," she tells me.

"Oh," I say, and dip my head in disappointment. I wonder if that was going to happen to our apartment building, too.

"Yeah. She says she saw outside some weird people checking out our neighborhood, and now, they're tearing everything down. But I would go out with you if I was staying. I always thought you were cute, too," she says with a smile that makes my heart flutter.

"For real?"

"Yeah. Here's something to remember me," she says. Then, she pulls out her school picture and hands it to me.

"Thanks," I say and stare at it like it's a treasure. I am going to miss her so much.

"You're welcome, Jarell."

To my surprise, she kisses me on the cheek. All hell breaks loose then. All my friends start running around and screaming and laughing, making a big deal of it. Her friends coo at us. All I can feel is my body tingling and my heart beating fast instead of fluttering. I had no idea she liked me as much as I like her. I just wish I'd talked to her sooner.

"I hope I see you again, Jarell. I'm going to miss it here."

"Yeah. Same. I'm gonna miss you," I confess.

"Yeah. I'll see you around, ok? My mom said I have to be in at six to pack," she says, and then turns and smiles at her friends to leave.

"Wait!" I call out. I step to her and grab her arm before she goes.

"Yeah?"

With no hesitation, I lean in and kiss Izzy on the lips. She easily accepts. Whatever hell that broke loose before got way worse. Now, the girls ran around screaming how cute it was, but surprisingly, all my homies stared at me with their mouths dropped. I smirked.

"Here, take this," I say to Isabella. I give her my love confession. "Here's to remember me."

She doesn't say thank you, but the look in her eyes tell me everything. Instead, her response is a laugh, and she runs away with her friends who are squealing and talking about it all.

I look back at my homies, and with a smug, I put my hand out and do this forward motion. They all look like they caught the flu.

"Run me forty-five dollars now. Me and my momma could use it."

~ ~ ~

"So, I haven't seen Isabella since that day, but I'll always remember that. They were so salty about losing that money." I chuckled.

"Jarell that was the sweetest memory. How does that memory make you feel?" Trisha asked, still writing quickly in her notebook.

"It makes me feel like I was the finest dude on Earth." I smirked, feeling my skin warm. Never thought I'd still feel that soft spot for Isabella. I hadn't thought about her in years. What did she look like? Would she still feel the same about me the way she did back then?

"Okay, I can see that! How would you describe how you're feeling right now?" she asked.

"Um… calm. I guess," I replied.

"What about that memory makes you feel that way?"

"I don't know… I guess just being in a place that made me happy and being around people who made me feel happy. Like … they made me feel like I was important," I said.

"That's very reflective of you, Jarell. I can even see you're more relaxed. Your muscles have loosened, and your shoulders aren't as tense. Are there any places or locations in your life right now that make you feel as calm and important as the basketball court did in Chicago?"

I bit my lip and pondered. Were there?

"I don't know. Maybe the paths I use to go hiking. I don't feel important there, but I feel calm. Or my bedroom. I don't feel calm there, but I feel important because of the origami I create. No place exists right now that would give me both feelings at the same time."

"Interesting," Trisha said with a nod. "We will unpack more about the origami in the next couple of weeks because on Tuesday, I'd like to talk more about your other hobbies. However, let's end our day with some coping tips and exercises I'd like to give you before you leave. Is that okay with you?"

I nodded.

"I want you to think about how you feel right now sitting here. In this moment. Whenever you begin to feel like you're ramping up or feel that rage rising in your chest that your mother wrote about in your profile, I want you to try and seek your personal location of calm or comfort. If you cannot physically get there, try these recordings of mindfulness activities that will help you begin centering yourself, becoming present, and aware of your feelings. I often don't say this to folks, but at some point during the mindfulness, let your mind wander to those moments on the basketball court or where you hike. That will help you lessen those moments of anger. So, let's practice that right now together."

And we did. For about twenty minutes, we completed the mindfulness activity that played from the app on her phone. I nearly went to sleep, but that was the most grounding shit I had ever done. Never felt so aware of my body and how stress and tension could exist in the smallest muscles. Even my feet.

I never thought life in Chicago could ever be the source of healing and happiness. Just thought it would make me sadder. Madder. Make me more ... hurt.

But as I left today's session, I felt none of those. Instead, I felt something rarer.

Pride.

Chapter Twelve

Point of View: Jade Williams

When I walked through the doors of Crenshaw High, I made sure all tears disappeared after doing the hardest thing I'd ever have to do in my life. How the hell was I supposed to function today after that breakup?

Once inside, the scene wasn't that much different than when I left it a week ago walking arm in arm with Jarell, protecting him from the harm D-Block would inflict due to their senseless anger after he beat up Martell.

Once I made it past the doorway threshold and metal detectors, it was like I stepped in a pool of superglue. My legs were cinderblocks as I surveyed the morning scene. Everyone buzzed around doing all kinds of shit, signaling that the end of the school year was here. Play fighting and sprinting the halls like a track field, multiple couples making out near lockers. Cliques and circles of the underclassmen twerking and playing music from their mini-Bluetooth stereos. Just a bunch of turning up, like no one gave a damn two of their schoolmates almost died in the pool down the hall just days ago. Nothing was somber about this place.

For the first time ever, as I stood here, no one gave me even a glimpse, and my stomach turned at it. Should I be grateful or deflated? Either way, losing the throne of the school was hard. Thank goodness it was almost over. Six weeks, Jade. Six weeks.

The weighty feeling of my legs lifted after I took a breath, lifted my chin up high, hauled my bag over my shoulder, and pressed forward towards my locker.

You got a job to do, girl.

Finish up missing work. Attend the remainder of classes. Graduate.

... and find out who kidnapped us.

That's it, that's all.

My presence brought more attention as I strutted down the hallway from the Freshman wing to the Senior wing. The older the kids in the hallway got, the more eyes landed on me, which was such a paradox. You'd have thought the younger ones would care enough to stare, but I guess this solidified the immaturity of this shitty school. Many eyes fixated on my hair in curiosity. Yup. I was still the baddest bitch here, whether everyone hated me or not. With long hair, short hair, no hair, I'd still be the one these bitches competed with.

But I never made eye contact or even much less smirk. I just kept it pushing. Didn't even know who was talking or what was said about me. Again. I was outta here in six weeks. Who cared about being the baddest bitch anymore?

At last, I made it to the Senior wing, and D-Block was just ahead around the corner. My legs slowed down, and my chest fluttered as if it would fly away and take my soul right with it. My fingers tightened around my bag before I reached the block. The last thing I needed was to start sweating, so I closed my eyes and bit my lip before continuing on.

I peeked around the corner, and the block was nothing like it used to be. Shit had a whole new feel.

Now? Several resource officers patrolled and posted up in the hallway like club bouncers. The same D-Block crew members and bullies who camped out here were still present from Martell to Erica to Tazz. But it wasn't the usual circus. At all. They were quiet and borderline bored as the group's circle conversed, but clearly not shit talking about someone else.

Down the way, the old graffiti decorating the halls with our infamous name was being scrubbed clean off the walls by one of

D-Block's rising junior "stars" Brent Richardson. Another basketball player who would likely take the reins of D-Block now that Mike and Martell were graduating. Didn't look like he would have much future control by the looks of it. Might be the ringleader of cleaning up the place.

Hmph. Wow. This school was on a mission to turn shit around. For good.

I must've been surveying the area too long. To my demise, Martell's eyes slammed into mine. As he death glared my way, his mouth moved with inaudible words, and others in the circle shot a look at me, too. Fast, I turned my head and kept moving towards my locker. *Fuck.*

I had to find my best friend, Laurie. The only person I knew I could talk to and trust. One that didn't hate me like everyone else did, even though she was the quiet member of my shit list.

As I approached my locker, there she was near hers, leaning up against the wall and talking with one of our cheerleading teammates, Arianna. Once I was in her line of sight, her bright smile and laugh at whatever Arianna said morphed into a small frown, burrowed brows, and overall concern.

"Arianna let's talk later," Laurie said, rushed. Arianna, whose back faced me, shifted around to follow Laurie's gaze and balked the second she saw me. Her eyes glazed over my hair before giving me a full-on mean mug and a curled lip before walking away without any other acknowledgement.

Yeah. Her ass was a part of the D-Block "let's hate Jade Williams" operation too. At least hers was a little more warranted. I had dropped her during an air stunt on the football field earlier this year on accident. That video was still getting likes and comments even six months later from all over the country. With how well known I was due to my dance career, it didn't take long for me to get tagged in it all the damn time.

"Jade... you cut your hair," Laurie said more than asked.

I rubbed my arm and looked away. "I think that's pretty clear."

"It looks good, but …why?"

"Long story."

"Well… where have you been? Didn't you get out a couple days ago? It's already Thursday. I thought you got out the hospital on Monday."

"Another long story. Listen. Why did you block me on Instagram?" I asked with a hand on my waist, cutting right to the chase.

She rolled her eyes. "Why is it that every time I ask you something, we have to sidestep it because you wanna talk about what *you* wanna talk about? Answer my questions first. Then I'll tell you why." She crossed her arms.

I gave her a long look, but she raised an eyebrow and shifted her weight in resistance, popping her hip to the air. Ha. Okay.

"Fine," I whispered. Before continuing to spill some of the beans, I gazed around to make sure no one was close enough to hear us. "Long story short, I cut my hair because Tuesday morning, like in the wee hours of the morning, Jarell and I got into some real serious shit with about five guys at gunpoint. One of them pulled my hair to the point many sections got pulled out. So, I just ended up cutting it even."

She gasped. "Are you serious?"

"Yes, girl. Don't know who did it, but I'm gonna find out."

"How'd you get away? Are you okay?"

"Now that, I can't tell you. Active criminal case. But I'm okay. I have a feeling some of these idiots here had something to do with it, and I'ma do whatever I gotta do to figure it out."

"No, Jade. Can I be honest?"

I blinked and extended my neck.

"The common denominator to all of your woes or whatever you wanna call it is that stupid ass retard Jarell. Why do you insist on staying and being around him? He was the reason you nearly died! And now, apparently, is also the reason you almost died again with five guys at gun point. Am I right?" she asked, her ocean blue eyes turning dark.

I could've screamed and pulled the rest of my hair out. *Why was everyone attacking him!?*

"Laurie, don't you fuckin' start..."

"It's true, Jade! Why don't you listen to me?"

"The same reason why you won't listen to me about Martell being a piece of shit, but you still fuck with him." I shrugged.

She straightened up and smacked her lips. "That's completely different, Jade, and you know it."

"Is it?"

She shook her head and waved her hand.

"No, no, no. We're not going there."

"Alright, well then we're not going there about Jarell, either." I popped my tongue.

"Whatever, Jade. I don't have time for this," she said, maneuvered past me, and attempted to walk away, but I grabbed her arm before she got too far. "What the... let go of me!"

"Chill, Laurie. I'm not even hurting you." I huffed and let her go before one of those stupid resource officers down the hall interpreted this as a brewing fight. "You gonna tell me why you blocked me or what?"

"Seriously? Are you really asking me that, Jade?"

"I wouldn't bring it up again if I didn't wanna know. What's up with that? Some fake ass shit if you ask me."

"Fake? Wow. You don't get it, do you? You and Jarell are the reason why this school has gone to shit and why the police now have set up shop in our hallway! You got blocked because we don't know who you're talking to, and we don't want you reading comments and snitching. All because you're trying to protect that creepy ass bum. You have the community going crazy, like we're this awful school and awful people. Yet, you won't tell everybody you used to be a part of it. You bullied Jarell too, but you want to act like some angel. You should be scrubbing those hallways just like Brent is."

With that, Laurie stormed away with her fine, thin blonde hair flowing behind her like a cape.

I closed my eyes. Welp. There goes my best friend. For now. She always comes around. I'll just give her time. Nothing ever tore us apart, and if she knew I had broken up with Jarell, she'd be singing a different tune.

The bell rang for first period class to start. English class. When I showed my face, late as usual, my teacher's eyes almost bugged out. With a huff and hand on my hip, I told him not to even start with me.

"No, I'm not going to do what you call 'start' with you, Jade, but I'm just… I'm glad you're back. And I'm glad you're alive and okay," Mr. George said. "Stop by during office hours to get caught up on your work. You've missed quite a bit, so make sure you're responsible and pick up your missing work and turn it in."

"Thanks," I whispered and then moved to my seat, avoiding eye contact with everyone.

The whole class was a snooze fest. It wasn't hard to avoid eye contact with everybody because I fell the fuck asleep. But best believe once again, when that bell sounded, I woke up and darted out of class, the first out even though I was the last to walk in. I didn't give a damn about being a C student for this last year. All these irrelevant ass books from Europe they had us reading was just doing the most. I'd much prefer History or any of the social sciences because at least it was relatable and the conversations fruitful. Science, Math… all that other mess could go.

I don't know why I was moving so fast though because where was I rushing to? D-Block was out. Maybe to my locker to pretend fixing my hair and outfit, but that couldn't happen after every class period. Jarell wasn't here to search for and flirt with. Laurie's mad ass wasn't an option.

So now what?

I paced the halls towards the courtyard to think alone before my next class started. On the way there, again, Mike Harrison was currently being swarmed by a brand new thotty who wasn't the red head witch from the mall. But this new one was even more hideous. I thought I ain't have no ass, but her love handles all by themselves could've padded her butt the way it needed to if the fat had grown in the right places.

I paused and swiped a hand over my face.

That was a mean ass thought. I shouldn't have been body shaming her. She wasn't even the problem. He was! What a hoe ass nigga. Glad I didn't have sex with him because now, who knew how many bodies he had? Except this time, I wasn't letting him slide without acknowledgement.

I moseyed up to them both as Mike smooched all over ol' girl's collarbone, and her head peeled back, giggling and giving him as much access as possible. When she saw me in her line of sight, her cheesy smile transformed into a scowl.

"Can I help you?" she interrogated.

"Not really because I ain't here for you. I'm here for him." I pointed past her as Mike's eyes shifted to meet mine. He did a onceover from head to toe of my body before he smacked his lips, mumbled something inaudible, and turned his head away.

She pulled away from him and sized me up. "What you need with him? Ain't you old news?"

"Girl, gone somewhere." I waved her off like the unimportant puppy she was. "You ain't his momma. What's understood ain't gotta be explained about the fact that I got a bone to pick with him. Run along now."

"Bitch –"

I rolled my eyes as Mike stood in front of her.

"Aye, aye, aye, now baby. We ain't doing all that fighting shit alright? We ain't got time to be dealing with all that, and I ain't in the mood for the extra," Mike whispered to her with his hands on her shoulders.

"Girl, I wish you would lay a hand on me. I don't know why you getting all worked up anyway. I don't want his ass at all, let's be clear. Everybody knows that, so why you feeling threatened by me?" I asked her.

"Mike, please let me slap her goofy ass. I've been waiting for the opportunity, and now that she ain't on D-Block, I would love to do it," she begged, but Mike kept pushing her away from me. "Stupid bitch!"

I just laughed.

"I'm not the stupid one. You ain't the only female he kissing on, but that ain't my business." I shrugged and surveyed my nails.

With pressed lips, Mike's hazel green eyes bore into me. A look that could kill.

"Lizet, just please give me a second," Mike requested.

"So, you're just gonna stick up for her? She can just interrupt what we were doing without consequence?"

"No," he said, a firm dissent. "I'm trying not to have you fighting, so let me see what her ass wants with me. It ain't got nothing to do with me sticking up for her."

I smirked and shook my head with my arms crossed. What a crock of shit.

"Whatever, Mike. I'm not going anywhere. I'm gonna stand right over here and wait," she said with her nose in the air and crossed arms.

"Fine. Whatever you gotta do," he said, and then backed up a few steps before turning back to me.

"I see this is the second female this week you're slobbering over. Didn't know you'd be so easy," I said under my breath.

"Jade, what the hell you want? I swear, life been smooth as fuck without you in my face every damn day wanting to talk about some shit, but here you are …"

"Mike, I'm not gonna let you ignore or disrespect me like we ain't been friends. Like we ain't ever kiss and hug up on each other. Man up and talk."

"Talk about what? Talk about fucking what? Get yo' ass outta here man, for real. Yo' annoying ass always tryna 'talk.' The shit is over between us, and you made that clear fucking around with Jarell," he said.

My eyes ballooned. "What? Um, don't try to alter the story! *You* made it clear we were done when you dragged me along without committing to me, and when you damn near raped me in the backseat of your uncle's car," I seethed.

"What?" he bellowed with narrow eyes. "Raped you? Now you know you lying! I hope you ain't one of those dumb hoes who ruin niggas' careers tryna get clout off fake rape allegations. If so, I swear to God..."

"I'm lying? I'm lying!?" I pointed a finger at my chest. "So, you ain't try to force me to fuck you in the truck Homecoming night when I wanted to go home or to a hotel? You didn't tell me 'You know you want this?' when I tried to stop? You didn't do that Mike? A'ight." I smacked my lips and nodded.

"I didn't rape you, Jade." Mike shrugged, the first tardy bell echoing throughout the hallway.

"You didn't, but barely! But that's not even the point. Just apologize, Mike! Seriously. After all the shit we've been through since Freshman year and being together, as former friends and even a former couple, the least you can do is apologize. I'm not trying to ruin your little bitty basketball career. What I'm mad about is you dogging me out, and had you not done that, dragging me along by your stupid strings, there might've been no Jarell to mess around with to bruise your funky little ego."

"I'm not apologizing for something I didn't do, so what's the real reason you came over here? Because you honestly don't give a fuck about us not being together at this point and neither do I. Be real with yourself," he said, stroking a brush over his smooth, black waves repeatedly and wiped nonexistent dust from his shirt.

My hand itched to smack him in the mouth. Bad. The lack of accountability on his end had me real hot, but instead, I gritted and grinded my teeth to contain the urge. When that was settled down, another desire rose to flee the situation all together so I could stew in anger elsewhere, but I had a job to do.

"What do you know about this past Monday night into Tuesday morning?" I asked.

His brows nestled into a frown. "Huh? Fuck you talkin' about?"

"Jarell and I got into some shit where we got set up and coulda got hurt, and I got a good feeling some of y'all got something to do with it, since y'all playing 'let's hate Jade' now and all of y'all blocked me off your social media accounts. Since Jarell beat your friends' asses. So how 'bout you be real with me. What you know about it?"

His eyes relaxed with indifference. "I don't know what the hell you talking about. You always in some fucking drama; I ain't got shit to do with that."

"Please don't play stupid. You're already not telling the truth or apologizing for your toxic shit, so at least be truthful about this. I could've died," I said.

"I. Don't. Know. What. You're. Talking. About. You speak English?"

"Don't insult me, Mike," I said.

He puffed and threw his hands in the air.

"A'ight listen, lil' shorty. And hear me loud and clear."

His hands gripped my shoulders. I looked down at his hands, and then back at him like he was crazy and pushed them away.

"After today? I don't want nothing to do with you. Don't come near me. Don't talk to me. Don't call me. Don't even fuckin' look at me. Every time you come around, it's always something new, and I ain't got time for it. I don't care anymore. I don't care about what we had. Most of all, I don't care about *you*."

"Mike don't you—"

He stepped to my face. Nearly nose to nose. "Shut up. I'm done. Take your Louis Vuitton, your pixie cut, and fuck off. Leave me and my girl alone 'fore I have her whoop yo' ass the way I wish I personally could but can't. Because you definitely due."

Before I could spew the venom on the edge of my tongue right back at him, he sidestepped me and walked away, bumping my shoulder along the way and grabbed the hand of the Latina girl who, as promised, still stood nearby watching the whole thing. She gave me a final snarl before disappearing down the hall with Mike.

With a tight fist and a loud, angry scream brewing in the pit of my stomach, I punched the locker and fled the hallway, moving towards second period Math in tears.

How the hell was I supposed to survive six weeks?

At this point, I'd rather beg Alise.

I'd rather plead for the next six weeks than to endure the trauma of this place.

Chapter Thirteen

Point of View: Jarell Hendricks

It was like night and day.

The anger that iced my veins last night and into the morning melted like a popsicle in the desert as I got on the crowded city bus to head home for the day after Trisha walked me to the stop just outside the therapy building.

For the first time in a what seemed like forever, I could legit feel my chest rising and falling evenly. My heart thumping. Various conversations between folks spilled into one another as different languages, Spanish, English, and Chinese, mixed together to create a sort of lingual song. There was one convo I heard over everybody else, though. Some OG nigga shared with his grandson these dramatic stories of the past as the little boy giggled and asked a million questions about what life was like fifty years ago. Even the stench of diesel bus fuel ain't bother me, plus, the soft pinging of the bell, signaling someone needing to be let off.

It's been a minute since I rode the bus, and I made a mental note to do it more often instead of walking everywhere to familiarize myself with new areas. No doubt, the bus was a dope experience, and as much as I didn't like people, today was different.

Mindfulness makes you more aware. Apparently. Last time I felt this way was when Jade and I gave ourselves to one another. Something that wasn't happening again.

No sweat though. Nothing could touch or shake a nigga up right now, so instead of wallowing in that breakup, I sat back and relaxed until the computer lady on the bus said, "Slauson and

Budlong," and pulled the string above me. I got off and walked the rest of the way home, dragging my feet down the road and touching familiar landmarks along with relying on my new OrCam glasses Jade bought me for Christmas.

Fluttering my fingers at my side and then raising my hands to feel the direction of the sun, it was close to being right over my head. Hmm. About ten in the morning. It was already proving to be a hot day, so going home without air conditioning was for the birds. Plus, my stomach rumbled louder than thunder, and going for a quick dance wouldn't hurt to pass the time and create less moments I'd have to sit sweating in my room. It would be the perfect opportunity to think about Chicago and resurfacing all those memories I had blocked after moving to California. Especially the great ones.

My three homies man... Rob, Alex, John...

What could we have been if things had turned out better for us?

Instead of turning the corner home, I took a twenty-minute trek over to IHop. I ain't have much money – only ten dollars – but that would get something small and off the ala carte menu. I wanted to be in and outta there anyway.

While eating, I debated on whether I should even go back to Chesterfield Square, the park Jade and I were abducted from. Hell, I ain't feel safe walking around on any street anymore, which just the thought upset me even more about Ma and her decision to kick me out. I mean, them mothafuckas wouldn't wanna do no stupid shit in broad daylight, right? They were under investigation. Laying low would be the smart thing to do. At least I would hope.

After demolishing two stacks of plain pancakes, I walked on over to the park in my favorite spot away from everyone to dance and let the drama of the last couple nights leave my heart and let the great memories of the past flow back in. I danced until the sun beamed right over my head and a little to the west as the weather heated to its peak.

"What time is it?" I asked OrCam.

"The time is now 1:37 p.m."

Yup. Time to head home now and rest up; my legs were close to giving out. Daydreaming on the way home about everything and nothing, mostly about things I used to be able to see that I would later transform into origami, the walk went smooth until I made it to the second house down from ours. Once I realized how close it was to home, I balked before heading towards the porch.

After everything last night, what was Ma gonna say now that I was home? Was she gonna tell me to get out again? That she doesn't want to ever see me again?

I took a deep breath.

I convinced myself Ma wouldn't do that. She wouldn't leave me out on the streets like a bum ass nigga, right? She loved me too much for that… at least that's what she said.

I continued towards the house and made it to the front lawn. Anticipation killed me for that front door to smash open with Kylah sprinting out of it, eager to help me inside. But it never came.

Hmm. What was that about?

After opening the gate, my gait slowed to a crawl. Maybe she didn't see me walk up to the house, or maybe she just needed a chance to see me in the front window, but now that I was here… fully here, she still didn't come. Now, I wasn't even trippin' about anything related to Ma and all the shit she would have to say. I just didn't want any bad news about baby sis.

"God, please just give me a break. Please," I whispered, bowing my head and resting my arms on my knees after sitting on the porch.

Maybe she was just taking a nap.

Maybe she was playing with her toys.

Maybe she was upset with me for arguing with Ma so much lately.

Whatever it was, I just wanted her to be a'ight.

I pulled my keys out of my jeans pocket, felt the ridges of each key to find the right one, and did our special family knock before I rattled the key into the keyhole to come in. I recoiled when the air of the house slapped me.

Smoke. Cigarette smoke. Man. The last time Ma smoked was the first time that piece of shit put his hands on her. It took her a minute to get out of the habit, too. Here we go again.

"You're back," Ma mumbled, blowing out a new stream.

"...yeah," I responded. My nails itched at my forearm as the scabs began closing up those skinny wounds she created. "Surprised you letting me come in and not kick me out again."

I held my breath for a response, but I wasn't afforded one. Instead, silence hung over the living room. The longer she said nothing, the more I felt safe to move deeper inside and put my keys on the hook in the kitchen. Somebody had to soften the discomfort.

"Where's Kylah?" I asked.

"In her room. She just got home from school. Why?"

"I just... she didn't come outside to greet me today," I said and walked towards Ma's voice again.

"She didn't know you were coming back."

"You told her I wasn't coming back?"

"No. I said you'd be gone for a while."

I crossed my arms and shook my head. This wouldn't be a problem if she hadn't kicked me out to begin with. Just had me on the street and didn't give a fuck. In my head, all kinds of names and cruelties came to mind about what I could've been calling her for acting like she ain't give a damn, but there was no more room in my heart to keep them.

"I had my first appointment today," I confessed, changing the subject.

"And how did that go?"

"S'cool." I shrugged, but inside, I knew I had never felt better. But I wasn't gonna get too excited. It was only one session. "Ma ... did you even want me to come back?"

This time, she drew out an audible stream of smoke.

"What kinda question is that?" I felt her body freeze.

"Well... the way you bl— ... never mind. It don't matter, and I'm not tryna argue anymore. I'm sorry, Ma. I'm sorry for what I said about ... about that day. I won't bring it up or say anything like that again," I surrendered. "It wasn't meant to blame you. I'm sorry."

I couldn't afford to lose her, so if surrendering the truth and how I felt about everything would meet that goal, then whatever. I guess.

"It's okay, Jarell. You know I wanted you to come back. I was just angry and upset," she admitted.

"Yeah... I know." Sarcasm was the name of the game. I changed the subject again before she could detect it and say something slick or flex her parent power muscle. "You shouldn't be smoking all that mess with Kylah around, you know. It's been a minute since the last time you smoked. Why now?"

"I can do whatever I wanna do in my house. I pay the bills."

Barely was on the tip of my tongue, but instead, I opted for another: "Yeah... I know."

This time, I didn't stick around and headed to the hallway, leading to my room and Kylah's room. I walked straight past mine and stopped at hers to check in.

"Kylah?" I called out and tapped on her door that made the sound of rain.

No answer, and a long pause ensued after.

"Kay Kay?" I tried again, my chest rising with concern.

"Yeah?" her tiny voice responded.

"Can I come in? It's Relly."

"Yes."

After a few seconds, the doorknob twisted, and the wind from the door opening whooshed over me.

"Hey. Can I come inside?"

"Yeah."

Taking a few careful steps forward since I didn't know what toy landmines she had this time, I came in before shutting the door and leaning against the wall.

"Why you in here all by yourself? I missed you outside. You always come to help me up the stairs and I had to figure it out all my own," I whined.

"Sorry Relly, I forgot," she moped.

"You forgot? Since when do you forget to come help your big brother?" I smiled and sat down on her bed next to her. Her knee dug into my hip as she sat pretzel style.

"I don't know."

"What's the matter baby girl? Is something wrong?" I asked with care after recognizing how down her voice sounded.

"Nothing."

"Oh, something's gotta be wrong. How was school today?"

"It was good."

"What did you do?"

"Nothing. Just colored, count by 10's, and we are learning new words," she said.

"What's so bad about that? Did you have morning recess to-day?"

"Yes, we played hide and seek."

"Did you get caught?" I asked.

"No, I won," she replied.

I chuckled. "Well, that's good! Something can't be wrong about school today. Is there anything else you wanna tell Relly?"

"Mmm… you and Mommy yell at each other a lot."

I sighed. Okay. I knew something was up.

"Yeah, I realize that. Listen. I don't mean to scare you with that. Mommy and I were just mad with each other. We won't be doing much yelling at each other anymore."

"Do you still love Mommy?"

"Of course, I do! Sometimes people just get mad at each other. You should never yell at someone when you're not happy."

"Jade said that, too."

I smiled a sad one. Fuck... I missed her already. "Well, Jade's right about that. You should listen to her."

"Relly?" Kylah called out.

"Yeah?"

"How come I don't have a Daddy? My friends at school have Daddies. How come I don't have one?" she pouted.

Woah. What? Where did that come from?

My heart tanked.

Damn. I had always hoped this question wouldn't ever come up, even though I've anticipated it for a while now. At five years old, Kylah was way ahead of her time in most cases, and this was no different. Grown as hell. I never had a prepared answer for her either to this dreaded question. How do you tell a little girl she was the product of horrific acts? Whose responsibility was it to protect her from that? Do I lie to her? Tell her who her dad really is? Which version of the truth would be best for her future?

"Um... well everybody has a dad..." I replied, pulling my t-shirt away from my neck.

"How come everyone has one except me?"

"Kylah, everyone has a dad, but sometimes, some people never get to meet him. Mommies are more likely to be known than Daddies."

"Will I ever meet mine?"

Fuck. Pausing, my mouth dropped to say I hope she never does, but I caught myself and let out a long sigh.

"Um... I don't know. Where is this coming from?" I asked. "You've never asked anything like this before."

"I just wanted to know my daddy."

"No. Where is this coming from?" I repeated with more resolve.

"Mmm... I can't tell you," she whispered. Her voice itself was the saddest version of her I had ever heard. A weird, ominous feeling settled in my chest.

"You can't tell me?" I frowned. "Why not?"

"It's a secret."

"What? Come on. You can tell your big brother, right? You tell me everything. Did Mommy say something about this?" I squinted.

Silence.

"Kylah, I can't read your body language, like if you're nodding or shaking your head. Remember, I can't see. You gotta use your words with me. Was it Mommy?"

"It's a secret," she repeated.

Pausing and gazing in her direction, a thick silence overwhelmed the room. My stomach flipped.

"Did... did you hear something I said to Mommy lately? Like yesterday or two days ago?"

A small squeak left her lips.

"Use your words..."

"Hmm?"

"Kylah, I asked you a question and you need to answer it. Stop playin' with me. Did you hear me saying something to Mommy? Or did Mommy tell you something about your dad?"

"Mmm..." she pondered; her hum was even shaky.

"Come here." I motioned with my hand. After a slight pause, she crawled onto my lap and laid her head against my chest. "Talk to me. Please. I'm serious. You need to tell me right now or else I'ma ask Mommy about this myself. Remember, when something is wrong or bothering us, we tell each other. You remember that?"

"Mmm hmm."

"So, tell me."

"My friends at school said I don't have a daddy. They told me to ask why I don't have one like they do, and that Mommy doesn't look like me."

"Okay... why would your friends care?" I asked with squinted eyes. "Why would that be a secret? Have your friends even seen Mommy?"

I doubt they did. Ma hated going up to the schools unless she absolutely had to. Kylah took the bus home, and the last time I remembered Ma going up there was to register her for school. And maybe a holiday program Kylah was in during the school day, but that was four months ago.

"I don't know."

"Kylah, are you telling me the truth?"

"Mmm hmm."

"Have you been talking to someone you're not supposed to talk to? Have you been talking to any strangers or people you've never seen before?"

She shook her head. "No."

"Kylah, please tell me the truth if you are. Relly don't want you to get hurt, and I want you to be safe."

"I didn't, Relly."

"Be honest," I pressed. "Did Mommy tell you to say that it was a secret so that you wouldn't talk to me about this?"

I felt her shake her head against my chest again. Fuck that. This wasn't over.

"Then what was it? Who was it?"

"My friends at school, Relly."

I smacked my lips and leaned away from her.

"No, I don't believe you. I think you're lying to me, and I don't like that. I'm tellin' Ma right now. Let's go," I said.

The second I said that, she flailed, threw a tantrum, and began crying. I lifted her up from my lap and put her on the bed.

"No, Relly!"

"Be quiet. Let's go."

"No! I'm not going."

"Kylah, I'm not playing with you. Get up or else I'm snatching the heads off your favorite Barbies. You make the choice, and if you make the wrong one, you'll be even more mad. Or, even better, you can tell me the truth so you can avoid getting in trouble with Ma or me ruining your toys."

"You can't see my favorite Barbies," she snapped back.

Ooooh... she could be a little shit sometimes, I swear.

"I don't care what I can't see. Keep talking, and I'll take all of them and throw 'em away. Get in here. Now."

Whining, crying, and stomping, she opened the room door to head to the living room. I followed shortly behind her.

"What the hell is going on now? Damn, I'm tryna have some peace," Ma mumbled under her breath, new cigarette smoke clouding the air.

"Somebody been asking 'bout her dad, and she won't tell me who it is. Was it you?" I asked.

She smacked her lips. "Why would I bring him up to her?"

"I don't know, that's why I'm asking. She's saying it's her friends at school, but I don't believe it." I frowned.

"Well, that isn't an unbelievable idea, Jarell. These kids know and ask more than you think. Think about when you and your friends were younger, getting into all kinds of shit."

"At five-years-old?"

"Um... yeah! You little niggas was always into something. Jar-ell, we lived in the projects then, and we live in the hood now. These kids ain't sheltered. She's probably picking up all kinds of crap at that school."

"Well, I still don't trust it. You sure you haven't said anything?"

"No, Jarell. I haven't."

"Mommy! Relly said he was gonna take my favorite Barbies' head off if I don't tell him!" Kylah cried in Ma's lap.

I smacked my lips and rolled my eyes. Here we go... tattling and shit...

"Jarell, now why the hell would you tell her something like that? That'll scare the shit outta her. Just because she ain't telling you what you wanna hear?" Ma snapped at me.

"She's lying to me, Ma! This ain't something to be messing around with. Especially about him! Somebody gotta do something!" I yelled.

"Boy, go sit your overgrown ass down somewhere and leave this girl alone. She's probably not even lying, and if you would worry about yourself and leave me to raise her, you might be better off."

"And you'll ruin her, too, like you ruined me," I mumbled and turned on my heels to walk away.

"What the hell did you just say, Jarell Alonte?" she yelled after me, but I had already made it to my room and slammed the door shut.

I shook my head. Hell naw. Something wasn't right. Somebody was lying. So now that I wasn't going to school anymore, I made a new commitment to drop Kylah off and pick her up from school every day. Except Tuesdays and Thursday mornings, since I had therapy.

I didn't trust anybody. Not even little ass kids.

Chapter Fourteen

Point of View: Jade Williams

The rest of the week had flown by along with the weekend, and now, it was already Monday morning again. Seven a.m.

I spent almost all of Saturday and Sunday at the studio perfecting Cardi's dance routine, preparing for this upcoming Friday's shoot in order to prevent from spending hours in the house crying about breaking up with Jarell. Alise periodically came to dance with me for a couple run-throughs and give her critiques.

Whole time? The vibe between Lise and I just wasn't working. The chemistry was off. Maybe it was just me who felt it because it wasn't like she had an attitude or anything. But that chip on my shoulder was bitter cold, and for a second, it looked as if she noticed it too, but wasn't sure. She never addressed or asked about it, either. Good. I didn't want that confrontation with her, but... I mean shit. Her ultimatum led to a lot of decisions I didn't wanna make.

Most of all, and rather the most disappointing, I barely got any updates from the detectives about our kidnappers. Only lead they had was regarding the SUVs those idiots had thrown me and Jarell into. The detectives had questioned people who lived in the neighborhood around the park about what they might have seen that night, and only a couple people said they saw two SUVs drive by, but they didn't know where they had come from. They didn't see any SUVs take anyone. Now, the police were "looking" for the SUVs. Supposedly. The part of me that often tapped into reality had zero hope for this case.

With an aggravated huff, my head hit the headrest of my car as I cleared my head of all thoughts and watched kids start to file into the school building to start the day.

This new feeling that settled in my gut when I parked in Crenshaw's lot now was something serious. Just seven months ago, I couldn't wait to come to school just to stand and hang out on D-Block. Now? It was like a boulder of anxiety brewed in the pit of my belly.

Lowkey, if I got approved for one of these apartments I applied for before being admitted to the hospital, I might make the choice to drop out and just take the L on having a career at Hip Hop Emporium. Anything would be better than here.

For a second, I paused. Then smacked my lips with a sneer.

Wait a minute.

My name was Jade fuckin' Williams. I never ran from anything. The one thing my momma did manage to get right – she refused to raise a weak ass bitch. I couldn't start being one now. After dealing with Momma for the last eighteen years, I sat here and acted like I couldn't get through what, five weeks with a bunch of kids? For real?

Girl... get out this damn car.

If anything, my promise to Jarell still stood. I was gonna get answers about our abductors. I might've broken up with him, but I refused to leave him out to hang on this one.

When I went into the building and made it to my locker, I created a list on my phone of people I needed to speak with about the kidnapping. Mike, I had already spoken to. Result? Epic fail. Laurie, I semi-talked to, but that shit wasn't over between us. Martell was next on the list. His vindictive ass, other than my mom, was probably the most likely culprit behind all of this. Even though Mike, who was his best friend, and I were a "couple" Junior year and into the early part of this year, Martell still, for some reason, didn't like me as much as he liked everyone else. I never understood why, but hey, I didn't like his ass either. He often did the absolute most – and not in a good way. Always tryna be seen.

But our mutual dislike for one another wasn't gonna stop me from harassing him with questions about the kidnapping. Because like it or not, he got his ass whooped for disrespecting Jarell, and he was in no physical position to harm me if he gets angry with my questioning. And I was plenty sure he wouldn't want to get another beat down.

So, after I finished doing what I needed to do at my locker, I went searching for Martell. I even took a ballsy move and went down D-Block past the old crew to find him. Of course, I didn't get the best reception, but since security was so tight now, the most I had gotten were dirty stares.

In my quick search there, Martell was nowhere to be found. Maybe he didn't show up to school today, but Laurie wasn't on D-Block or the rest of the Senior wing, either. Hmm. Her car was in the parking lot, though. She was the only one who likely knew where he was.

Oh. Wait. Maybe she was in our hideout spot?

A couple years ago, Sophomore year, Laurie and I had gotten a hold of some crazy weed that had to be laced for the low from our then mutual D-Block friend Tazz. I don't even know why, but we smoked it at school on some dumb shit. Guess it was the excitement and adrenaline of getting caught. But before we did, we had to find a spot in the cut to do it. We searched the school high and low and found this ducked off room in the back of the school theatre. Something like an equipment room or storage and smoked our souls away.

Every now and then, Laurie would still go and get high without me whenever she'd get a bag. The day we found that room was the first and last time I hit the blunt because I ended up being a paranoid mess after smoking that strong ass shit and never wanted to feel something like a crack fiend again.

Maybe that's where Laurie was.

I trekked over to the performing arts center and went on back in the dark. The moment I stepped behind the stage, small noises came and went that didn't register to me right away, so when I slowed my roll, I bent my head forward and stared out into space to catch the sound again. A few more weird sounds and panting became more apparent. Oh God…

Turning the corner into our spot, there lied the sound's source without even a hint of hiding.

Martell stood tall with his neck still in a brace from the beatdown he took from Jarell. His jeans wrapped at his ankles while he bit his lip and looked down with his eyes full of lust at no one other than Laurie. On her knees.

I shook my head.

The fuck? Home girl couldn't wait 'til lunch and go to her car?

I stood unapologetically with my arms crossed, waiting for Martell to either reach his climax, or for one of them to notice me. Martell was so into it that he had no inkling of my presence lingering in the shadows.

I grinned.

Because I disliked his bitch ass so much, I was gonna wait 'til he was on the brink of release and then interject. I should've whipped out my phone to record the whole thing. One, for Laurie being fake and blocking me off social media because she wanted to save her ass with D-Block instead of being a real friend, and two, to show the world how much Martell wasn't as well-endowed as he bragged about himself to be. *But revenge porn was illegal.*

Tuh. Laurie's an idiot. Martell didn't give a shit about her the same way Mike hadn't given a flying fuck about me. They were best friends for fucks sake; birds of a feather flocked together. So, the fact that she was on her knees like this made me want to slap some sense in her.

"Damn, Laurie," Martell whispered, his breath quickening as he gripped her hair.

"Ahem." I cleared my throat and shifted my weight to the other leg.

Screaming, Laurie tumbled onto her butt as Martell buckled and leaned forward to hide his junk as he grasped at his jeans but missed several times because they were so low past his shins.

I bit my lip and inner cheek to stop from laughing.

"What the fuck Jade?" Martell growled as his eyes grew dark with a sinister tint.

"Jade?!" Laurie gasped.

"Fuck do you want, man? I swear to God yo' mousey ass always fuckin' shit up! Dumb ass bitch," Martell hissed as he finally got a hold of his pants, scrambled to pull them up and button them back together.

"Boy shut yo' little ass up. I ain't worried about you getting off more than I'm tryna find out what the hell you know about Jarell and me being put in a situation where we coulda got hurt the other day."

"What the fuck are you talking about?" Martell looked at me like I was chattering out my ass.

"You know what I'm talking about! There's no coincidence that all of y'all got me blocked off social media, and y'all removed me from the GroupMe. Y'all gotta know something. Both of you."

"Man," he groaned and looked away from me. "You don't even be on social media other than posting dance videos and signing off anyway, so why do you give a fuck?"

"It don't matter! Have you talked to any detectives at all? Tell me what you know."

"Laurie, you better get your friend," Martell mumbled, looking dead at her, yet pointing a stiff finger at me.

"Jade, stop harassing him. It's bad enough that you come barging in on what we're doing. You need to get outta here. You and Jarell have already caused enough trouble for him."

"Girl... bye. I'm tryna figure out something way more important, alright? You need to go brush your teeth after having that dirty ass thing in your mouth."

She scoffed with her mouth dropped.

"After everything you and Jarell have done, what makes you think he's willing to answer anything you have to ask?" she yelled with her arms flailing in the air.

"Answer the question Martell," I demanded, ignoring Laurie.

"Who the hell you supposed to be?" he seethed, looking me up and down. "So glad Mike stopped fucking around with your ass, so I don't have to see you. I swear if you even think about making your way down the Block, you gettin' yo' ass whooped because don't nobody fuck with you. At all. Just wait until security lets up."

I rolled my eyes, feeling an invisible punch to the gut. Despite it, I stood tall.

"Which will be never. I see you mighty quiet with the answers, so obviously you got something to hide. Or maybe I'll just turn your name into the detectives myself." I crossed my arms again.

"Call 'em! I told you I don't know what you talkin' about, but thanks for giving me the idea. Whoever it was to 'hurt y'all,' if they ever come back, I hope they dump your annoying ass in the ocean somewhere along with that pussy ass nigga Jarell. Fuck outta here," he uttered and walked out, bumping me hard on the shoulder on his way. "Bald head bitch."

And with that, Martell exited stage left. Literally and figuratively. My fists balled. Oooh he so lucky Jarell wasn't here anymore. I would've loved to see Jarell pound him for talking to me like that whether Martell was still in a neck brace or not. Mike might as well be added to the list because he had walked away from all his bullshit unscathed.

When he was clear out of the room, Laurie turned to me with an ominous frown. It creeped me out, but I wasn't scared of her. She didn't even defend me.

"You have some nerve Jade..."

"Girl, I want all the smoke. I just told you the other day about what happened, and you know I'm trying to figure out who. And yo' ass just sits up here and defends him?"

"No one cares about this whole thing with Jarell, Jade! You need to leave Martell alone and respect boundaries. Especially coming up in here to our secret hang out spot to crash our party and embarrass us. That's not okay, and I'd like an apology! I'd also like an apology for just disregarding what I had to say like I was trash."

I raised an eyebrow and nearly laughed.

"An apology? Girl you shouldn't be doing anything sexual at school anyway! You lucky it was me and not a teacher!"

"That's not the fucking point, Jade. Whether I decided to do this to have fun and be risky or whatever it is, you had no right to do what you just did. Why don't you ever own up to anything? You never take any accountability, and I'm not just gonna sit idly by like your puppet sidekick anymore and let you run all over me and tell me what I do wrong, yet I can't do the same with you. You're not squeaky clean!"

"A puppet sidekick, huh? That's what you think of yourself and our friendship?" I huffed, trying to back her in a verbal corner.

"Stop. You need to be a better friend, Jade! You don't respect me at all, and you don't care about how I feel about anything! Every time I tell you something or do something, you wanna say I shouldn't be doing it or that I shouldn't think that way. I should be able to share things with you without feeling judged. You're not my mom or this perfect bitch."

"Stop acting like you're the victim all the time! I felt judged whenever I'd talk to you about Jarell. So, stop doing dumb shit, and maybe I wouldn't have seem like a 'mom' or you wouldn't have to feel like a sidekick!" I roared, my arms flailing in the air.

By this time, Laurie's face turned red as tears popped off her face and onto the ground.

"No! I've always been your 'sidekick' and not your friend. Ever since your NBA player stepdad got you all those connections with dance and you've raised your status in the city, you act like you're too good for anybody and everyone else's choices aren't right except for yours."

"That's not true," I countered.

"Shh! Let me finish." She sniffed. "Most of all, you act like I'm some dumb blonde who can't make decisions for herself because I don't have life figured out the way you do. If you can express your disagreement about me and Martell, then I can say whatever I want about Jarell."

I shook my head the entire time she spoke as she continued.

"I'm always in cheerleading practices defending you from attacks, even when they'd attack you about Mike. I stuck up for you when they made rumors about you and Jarell, when apparently, they were true, making me look stupid. I was there when your mom slapped the shit out of you at the football season opener while everyone else laughed and recorded it. I was there when you thought I never was, and this is what you do to me? You're a horrible friend!"

"Laurie. I saved you from being raped by Martell when you were drunk at a party. He doesn't care about you, and you can't even see it. You're not a victim of a bad friendship," I said, rubbing my arm without giving her eye contact and biting the inside of my cheek.

"I don't wish to be. Martell does care about me, and if he doesn't, let me find out on my own. I wish you would be the same kind of friend I am to you. If you were on your knees pleasing Mike, at the time when you actually liked him, I would be cheering you on quietly as I walked away to mind my business. And you know for sure that's what I would've done. Give me the same fucking respect!"

"Ladies!" Another voice shouted and silenced us. Turning our heads, it was Ms. Jenson, Jarell's old special education teacher. "You both need to stop screaming at each other. What are you doing back here? I heard you both all the way in the hall!"

Neither of us answered. We just stormed out the back room in separate directions.

This wasn't over between us. As mad as I was with her? We had to make amends and work this out. I wasn't willing to lose anyone else in my life.

Chapter Fifteen

Point of View: Jarell Hendricks

"Welcome Jarell. I'm happy you came back, and you didn't think I was too crazy, or I scared you away."

Yup. It was that time. Tuesday morning with Trisha as I sank into what was becoming my favorite sofa in therapy. Even though last Thursday was only my first day.

I swear, when I was through with this lady by the time these six weeks were up, I was gonna leave here sounding like a deep south redneck. Either way, I didn't give her any verbal acknowledgement. Just a nod.

"How are you this morning?" she asked.

"I'm straight."

"How was your weekend?"

I lifted my left shoulder, and it came back down.

"S'cool."

"Hmm. Okay. How's home? I read in your profile that you have a little sister named Kylah that you look after."

"She's fine."

Why she asking so many damn questions? Shit was already getting annoying, and it had only been two minutes. What did Ma put in that profile? Hell, did she add my baby pictures, too?

When she mentioned Kylah, I hoped she made it to school okay, which, I mean, I know she did, but... ever since she asked about her dad, I kept my promise to walk her to and from school.

Whenever Kylah was presented with *anything* straying from a previous norm, it was like this earthshattering big deal. She relished this new routine and was more excited than I anticipated.

She even showed me off to some her Kindergarten friends, who then turned around and asked why my eyes looked the way they did. At first, it made me squirm, but when Kylah told them I was blind like it was the coolest thing in the world, my whole outlook changed.

Then, my old friends back home came to mind.

No one in my life was as proud of me as Kylah was *except* for my old friends, even through the arguments, fights, and disagreements. We had a brotherhood. A bond. Too bad, I didn't have a single person I could call a friend anymore. Not even Jade.

"Let's get started for the day," Trisha said, cutting right through my thoughts. "Last time we talked about locations and spaces, both physically and in our mind that we can travel to when feeling angst, anger, rage, sadness, and more. We practiced some mindfulness on Thursday to help you become more aware of energy and space and allowing your mind to wander to those spaces and locations where you experience happiness. So today, we're going to talk about actions. Positive actions. Based on your profile, it says that you've dealt with a lot of trauma, and you have currently been dealing with thoughts of suicide. Can you tell me more about that?"

Ha. Was she serious? She was getting a little too comfortable. In response, I smacked my lips and shrugged.

"No."

"Okay…" she said as if calculating her next move. "What do you do when life is too much? Do you express your emotions? Who do you speak with?"

"I don't."

"You don't what?"

"I don't express my emotions. Sometimes I write poems, though. Especially if I'm in a place where I can't dance or do origami."

Her jewelry jangled, signaling a nod. "Dance, huh? We mentioned it last week but didn't dig deep. Say more?"

I rolled my eyes. "Let me guess. Someone wrote in my profile that I was some phenomenal dancer…"

"Actually, no. Your profile just shows your interests, and it says you like to dance, but it didn't say anything about you being a phenomenal dancer. Is that how you view your identity as a dancer?" she asked.

She think she "got" me. I hear the faint little smirk in her voice.

"I don't view myself like anything. I just… thought that's something Ma would've put in my profile since she's revealing my whole life story in there."

"I don't think you'd say she put 'a phenomenal dancer' if you didn't believe that about yourself."

"You can think what you want," I shot back with hostility.

"It's okay to view yourself positively, Jarell," she responded, her voice now as soft as a pillow. "There's nothing wrong with that. Even when people don't think the same about you."

I paused, and then looked away. After her pen scribed in her notebook, for a moment, she stopped and then spoke again with caution.

"When was the last time you danced?" she asked.

"After therapy last week."

"Okay, that's good! Was it because you felt stress? Was it because you were upset? Or because you love it? What was the reason?"

"None of that. I was feeling real numb last week, but before I went numb, I almost exploded. I actually forced myself not to," I explained.

"What do you mean by numb and exploded? What happened?"

"My ma kicked me out the house and left me on the streets overnight." I frowned. My skin bubbled just from the thought.

"Would you like to elaborate?"

Man. She always wanted me to elaborate on some shit. It wasn't her business, but damn... when would I ever have the opportunity to express my truth about Ma and someone would actually listen? I didn't have a dad. I didn't have grandparents. I couldn't talk to a five-year-old. What choice did I have?

"Well..." I started. "She don't listen to me. She never has, even when her choices fucked me up in the end. She only thinks about herself. Anything I have to say about shit she doesn't agree with, she shuts it down. Always telling me, 'I'm the parent, and you're the child.' I'm so tired of that bullshit argument, man. To me, that's an excuse to make bad decisions and not be held to task about it because you know a kid can't do shit about choices adults make. But I'm grown now, and I'm not letting her just slide with doing whatever anymore. Especially when and if it affects me, and she doesn't like that I'm fighting back now."

"Can you give me an example?" Trisha questioned.

"We got into a heated argument last Wednesday night after she pulled a move that would put our family in danger. I ain't going in detail about that. But the second I called her out and tried to have a conversation about it, she shut me down. It escalated, and in the end, I brought up her abusive ex and a bad situation that happened with him. Then, she just snapped on my ass. She punched me, scratched me, hit me, and then kicked me out."

"So, what did you do?"

"I walked around town. It ain't like I had anywhere else to go. I walked for a long time until I just sat on the edge of a curb and fumed until... I didn't feel anything. Then after therapy on Thursday, I danced about it after we did mindfulness."

"What do you mean you 'didn't feel anything?'"

"I just didn't. Like I said, I went numb. Like … I don't … it's just that my body is here, but my mind isn't," I tried to explain. "I don't know how else to put it."

"When you feel emotionally numb, do you usually dance? Is that your go to?"

"Iono. Maybe. To be honest, I dance when I'm tryna get away from something or when I'm tryna keep from tearing everything apart. Or saving someone from getting they ass fucked up. By me."

"When did dancing become a habit for you?"

"I never saw myself as someone who would dance, and when I started, it came at a hard time in my life. When things started to go downhill for me and Ma back in Chicago. Before that, though, I handled a lot of my problems by fighting. I was always whooping somebody's ass."

"Fighting? How did that work out for you as far as conflict resolution?" she questioned.

"Sometimes it worked, and other times it didn't. It definitely didn't work for Ma. It made things worse for her. Eventually, I stopped fighting so much because I promised Ma I wouldn't stress her out anymore," I said. "I told her I would dance instead."

"Do you remember the day you made that promise? What happened?"

"Yeah. I was just messing around, but it was Ma who noticed it and said I should continue to use it as a release. This is random, but the only reason why I actually remember this day was because it was the day Michael Jackson died…"

Chicago, IL – June, 2009

"Hey, did you know Michael Jackson died?" Robert asks, running up to the court all out of breath.

It's the first question we get for the day as I play Horse with my boys Alex and Jonathan. On any other day, it was me who was late to come to the court because of my mom, but today, it's Robert. His eyes are as wide as saucers that were kinda moist, like Michael Jackson was the homie or something.

"Is that why you so late?" I ask Rob as I shoot a shot up for play, but out of nowhere, Alex blocks it so hard, it flies into the stands. I smack my lips and give him a dirty scowl. He just laughs and so does Jonathan.

"Yeah! My mom and brother were watching the news. You don't like Mike?" he asks, surprised none of us are as hurt as he is.

"Of course I like him, but it ain't like I know him." I shrug. "Plus, I doubt he's dead."

"Man, it was all over the news! It's gotta be true!"

"Man, come on and let's play ball, dude. Michael Jackson ain't dead," Jonathan says and pushes Rob onto the court.

"How'd he die anyway? If he is dead?" I ask.

"Who cares, stupid," Alex responds. I pause and stare at him. I'm about ready to punch him in the jaw because he's been picking at me all day. For no reason. "It ain't got nothing to do with this Horse game. He ain't dead."

"Man whatever. Y'all gon' be salty when you see he is," Rob says.

I just laugh at Rob and try to ignore Alex. Rob's so dramatic sometimes.

I mean, I can't lie. It would suck if Michael Jackson is dead. Mommy and I watch Michael Jackson sometimes because that's one of her favorite artists. His music is okay, but I'm more interested in his dance moves. I've always wanted to dance like him and look as cool as he looked, but I never tried it.

Hey. Speaking of dance moves, I always wanted to ask Mommy about something weird I experience.

For some reason, every time I watch Michael Jackson dance, the world slows down. Like he's moving in slow motion. It's strange, but it's like I can see and calculate every step. For some time, I noticed it, but then, it kept happening every time I saw someone dance. Especially if they're great.

My favorite guy artist is Chris Brown. The whole 'world slowing down' thing happens when I watch him dance, too. I never understand why. It isn't like I'm trying to be a dancer or anything. I love basketball. And girls. That's it. Don't nothing else got my love.

We drop the whole Michael Jackson topic and start playing two against two. Me and Rob against Jonathan and Alex. Game to eleven.

It's a pretty even and competitive game. Except today, Alex is guarding me super hard. What's his problem? I went for a couple of layups that missed because he fouled me, but I didn't call it. I ain't no punk, but it isn't going to last much longer with him fouling and me not calling it.

The game is tied eight up, and I have the ball. I cross over and dribble in between my legs a few times to set him up to take him to the rack when he reaches for a steal, nearly tackling me in the process and takes the ball away from me.

"Foul!" I shout.

Alex smacks his lips with his arms out, picking up the ball to stop the game.

"What? Foul? Ain't nobody foul you. You just being a punk," he says.

"I don't call fouls like that and I ain't call 'em all game, so if I call foul, then you hackin'," I respond.

"Nope. You just being a pussy like always." He shrugs.

"What's wrong with you? I didn't do anything to you, and you've been acting all pissy. I thought we was cool?"

Alex been acting funny ever since Isabella and I kissed before she moved away. Crazy part about it? He and I were the closest out our group.

"Nothing's wrong! You just think you the shit and I don't like it."

"Huh? Oh, so you hatin'?" I raise an eyebrow. "Just say it if that's what it is."

"Why would I be hatin' on you? You and your momma ain't got no money," Alex says, and I shake my head with a smile.

"Come on, Alex. That ain't cool," Rob says, stepping in between us.

"You live in the same apartments, dumb nut. You ain't got money either," I shoot back. "Look at you. You ain't out here with new clothes. You wear raggedy clothes just like everybody else."

"Jarell, chill," Jonathan says. "Just leave it alone."

"What did you say?" Alex threatens with tight lips and walks up to my face. "I'll show you a dumb nut…"

"Come on, y'all. Don't fight. Please," Rob begs. "Let's just finish the game, bro."

"Oooh I'm so scared," I taunt, and then turn to Rob. "Bro, I ain't do nothin' to him! He hatin' for no reason! I'm not about to just let him keep punkin' me," I say.

"I said I ain't hating on yo' ass! I don't like how you act like you so high and better than us. Like you can just get any girl you want!"

"What? He doesn't act like that, bro," Jonathan says.

I smacked my lips. "He just mad because all the girls he like told everybody they like me at lunch on the last day of school. I don't want them. I like Isabella and she's not even here! You can't get mad at me because they don't like you. Ain't my fault you ugly."

With no time to breathe after those last words, Alex's arm stretches over Rob's shoulder and his fist meets my nose. Dead in the middle. It doesn't take long for it to start burning… then, trickling fluid.

I can't believe someone who I call my best friend just did that! Punched me that hard! Dude is that mad over these girls? We're going to middle school. Why would I care about getting a girlfriend that isn't Isabella?

"Now what?" Alex taunts.

I smack my lips and take a step back, pulling my shorts up.

"Come on, Jarell bro. Don't fight," Rob says, but Jonathan pulls him out of the way.

"No. Just let 'em fight. They'll hug it out later like they always do," Jonathan says.

"I ain't hugging shit out!" Alex shouts. "Let's go!"

And it happens again. That weird "slow down" effect happens during fights too. Everything becomes slow motion.

So, we scrap it out. Like we were never friends. Like we're strangers. We throw several punches that hold some weight, but we both miss because we duck and dodge too quick. After a while though, those swings start to land. When I think I have the advantage, that I'm winning this fight after a good three or four piece, he comes back with one strong punch somewhere in my face that nearly knocks me off my feet. Rocks my whole world. That happens at least three times, but I battle to stay awake. And then, I find an opening with his guard down and I punch him hard enough to get him on the ground. But he scrambles back up. Next thing I know, my legs are being lifted, and he slams me before I can get on top of him to wear him out.

I break the impact of the slam by grabbing his shirt and taking him down with me. He gets on top of me ready to strike, but I'm never one to get pinned down either so I toss him off me and get back up. Now, we're squared up all over again.

"Come on, punk!" I say in my fighting stance.

"Bring it on, pussy!" He does the same.

Dang, he's tough! I'm not surprised though. Me and Alex are known at school to never lose fights. Ever. We be tag teaming the hell outta people when we walk home from school because someone always tries our numbers since we're both smaller dudes. And in the projects, people always test you to see who they can mess with and who they can't. Me and Alex both ain't one of those people because they know they'll get beat down.

The both of us attack each other again, getting a few licks in before we're torn away by two strong forces.

"Alright, alright! That's enough! Stop, you two!" some lady voices scream over the chaos.

The world comes back to normal speed. One of the ladies is my mom. The other is Alex's mom, Lynette, and they're best friends. Almost like sisters. I huff, out of breath and take a look around. Woah. All our neighborhood friends had gathered around the basketball court to watch. All I hear is the fight was a tie and nothing else.

"Why y'all fighting? Y'all supposed to be brothers!" Ms. Lynette yells.

"He hatin' on me!" I shout, spitting out a tooth and blood built up in my mouth.

"Man shut up. No, I'm not! He thinks he's all that!" Alex screams back with a bloody nose and tries to come for me. Just as he did, I went back at him too, but our parents tear us apart again.

"Stop it! Both of you!" Mommy shouts.

"Why did you let them fight?" Ms. Lynette looks at Rob and Jonathan with a glare they flinch at.

"Alex punched him first and busted his nose, so I knew stopping them wasn't gonna happen." Jonathan got to talking real fast with a shrug. "Plus, we know they'll hug it out later anyway."

"That's true, Alex?" his mom asks.

"Yup!"

"See! He hit me for no reason!" I shout.

"Shut up, you wannabe tough Momma's boy!" Alex responds.

"Listen, Radiya, we'll work this out later. We just need them to get away from each other. Let's go Alex. You have no business punching him!" Ms. Lynette shouted.

"And you have no business probably being an asshole to him, Jarell. Let's go," Mommy says and drags me by the shirt towards the apartment complex. Why does she always have to embarrass me?

"The hell is wrong with you boy? Get yo' black ass in the house. Now!" she growls with a tight jaw.

The entire time, she cusses me out until we get inside, much to the amusement of everybody else. Then, she finds a belt and jacks me up hard against the wall, causing some of the wall paint to chip.

"Why do you keep fucking fighting, Jarell?" she screams with a stiff finger at my nose. All warmth drains from my body; her eyes are frostier than I've ever seen. "You are eleven years old. That's like the sixth goddamn fight in the last three months either at school or on the playground. And now you're fighting your best friend?" She slaps me upside the head.

"Did you not just hear that he hit me first!?" I yell. "And it's because I'm short, so people try to rob me or punk me in this stupid neighborhood! People always try to pick on me!"

"Boy don't you ever talk to me like..."

Without another word, she raises my arm violently in the air and strikes me over and over with her belt until I fall to my knees. She quits once I do. I don't start crying until she's done. I can't believe I'm getting a whooping because of something I didn't do. I rarely even got whoopings. This is probably the second one in my whole life.

"Nobody else's kid fights as much as you do, damn it," she says and throws her belt onto the couch.

"That's not true!"

"Shut up. I don't care. I'm tired. I don't even care what you're fighting about anymore. Find something else to channel your anger. Go to your room before I whoop yo' ass again. I don't even want to look at you right now. And tomorrow, you're going to apologize to Alex. I don't care who started it. Get out! Get out, now!"

I stop crying, get up, and mope to my room. I shut the door, not wanting to cause any more trouble. Man, I hate making Mommy mad at me. Or worrying her, but this was the angriest I've seen her. But I was honest. I fight so much because of where we live. There are gunshots around here every night. Ugly dudes on the front porch of the apartment complex cat calling at her any time she walks out. A new kid or person dying every day from getting beat up or from a gun. I have to learn to fight. I have to protect myself. And her. Nobody was going to punk me. Ever. Not even from Alex.

I sit on the bed and look in the mirror.

I look horrible.

My nose and lip are still bleeding. My left eye will be black to-morrow probably. But I smile at myself anyway and see my missing tooth. Nobody was taking me down without a fight. Was Alex hurting just the same? I gave him a good run for his money, so ... hopefully he is.

I walk out my room and go to the bathroom to clean my face and gargle some saltwater like I always do after a fight before I come back and turn on the TV. She didn't say I was grounded, so TV is fair game.

First channel that pops up is MTV. On the bottom of the screen, a tagline runs ....

"Michael Jackson died of cardiac arrest."

Dang. Rob was right. Michael Jackson did die. That sucks. He was a legend. I turn on BET to confirm my doubts, and they are play-ing all his music videos. As I watch, it happens again.

Michael Jackson's dance moves slows down. All the way down.

I squint my eyes and then rub them to see if my mind is playing tricks on me. But it's not. He still dances in slow motion.

The more I stare and study, the more I want to be just like him. He's so smooth, sharp, yet elegant and... I don't know. It's just cool. The way all those girls pass out over him. Ha. Maybe if I did some of those moves, girls will pass out over me too.

I get up from my bed, and I try out some of his moves. They come so easy to me. Everyone makes it seem like it's hard, but it actually isn't. The kicks, the floating, the popping and the locking... it is sur-prisingly simple.

And then, I finish one dance video. Then another. And another. And then I dance to another one. This time, it's Remember the Time. This is my favorite video of him that I've probably watched the most. These Egyptian-like moves are unlike anything I've seen anyone do, but I try them out anyway.

"Jarell!" I hear from behind me.

I jump out of my skin at Mommy who is standing in my door-way. She's staring at me with wide eyes, like I had morphed into someone completely new. I hold my breath. What did I do now?

"Yeah? I can't watch TV, huh?" I ask. "Sorry. I'm probably on punishment."

I take the remote with shaking hands, fumbling it before I turn the TV off. She is still staring at me like I'm some alien.

"Jarell how the hell did you learn to dance like that?" she said in awe with a smile.

"Huh?"

"I know what I saw. How did you... when did... what..." she stutters with a washcloth and peroxide in her hands.

"Ma, I was just messin' around," I say, my shoulders relaxing.

"Like hell you were! That was amazing!"

"You embarrassing me."

"No Jarell, I'm serious. I've never, ever seen anything like that before."

"Ma, please don't think that I'm going to be some dancer or something."

"I didn't say that, but... you should keep dancing and investing in it. I'll just leave it at that," she says and then walks into my room. She sits on my bed and pats an open spot next to her. "Sit down."

I sigh and obey. She has a warm look on her face, but also something else. The story is all in her eyes, and I can't translate it.

"I didn't want to whoop you, Jarell," she says after a long pause. She brings my head to her chest and hugs me. Then she kisses my forehead. I smile small and wrap my arms around her waist and hug her back.

"It's cool, Mommy. I deserved it."

"Yeah, but I should've handled that different. Whooping you has never been my thing to raise you, and I don't want to start. I just don't want you to get hurt, baby. I get scared when you fight so

much," she whispers, and puts a towel saturated with peroxide up to my eye. "Your eye is black. Alex must've got you good."

"Yeah, he kinda did. I think I lost that one, Mom."

She laughs.

"Nah, when I got out there, you gave him some pretty good licks and punched him to the ground. Whew. You are a true boy. Super physical. Both of you."

"Yeah. I still want to be friends with him, Ma. I think he's mad at me because of the girls at school."

"Over some girls? Yeah. I don't think you'll be at odds with each other anymore. But listen baby. I want to tell you something. I whooped you out of anger and I shouldn't have," Mommy confesses, and gives me a long, sad glare.

"What's wrong, Mommy?"

She takes a long, deep breath.

"You know your crush Isabella and her family moved out of their apartment, right?"

"Yeah."

"Well. We are being removed, Jarell. The same way they were. We can no longer be here anymore."

I blink several times, trying to understand what she just said.

"Why?"

"They are tearing down all the projects in Chicago and remodeling them, baby. They're raising the price of rent by hundreds of dollars, and I can't afford it."

"So ...what are we gonna do?" I ask.

"I don't know, honey."

"When is this supposed to happen?"

"At the end of next month," she says and dips her head. She's trying hard not to meet my eyes.

"So, we're gonna be homeless..." I say this time instead of asking. She doesn't say anything for a while. She just nods.

I don't know what to say.

I would have never guessed that I'd ever be homeless. What would I do with all my clothes? My basketball? All my shoes? We were gonna have to stuff them in a bag and just drag everything around?

"Jarell, everything is going to be okay. We're going to make it through this."

"But... what about other family?" I ask. My breathing becomes quicker. I don't want to live on the streets.

"Jarell, you know I was a foster child..."

"But... there has to be something."

"There isn't, baby. I called government assistance a while ago, and they've set up arrangements and a meeting. I don't have much detail yet until they call me back."

I sigh. Now I gotta make it up with Alex and the rest of my boys because after July is over, who knew if I'd see them again?

"Well, I hope we find something else before then."

"I hope so too, baby. But here's what I want you to do. I don't want you getting into any more fights. Actually, I want you to dance more often. Dance when you get angry. Can you try that for Mommy? It'll make me feel much better with all this stuff that's going on."

I don't hesitate.

"Of course, Mommy. I'll do it."

~ ~ ~

"That's the story behind the dancing instead of fighting. Like I said, I never planned on it, but it just kinda happened. The world always moved so fast, you know? Like being hit with news that we'd be homeless and the next thing I knew, we were on the streets and... dancing was the only thing that slowed everything down. It still does," I explained to Trisha.

"Jarell, that's an amazing story behind such a strong, productive coping mechanism. I'm glad your mother recognized it at the time and encouraged it. I hope you continue to dance, Jarell. It seems like a great outlet."

"It is," I agreed. "I ended up getting good at it, too."

"Good. Well, let's end our day together with some mindfulness again. We will do this at the end of every session," she said as she shuffled to stand to her feet. She walked towards the opposite wall where the door was and pulled down the yoga mat that hung up beside it.

"This time, we will complete mindfulness laying down. Sometimes it's better that way. Today, I want you to focus on allowing yourself to feel self-compassion and patience, especially when you've become numb. It is an important part of healing. The goal of today's mindfulness is to allow yourself to undo numbness. We will talk deeper about feelings and unpacking that for next time. For today, think about those times you wanted to fight or explode, or forced yourself to feel nothing and try shifting that over to the way your body feels when you dance. I want you to think about how you can develop compassion for what your body is able to do. How does that sound?"

I took a deep breath and shifted down to the floor once she had the yoga mat set and ready. "I don't got no choice, do I?"

She chuckled, and then said in jest, "You always have a choice. But today? I say you don't."

"Well then here we go, boss!" I laughed and she did too before starting the recording, and I allowed myself to float away for the day.

While eerily somehow, remaining present.

Chapter Sixteen

Point of View: Jade Williams

I still owed my stepdad Corey an explanation.

It was the first thought to come to mind after I left the school Wednesday afternoon before heading over to Hip Hop Emporium to finish our last dance run throughs before shooting Cardi's video this Friday. At first, I was gonna figure everything out with Laurie and how to make things right. She was still steaming about me crashing her little intimate party with Martell and ignored me like I was Casper at school. But when I realized it had been two weeks already since Corey picked us up from Fresno, I wanted to slap myself. He still deserved a follow up because Corey wasn't anyone to play with when angry.

And not telling him shit about what happened would take him there, knowing it had happened to his "baby girl."

So instead of heading straight to the studio to prepare for rehearsal, I took the long drive out to the outskirts of LA. I was gonna make this quick because traffic was insane, and I still needed to be at the studio in time for practice at seven.

Arriving after getting out of a traffic jam and rolling up into the gated community, I buzzed into Corey's estate and parked next to his Range Rover. As soon as I walked inside, he was already standing in the living room area expecting my arrival.

"Hey, you're a surprise!" Corey beamed as he paced towards me for an embrace. "How's my baby girl?"

"Hey Dad." I returned the glee, letting his big body encase mine as he planted a kiss on my forehead and then chuckled.

"You gotta come visit me more often so I don't have to be so stunned and excited to see you."

I giggled. "Yeah, I know."

I made my way deeper inside his hillside home, the wind of the vaulted ceiling fan whooshing through my pixie cut as I sat on the couch. Every decoration around me seemed to sparkle as if it had been scrubbed thrice over. Even when hanging at home, for Corey, no beard hair was out of place, no eyelash was out of sync... little shit like that that attracted Janet to him. Because she was the *exact* same way.

His shiny bald head and clean-cut caramel skinned look, donning slim fitting suits and stayed with the latest Stacy Adam's, Corey had always reeked regal. I always remembered Momma being unable to keep her hands off him and unable to take the heart out her eyes when I was a little girl. You know... until things went south.

"So, what's up? I hope you got some news for me..." he started, sitting across from me and lighting a cigar.

"Yes... and no..." I trailed off, sinking my feet deeper into the plush carpet. "I'm just stopping by. I know you wanted updates, but it's not like I have much to say to be honest."

"Alright, well I ain't gone make you jump right in. I want to see how you're doing first. How's everything? Since I last dropped you off at ... what's his name again?"

"Jarell."

"Yeah, your new boyfriend."

"Not anymore," I mumbled, breaking eye contact.

He paused. I felt him give me a look. "What happened? Everything okay?"

My head fell back, and I rolled my eyes to the ceiling to avoid the familiar burn of tears. I had never cried so much, and I was just sick of shedding them. I cried more this year than every other year of my life combined, and I just didn't want Corey taking me there.

"I take that as a no," Corey concluded with wrinkled brows. "Did he have something to do with what happened with the kidnapping?"

"No. It just isn't the right time for us to be together. I don't wanna talk about it, Dad," I said, giving him my eyes again once the tears cleared.

He shrugged. "Mmm, well alright. You know there's always better out there if he wasn't right. I'm always here if you want to talk. Even about boys, although I know you won't like that."

"Yeah, I don't need you telling me you're trying to kick Jarell's butt over something unnecessary."

"Damn right." He nodded and let out a thick puff of smoke. "How's dance going?"

"Ayyye!" I stuck my tongue out. "That's more like what I wanna talk about. It's going fine. Alise and I are getting ready to shoot with Cardi B on Friday for her new single. Everything's gonna drop in the summer."

"Aww shit, that's great, Jade! First Chris Brown and now Cardi? I'm so proud of you. I remember always taking you to ballet practice when you were about three or four years old, and now you're taking off with the biggest artists. I mean, you were always with big names early on, but ... I'm never less amazed by what you do."

I blushed. "Thanks Dad. I appreciate that."

"Just text me when the song drops so I can share it with everybody."

"Will do. I also am gonna be starting up with being a youth choreographer right after graduation, so I'm excited about that. It's pretty good money, too. I've been applying to apartments, and I think I might have gotten accepted into one. I got a phone call at school today from them and an email. I just haven't checked it yet, so I'll be set to pay my own rent and everything. If I got it, I hope you can help me move big furniture I've already ordered on Saturday."

"You know I'll help. So... no college?" he asked, shifting the subject.

"Nope. I got everything I need at the studio. No reason to go in debt when I'm already doing what I love."

"No back up plan?" He raised an eyebrow.

I blinked. "Did you have a backup plan before you went to the NBA?"

"Nah. That's why I'm asking... so that you don't make the same mistake," he said, putting out the remainder of his cigar in the ashtray.

"Never thought about a backup. I can't imagine doing anything else in my life except for dance. I guess I'll cross that bridge whenever it comes. If it does."

"A youth choreographer, huh? You like kids?" He gave me a suspicious glare and then laughed at me. I laughed right with him, the unspoken answer lingering in the air. If it meant I could continue making an influence on the dance industry, I could adapt and learn to like them when need be.

"What else is up? How is school? You ready for graduation? Prom is coming up too in a couple weeks, ain't it?" he asked and kicked his feet up on the coffee table and stretched his long arm along the top of the couch.

"Yeah, and I'm not going to prom."

"Why not? You know you would likely be that queen bee, right?"

I shrugged. "Maybe."

"What's up with you? Why the sour attitude about your Senior year?" he questioned with a side eye.

"It's a long story."

"Damn girl, tell me something! Everything is a long story to you. You weren't gonna go with your boyfriend? Well... now ex-boyfriend?"

"No, Dad," I responded, now getting annoyed. "Jarell wasn't gonna go to prom whether I was going or not. He was never going to be my date."

"Why?"

"Crowds, dances, all that extra just isn't his thing. Especially since he's blind. Anything else?"

"Shit I'm just tryna figure out what's wrong. You were always excited about school, so I'm just wondering why the long face about it. I'll leave it alone. What I won't leave alone though is about the whole kidnapping thing. What did the police say? Any updates? You never did tell me what actually happened."

This man had me out here like it was an interview. All these questions!! Guess it was my fault though. I never contacted him or updated him about what was going on in my life on the daily basis. Corey had missed a lot from sixteen to now, eighteen.

"I don't wanna talk about it. It's out of my dreams and nightmares, so I don't wanna talk about it to bring them back. But as far as updates from the police? Nope. Just information about the SUVs that took us. They're still having a hard time tracing it to a particular person since there were no surveillance cameras."

His shoulders dropped. "Are you serious? Good for nothing fucks."

"They don't care about Black folks, Dad. It's South LA. Jarell and I got taken away from Chesterfield Square. So, I know they're not going to care whether they find these people or not. Anyone who lives off Slauson or anywhere near Crenshaw don't get the time of day by police."

"What? Chesterfield? What the hell were you doing over there?" His voice deepened. "Your mom doesn't live anywhere near there."

My eyes widened, feeling my heart beginning to race. He never talked to me with such a scolding tone.

"Dad, Jarell lives near there," I explained. "You know that."

"Yeah, but over at Chesterfield that late at night? You know that's not where you should be going."

"That doesn't excuse the behavior from them, Dad. These White folks just as crazy here in the valley. It could've happened here, too," I retorted. Dad lived in rich ass Calabasas along with many other celebrities, and these non-celeb White people were just as slimy. They just got away with it, and the fact that he was acting like this because I was around an area where I attended school was just silly.

He took a deep breath.

"You right. My bad." He swiped a hand down his face. "You know I'm from the Chicago area, so I only go by what I hear about neighborhoods in LA."

"It's cool."

"It just pisses me off that they ain't got no damn leads. I just… I don't understand it, Jade. I know you don't wanna talk about it, and that's fine. Well, it's not fine, but I'm gonna have to be fine. I just want things to be okay, and if I gotta handle fucking business to take care of these mothafuckas, I will. I ain't never been so scared in my life when I got that phone call from the police station…"

"Trust me. I'll be the first to let you know if I need you to handle somebody," I assured.

"Did you tell your mom yet?"

I huffed and dipped my head. Fuck. I knew this was coming.

"I went over there to ask about her involvement, but I didn't give specifics. I kept it real basic. I'm not telling her anything." I crossed my arms.

"Why? What's going on between you two? Y'all were always very close. Tight."

"Nah… my turn to ask questions." I sat up and leaned forward, drilling him with my gaze. "What happened between you and Ma? Why y'all break up?"

"Is that what this is about? Your mom and I separating?" he asked with remorse.

"Partially. Spill."

He sighed and whipped out another cigar from his pocket. A long bout of silence shortly followed. Cool. I had all the time in the world.

"You know..." he started, and then a puff of smoke. "I um... I still love Janet dearly, Jade. I do. It just... we weren't on the same page."

"Say more," I ordered.

"I just... I never wanted to tell you this way, Jade. I still don't. I don't ... I never want you to look at your mom in a negative way. She's all you have as family other than me."

"To the point Dad." I motioned with my hand.

He took another deep breath as his shoulders dropped and closed his eyes. Then he opened them with this inscrutable look I had never seen before. If I could describe it, it was filled with regret and angst. His eyes halfway blinked as if he was intent on holding back more hurt that would seep through.

"Your mom and I separated because I... it wasn't because neither of us cheated or didn't love each other. I loved everything about your mom. Her ambition, her style, her cleanliness, her beauty, her no nonsense attitude... I needed someone like her in my life. I needed someone strong to hold it down while I was on the road in the NBA and someone who knew how to wield off other women who would throw themselves at me, you know? She was everything I needed. And then, there was you. You made me the father I always wanted to be. I wanted a future with your mom, Jade. And you were practice for how I was going to be a good father to my own seed."

My heart warmed and my belly fluttered at such a sweet statement. But I couldn't fold. "And then?" I asked with a straight face.

He pressed on. "Ultimately, when she and I began discussing our future together as potential husband and wife, her values and my values weren't on the same page with how to raise kids. She had such a top-down attitude towards you, and she was very hard on you in ways I just didn't see as fair. It was like she was obsessed with you in every way imaginable, and it was gonna be her way or the highway. Worried about schooling, worried about you becoming pregnant, worried about what boy you'd be seeing, worried about how much money you have, worried about your sex life that didn't even exist, and all this shit that just seemed to be unnecessary."

"I can see that now," I whispered, the tears forming already. Even Corey saw her ways and never told me...

"But here's where the bigger issue came. I knew you would rebel and go your own separate way and see her for what and who she really is. I knew her controlling ways was because of her own history of getting pregnant early by some lowlife, getting kicked out, and having to figure it out on her own.

"But around the time you were sixteen, she got pregnant with my kid. And we still never got on the same page about our views about raising kids and what we would and wouldn't allow. I told her I didn't want my future son or daughter being on this invisible leash she constantly held like she did with you. So, we had a big... no *massive* argument about that and a whole lot of other shit while you were at dance practice one night. Long story short, in the end, she told me we just didn't have a future together. Basically, broke up with me and a few days later... she aborted my kid, Jade. She aborted it. Said she didn't want to be a single mother twice."

I gasped, my inner temperature shifting from zero to a hundred. How dare she...

"I'm friendly and cordial with her only because of you whenever I see her. I just... I don't want you to see her as some nasty person because I didn't want to plant those seeds for you. She's always been great to me and what we had was amazing. I still have love for her, but I'll never forgive her. I never will."

"Dad... I ... I'm so sorry," I whispered. "I can't believe she would do something like that."

"I know. I didn't believe it either," he said, putting out the last butt of the cigar in the ashtray again.

I shook my head and clenched my fists along with my jaw. I couldn't believe her. What a conniving ass … she aborted his child simply because they couldn't see eye to eye? There was no one more selfish and self-centered. And that's how she was trying to raise me to be. Fuck that. If I was Corey? I woulda choked her ass out. But I had to calm myself. I couldn't be angrier than Corey himself. Or could I?

Shifting, now feeling uncomfortable, I sat up, forward, and rested my elbows on my knees, giving Corey a serious look.

"Whether you want me to hate Momma or not, I do. I hate her. Momma *is* a nasty person. There's a lot of stuff I won't forgive her for, but this isn't the first person she's tried to kill. The real reason I won't talk to her is that I think she's a suspect in us getting kidnapped, Dad."

He huffed with wide eyes. "What?"

"Yeah. Trust me. I think she's got something to do with it. She wasn't there when it happened, but I'm sure she had a hand in planning it. I confronted her about it last week and she took forever to deny it. She can't stand the fact that I was dating Jarell. I've never watched someone hate another person as much as she hates him. The fire and … I don't know… contempt in her eyes for him … I've never seen her look at anyone like that."

He put his hand up to stop me as he shook his head.

"Woah, woah, woah. Alright. Hold up. No matter how we both feel about your momma Jade, she ain't that damn crazy. She loves you too much to put you in any sort of danger like sending out folks to kidnap you both. Not with you in the mix. Like I said. She's obsessed with your life and controlling it, so she wouldn't try to end it by doing some shit like that."

"Yeah Dad, but what if she was sending for Jarell, but those guys also decided to take me, too because they knew if they didn't, I would be free to snitch or go to the police?" I countered.

"I still don't think she'd go to that extreme. I know your mom."

"I can't trust her. I don't trust her. At all," I pouted and slid down the couch a bit with my arms crossed.

He paused, and then stood up to move my way and sat down next to me. He placed a comforting hand on my thigh.

"Look at me," he said.

I shifted and gave him exasperated eyes.

"Listen. As fucked up as she can be, one thing I can say about Janet is that she would do anything to protect you and keep you away from landmines that would blow up your life or your opportunities. I don't think she would wanna screw up her own career by being an accomplice in an abduction either. She has her clothing line going, and I don't think she'd be that stupid. At the end of the day, abortion is legal, so the way she did me? That's a different story."

I rolled them this time and looked away. Maybe he was right. I watched Momma have a whole meltdown once she realized I wasn't going to listen to her. Just from remembering that, I now felt the guilt I felt that day nestle in my chest again.

"Are you sure Jarell ain't got cats looking for him or want his number?" Corey asked.

"Yeah, and they're from school. He beat up two people for bullying him. Marcus and Martell. So, it could be that they told some of their people to go after him. That's the only other option left because those guys who kidnapped us weren't from school," I said.

"How do you know?"

"I know what folks from school look like even without seeing their faces. I know their body types and their skin tones. I know their voices. These guys were nothing like the people at school. They had grown man strength. Especially the way they manhandled Jarell," I replied.

"So yeah, they must've hired some hitmen," he concluded with a finger on his chin.

"I can see Marcus doing that, but not Martell. Martell is a wannabe hard ass, but he's soft as ever," I scoffed. "Martell ain't got those kinds of connects the way Marcus does. Martell wants to play basketball too bad to do all that."

"Yeah, but those are the kinda niggas you need to watch out for. If he already got beat up by Jarell and didn't think he would, those are the kind of niggas that will go out their way to prove a point to maintain their image. Prove that they are who they portray themselves to be."

I nodded. "Touché."

"So yeah, it's gotta be that one of them hired those hitmen. The police will find them soon enough. I just need you to know that it likely wasn't your mom, Jade. Janet loves you, even if it doesn't seem like it. She will bend over backwards for you. You have to remember where she's come from. Coming from a family, her mom and dad, who turned their back on her after getting pregnant. Having to move across the country to chase an opportunity for designing clothes and taking a risk with you at her hip. That's why she's so protective of you, even if it's toxic. She would never, ever put you in a position to get kidnapped, Jade. Please know that," Corey explained.

I rolled my head back and exhaled. I hated that Dad was fucking right all the time. And so rational. I hated that shit.

"So, what should I do?" I asked, giving him a pleading look. "I cut ties with her. She thinks I'm pregnant by Jarell."

"Well... are you?" he started, taking out another cigar.

"No."

"Okay then. First off, you ain't severing shit. She's all the blood you got that you know. Secondly, you need to go make it right with her. Talk to her to figure out why she's trying to control you. Let her know you have your own life, and that if she wants the relationship between the both of you to return, then she's gonna have to back off."

"She's not gonna listen, Dad," I said. "Last time I tried that, she slapped me."

"Bet. I'll talk to her then, and I'll let you know when it's clear again to talk to her. She won't slap you this time. And if she does, let me know. I'll deal with it." Another cloud of smoke rose to the ceiling.

"Okay." I stood up. "Thanks Dad. But I should get going because I have rehearsal tonight at seven and you know how the traffic is. Keep me posted about your conversation with Momma."

"Alright baby girl. Gimme hug. You take care now. Be safe. Call me if something ever happens, okay? You keep me posted about the case," he said, pulling me in for a final hug after putting his cigar down.

Once we gave our final farewell, I walked towards his door and said, "By the way... you and that cigar stink." I laughed and so did he before I left. When it came to Corey, I never minded his occasional smoking because he did do it in moderation.

I just never knew how someone so clean could develop such a dirty habit.

Chapter Seventeen

Point of View: Jarell Hendricks

For some reason, Jade been on my mind heavy today.

Even when walking Kylah to school, her usual babble about everything and nothing would keep my attention long enough to engage, but this time, it went through one ear and out the other.

I couldn't stop thinking about her. Stop missing her.

Why did she have to leave me?

For the first time since we broke up, it finally punched me in the face that she let me go. I had gotten so used to talking with her, hugging her, flirting with her, and being around her every single day for the past seven months, and now for it to just return to the way things were before I could call anyone a friend rattled me.

But once Kylah was in the school and I took the bus further into the city towards downtown, I suppressed all that feeling shit. I didn't know what to expect from therapy today, and showing Trisha much of anything coming in wasn't an option because then, she'd ask about it. Talking about Jade was off limits.

Now, I sank into the velvet couch right across from Trisha, ready to start my third session. The shit felt like I had been here for weeks already.

"Alright, Jarell," Trisha started. "Today will be a little more intense as we dig deeper into the things that have been causing you to feel distress, anger, or apathy."

I took a deep breath, rubbing my forehead with one hand. Here we go.

"I know the last couple sessions were getting to know you, your hobbies and current coping mechanisms, but now, I think it's about time we talk about how to marry those coping strategies and hobbies with thinking about root cause and unpacking your feelings around grief and loss. How does that sound? That we begin to go this route today?" she asked.

"Ain't that why I'm here? To be fixed and talk about all this so I can be better?"

"This isn't about fixing you, Jarell. There was nothing ever wrong with you," she said softly. I shifted my eyes from her direction when the peace grew too loud.

"So," she said, slicing the tension. "To you, Jarell, what does it mean to lose something? Can you explain that to me?"

I huffed. What kinda question was this? Isn't the definition of loss obvious?

"To once have something and now you don't. Or you can get it again if you find it."

"Okay…" she trailed off, scribbling in her notepad. "And what does it mean for you to grieve something you once had, but now you don't? Something that will never come back?"

"Grieve?"

"You know… mourning. Like, your immediate and long-term response when you lose something. What does grief mean to you? Is it necessary to grieve?" she encouraged.

"It doesn't mean anything. Loss just happens. There's no real meaning behind grief. It just fucking sucks."

"Have you ever reflected on how you truly feel when you lose something?" she questioned.

"It depends."

"On what?"

"The loss or if I care enough about the loss. Like I said. Loss just happens. There's no elaborate reflection about it for me. At least from my own understanding of what I think you tryna say."

"Okay. Here's what I would like you to do. With braille paper, slate, and stylus on the table I provided, I would like you to create a list of things you've lost that you deeply care about. Can you do that for me? I'll give you five minutes."

Poking out my lip, I rose from the velvet couch and dragged myself to the circle table. Grabbing the stylus and paper, I wrote my losses. It came quick to me. Didn't number them. Just kept going until I reached the bottom of the page. When Trisha's timer pinged, I put everything down.

"Done?" she asked. I nodded. "Can you read it to me?"

I opened my mouth to speak, thinking this would be easy to just read out loud, but as soon as my fingers brushed against the first valuable thing I had lost, I stuttered and stumbled. Swallowing, I cleared my throat and tried again, but only air came out. Fuck. I didn't realize how different this would hit to name all this shit out loud with intention. To admit how much I didn't have…

"Take your time," Trisha encouraged.

"I… I… lost… everything." I quivered. My chest tightened and my shoulders stiffened like they were gripped by an invisible wrench.

"I lost my pop before I was born. I lost my old home. I lost Chicago. My best friends. I lost their moms who treated me like a son. I lost my old school and the teachers who loved me. I lost basketball. I lost my childhood. I lost my eyesight. I lost my fertility. I lost my innocence. I lost my ability to process physical pain because of the beatings from my Ma's ex-boyfriend. I lost my girlfriend, Jade. I lost trust in my mom. I lost control over almost anything in my life. I lost everything I ever loved or cared about and kept all the shit that don't mean shit."

The silence that followed swelled like a tumor. Didn't know if she sat there feeling sorry for me, or if this was an intentional way to honor everything I no longer had. It grew thicker and thicker and wider and wider, pushing up against the walls until I finally whispered:

"Trisha. *This* is why I want to die."

Now the air felt like a bomb was in the room. I could've melted and became one with the floor. Trisha went motionless for a moment.

"S-So… you also want to lose your life? You want to add to that exhaustive list?" she asked.

I rocked my head from side to side and licked my lips. "It would be the one loss I can control. And then I won't have to ever go through another one. That's all I want. To not lose another… fucking… thing."

Another stretch of stillness. I wished nothing more than to see her face or her expression right now. Only thing I could get was the pen scratching against her paper. Again.

"Jarell… can you tell me what you have? What you possess that you care about? Can you create a list of that for me? Same process. I'll give you five minutes to think."

"I don't have to write it. I don't have much. I have my sister, my mom. A home and a bedroom. Clothes. Shoes. A functioning body. Ability to dance. Ability to create. Ability to move through the world differently. I have the ability to dream. That's all I can think of," I said.

"And those don't outweigh your losses?"

"No. I don't care about this new place called California. Dreams don't matter. Creating is a choice. Home now means so many different things… shit outside on the street in fucking blizzards was home at one point. The only ones I would say that actually matter are my mom and my sister."

"I noticed you didn't write down life. That you have life. Why?" she asked.

I shrugged. "Even though my body functions, I guess, half the time I don't feel like I'm alive anyway," I confessed.

"Let's unpack the whole 'feeling' concept. You often mention feeling emotionally numb or that you're just not present. Or that you don't feel affected. However, I can see that you feel some type of way about everything you've lost as you're sitting here right now. I can tell that you feel angry. Bitter. Resentment. Helpless. Stuck. Traumatized. Those are feelings, Jarell. You may not recognize them all the time, but I see them in your eyes. Can you elaborate on what you feel when you lose something in the moment? And has that feeling lingered longer than the moment you felt it when it happened?"

"Um... I don't know if I understand the question."

"I'll say it like this. When loss has happened, how did you deal with that loss the moment you realized it was gone? What do you feel?" she reframed.

"Uh... I don't deal with anything. I just... I'm always forced to move on and keep living like it never happened," I responded. "I may cry in the moment. Might scream or get mad, but I don't deal with the actual loss. As far as the feelings? They come and go because I always have to focus on surviving the next moment. I don't have time to accept or reject a loss. I just... move on I guess."

"Have you ever had plans to accept or reject your losses?"

I smack my lips. "No because it's always one thing after another. All the losses are smashed together. And now? If I do feel anything about it, I block it out by either forcing myself to, by dancing, or by doing origami because I can focus on the actions of my body rather than emotions. Other times, the shit boils over and I kinda rage out until I hurt someone else. The fighting I told you I tried learning to avoid."

"Rage is a feeling," Trisha commented. "You do feel rage."

"I don't feel rage. I act rage. The last time any real emotion came out was when I told my ex-girl about what happened with my eyesight and when I told Ma I wanted to off myself," I confessed. "Those two days were the most that had ever come out in years. I learned to block all that feeling shit. Somehow it spilled over recently."

"So, you're telling me you've finally let yourself grieve and feel sadness recently? Over at least one of the losses on that list?" she asked.

"If that's what you wanna call it. At that time, I was on the verge of losing Jade after she saw what my rage could be. And I couldn't take suffering a breakup after a bad day in jail and after pouring my heart out to her. The shit didn't fuckin' matter because I ended up losing her within a week anyway," I hissed, shaking my head. "Shit is lame, I swear."

"You're feeling bitter right now," she again commented.

"Look, why the fuck do you keep doing that!?" I boomed, feeling smoke coming out of my nose and my fists balling. "Didn't you say at the beginning that you wouldn't tell me how I should feel? Stop telling me how I fuckin' feel!"

"Anger. Jarell... I'm just trying to get you to pause and identify your feelings the second they come on, okay? Sometimes it's hard to identify them when you're expressing yourself. Attaching a name of a feeling to verbal expression can help you process your pain. Process what's going on deep inside of you. Help you heal. And that's when our practices of mindfulness come in," she explained with a calm tone.

"Well, I don't like that shit. Don't tell me how I feel, Trisha. You're not me," I countered. "This is the one time I finally wanna talk to you, so you need to let me fuckin' talk without you also tryna assess me. Or I'll leave, and I won't come back."

She sighed, scribbling more words in her pad.

"You're absolutely right. That's my bad. I apologize, Jarell," she said. "I didn't realize I would make you upset. I'm sorry."

Whoa.

That fast? An immediate apology? A sincere one. One that didn't sound like it was to take the heat from herself to put it back on me. It wasn't condescending. Wasn't a mockery. No excuses. No extra explanations. No ifs, ands, or buts. Not sorry because she felt pity. Not coming around days later to say sorry, either.

It was a real apology. A simple one. A straight one, no chaser.

And not because I asked her to.

Woah.

I blinked, pausing for a second, giving a suspicious look her direction before I began speaking.

"Were you serious about apologizing?" I asked. "Just now?"

"Of course. Why wouldn't I be? I harmed a client on the clock and broke a promise. That's not something I would play or joke around about," she said, and for the first time, her calm demeanor cracked.

"It's just... I- I never heard anyone apologize to me so direct and so quick. Ever. No one ever cared to."

Weighty pauses were the theme of today. One that allowed us to both sit in discomfort, I guess. At first it was deafening, but now, I was beginning to lean into it. Fuck man. These were the moments where sight would be great to gauge the room, yet I was only left with the energy in the air.

Trisha spoke.

"Jarell, I'd like to open up this space today to allow you to grieve. Just so you're able to recognize, validate, and accept your emotions when you do. Remember, I don't want to retraumatize you or anything like that, so I will let you choose the moment to reflect on. Let yourself truly miss what is now no longer here. I know our society doesn't allow for that sometimes. Especially Black men. The only way we can move towards accepting loss is to identify, accept, and acknowledge your feelings about it."

"Okay..."

"Think about one of the things you've lost from that list that you've never thought about. Share about that time and allow yourself to feel whatever you want to feel about it. We will unpack it when you're finished and engage in mindfulness activities. If it gets to be too much or re-traumatizing, you can absolutely stop, and we can go another route. You let me know what's best for you."

"I guess I'll talk about the day I lost my friends and my home at the same time. Back in Chicago before we came here. I guess I can continue where I left off last time. Around when I was about eleven," I said.

"Alright. I'm a fly on the wall..."

Chicago, Illinois – July, 2009

POW! POW! POW!

I jerk awake at the explosive sound from outside of my window. My heart pounds out of my chest, and I break into a full sweat. What the heck? I turn and gaze at my alarm clock, which is now blurry. I rub my eyes and try to read it again: 3:58 a.m.

I take a deep breath. I'm thankful we're on the third floor. Slowly, I get out of bed and walk towards the window to see what's going on.

POW! POW!

I duck and cover my head as my knees strike the floor.

"Mommy?" I call out in a panic. I crawl away from the window, burst through my room door, and head straight for Mommy's room next door. She hates gunshots, so I have to make sure she's okay. I know she heard it.

I rush to her room and the door is already opened. She's sitting up in bed. Her light is on, and her eyes are bloodshot red. I freeze and blink. What happened with her?

"Mommy?"

She cries even harder when she looks at me. Okay. She's scared of gunshots, but I've never seen her cry over it.

"Mommy..."

I walk to her bed and give her a hug. As soon as I touch her, she breaks down in my arms, sobbing out loud. I tear up. I hate seeing Mommy this way. It's the worst thing in the world. I would rather experience anything else.

"Mom, it's okay," I whisper to her. "The gunshots are gone."

"It's not that, baby," she sniffs, pulling away from me and wiping her eyes. "I should be protecting you."

"What is it?"

She shakes her head and looks up at the ceiling as if she's holding something back from me. I look around, trying to find answers. But then, I notice she's holding a piece of paper in her hand she tries to keep away from me.

Slowly, I take the paper away from her and read it.

Ms. Radiya Hendricks,

NOTICE!!!!

As of June 2009, the Department of Housing and Urban Development will be demolishing and remodeling the final sections of the Ida B. Well's homes and upgrading all housing units. This project will be completed by March 2011. When completed, housing costs/rent will increase by as much as $1,000. If you are planning to remain a resident of the Well's homes, please see the property manager to sign a contract to continue your lease and we will reserve housing for you in the meantime. You must pay the new property's rental rate of $1,743 for a two-bedroom apartment. From our records, we have notified you January 19, 2009, and you have not signed a contract. If you do not sign your contract by July 30, 2009, your lease ends on July 31, 2009. Thank you for your cooperation.

I look at the calendar that Mommy always has on her wall.

It is July 31st.

What does all of this mean? I don't understand all the language. I dip my head low, and I hug her again. She cries all over again, but I have to stay strong. Someone has to.

"Does this letter mean we're being kicked out?" I ask.

She nods.

"What about all the other apartments?"

"They've all been remodeled, baby. We're the last of the housing projects," she tells me. "There's nowhere for us to go in the meantime. I've applied for Section 8 housing a while ago, and we're on

the waitlist. I haven't been approved for any other housing yet. So, they will probably give me a voucher for us to live in a hotel until they can find something good for us."

I take a deep breath and just give up trying to come up with any other option. I guess I need to prepare myself to live on the streets or this hotel Ma's talking about. Just the thought sinks me into a sadness I've never felt before. What about all my friends? What were we gonna do with our belongings? Now, I'm scared.

"So, we have to pack?" I question. My hands are shaking, but I hide them behind my back.

She nods.

"Let's take only what we can carry, okay? I want you to go to summer school in the morning, though. Say bye to your friends. Please try to have the most fun you can have, alright baby? I don't know what's next from here, but we're in this together."

I nod. I don't know what else to do or say.

"Try to get some sleep. We have a long day ahead," she tells me. "Sleep well in that bed, Jarell. Seriously. With your blankets. We may be able to find better shelter after the hotel, but there's no guarantee."

I sigh and obey, walking out of her room. I snuggle into my covers and smell them. Man. I never felt more grateful to have a bed than I did right now. I close my eyes and try to sleep, but my mind runs miles per minute. Thinking about all the memories in this apartment. I remember being here my whole life, and now, it is going to all be taken away.

I keep these things on my mind until I fall into a fitful sleep.

—

Summer school was a dud. Too many people around me were happy and giddy, and I was just depressed. I didn't want to talk to anyone. My friends and teachers had kept asking me what was wrong and if I wanted to talk about it since on any other given day, I was happy and social, but I just told everyone nothing. I didn't wanna talk or think about it.

Then, one of my teachers found out from the office that it was my last day of summer school there. She had pulled me to the side to figure out why.

"Jarell, are you leaving us?" she had asked with a concerned look.

I didn't say anything. I just blinked, hoping the hurt I felt didn't show.

"You live in Ida B. Wells, don't you?"

I blinked faster because I didn't want the tears to fall, but they puddled in the bottom of my eyes.

"Oh Jarell..." She sighed.

"We're going to be homeless, Ms. Smith," I had said, keeping my tears to myself. I didn't need to show nobody any signs of weakness.

She looked at me with pity and sadness and pulled me in for a long hug.

"Listen to me, Jarell," she had said to me. "Look at me. You're the strongest, most confident little boy I know. Keep that edge about you, Jarell. You have a fighting, competitive spirit about you that I see so rare in kids your age. You have fire in your eyes. Stay strong. You will make it out on top, okay?"

I now sit on the bleachers at the courts of the apartment complex, thinking about what Ms. Smith said. I don't believe it, but somehow, it sticks with me.

I sigh and gaze around at everything around me. On the other side of the complex, I see construction trucks and cranes. Behind me, other kids are outside playing on the actual playground, laughing and screaming. I scoff and look away.

A game of five on five is goin' on with some grown men right now, taking advantage of the courts before all the kids get home from summer school. Whenever they play, I usually watch real close, taking note of their every move because I want to become as good as them someday, but my mind is so out of focus. I just look around and appreciate the memories that I'm leaving, trading it off with the unknown.

I'm so lost in thought that I don't even see Alex, Rob, and Jonathan coming my way until the last second from the other side of the court. They, too, are quiet when they reach me. They say nothing at all. We all just sit as an unspoken brotherhood and watch the guys play ball as if we all are thinking about the same thing.

"You good, Jarell?" asks Rob as he scoots closer to me. He has a sad glow to his eyes, and I smile small. I don't want him feeling sad either, so I try to lighten up the mood a bit.

"Yeah," I respond.

"What's wrong?" he questions.

"Nothing, man."

"Hey, something's wrong with me. I ain't told y'all yet, but I'm moving tomorrow. Down to my uncle's house a couple blocks away. I mean, I can still walk over here to visit y'all, but it ain't gonna be the same," Rob confesses.

"Word? I'm moving too! Tomorrow. To my grandma's on the West side! My moms won't even tell me why. She just made me start packing," Jonathan declares.

"For real? That's why we're all sad! We're all moving! My mom said she's moving us out too. She plans to move out of the state in a couple of months. She said she don't know where we're moving until then, and that we'll probably crash at my aunt's house. She won't tell me why either," Alex butts in.

I sigh and shake my head. Yeah. All their parents got put out, too. But at least they have a plan, even if it is somewhat of a plan. They know where they are going. Mommy has no family, since she's a foster kid. We don't have a grandma we can just go to. Or a cousin, or an aunt. We have each other and that's it. My dad is dead. We have nothing. No plan, no nothing.

"Everyone's moving. My mom told me that they're tearing down our apartment and remodeling it. I read the note. So, everyone is going somewhere else now," I reveal.

"Ohhh. So then where are you going, Jarell? Are you gonna come back here?" Rob asks.

"Don't know. Ma says some hotel for a while." I shrug.

A pall hit the conversation. They all look at me with this stupid "I feel sorry for you" look that makes me squirm. I shift my eyes away.

"Stop looking at me like that. We'll be a'ight just like any other homeless people," I huff.

"Well, let us know if you need food to take, bro," Rob says. I shake my head with pride.

"Well, since we here and all moving away," Alex says and looks at me with sadness, "Rell, I know we haven't talked since we fought. And I just want to say, I'm sorry."

He holds his hand out towards me to come to a truce, I guess. I look at his hand and give him a small grin. Man, no matter what, Alex was always gonna be my homie. 'Til the wheels fall off. All of them. I accept his hand and shake it.

"Thanks. I'm sorry too. I was never mad at you," I tell him. "You messed me up bad though, I'm not gonna lie."

Alex laughs and so does the other two, nodding their heads.

"Yeah, he tagged your ass," Jonathan says, and I laugh. "You hung in there, though!"

"I did, but it wasn't easy! Man, I've never had such a hard time trying to fight somebody before! Like you got a machine gun fist!" Alex says.

I chuckle and shake my head.

"You was wrong for hitting me in the first place," I say.

"I know. You were right. I was actually mad about those girls."

"Man, you ain't never heard the term bros before hoes? My uncle taught me that," Jonathan says, and we all start laughing. Man. This feels so good to be around my friends like this again. All four of us. With no one fighting. No anger. Just like the way it used to be.

"Y'all should hug it out, now," Rob says and pushes us together.

With no hesitation, Alex puts his hand out and we slap hands and pull each other in for a hug. Jonathan and Rob smile with a satisfaction that made my own heart smile.

"So, check this out," Alex says to all of us with excitement, so ready to move on from this kind of sappy moment. "Since my mom and I don't have a plan either until like October, guess what?"

"What?"

"I joined a gang." He smirks like he's made the best decision of his life. I look at him like he's crazy. Because he is! Alex shouldn't be a part of no gang. We know what happens to people who do. Well at least I do. I don't have a dad because of one.

"And why is that so cool?" Rob asks.

"Right!" I agree with Rob.

"Listen! It's just me and my mom, right? Just us two. I talked to my older cousin who visited from out of town. He's in it and he said we gotta have some protection until we move. So, I made a plan. I joined the gang so that me and her can be protected and have a place to stay until we leave. It's smart, y'all. For real."

"No, it's not," I say and shake my head. "You're gonna end up dead. And the gang not gonna let you pick up and move so easy. It don't even work like that. At least that's what my mom said."

*"No, I ain't gonna die. **You** and your mom are gonna end up dead living on the streets with no one to protect you, Mr. Know-it-All."*

I smack my lips and shake my head, not even wanting to argue with him. I don't want us to fight again. Because this time I'll actually win.

"How'd you get in the gang?" Jonathan asks. I almost want to smack him because he sounds like he's thinking of joining one, too.

Alex smiles a sneaky one, cutting his eyes at all of us.

"I had to do some crazy stuff. My cousin made me go around and spray paint different taglines around the hood. Then, I had to steal stuff for some members at the corner store. Then, last night, I had to be on the lookout when another dude got robbed. It's been

crazy, but they said I'm in and they will protect me and my mom as long as I'm loyal and do what they tell me to do."

I feel sick to my stomach. "I don't like this at all, Alex," I say.

He just shrugs.

"Who cares what you think. You should do it too, Jarell. Don't you want protection?"

"I can protect myself."

"I can tell my cousin about you. Especially since you can fight. Plus, I'll get you a gun. My cousin said he's gonna teach me how to shoot. I'll teach you too."

"Just because I can fight doesn't mean I'm going," I rebut. "And I'm not shooting no damn body."

"Stop being a wimp, Jarell. Come on!"

"I'm not! I'm not trying to end up in jail or like my dad. I don't want no parts of that. I just wanna hoop and that's it."

POP! POP! POP... POW!

"Get down!" screams one of us, and immediately, I duck into the bleachers.

My entire world slows down again, and everyone around me is sprinting away in slow-motion. I look into the direction of the gunshots, and I see a white sedan. Its window is rolled down with someone holding a long barrel of a gun with a black bandana over his face. He points directly at the guys on the basketball court as fire bursts from his car window, spraying the entire court.

POP, POP, POP, POP, POP, POP!

I reach up to my ears and plug them as I duck and whip my head over to the guys on the basketball court who start shooting back as smoke rises in the air.

"Ahh!" I hear someone near me scream. Actually, two voices.

I shift my gaze from the court and into the direction of the screams.

"Oh no," I whine.

They were too late. They didn't duck fast enough. My mouth drops and I blink several times, praying I'm not seeing what I'm seeing.

There's Rob. Lying next to the bleachers in a huge pool of blood and a deep, deep wound right in the middle of his stomach. My world speeds up and I sprint to Rob, kneeling to him. I instantly start crying. My hands are shaking like I'm frigid. I reach down and pull him in my arms.

"Rob, get up!" I cry. "Seriously. Get up."

His eyes are wide open, but they seem to see nothing. The light of life dims quicker than I can think about what's happening to even try and save him. He moves his mouth like he's trying to say something, but nothing comes out but a stream of blood.

"Rob... Rob, please," I whimper. "Say what you were gonna say. Say it."

He no longer moves. His body is a boulder in my arms.

"Rob," I cry his name for the last time.

I can't even think about the screaming going on just steps away from me. I look over, and it's Jonathan, clutching his arm in agony as it gushes out blood as well. This time, Alex is over him, trying to get him to calm down as he puts pressure on his arm to stop the bleeding.

"Somebody help!" Alex screams out, and I am just frozen.

I look down at my arms and Rob's eyes are still wide open, staring at me. I close my eyes and begin to just weep with my forehead against his. How could I lose both my home and my friend in one day?

"Somebody get some help!" Alex continues to shout.

No one seems to respond. And then, a woman's scream shatters the silence.

"Jarell! Oh my God Jarell! Baby, answer me! Where are you? Get away from me. Jarell!"

I can't bear to move myself away from Rob. I need to stay here until help comes.

"Jarell!" Mommy screams again, this time, closer. I look up to see her sprinting full speed at me as I hear sirens wailing in the distance along with Alex's mom screaming for him as well.

"Jarell baby. Are you okay? Oh my God. Please be alright. Please... all this blood..."

Mommy swarms all over me to make sure I'm alright. I am, but I'm not. She notices I'm not wounded, but she realizes the pain in my eyes. Then, she takes one good look at Rob and squeezes her eyes shut.

"Oh Jesus, Rob," she whispers.

POP, POP, POP, POP, POP, POP!

I duck again, but my mom snatches my shirt, ripping it, forcing me to get up.

"Get up, Jarell!" she screams.

"No! I'm not leaving him there!" I scream and try to fight my mom off of me. "He's my friend!"

"Jarell, damn it, he's dead! Let's go before you get killed!" she shrieks and picks me up and over her shoulder.

"Stop!" I scream, punch, and kick, shouting, trying to get away. But she has me gripped too tight.

She just sprints away with me over her shoulder as Rob's dead body gets smaller and smaller in the distance. And so does Alex and his mom, as they sprint in the opposite direction, leaving Jonathan screaming on the pavement as blood spills from his body.

I know it's the last I'll ever see of my friends again.

And that hurts.

It hurts so bad.

~ ~ ~

"And I was right, Trisha. I never saw or heard from any of them ever again," I whispered, as now, the tears fell into my lap. "This shit still haunts me. Ma didn't even let me say goodbye or anything. I mean, I knew it wasn't safe, but ... I never got closure with that. They were the brothers I always wanted. And now they're dead, and now I don't have any friends. I don't have anyone I can talk to or trust. People don't know me here, and if they think they know me, they bully the shit outta me. And I try to keep my distance because..."

My words simply blended with my sobs and disappeared. And I just grieved. For a while without much of a sound, but the tears came heavy. I barely sniffed. Barely hiccupped. Just flat out cried. Trisha just sat there without a single peep until I approached the finish line.

"What do you feel right now?" Trisha asked.

"Sad. Pissed. Aching... I don't know..." I sniffed.

"Good. And where on your body do you feel it?"

"I don't know."

"Alright. Let's do some mindfulness so you can identify that." Trisha went to the opposite wall and grabbed the yoga mat again, placing it on the open floor just ahead of me. "You ready to begin?"

I nodded, wiping my face dry with the back of my hand.

Once I got settled, she led me through another thirty-minute session. By the time it was over, my stomach unknotted. My shoulders relaxed. My arms softened. My chest opened. My jaw loosened.

As I was on the ground, almost sleeping by the time mindfulness ended, Trisha shook me to full consciousness.

"Jarell, that's it for us for the day. Time to walk you to the bus stop," she whispered.

Rising up from the floor, I got my stuff together like my glasses, keys, bag, and all that with her assistance that I needed to head out. Neither Trisha nor I said much of a word to one another from the building to the bus stop. Our lack of communication ended once the bus arrived, and Trisha gave me a farewell.

I gave her a respectful nod and moved up the bus stairs. Before it closed behind me, I paused and turned around. "Trisha?" I called out before taking the last step.

"Yes?" she responded with that thick drawl.

"Thank you."

Chapter Eighteen

<u>***Point of View***</u>: Jade Williams

I couldn't believe it.

I really had my own apartment. Mine. My own set of keys. My own kitchen. Closets. Living room space. Master bedroom suite. It was mine!

I gazed around the space with boxes up against the walls in awe, nearly in tears. No other girl I knew at my age, before graduating high school, had their own nice, upscale spot like this. Corey helped me move in the big stuff like my TVs, couches, tables, and other furniture yesterday, so I just had the small things left to put up. I couldn't wait to have Laurie and Alise over to help me unpack and spice up the place with decorations. It was the perfect opportunity for Laurie and me to connect, make amends and move on after a rough couple of weeks. She would get over the whole Martell thing. I was sure of it.

Not only that? Once we were finished decorating the place, I'd have my first mini Sunday night music video watch party too as a housewarming activity! Alise and I had finished our video shoot with Cardi this past Friday, and Cardi released the pre-release version to us. I couldn't wait to see the results and final edits. That shoot was a piece of work because it was a full three-minute straight dance routine. No stops, no camera shifts, no nothing. Just Cardi working the scene and Alise and I dancing on her left and right sides. Almost like "Single Ladies" vibes, but of course, way more hood and in an urban setting. And Cardi didn't dance as much.

It was the first music video I had ever done in which I had learned the routine in just ten days and the longest I had danced straight through in a video. Thank God I was already in tip top shape. If it turned out the way I imagined, it would be by far my favorite piece of work. Of course, in hopes of me being able to dance with Beyonce one day. One day.

I had tonight all planned out. But as of about fifteen minutes ago it was gonna change.

I had gotten a phone call earlier from Jarell's mom asking if I could come pick him up. At first, I was skeptical because it seemed like she didn't even know or realize Jarell and I had broken up. Plus, I didn't want to be put in a position to take him back again in a moment of weakness, especially when thinking about everything Kim and Alise had said.

But then, his mom begged me.

"Jade, please. It's his birthday today, and he needs to get out the house and be with someone other than us," she had revealed. "You weren't gonna hang out with him already as his girlfriend?"

At first, I was gonna ask, "It's Jarell's birthday!?" because I had no idea. But instead of revealing how bad of a girlfriend I was for not knowing that information about him even when we were together to begin with, I had no choice but to tell the truth.

"To be honest Ms. Rachel, Jarell and I broke up."

"Oh... I didn't know..."

"Yeah."

"But you're still friends. Right?"

"Yeah. If he doesn't hate me," I had responded. "I haven't talked to him since the day we broke up, which was a couple weeks ago."

"He hasn't said anything to me about it. So how about this. Would you allow him to be with you? I really want him to celebrate this year. I've seen my son and his feelings for you. He's never gonna hate you. Please."

"Alright, well. I just got a new apartment, and later, I'm having a mini music video watch party for my appearance in Cardi B's video for her new song. I'm having a couple friends over, so I'm sure we can make it a dual celebration. Plus, he can get familiar with my place before people get here."

"That sounds like a great plan. Don't worry about picking him up. I'll find a way to get him over there," she had offered.

"No, I'll come pick him up. I got some things and updates I wanna talk with him about anyway. No worries. How does twelve sound?" I had asked.

"Noon sounds great. Thank you so much, Jade. This will probably be the last time I call you because I got him a new iPhone for his birthday so he can use Siri to call you. I also made a cake for him while he was in therapy Thursday morning. I think he'll love it, so make sure you come grab the cake too when you get him. Please don't tell him I called you to do this. Just … act like you were gonna do this all along."

"Sounds like a plan. I'll see you soon."

Yeah. And so now, I was about to head out the door to pick Jarell up with little time to mentally prepare to see him for the first time again in nearly two weeks.

Taking the thirty-minute drive to the southside, I pulled up in front of Jarell's house. His mom was already sitting on the porch with the cake in her lap and stood the second I got out the car. Pacing up the walkway to the porch, Ms. Rachel spoke.

"Thank you so much for doing this, Jade. Especially when… you know… y'all are no longer together," she said, shifting her eyes away from me. "After this, you don't need to feel like you should be around him or connect with him anymore."

I put my hand up to stop her and shook my head.

"It's not a big deal, Ms. Rachel. Jarell and I aren't enemies," I said with a smile and took the cake from her. "Thanks so much for calling me. I'm glad Jarell has a phone now. What's his number so I can add it to mine?"

"It's 213-555-0942."

With my other free hand, I whipped out my phone from my jean pocket and entered in the number.

"Cool. How's Kylah doing?"

"She's great! I sent her to her room so she wouldn't see you coming up the walkway from the front window and blow our cover." She giggled. "That girl something else, and she misses you. She asks me about you sometimes."

"That's so sweet. Tell her I said hi and that I miss her too. I want to come see her one of these days," I offered.

"She would love that. But let me go on inside and grab Jarell, and you can go ahead and put the cake in the car. Will you be able to drop him off back here later?" she asked.

"Yep, I got it. I'll see you soon. Thanks again for calling me. I hope I make his day special," I said. I meant every word.

"I do too. I'll see you later," she said, and I went back to my car.

After about five minutes, Jarell came outside and walked towards the curb with a pensive look. He sported a long-sleeved black t-shirt, his favorite black sweatpants, and a pair of old knock off sport slides. It was refreshing not to see Jarell in his old, oversized Black hoody he used to wear every day with that hood up. Without it, he looked so much more open and freer.

And sexy as all hell.

There was nothing more beautiful than Jarell's rich, deep mahogany skin, growing beard, and his new eyeglasses. His gait and swag were even more pronounced without the hoody – a kind of thick, mysterious energy surrounding him that initially attracted me to him from the beginning.

Yet, he had no clue ... even an inkling of his own appeal.

Somehow, that's what made him a magnet even more. At least to me.

Fuck.

I had to get this out my head. I had to be strong and keep him in the friend zone. I couldn't fold. Not today.

He finally reached my car and pulled it open.

"Happy birthday, Jarell!" I said with excitement as he got in.

"Thanks," he responded, not even close to matching my vibrance. In fact, he shook his head with a straight face. "I can't believe Ma called you to do this. She ain't have to do all that."

"What? She never called." I frowned.

"Jade, you ain't gotta lie to me. I know she did because I never remembered telling you when my birthday was. Unless she told you a while ago or some other time when I wasn't around," he replied.

"Yeah. She told me when she got me into the hotel she works at after getting out from that kidnapping situation," I said, pulling away from the curb and down the road. "She said your birthday was coming up. April ninth."

"Oh, okay. Well then in that case, I'm glad you cared enough to celebrate with me. You know, since you broke up with me and shit," Jarell declared, cutting a snarky glare my way.

"I told you I still wanted to remain friends, Jarell. I meant that. I just didn't know how or when because... I thought you'd still be upset with me. I was scared to talk to you again. I wanted to give you space." Now that was the truth.

"And you were right," he admitted with a nod.

"Good. So that means I'm glad you're in a better headspace to hang with me now for your big day, right? You're nineteen, huh?"

"Yup."

"That's wassup. You a old man," I joked.

"I know. Feel it in my joints every day." The corner of his mouth on the left side lifted.

"Yeah, whatever."

"Speaking of kidnapping," Jarell started, "did you get any updates about who did that shit to us? I'm serious about getting even. Shit gets me worked up every time I think about it, and I honestly been trying real hard not to think about it."

Damn it. I was hoping he wouldn't bring that up. It was the last thing I wanted to discuss.

"About that…" I sighed, gripping the steering wheel tighter. "I don't have much news. The only thing the police have is that they found the two SUVs, but they're having a hard time tracing it back to who owns them. I think those trucks were stolen."

"What the fuck? What are they doing, then? How we supposed to get even when we have no leads?" Jarell smacked his lips. "Man, they ain't finna find nothing. They don't care."

"Relax. You know I've been taking matters into my own hands. I've talked to everyone I can think of already. I talked to Mike, Martell, Laurie, and Momma. None of them gave me vibes that they did it. Maybe my mom a little bit, but… I don't know for certain that she did it or at least planned it. Not enough to warrant her arrest. Only person I haven't gotten to yet is Marcus, and to be honest? The way Marcus gets down on the streets? I think he might be the person who hired hitmen. Because I haven't seen his ass since I've been back to school."

"Well, I need you to find out for sure that it's him."

"What are you gonna do if it's him? What's your plan?"

"Haven't decided yet," he said without emotion.

"Listen. I know we both want revenge, but don't do anything too crazy." I looked at him sideways. "I don't want you ending up in jail because of someone else's shit. He's the one that needs to go to jail."

"Can't promise you that."

I rolled my eyes and shook my head. For all the shit Jarell had gotten himself into over the last couple of months, you'd think he'd try to steer clear of mounting more crap on himself. I just prayed that when the time presented itself and he stared revenge in the face, he'd make the right choices to save himself. As much as I wanted payback too, I still felt like him staying out of jail was more important.

I left Jarell's words unchallenged, and the car fell silent until we reached the parking lot of my apartment.

"I've been wanting to tell you some good news. I finally got approved for my new apartment! And we're here now! All mine, no roommates. I just got the keys to it yesterday. I thought it would be nice to bring you and let you be the first one to check it out and become familiar with it and let you play a part in decorating. I'd love to have some of your origami pieces up in my room," I offered with a soft smile.

His eyebrows raised.

"So, you saying I'm gonna continue being in your life? Even when you broke up with me?" Jarell questioned with a dubious glare. "Or is this just a one-day birthday situation?"

My eyes shifted and head jerked back. "We're back on this again? How many times do I have to tell you I want us to remain friends? When it's time for us to be more than that, I think we'll both know. Stop making me feel guilty for doing what I felt was right."

"I ain't tryna make you feel like anything. I just don't wanna set the stage for any confusion about where we stand and end up going back and forth about it. For the record, I'm not the one who wanted to remain 'friends.'"

"Who said anything about going back and forth? I swear you can be the most frustrating person," I whispered the last sentence, opening the car door and slipping a leg out.

"I'm just bein' real." He shrugged.

"Look. Here's where we stand. We're friends. And that's that. There's no confusion. There's no misunderstanding. That's pretty damn clear. What's hard to get about that?"

"Yeah... a'ight," Jarell mumbled and got out of the car as well. "Let's see how long that fuckin' lasts."

"What's that supposed to mean?"

"It means what I said. You know you or me can't hide how we feel about each other for you to be bringing me up to your new spot where it's just the two of us alone, but aye. You got this in the bag." He said with a sarcastic smile and leaned on my car.

With a sigh and a smack of my lips, I got out and shut the door. Whatever. I wanted this conversation to be over. Mainly because I didn't want him to be right. Again. The way he always was.

I was tired of fuckin' never being right.

I didn't want to bring his mom's cake in just yet, so I left it in a cool, shaded place in the trunk so that the frosting wouldn't melt. I still needed to think of a good way to surprise him first. Maybe discuss it with Alise when she got here. If she didn't have any questions or hostility about him being here.

Jarell and I walked up the stairs to the building and into the elevator.

"So… how's therapy going?" I asked after a long bout of peace and nudging him with a playful shoulder.

"S'cool." He shrugged again without expression.

"Are you learning anything useful? Is it worth your time?" I asked, trying to coax more info out of him. He never ceased to kill me with these one-word responses or unelaborate answers.

"I don't wanna talk about therapy," Jarell said as the elevator stopped, and he followed me out.

"I can respect that," I said in disappointment, but hopefully, he didn't pick up on it. Without much else, we reached my door, and I opened it, letting the both of us inside. "Well… here's my new spot!"

"Damn, it feels big and tall. Like the ceiling is high," Jarell said, walking around and dragging his feet across the silky wood.

"It is." Jarell always amazed me at his ability to feel energy and space of a room. "How'd you know?"

"The echo. Open concept?" he asked.

"Yup!"

"Yeah, I feel it. I ain't run into counters or walls yet," he replied, his arms now stretched wide.

"Yeah, and I'm happy that you're one of the first to be in it! But I gotta tell you something. We won't be just the only ones here. A couple people are coming over to help decorate the place soon. And then we're gonna have a watch party for the new Cardi B video Alise and I are in. We shot it on Friday, so we're gonna celebrate with snacks, pizza, and just some chill time. One of those people is Laurie. I'd love to make your birthday a part of our celebration too, Jarell. I hope that's okay."

Jarell nodded.

"Sounds like a fun night. As long as you check your home girl," Jarell replied.

"Don't worry. I got it," I said. I walked over to a box that had office supplies in it. I opened it, pulling out some paper and putting it on the coffee table in front of him. "Origami? Wanna teach me some more again so we can hang them in my room? Like I said, I want you to be a part of decorating the house, too."

Jarell froze and then laughed with a reminiscent twinkle in his eyes.

"You know what happened the last time you wanted me to teach you origami, right? You tried to fuck me on your bedroom floor," he joked and then followed with a teasing snicker.

I huffed with a twisted smile. As much as I desired to punch him for even resurfacing the memory, his laugh melted every inch of annoyance that grew in me. It was the most beautiful sound, considering it was so rare. And so was his smile, which brought a kind of light to his features that made him glow like the king he was. *Whew.*

"I promise I won't try to have sex with you this time. Remember, we're friends. Okay? Don't embarrass me by bringing that up." I blushed.

"You wasn't embarrassed when you was kissing on my neck," Jarell said with a wicked, yet facetious glare. "We were 'just' friends then, too when I gave you the real thing. Don't get amnesia."

"Jarell!" I squealed. I could've melted to the floor. "C'mon, really?"

He chuckled, this one completely genuine. "A'ight, a'ight. Come on." Jarell gently motioned me over to the couch, which he had already found while making me the butt of his jokes.

And it was just that. Us having a blast together creating origami without sexual tension, without any animosity about breaking up, and most of all, forgetting about everything we had been through. Like we had known each other for years as childhood friends and this was a reminder of the old times.

Yet, though romance and open display of affection was absent from the space, *still*... there was something about our intimate energy... it was almost tangible. A vibe I just couldn't explain but could only perceive. Did he feel it too? Damn. How the hell could I hang on with keeping him in the friend zone?

Ugh. He was right. Again.

KNOCK! KNOCK! KNOCK!

"It's them," I whispered to Jarell and put down the paper I was working on. "Once again. Play nice with Laurie, okay? You both are important people in my life. Plus, maybe without all the pressure to not like you because of people at school, she'll open up and try to get to know you."

"I'm not the issue, Jade," Jarell countered, switching out his eyeglasses for his sunglasses.

"I know, but you know what I mean about playing nice."

"Yeah." Jarell nodded with cynicism. "I'll give her a chance."

"Okay." I smiled. "You are the best, Jarell. How great would it be if all three of us got along?"

He shrugged like he believed none of it as I went to the door and opened it.

"Ahh!! Hey sis!" Alise squealed and rushed inside, twirling in a 360 circle. "Damn girl, this spot dope as fuck! Even the lobby cold!"

"I know, ain't it!?" I beamed.

"Hey, Jade," Laurie said with a wry smile as she walked inside. "I'm happy for you. It is a good-looking place. Now I guess I have somewhere to go when I don't have to deal with my helicopter parents."

My shoulders dropped as I sucked the inside of my cheek, giving a long gaze at her sullen, yet chippy demeanor.

"Yeah. Hey. Listen, before you go any further inside," I whispered, grabbing her arm and pulling her aside as Alise took herself on a personal tour and marveled at the apartment. "First, thanks for being willing to come. Especially after everything. I'm sorry about crashing your... thing backstage with Martell. I was wrong for that. I know you wouldn't do that to me. I was looking for answers about something and was only thinking about myself. I don't want you to feel like a sidekick and that I'm perfect and you're not."

She nodded.

"Thanks for apologizing," she said with a small grin and giving me full eye contact. "I appreciate that."

"Cool. And I mean the apology too. I'm not just saying that," I said. "I miss the way things used to be with us."

"I know. I feel that, too." She continued smiling, and then her eyes left mine to explore the scene and apartment around her. "You did luck out. This is a nice spot!"

"Yeah, it is. Let me show you the living area," I said, pulling her away from the door and towards the living room when she balked in her tracks at the sight of Jarell sitting on the couch.

"What the..." she trailed off.

I yanked her back to where we were where Jarell wasn't visible.

"Yes. Jarell's here. Okay? Please don't make this about you or your dislike for him. I already talked to him, and he said he's willing to give you a chance, alright? I apologized about what I did with Martell, so I would like you to play nice with Jarell. Let's make this about the new apartment."

"Hmph. Now I see the only reason why you apologized in the first place was because you knew he was here and I'd give him a hard time," she said, giving me a disappointed head shake.

"No, it's because I actually meant it, and I don't want to fight with you anymore."

She dished me a mocking nod. "Okay, Jade." Moving away from me and back out to the living area to check out the rest of the apartment, she said, "Tell me which part of the house you'd like me to decorate."

"Sup, Laurie," Jarell called out to her, nodding his head. I wished I could read his tone. It wasn't rude, sarcastic, or patronizing, but it also wasn't excited, happy, or bright. It was simple and without affect.

"Mmm," she hummed in response and walked right by him to examine the labels on the boxes against the wall.

"You can start with the bathroom," I said with frustration, and Alise came rushing out from the back of the apartment, oblivious that her appearance had eased the tension.

"Girl, that master suite is nice! I might have to move over here. I thought my apartment was nice…"

"Alise, your apartment is way better than mine, and you know it. You make twice as much money as I do."

"Still! This place is so you," she said, hugging me.

"Thanks." I smiled.

She didn't let me go but whispered in my ear instead.

"And um… what's he doing here? You didn't break up with him, huh? I knew it."

I smacked my lips and pulled away, giving her a scowl.

"Jarell, Alise is also here. Remember her? I know it didn't end well when you were at the studio, but here she is," I said aloud, busting up her moment of secrecy and suspicion.

Much to my surprise, Jarell perked up with a smile. "Oh. Yeah, I remember. Wassup, Alise. My bad about that day at the studio when I came. I was in a bad head space, so I hope we can start over," Jarell said, stood up, and held his hand out.

At that, her exasperated glare at me morphed into shock. With an "okaaaayyyy" look, she walked over and accepted his handshake. Hmm. Therapy might've been doing him some good.

"Apology accepted. I don't mind starting over," she replied. Whew! I was so glad she was so much more forgiving towards him.

"Good." Jarell nodded.

Alise turned around and whispered in my ear again.

"Girl, you were right. The nigga fine as hell. I see the big deal you put on about him now." She giggled and I pushed her away, giving her a somber gaze.

"Nah," I uttered. "We're *friends*. Let's go downstairs for a second. I got something from the car to get, and I want you to come with me."

"Oh...okay," she said as I pulled her arm and dragged her out the apartment, leaving Laurie and Jarell alone. Hopefully a great thing and an opportunity for them to hash out their differences.

"What's this all about?" Alise asked. "Why you bringing me out here?"

"It's Jarell's birthday today. I have a cake in the car I want to surprise him with. Plus, I want Jarell and Laurie to make up and have some time alone to do that."

"Oh, they don't like each other?" she asked.

"She doesn't like him. Long story, but it's for no reason. But I wanna give them some time to talk everything out so we can have a good night without any awkward shit going on. So, let's go get this cake, and when we get back, listen in. If they're talking."

"Cool. Let's do it."

~ ~ ~

We made it up the elevator again and to my apartment door with the cake in hand as Jarell's voice filtered through the walls.

Maybe my plan was working. Alise and I both looked at each other and nodded before we leaned our heads forward to listen in.

"Laurie, I don't know what your problem is, but you don't know me," Jarell said. "I ain't done nothing to you. Don't even know you enough to dislike you, so what makes you think you know anything about me? We can squash this petty shit right here right now."

Oh God. What did she say to him?

"Get along with you? Um, no. My issue is that you ruined my best friend's life," Laurie retorted. "You fucked up our school. You ruined my boyfriend, Martell. You ruined D-Block. You caused Jade to nearly die. You're not cut out to be her boyfriend. At all. You have nothing to offer."

"Who are you to tell me what I'm cut out to be and what I can offer? Y'all ruined your own shit by fucking with me for no reason. You just mad it backfired," Jarell said. "Like I said. You don't know me."

"I know enough. You're a crack baby with a crack head mom, you're a dirty, homeless bum who needs a bath, and you're a low-life who has no friends. You probably steal everything you own. You're probably a rapist. There's a reason why no one talks to you," Laurie snarled. "You're a creep. You wear those sunglasses because you wanna hide your demon eyes."

A long pause. Uh oh. Shit. I pressed my ear closer to the door.

"A'ight," Jarell started, the threat evident in his voice. "I heard that shit a million times so you ain't hurting nobody, Laurie. You only coming for me because you see everybody else do it, so you feel like you can fuck with me, too. Only reason why you get the time of day is because you ride Jade's ass. If she didn't invite you here, you'd probably be somewhere with a dick in your mouth for attention. Clout chasin' ass girl."

Oof. Ouch. That was a dagger to Laurie's soul. They couldn't keep going back and forth like this because it was a fight Laurie was a thousand percent sure to lose. Jarell's clap backs were too hard to recover from. Verbally or physically. And he wasn't one to hold back when he got started.

"Yo, he ate her ass up." Alise laughed, but I gave her a dire look.

"Not funny. Jarell is a loose cannon. Let's get in here before shit starts popping off," I whispered, handing Alise Jarell's cake.

Alise and I burst through the door in time to see Laurie slapping the shit out of Jarell to the point where his sunglasses tumbled.

"Laurie!" I shouted and ran to separate them, but I was too late.

Without even blinking, Jarell snatched Laurie's shirt in his strong hands and yanked her to his chest, hemming her up in retaliation. Laurie couldn't even scream; he did it so fast.

"Jarell, stop! Let her go!" I yelled as Jarell's lip began to bleed. Damn, she hit him *hard*. Didn't think she had that in her.

"She stupid as hell thinking she can put her hands on me knowing what happened to her wannabe boyfriend," Jarell barked and lifted Laurie up to the tips of her toes as fire filled his eyes. "I put that nigga in a neck brace, damn near suffocated his cousin in broad daylight, and she act like she don't know what the fuck I'll do to her. She thinks she's invincible because of you, Jade. Either get her the fuck outta here, or I'll fold her ass up and throw her off the patio."

"Oh shit," Alise whispered, freezing in her tracks with his cake as Jarell dragged Laurie over to the open patio door. Aw hell. Jarell couldn't do this. I lived on the seventh floor; he couldn't shove that girl to her death off the balcony. No way. Not on my watch.

"Jarell, you don't wanna go that route," I warned as calm as I could while moving swiftly towards him. Laurie screamed and tried to move, but he had her shirt gripped too tight and drew her too close against him to allow for escape. She couldn't even flail, knee him, or anything. Only thing she had was her forehead, but Laurie was too stunned to use it. Shit, where the hell did Jarell learn all these lock holds?

"Jarell. Let her go. I'm sorry. I didn't mean for this to happen," I said, trying my best to stay composed. "I thought if I tried bringing you two together outside of school and away from peer pressure that she would let the bullying go and make a connection with you, but I was wrong. I'm sorry I left you both alone. Let her go. Please."

With a frown, Jarell threw her to the ground at the patio door like she was featherweight as her hands slapped the floor.

"I'm out," Jarell mumbled and moved Laurie out the way with his foot before he stepped over her. Whew. The disrespect. "Where's my fucking glasses?"

Alise hurried to pick both sets up and handed them over to Jarell like they were hot potatoes. He snatched them without remorse.

"Where's the door?" he growled as Alise rushed to walk him out.

"Jarell wait!" I screamed, but he didn't stop as Laurie roared and tried running after him, but Alise held her back at the door. When she looked to be too much to handle for Alise by herself, I swooped in to stop her as well.

"I'm gonna kill you, you asshole!" Laurie shrieked after him.

"Would you shut up and stop?" I yelled, pushing her deeper into the apartment and down on the couch. "You trying to get me kicked out my place already with a noise complaint?"

"Fuck you, Jade! You're just gonna let him do that to me?" she wept.

"You started that shit! He's didn't do a damn thing to you, Laurie! I heard the whole conversation before it escalated and he wanted to make things right with you."

"So?" she shot back.

My jaw clenched. "Look, I know you think you're invited to the BBQ and you think you got a lil' Black card because you hang with me, but you don't know nothing about being hard. You don't know anything about talking shit to anybody from the hood or anybody on Jarell's level. Only reason why you think you're safe doing it is because you're protected by the system, school, and your parents. You really think Jarell won't destroy you? Don't you see what he's done to people three times stronger?"

"I don't care," Laurie cried, whipping out her phone. "I don't care about any of that! He almost threw me off the balcony! He's fuckin' crazy! I'm calling the police. He needs to be thrown under the jail; he's already got charges against Martell."

"The hell you won't," Alise said, yanked Laurie's phone away, and threw it to the floor, the screen cracking into hundreds of parts. "You started that shit. There are two witnesses, and he never hit you. He didn't even make it outside to the balcony."

"I can't believe you would take his side over mine!" Laurie whined, giving me a baffled look. "And you're buying me a new phone!"

"Girl, I ain't buying your entitled ass shit. You lucky I don't beat your ass for tryna play victim and for using the police as your personal avenue for revenge against something you honestly deserved," Alise seethed as her skin began to heat red.

I sighed and stepped in front of her.

"Alise. I got this," I said, putting a hand up.

Alise shook her head, squinting her eyes and balding her fists as she moved away from the two of us. I closed my eyes and took a deep breath before death glaring Laurie down.

"Laurie... listen. It's a wrap. Our friendship ends here. I don't wanna have anything to do with you. You think you're tough, but you hide behind me like a coward. I just saved your life, and you wanna whine to me about some shit you started? I care about Jarell, and you haven't ever showed an ounce of respect to him when he's shown respect to you out of respect for me. You did this on his fuckin' birthday. Bitch. Get out. Don't you ever call me or come back."

With a long, shameless look, Laurie stood up and straightened herself out. Then, she walked towards me with a deliberate steadfastness I raised my eyebrow at.

"Don't walk up on me if you don't wanna get your ass slapped," I warned. "I don't give a damn about you callin' the police. I'll call 'em for you."

"Fine," she mumbled in my face and proceeded to walk out the already opened door. "Be like that then."

Once the door slammed shut, Alise huffed as her lips pressed thin with a wild gaze. "I can't believe her ass did that. She tried it! Oooh, she lucky I didn't kick her ass. Are you good?"

"Bitch, you ain't in the clear, either!" I roared at Alise and pointed an index finger at her. "No, I'm not good!"

"What?" she whispered with this fake offended look. "What I do?"

"You saw what Jarell was up against. This isn't an isolated case. He always takes the nice route while everybody just shits on him, and you made me break up with him. You made assumptions just like everyone else, and I listened like an idiot. You can get the hell out, too," I said as my tears wound up.

"Jade..." she started, her brows wrinkling as the hardened look in her eyes softened.

"GET OUT!" I bellowed. "Please. Get out."

With a glare, yet no words, she grabbed her belongings and exited, closing the door quietly behind her. As soon as she was clear, a sob escaped my chest.

There was no way Jarell would ever want to speak with me or deal with me again for putting him in that position. Not only that? I was pissed at myself because I called Jarell a loose cannon and not Laurie. I wasn't going to demonize him in any way anymore. Ever! It was *always* everybody fucking else and my dumb ass always trusted they'd do the right thing to him. This was the last straw!

Chapter Nineteen

Point of View: Jarell Hendricks

"Trisha, I fucked up. Big time."

This was the very first time I spoke first in therapy. Never thought the day would come, especially on a Tuesday. But after my birthday, there was no way I was letting this shit slide without talkin' 'bout it. Who knew what Laurie had up her sleeve? She coulda been pressing charges on a nigga right now and I would have more shit tacked onto my assault charges on Martell.

DAMN IT!

Why did Jade think bringing her there was a good idea? I understood her intentions and all, but she knows her friend better than I did. Why didn't she know she would do something like that?

"What do you mean you messed up, Jarell? What happened?" Trisha asked.

With a whole lot of irritation, I gave her the rundown on everything from Jade picking me up that afternoon to Laurie asking me why the hell I refused to leave Jade's life when Jade and Alise left us alone, which led to the confrontation. After I left, I had found the nearest park, sat on a bench, and thought about the whole situation before a quick dance. Then, I took my ass home on a two and a half hour walk just thinking about how screwed I was.

"Thanks for telling me, Jarell. Before we dig into this, I want to recognize your openness and honesty. I just want you to know I appreciate that," Trisha said once my soliloquy finished as her pen whisked over the paper in her notepad. It caused my chest to stop fluttering for a bit. "Now, I don't think you messed up as bad as you think you did. Right now, it sounds like you're feeling guilty or ashamed. I don't want to make assumptions, though. Am I accurate on that?"

I nodded. "Yeah. Spot on. I shouldn'ta put my hands on that girl." I sighed, swiping a hand down my face in disgrace and looked from Trisha's direction. "What if she calls the police? Can she call the police on me?"

"She can, but if she did, there wouldn't be much of a case," Trisha said. "From your version of the story, it doesn't seem like you hurt her enough to have an arrest warrant. Not even close."

"Yeah, but still. I fucked up," I pouted.

"Remember our last session together. Compassion, Jarell. Compassion for yourself. Patience with yourself. Now that you've thought about what you did, let's consider what you didn't do. What are some of the things you chose not to do during that situation?" she asked.

My index and thumb squeezed my chin as my brows furrowed.

"Um… I didn't hit her back. Didn't throw her off the balcony. Didn't yell at her. I didn't injure her, didn't throw anything, or punch walls after the fact. Um… I didn't go crazy," I listed. "There's probably more, but I can't think of anything else."

"Nice work. Do you believe one of those things would've happened if you weren't as mindful of your emotions and actions in the moment?" she questioned.

"Honestly, yeah. I woulda did something a lot worse," I admitted.

"Then you won, Jarell. You won in that situation. You paused and were conscious of your actions or lack thereof. You acknowledged and became aware of your anger. You were in tune with your mind and body when you let her go and didn't mindlessly rage out afterward. You realized it wasn't worth it. You reflected on the situation after. You still have some work to do with being compassionate and patient with yourself, but this situation was a step in the right direction. I'm so proud of you, Jarell. I am," Trisha lauded.

Goddamn. I felt like a man on top of the world. The way she just framed everything and put it in perspective was crazy.

"I have one more question for you," she said. "Did you feel emotionally numb during that whole thing or any time after?"

My eyed ballooned. Woah.

"No," I answered. "I didn't feel numb at all."

"Mmm." The energy of her smile weighed the room. "Now, for your homework to bring back on Thursday, I'd like you to think about how you would've handled that situation differently if you could start all over. Think about some of the things you did that you weren't proud of and think of an alternative scenario in which you would've made even better choices."

"I don't know if I could've done any better than I did," I confessed.

"There's always a better version of ourselves and our choices, Jarell. Sometimes it's hard to imagine, but it's true."

"I believe you," I said. And meant it.

She didn't say anything else for a while. I took that time to lean back and sink into the velvet couch and become more comfortable in the room as the incense burned behind her. For a while, I hated that damn smell, but now, I didn't mind it as I listened to the scribbles and scratches over the paper until she flipped another page and continued.

"Trisha, what do you be writing in that notepad?" I asked suddenly, my question laced with humor. "Like, you be writing a whole novel."

She chuckled.

"I'm just documenting your homework assignment. That's all. Other times, I'm just writing notes for myself to remind me of what we discussed and then that's when I think of next steps after you leave," she replied.

I nodded. "Oh, okay."

"I'm done now. Let's get to what I have planned for today. I think what happened on Sunday is a perfect sègue into talking about how to deal and cope with other people's choices. This girl, Laurie, or whatever her name was, made a choice to hit you, right? She made a choice to insult you, and you had to cope with that. And you handled that to the best of your ability. So now, I want to dig deeper into other areas of your life that have had you bound by chains and have developed a sense of resentment inside of you because you had to cope with their choices. I want to talk more about your mother today."

"Fuck," I whispered.

"Yes. And your stepfather. Or mother's ex-boyfriend, I should say."

"Double fuck," I said, rubbing my temples.

"If that's the word you need to help you transition to that state of mind, I'm all for it," she said, the jest underneath. "In your version... can you describe your mother's ex-boyfriend? Who is he and how do you perceive him?"

I swallowed as my body shifted into a deep freeze. Damn, this was too soon.

"I ain't sayin' much because the mothafucka ruins my day every time I think of him, but he's a monster. A rapist. An abuser. He skipped town when we called authorities on him for doing some of the dirtiest shit to my mom and I, and the authorities dropped the case. He deserves to die, and I hope he is dead somewhere. That's all I gotta say."

Trisha logged her notes in her notebook before she spoke again.

"Okay. A couple of sessions ago, you mentioned your mom making poor choices and not listening to you when her choices affect you. Can you tell me a little more about your perception of your mother? What led you to believe that she's a poor decision maker and some of your history with that? I know you've been letting me inside quite a bit with your past in Chicago, and it seems like you and your mother were close. When did the distrust begin?"

"Man…" I slouched down in the couch even more. "It's one long ass story, but I'll try and make it short. If you care to hear all of it."

"I'm all ears. You talk as much or as little as you want."

"I guess," I hesitated with a lazy shrug. "You remember when I told you after my friends died from those gunshots that she ran off with me right? In the middle of gunfire?"

"Mmm hmm."

"Well, that was the start of everything. It was like I ain't know Ma anymore. I don't know if she did this legally or not, but she even changed her real name from Radiya to telling me and everyone else to call her Rachel. She usually told me everything, and we was hella tight, but the second we were homeless, it seemed like she held secret after secret."

"Like what?" Trisha asked.

"For a while, after that gunfight, we lived in this dirty motel waiting for a new housing unit from the government. She left me in that raggedy ass place from about five at night to about three in the morning. She would come home, go to sleep, and I would wake up a couple hours later to catch the bus to my new school. When I got home, she'd only be there for about an hour and then off she went. I always asked her where she would go and tell her that I missed her, but she told me it was 'grown folks business.' Said it was to make money for us to get outta there. I ain't ever see none of that money because it ain't like I ever have shit. No new clothes, no new shoes, nothing. But sometimes, she'd come home with her nails done or new wigs. She never asked me about school anymore, never talked to me… it was like she didn't care about me or love me anymore.

"One night, she just up and decided we weren't gonna stay in the motel anymore because she caught me passed out in someone else's room. Let me tell you about that. For a stretch of time… maybe about two or three days, Ma left me in that motel with no food; I was hungry as hell. We ain't have anything to eat for a grip, so I went knocking on people's doors asking for food while she was out doing whatever. I lucked out and this one guy let me in because he realized I was her son. I didn't even know how he knew her, but I trusted him. Turns out, dude fed me about three of four strong ass weed brownies that were laced with another drug. Knocked my ass out.

"The killer part is before he knocked me out, we were talking, and I find out from him that Ma was a prostitute in the motel. That's what the fuck she was neglecting me to be. So, you know, as I got older, I connected the dots and knew that shit to be true because how else would she have found me passed out on his bed later that night? She was probably heading to him to give him favors and saw me laying there. I don't know what happened when she found me, but she took us out the motel that night and had our ass living on the streets ever since between different shelters until the government could get us in a new unit. But we never made it to one. Ever since, it's been hard to trust her. She should've never neglected me like that."

Trisha, again, continued penning in her notepad without saying another word until she was finished.

"How did your mother meet your stepfather?" Trisha asked.

"I don't know. Probably through being a prostitute. She said she knew him way before I met him, and I didn't meet him until the day she damn near died out in a blizzard when we couldn't get shelter."

"Can you tell me more about that?"

"Yeah... strap your seat belt," I said as the memory played back like a film.

Chapter Twenty

Point of View: Jarell Hendricks

Chicago, Illinois – February 2010

It's February and I ain't got nothing to smile about. Neither does Mommy. The wind is howling, and the air is white. My teeth chatter against each other as the wind strips my skin to the bones. I could always handle the cold here because I always walk to the bus in the winter back when we lived in the Wells. But today hurts. This is a cold that really hurts. And we have nowhere to go – all the waiting lists were filled for a shelter.

We knew the winter storm was coming with subfreezing weather from all the other homeless people on the street. Thing about it? They were smart. They got into the shelters and got their names on the lists ahead of time. Unlike Mommy.

Day after day before the blizzard hit, I tried to find warm clothes on the streets. I haven't found any yet. We had no Salvation Army or Goodwill around where we stay, so now I'm in a t-shirt and jeans today with a blanket. For as long as Mommy was out being a 'prostitute,' or whatever, I have never seen any money or any of our things be replaced that got stolen some time ago. I never ask her about it because I am trying to trust her. As hard as it is. Because who else am I gonna trust? I don't have anyone else.

"Mommy?" I call out to her.

She doesn't respond. It's been like this for hours. Each time I've called her name today, I got nothing. And every time I call her, I feel some sort of hope that she will respond only to be disappointed.

"I'm gonna find us a place to stay, okay?" I conclude.

She's just sitting against the wall of this little lodge at this park with her head down and shivering. I can't blame her. We've walked for miles today, and she's probably disappointed that all the other shelters are too full. I know she's tired, but I just want to keep trying. We're going to die if we stay out here today, and someone has to be strong.

Where to start? Which direction do I go?

I try to make a decision. My stomach is searing, on fire. Like it's caving in, and I'm trying to focus on the next place we can go for help, but I can't even think. My head is pounding. I've dreamed about food each night I go to sleep. I pray for something small to come today. From somebody. Anybody.

I step out from under the park pavilion, and I nearly get blown away. The wind is so much that it rips my t-shirt into two.

"Fuck," I whisper.

I take another step forward. The snow is unbearable, and I can't even take more than a few steps without fumbling and stumbling.

I make it to the playground because that's the only thing in sight, and I try to see past it, but I have no idea where I am. Everything is completely white. My hands are ashy and stinging. My feet are numb and throbbing at the same time. My shirt is torn, and my underwear is wet because of the snow falling into the holes of my jeans.

With the little strength I have, I climb onto the playground and snuggle inside of a slide with my blanket.

I just break down. The tears freeze against my cheek as they pour. I just want a home. I want things to be the way they used to be. I want my friends. I want my basketball. I want my old bed. I want something. Anything. But not this.

"Hey, someone in there?"

I look up, and there's a man. A Black man with a thick coat, hat, gloves, scarf, and every fucking thing I don't have staring up the slide. I turn my head away. It hurt too much to look at someone who's warm.

"Kid, you alright?" he calls out to me. I ignore him. "Aye, come on out. I heard you crying. Where's your parents?"

I back away, further into the slide. I don't trust him. I don't trust anyone. I would rather die here than to be taken away from my mom. Because I'm sure he thought I was by myself.

"Listen. I won't hurt you. I just want to make sure there is an adult around and that you're okay."

"My mom's at the pavilion," I say, shivering. I can no longer feel my body, and everything inside of me seems to head into a complete frost.

"Okay. Here. Please come out and take this. It's something that will keep you warm. Come on out. Please," he begs.

I look down at his face, and his eyebrows are wrinkled with a deep concern that I somehow begin to trust. His eyes are soft and caring... a look I haven't seen from anyone in a while. Not even Mommy.

I buckle at first, but I come down the slide. I take a look around. From what I see through my squinted eyes, there is a van or truck of some type. But then it disappears into the whiteness. The weather has gotten worse. Snow is blowing everywhere, and the wind breezes so hard that it pushes me into the man with a thud. He reaches a hand out to me to steady me, and then I look down. He holds a thick piece of cloth.

"Here. Take this."

I stare at it for a while, and then I look up at him. His soft, brown eyes have shifted from concern to sorrow.

"Take it," he says.

With trembling hands, I grasp onto the cloth and open it up. It's a huge black hoodie.

I stare at it with my mouth open. I haven't had a hoodie in months, much less anything with long sleeves. When the reality of it sinks in, I gasp, fall to my knees, and weep while snuggling with the thing.

"Let me help you put it on," he says and lifts me to my feet.

The man takes the hoodie away from me with a struggle because I'm afraid he'd take it away for good, but he doesn't. He puts it over my head, and it drags in the snow.

"Sir..." I start to say it's too big. The cold air has so much space to move within it.

"Shh," he replies, and then takes my old blanket I still carry and wraps it around the hoody to eliminate any air pockets. To secure its fit. And just like that, the icicles my blood formed inside melts away. It's so cozy and secure. I had never, ever had a piece of clothing that made me feel so safe. And even when this blizzard is over, I know I'd never want to take it off. It's now my most prized gift. From a stranger.

Without another word, the man pulls the big black hood over my head. I become even warmer.

"Don't take this hood off, okay? It'll keep your head and ears, safe. Don't lose this thing."

"I won't," I assure him.

"I know this may seem a little gross, but this is all I got for food," the man says and gives me a box. It's a slice of pizza that's half eaten. I don't care. I'll take anything. "And here's a ten-dollar bill. Give this to your mom. Also, here's some information about a hotel that's taking in additional people. I wish I could take you, but we're doing some filming for a short indie movie. A winter scene. Take care. Good luck, lil' man. Please go find your mom. You have to get out of here before you die."

I nod, and my body rushes to snuggle with him. He wraps me into his large body and hugs me back. I don't say anything else, but I take his offerings and run away to Mommy.

"Ma," I call out to her.

She's still sitting up against the park pavilion's wall next to the bathroom with her head peeled back, staring out into space as a blanket wraps her shoulders. I don't know what she's feeling or thinking, and her body language doesn't give me clues either, but she doesn't answer me. Again.

"Mommy, say something," I beg. "I have something to tell you."

I sit next to her and push the pizza box her way. Maybe she's hungrier than I am, and she can't think or talk through it.

"I found some food," I squeak out, but when she doesn't look at me or even acknowledge any part of what I said, I lower the box as tears come and freeze once again. **What do I have to do? What can I do to have my mom back?**

"Mommy, you gotta answer me. Please."

Nothing. She just blinks. Little icicles have formed on her eyelashes. Her skin is pale. My heart races, and I struggle to keep calm.

"Ma? Are you okay? Come on. I need you. I can't be alone," I say as I put my head on her shoulder and cry. "Please. Can you just say something? Say you're here? Say that you'll eat this pizza? I don't need it. I can wait. Please."

And she says nothing.

Oh God. Oh no. I lift my head from her shoulder and try to shake a response out of her, but she falls over.

"Mom!" I scream as my throat closes.

As she lays on her side, hanging onto consciousness by a hair, she's still breathing because I see the cloud when she does, but it's very small.

"Mommy. Please. Get up." I wheeze and push her back up to sit against the wall, but she slumps. I shake her again, but this time, she does fall over.

"Help! Someone help me!"

I scramble up and high knee through the plush snow to the playground, praying that the man was still there. When I arrive, there are two guys this time, one tall and one short. The short one is putting away something like camera equipment in a van. The tall one is the same man who gave me the hoodie. I tap him right away.

"Hey, I need help. Please!"

The other guy also turns around. He's a Mexican dude with dark hair, and he looks just as concerned as the guy who gave me everything.

"What's wrong, kid?" the Black man asks.

"My mom isn't responding. I think she's dying. I need help. Can we put her in that van for a second? With some heat so she can warm up? Please," I beg, and the two guys look at one another.

The guy who gave me the hoodie gives him a look that said to just do it. The Mexican guy rolls his eyes and smacks his lips, and nods his head anyway. The van must've been his, or he must've been driving it.

"Alright. We'll see what's wrong with her, but then we have to move. We're working and we have to get out of this weather. Okay?" the Mexican man says.

"Thank you," I whine. "She's over there. She won't move, but she's still breathing. I see her breath."

"We got it," says the Black man.

All three of us scramble to Mommy through the thick snow. The money, pizza, and the paper with the shelters have blown away in the wind. I feel bad for wasting the man's money and food, but I hope he understands.

The Black man picks Mommy up with no effort at all and takes her to the van. The Mexican guy follows and escorts me, making sure I'm okay.

We get there, and it's already running with the heat blowing. The warmth I had already started to feel in this hoodie just got warmer as they lay Mommy across the back seat. I crawl up the middle of the van and sit next to her. Her skin is still colorless, cold, and she's barely blinking.

"We're somewhere warm, Ma," I whisper and brush the snow from her hair.

As I encourage her, the Mexican man comes back with a thick blanket from the trunk and lays it over her. Then, his fingers go up to the side of her neck as if searching for something.

"What are you doing? Why're you touching her like that!?" I yell at the man and almost push him away, but the Black man stops me.

"He's just checking her pulse. That's all. Relax, kid," he says, calming me down.

I take a deep breath with closed eyes. Man. I'm too on edge. These guys are just trying to help, and they could've said no to me.

"Her pulse is low," the Mexican man says. "We gotta get to a hospital. She needs fluids, food, and more warmth. She's gonna die here if we don't."

"Alright, let's get a move on then. We'll do our scene in the blizzard later. Let's help them out," says the Black man.

"Please take us! I don't want her to die. I don't wanna be alone," I weep, hugging Mommy close to me. I take a deep, deep breath of her scent, just in case she left me here to figure life out by myself.

"We're going lil' man. We just need you to try and relax, okay? Don't know how long it's gonna take to get to the hospital in the snow, but we are going to try our best. Okay?"

I don't even answer. Don't even know who said it. I am too busy crying into Mommy's heart.

~ ~ ~

"Aye. Aye, kid. Wake up."

I hear a whisper. Then, my body's being rattled by some force.

"Wake up, lil' man."

I bat my eyes open, and the Black man is towering over me. I rub my eyes and look all around. I'm still wearing this huge, black hoodie covered with my blanket. Surrounding me is a waiting room of some sort as other people are sitting and looking at magazines. And then, my last sense kicks in. I smell a hot meal.

"Here," he says. "Something for you to eat."

I look down, and he's holding a brown bag, and there's the infamous big yellow M. My mouth waters to the point of drooling. I snatch the bag away from him so fast, his head probably spun because if I don't, it's gonna get taken away.

"Take it easy. Don't eat too fast. You'll throw it up."

I don't listen. I just rip open the wrapper of the entrée, and my teeth sinks into heaven. My tongue bursts like fireworks with flavor. The tanginess of the ketchup with the almost sour blend of mustard and pickles. I chow down the small, crunchy, flavorful onions. But most of all, the cheese. It just melts in my mouth along with the seasoning and meat juices.

I close my eyes.

"Mmm, my God," I whisper and take another huge bite. My tongue bursts again with the same flavors, except intensified.

"Oooh wee, this is good."

I reach in the bag and pull out a handful of fries. I stuff them in my mouth, and my senses go insane. The soft, greasy, pillowy texture makes my heart flutter. Man, were they perfectly salted.

I eat everything in about six or seven bites. I barely chew. Once the food disappears, I burp out loud with an unapologetic satisfaction. I look up, and the Black man gazes at me with both awe and sorrow. I roll my eyes because I don't have time for him to be feeling sorry. Ooh. I hadn't even seen that drink! Perfect to wash this down. I reach out and yank the soda he has in his hand away and suck it up. It's a sugary bliss of Orange Hi-C. Nice and cold.

"You're going to throw all of that up, lil' man," he says.

I shrug and continue to slurp the orange liquid gold until you hear me slurping the last bits at the end of the cup.

"Thanks for the meal," I say once I'm finished. I crumple up everything along with the brown bag. I slouch in the chair with the -itis when suddenly, I realize something.

"Hey. Where's my mom?" I ask, sitting up in a panic.

"She's doing great. We just found out that she's doing alright before I gave you the food. I've been sitting out here looking after you because you fell asleep," he says with a small smile, and then he sits next to me.

"Wait. What's your name?" I ask. I squint my eyes because I still don't trust him fully. He's too nice to be a stranger. He gave me a hoodie. Brought my mom in. Brought me food and drink... I know

this just from living the streets for a while. Strangers don't care about you unless you're giving something to them.

"My name is Gregory but call me Greg. What's your name, kid?"

"None of your business," I say and then stand up. The hoodie drops to the floor like a gown. "I don't know you."

"Okay. Street smart. I get it."

"Who's with my mom? She by herself?" I ask.

"No. When I went in to check on her, there was another guy in the room."

"What? Who?" I interrogate with a frown. If it isn't him or the Mexican dude who had left us a while ago, then who is it?

"I don't know. He's a big guy, though. Tall, kinda blonde hair. Blue eyes. Well put together... you know anything about him?"

"No. And she knows him?" I ask.

"Seems like she does by the way they're interacting."

"Oh." I pause for a moment, and then look at him through even narrower eyes. "You from here?"

"Not exactly. Close, though. I'm from Indiana."

"Oh okay. Well thanks for everything. You didn't have to help."

"No problem, kid. Are you ready to see your mom?" he asks.

"Yeah."

And with that, I follow Greg to Mommy's room. It seems like we walk all the way across the hospital campus until we reach her room. 4107. As soon as we get here, my stomach bubbles, but I ignore it. I don't want Greg to be right.

When we open the door, Mommy's lying in the bed. She's halfway sitting up, and she looks okay. In fact, she's smiling and laughing with a guy who's talking to her. Like they've known each other for a while. He was a big, tall blue-eyed, blondish brown-haired White guy just like Greg described him. His skin was a little darker, which made me think he was mixed or something. Closer to White though. But his eyes were as blue as what I think the ocean looks like. But there's also an iciness to them like the snow outside. It's weird...

"Hey, Mom," I call out to her with suspicion.

Both Mom and the guy turn their heads to meet my voice. The guy looks a little curious, but I don't care about dude. I want my mom. Her eyes become doughy and her nose flares as if trying to keep her tears away. Without another second staying still, I rush to hug her. She hugs me back. Tight.

"Oh baby… I'm so thankful you helped your Mommy." She kisses my forehead.

"Oh… you have a son. Didn't know," White guy mumbles, thinking I don't hear him, but I do.

Mommy doesn't need to thank me. I'm just so happy she's still here. Alive. I do not let her live in her happiness too much longer, though. Because now, what's gonna happen when she gets released from the hospital?

"So now what? Are we going to find some place warm to stay?" I ask. *"And what about the hospital bill?"*

"Don't worry about that. Let the grown people think about the bills. You stay in a child's place," she says.

"I'm not going back out in that snowstorm," I say with my arms crossed. *"We almost died."*

"Little guy," says the big, tall, blue-eyed White guy. He walks over and stands over me. He's so big, I have to take a step back and lean my head all the way back to see him. *"All your fears won't be fears anymore. I'm taking care of your mother's hospital bills. And what do ya say? That you won't have to experience Chicago's horrible winter or blizzard ever again? I'll take the both of you to paradise."*

"Who are you?" I ask with a serious mean mug.

"Jarell, be polite. This is my friend. Nathan."

"Friend?" I raised an eyebrow.

"Yes. Friend."

Hmm…

"So whatdya say, kid? That I take you to paradise and away from this snowy trash?"

"Speak English," I demand.

"California is much warmer. Palm trees, dry heat, Hollywood," he bribed with a soft look at my mother. Mommy blushes and giggles like one of my friends at school.

Oh boy. Was Mommy crushing on someone? This dude? I mean… he is about to pay for her hospital bill, so I get it. But I'm not going. I'm not going with no stranger that I've known for less than two minutes. Especially no White dude after what happened to us at the Well's.

"We ain't going nowhere with you. You're White, and I don't trust you," I say with my lip turned and an eyebrow raised.

"Jarell! Excuse me? Don't be rude or a racist. I ain't ever taught you to talk like that! The hell is wrong with you?"

"Don't be saying my name out loud either!" I yell at Mommy.

*"Well, it's too late, **Jarell**," she emphasizes. "I think these two men deserve to know who we are, considering we owe them our lives."*

"Yeah, well they were doing the right thing. Doesn't mean we need to tell our business."

"That's a smart kid there. And too grown," Nathan whispers to Mommy, pointing a finger at me. Then, he looks my way. "By the way? I'm a quarter Black. Just White passing."

I cut my eyes at him. Something about him rubs me the wrong way. Greg and Mexican dude seem much more genuine and real.

"Yeah, that's my baby. He thinks he's grown, but I show him every single day that he's not. And what the hell are you wearing, Jarell? It's like four times your size," Mommy asks, looking me up and down.

"He gave it to me." I point to Gregory.

"Oh. Got it. Are you going to give it back to him?"

"No. He can keep it," Greg responds waving his hand.

"Oh. Well thanks! We needed that. Someone stole all our clothes some time ago. We literally have nothing anymore."

"Stop telling our business," I warn her, but both Nathan and Mommy talk over me.

"So, the doctors said that they're going to release you tomorrow morning. Why don't I take the both of you to the mall? Restock your wardrobe," Nathan offers. "Wait for the snowstorm and plows to pass. Then we can go. How's that?"

"We don't need your help," I interrupt with a mumble, but they ignore me again.

"That sounds amazing. I can't thank you enough. We had all our stuff stolen a while ago. Hell, today's the first meal I've had in days."

"Stop telling our business!" I scream, and Mommy whips her head towards me so fast with a look that could slice me in half. I don't back down because it's not like she can get up from the hospital bed. She's foolish right now, looking at this stupid guy with heart eyes. It's like she can't see anything else past all the good stuff he's offering to us.

"Jarell, you seem to forget who the goddamn parent is. It's me! You're eleven years old without a single chin or chest hair in sight. Sit your Black ass down."

"Listen, I think we should give Rachel and her son some time alone," Greg says to Nathan, but he's drowned out by Nathan continuing to speak. I see what Greg is trying to do, and I'm thankful. But it doesn't seem to work.

"I'm glad you're finally letting me in your life fully to help you, Rachel. I hate the stories you tell me about everything you've been going through. So, after the mall, I'll rent you out a hotel room for you to stay for a little while. So that you don't have to worry about your new belongings getting stolen. How about it?" Nathan asks my mom.

"That all sounds great Nathan. I'm all for it, but I'd like to talk to my son alone, please. Don't leave. Just stay here. I just want to talk to him first," Mommy says, and he smiles.

"Sure thing."

"No, you can leave the whole hospital. We won't need you any-more," I reply.

He laughs and then saunters over to me. He reaches his hand out and wiggles my head. I slap the shit out of his arm.

"Don't touch me."

He laughs.

"Rachel, your son is something... unique. You'll never have to worry about being unprotected, that's for sure. But hey, kid. I'm just trying to be nice. Trying to put you in a better situation, alright? I'm not your enemy," he states close to my face with a look in his eyes that I can't read. His eyes seem like they're without feelings. I'm good at reading people and seeing if they are genuine or not, but he's kinda hard to make out.

"Yeah whatever," I mumble.

"I'm so sorry about my son. Please. Just give us a second. Again, thanks so much for your help. And Gregory? I owe you my life."

"I'd do it again, ma'am. Take care. I'm 'bout to head out," Greg-ory says with his thumb towards the door. Then, he kneels to me and whispers, "Be smooth, Jarell. I wish the best for you and your mom. Keep ya' head up. You're right to question him."

"Thanks," I respond. He gives me a small smile, daps me, and walks towards the door. I want him to stay so bad. I want him to get Nathan out of the picture, and I want him to take us with him. The way my shoulders sink though shows what the reality of this is.

Without another word, Nathan and Greg walk out of the room. As soon as they do, Mommy gives me a glare. Then she blows up as soon as the door latches shut.

"The fuck is wrong with you, Jarell?" she asks with clenched teeth and balled fists. "You better be lucky I'm too weak to get up right now because I'd put my fist so far down your throat that—"

*"What's wrong with **you**? Who is he? I never even met him, and you're already talking about letting him take us to a different place," I interrupt.*

"I've known Nathan for a while now, Jarell. He's a nice guy, and he's been wanting to help for some time. I'm to the point where I can't be prideful anymore. We are in a tough spot and I ain't in no position to be turning down no favors. I think we should give him a chance."

"What? Where'd you even meet him?" I ask. "To me, he's a stranger!"

"It doesn't matter, Jarell because it's none of your young ass business."

"It does matter! Did you find him while being some stripper? Or a prostitute? I'm not going! I would rather find someplace else to stay."

The rage in her eyes rises.

"Boy, you better shut up talking about shit you know nothing about. You ain't grown and you ain't got no better options. You want us to keep sleeping around on these streets!?" she screams, and I grit my teeth, trying to hold my tears back.

"We wouldn't be sleeping on the streets if you weren't being a prostitute at the motel."

Mommy's body turns to ice after those words seep out and her glare is the icicle. Worse than anything going on outside right now.

"What do you know about that? Huh? From that fucking idiot who gave you those edibles that knocked your ass out and could've killed you? You're gonna listen to someone like that? You don't even know what a prostitute is." She squints.

I cross my arms. "Yes, I do. He told me. It's when someone sleeps with other men for money. I bet it's true what he said, too."

I hate knowing what Mommy does to make sure we survive. It's embarrassing. But that doesn't mean we should just accept any old person to help us and take care of us.

She placed a hand over her forehead. "Jarell, you don't know shit, alright?"

"And we don't know that guy out there," I say. "I'm not going anywhere with him."

"I know him. That's all that matters. And for him to save our lives like this, offer a new wardrobe, and a hotel for a few days, there's not much else we need to know right now. We just need to get out of this situation."

"I wanna be comfortable with him, too," I respond.

She smacked her lips. "Jarell. I'm the parent. I'm calling the shots. And if I feel like our situation will be much better with Nathan, then that's what'll be. You don't know the conversation we had prior to you coming to my room. Or any conversation we've had for that matter because he's been around much longer than you even know. What you need to do is stay in a child's place. You need to trust that I'd make the best decisions for us. Alright?"

I close my eyes and sigh in defeat.

"Fine. But can we at least see how he treats the both of us before you decide where we go?"

"That's a request I can live with."

"Okay."

I roll my eyes, knowing that she won't even care or taking my feelings into account no matter what Nathan does. All I can do is pray to God that Nathan truly is heaven sent and what we need for our lives.

~ ~ ~

"Trisha, this was the beginning of everything. All the turmoil. My mom put us in a situation that screwed us over for not only the next couple of years, but she fucked up my entire life. Had she just listened to me, we wouldn't have been in that shit with that bastard," I said with my lip turned up. "I knew he wasn't shit, but she sat in that bed and persisted that we leave with him."

"Jarell..." Trisha trailed off. I had never heard her sound so shaken. "How old is your mom?"

"Thirty-five."

"Okay, so sixteen years older than you, and eight years ago, she was only twenty-seven. Has your mom ever considered therapy for herself?"

I huffed with a deep, sardonic laugh. "Ma? Therapy? Hell naw. She's quick to tell me that I need to go, but she won't hold her own self accountable. She never will. Accountability is something she avoids any chance she gets. She keeps telling me that my issues are with Nathan and not her. Like she ain't play a role. Why do you ask?"

"No reason I'll divulge right now. We'll travel that road later. Here's my question to you. What other options or choices do you believe were available for your mother during that time? Considering she was a former foster child with no family?"

"Um, not leaving with that snow bunny was the only logical option. Especially since he was a complete stranger to me." I crossed my arms.

"To live or go where? You were living on the streets in the dead middle of winter."

"I don't know. Another motel where she wasn't thottin' around," I snarled.

"Do you believe she would've found another one if she could? If you were living in a motel, she likely got a voucher from some emergency homeless assistance program to stay there until a government housing unit opened. These vouchers are rare and in high demand. Especially in a big, urban city like Chicago. It's unlikely that you can get another voucher quick enough to live in a different motel if you don't like the one you're in," Trisha explained. "So now, the option for another motel is out. What other options do you believe she had?"

"More shelters maybe. I don't know! She's the adult. She gotta figure that out, and she needs to make sure the choice is safe for me. She shouldn't have been fucking niggas around the way to ruin the spot we had!"

"Okay. I'm going to provide something else to think about. Based on what you told me about your mother and how you feel about her, you expressed that you don't like it when she throws the 'I'm the adult and you're not' card in your face. Am I right?" Trisha countered, and I nodded. "Okay, so I need you to clarify something for me. Were you looking for her to take your input about alternative options to make your living situation safer? If so, you've already exposed eight years later that you still don't have any viable options she could've taken, which means you definitely didn't have any solutions as an eleven-year-old, either. Or, do you let her decide what's best as the adult in a tough situation?"

I smacked my lips. What the fuck. "Trisha, are you my therapist or hers? She fucked up. I didn't."

"I know. You have every right to be angry with her. I'm just trying to put things in perspective to help you develop patience and compassion when coping with other people's choices. This is all a part of healing. You don't have to answer my questions right now, but we will continue exploring these things during our time together. Here's my final question for the day before we wrap things up. What is it that you want from your mother? What could she do to gain trust with you again?"

"I want her to listen to me," I said. "It's that simple."

"Is it? We just established that adult choices sometimes happen without children input because children don't know enough to help make an informed decision. I want you to be honest. What is it that you *truly* want from her?"

"I don't know. I was serious the first time. I want her to listen and acknowledge that her choices destroyed my life," I said.

"And what do you want her to do with that information? What do you want her to do when she does acknowledge it?" Trisha asked.

"I don't know..."

"Okay. If you don't mind, I'm going to add to your homework today. On Thursday, I'd like you to come with a poem or a journal entry about the following: List everything you believe is your mother's fault that you felt has destroyed you. Then, I'd like you to list whether you believe the choice she made was in her control. Once you get your vices out, I'd also like you think about what areas you can show compassion for your mother. You don't have to write that down because we haven't quite defined compassion fully yet, but still. Please think about it."

"You taking sides again …" I trailed off. "You're putting me in the wrong and making me feel like I shouldn't be mad at her."

"I recognize it feels that way but trust me. This is about you healing the resentment you feel inside with her. Forgiveness is about you. Coming to terms with the past is about you. We will talk more about forgiveness down the line, but right now, I don't think we're ready for that quite yet."

"A'ight, Trisha," I said and got down to the floor to start mindfulness because I didn't wanna talk about this shit no more. "Fine."

Chapter Twenty-One

<u>***Point of View***</u>: Jade Williams

"You have reached the voicemail box of..."

"Uuuughhhh!!!" I roared and threw my phone on the couch.

Jarell wouldn't answer any of my calls, and it's been a whole week! Sunday to Sunday. Sometimes, he straight up ignored my call by sending me to voicemail on the first ring. Like he did this time. Every fiber in me wanted to roll up to his mom's place unannounced to apologize about everything that happened on his birthday, but I didn't wanna face his mom at all either, knowing that Jarell didn't even get any of his cake she made for him. 'Cause I was already knowing that she would wanna know how his birthday went.

God!!!

I wanted to strangle Laurie's stupid ass, but she lucky it was the Lord's Day today. Easter. I had gotten a call from Corey on Friday telling me he had spoken with Momma and that I had the green light to go see her and make amends. I didn't mind it all because I feared spending another holiday alone. I was already ditched on Christmas, so maybe Easter would turn out better for me. Alise was heading to spend the day with her own family and her boyfriend, leaving me out the picture. Plus? A bitch just wanted some good food! Yeah, I was working on that bottom row for a six-pack and all, but I couldn't tell anyone the last time I had a fat soul food meal. Last Thanksgiving wasn't it either since I was preparing to be in Chris Brown's Christmas concert. We had to make something work, period. Especially since Momma was a good cook.

I got dressed in a cute pastel colored dress with some chunky platform heels and left out from Alise's place, taking the drive deep to Baldwin Hills, closer to Ladera Heights where Momma stayed. When I pulled up and walked to the house, her car was in the driveway, but when I rang the doorbell, no one answered.

"Momma!" I yelled and this time, knocked on the door a little louder.

No answer.

I huffed. I know she wasn't ignoring me. Right? Good thing I knew where she kept a spare key.

Underneath the tiny home mat in the bushes on the right side, I dusted the spare key off and opened the door, letting myself inside.

"Mom!" I called out, but my voice echoed off the walls.

I checked the kitchen and dining area, and she was nowhere to be found. Checked the bedrooms, the back patio and pool area, bathrooms, living area, garage... nowhere. Empty.

And then it clicked.

She must've been celebrating Easter next door with Laurie's family.

My head fell back.

Going over there was the last thing I wanted to do, but if I could even just put a bug in Momma's ear that I wanted to talk to her soon, that would be good enough. I didn't need to stay, and I didn't wanna call or text Ma to tell her I wanted to talk because then that wouldn't seem as genuine. It was hard to tell someone no when you were in their face.

I walked through the thin line of grass that divided the two homes and sucked it up, not even worrying about seeing Laurie and dealing with her bullshit. Laurie knew I would mop the floor with her ass if given the chance, so she wasn't gonna be an intimidation factor.

I knocked on their white wooden door about four or five times and stood back to await a response. The door whipped open, and Laurie's face was all bright and happy, but it dissolved when her eyes met mine. I huffed and puffed. Why the hell did she have to be the one to open the door? She never opened the door any other time.

"Other than coming to ruin my holiday, how can I help you?" She raised an eyebrow and shifted her weight to one leg.

"Girl ain't nobody thinking about you. To answer your question? Yeah. You can help. By getting out of the way so I can see my mom," I shot back.

She scoffed. "Typical rude ass Jade. Remember, you're in my territory. Not yours," she mumbled and moved out of the way.

"Yeah, a territory you don't own or pay for."

Bumping Laurie on my way in, she whispered something along the lines of, "Your mom doesn't want to see you anyway," but I ignored it before she caught a fist to the mouth. Again. This was the Lord's Day.

As I moved deeper inside, festive voices filled the house from various directions. Some people occupied the dining area, some hung out in the kitchen, and some were elsewhere in the house I couldn't identify. Thank goodness I didn't have to go too far because Momma was coming out of the kitchen and approached the living room.

The second she noticed me, she hesitated before her eyes went straight to my stomach before addressing my face. I shook my head.

"Oh, this is a shocker." She blinked and then pressed her lips together. "Thought you said I was cut off."

"Yeah. I know." I rubbed my arm as my eyes wandered away from her hard stare.

"So, what do you want? I know it's not to celebrate Easter with me," she said.

"We weren't celebrating holidays before Easter anyways when you left me on Christmas, but that's in the past now. Momma, Corey told me he called and talked to you," I replied.

"Yup, he did. And? Is that who told you to come over here?" Her eyes bugged.

"No. I wanted to do it myself. Did he play a part? Yes. I had a long talk with him, and he made me realize some things. Can we sit down soon and hash things out?"

"Hash things out, huh?" she said.

"I know the last time we talked, it wasn't... it wasn't cool. Both of us were outta pocket." The entire time I spoke, I still wouldn't give her eye contact. The last thing I needed was to be discouraged, chicken out, face her wrath, or watch the 'I told you so' rise in her expression.

"The only person 'outta pocket' was you. Speak for yourself. And when would you like this 'talk' to happen?" she asked, using her fingers to simulate air quotes.

"Whenever is right for you," I responded. "I know today is not the best time, obviously, but can we do it sometime this coming week?"

"Sure. But you need to tell me that you've left Jarell alone and get rid of that demon child in you." She shrugged with pursed lips.

"Momma, the ultimatums aren't necessary, okay? I'm grown and can make my own choices. This ain't got nothing to do with Jarell. You're giving him way too much ammo."

"I'm dead serious. Make the decision," she said.

"Listen, Jarell and I aren't together anymore, and I was never pregnant to begin with. I just said that to get under your skin, so you can stop with all that. I broke up with him weeks ago."

"How do I know you're not lying to me?" she questioned. This time, her look softened a bit as the strained lines around her eyes disappeared.

"Momma, the worst thing in the world is to admit to you that I broke up with Jarell, alright? Trust me on that."

"Whatever. As long as the punk is out the picture," she said. "How about we chat next weekend? I'm heading out of town to New Orleans this week for their jazz festival and to do some fashion design work."

"That's fine. Next Friday or Saturday works for me."

"Okay." Then, she strolled towards me with a measured glare and stopped until we were nearly nose to nose. Her mouth tightened again. "And let me tell you something. After we talked last time? Don't you ever in your life think you will ever come up in my house and disrespect me the way you did. You need to do the work to build trust with me again because as a child… my child, you were out of line. Next time, you'll get slapped. Try me," she said pointing a finger at me, and then walked away before I could even have a chance to take a breath to respond.

My fists balled, and my teeth clenched. I could've killed her. She was doing the most. She could never just leave a situation without conflict, even when the other party tried to avoid it. Before I turned to head out, Laurie stood against the wall with a grin. Oooh, a punch to her face tugged at my core. That bitch had some nerve.

Instead of giving her any satisfaction that she ruffled my feathers, I left the house and stood on the porch to calm myself down. Wow. For the life of me, I will never understand why someone as nice as Corey would ever wanna spend more than an hour around that woman.

This wasn't a good idea. I loved Corey and all, but he just didn't understand how difficult it was gonna be dealing with Momma as her daughter. Making amends would give her another bridge to try and control my life, and, what I needed were boundaries. Not to be buddy-buddy with her.

So, I made the choice.

If I was gonna tell it to her face that I wanted to talk, I was gonna tell it to her face that coming by to suggest we squash the drama was the biggest mistake I made this week and just cut ties with her.

Turning I knocked on their door again to do just that and end everything once and for all. Corey was gonna be upset, but oh well. He had a whole different lens than I did.

This time when the door whipped open, I stared into the chest of someone I had never seen answer their door before. Leaning my head back as my eyes traveled up to his face because he was so tall, my heart shot to my throat and stayed there.

Wait a minute.

Those blue eyes… where did I see them before?

Holy hell, wait… this couldn't be…

One of the guys…

Wait… were these the same eyes watching everyone else do the dirty work in that abandoned warehouse in Fresno?

My chest began to constrict, and I felt a bout of panting begin, but I caught myself and held it instead. My gaze roamed quickly over the rest of his features to put the whole puzzle together. If scruffy was a person, it was him. His half-greyed beard went every direction but neat while his natural hair color donned a light golden brown. He had a messy comb over with receding hairlines, a long, pointy nose that was red at the tip, and thin lips.

He looked like the damn devil.

My first instinct was to clutch my phone to dial emergency, but once I reached for it, his eyes traveled to my hands and then back at my face. I dropped them faster than lightning strikes.

"You're looking for someone?" he asked, yet his hard tone wasn't at all subtle as he gave me a onceover from head to toe.

"Um… yeah. I uh…" I swallowed, and when he was done with his complete scan, he dished me a long, inscrutable look that made me stumble over my words even more. "I-I-I'm the neighbor. Next door." I pointed. "I-I was just here to see my mom."

He didn't say anything after. He moved out the way and opened the door wider to let me inside. I let out the air I was holding and accepted my cold welcome for the second time. As I followed alongside, I managed to take out my phone without fumbling it on the ground and took a quick picture of him. I attempted to breathe as normal as possible as he led me into the kitchen/dining area where honey ham roasted, garlic potatoes steamed, and sweet corn slow cooked in a crockpot. Many members of the Schmidt or Kaminsky family sat at the long dining table – Laurie, Laurie's dad, my mom, and many more folks I've never met as they laughed at someone's joke I didn't hear. When they were finished, all eyes landed on me.

"Oh, Jade! What an Easter surprise!" Laurie's mom Stephanie greeted, stood, and dashed to hug me. "You cut your hair. Beautiful! How have you been? We haven't heard from you since Laurieanne told us you went to the hospital and told us about the entire situation with your boyfriend at school! We hope you're done with that guy. He harmed a lot of people. We were so worried about you!"

Stephanie was super hyperactive who ran her mouth a million miles an hour, spilling everyone's business while at it. And likely high off that shit – either coke or meth. No other way around it because no normal person was as fidgety, alert, and high strung as she was. Her presence alone either made my heart race or tired me out every time I saw her. Don't know how her and Momma were even friends. You know... unless Momma was getting high too.

"I've been okay. Thanks for your concern." I tried responding without seeming bothered as I hesitated to hug her back.

"We're so happy to have you here. We have enough food for everyone and more! Come and take a seat."

"N-No, Ms. Stephanie. It's okay. I'm not that hungry." I bit my lip. "I was just coming to tell my mom something."

"Okay, well you let me know once you're ready for a plate. We have a lot of people here to introduce you to! Have I introduced you to my brother Nathan before? He got the door for you, right?"

She beamed. "He's in town from Chicago again for a couple months. We're so happy to have him back. He's always on the move with work and never tells anyone when he comes and goes. It's a surprise he's with us today, and I suppose you're the other surprise!"

Beads of sweat shot across my forehead. Who I now knew as Nathan stared at me with a smile, yet his eyes told a different story. A story I couldn't read. Again, he had barely come in contact with Jarell or me that night of the kidnapping, yet he had the most domineering, threatening presence. And as he sat at the dining room table today with a plaid collared shirt and jeans rather than all black gear, he was still just as intimidating.

I swallowed. I wasn't trippin', was I? Nah. Those eyes were like no other, and they were his. Are his. I know what the fuck I saw! *Trust your gut, Jade. Trust it!*

"Jade? Have I introduced you to Nathan?" Ms. Stephanie repeated.

"N-No, you never introduced me," I labored.

"Well, big brother Nathan," she started, slapping his big chest playfully with a devilish grin, "this is Jade, Janet's daughter. You remember us telling you about her, right? That awesome celebrity dancer who is Laurie's best buddy?"

"I think I'm familiar," Nathan nodded with a smirk. Then, he held his hand out, waiting for mine to be encased in his. "It's a pleasure to meet you, Jade."

What do I do? Do I run outta here and call the police? Do I expose him in front of everyone? Wait, I couldn't do that. I didn't have proof that this was truly him that kidnapped us! I couldn't just put someone in jail or accuse him of something without having concrete proof he had done it.

But wait, I gave the police descriptions of all people involved to the best of my ability. Those descriptions were public knowledge with a reward attached, but how many tall, blue-eyed White males were there in this damn city? So many of them could've fit the description.

Oh my God!

Before his empty hand was out too long before it would've become suspicious to the rest of the guests without me returning the gesture, holding my breath, I stuck a weak hand out to shake it. He squeezed me tight enough for it to hurt, but not enough for me to yelp.

"And that's my sister-in-law Sarah, her son and daughter Cody and Rebecca, and that's my aunt Bethany, and Grandma Meredith..." Ms. Stephanie went on and on, and I was just standing trying to stop my head from spinning.

"Jade are you okay?" Ms. Stephanie asked. "You look stressed."

Blinking and shaking my head out of stupor, I plastered a fake smile.

"Y-yes. Yeah. I'm good." I nodded, releasing the air stuck in my chest.

"Are you sure?"

"Yeah. Nice to meet everyone! I'm... I'm gonna go to the bathroom real quick. Be out in a second," I said, waving to everyone before I walked away.

Everyone returned the greeting except for Laurie, who sat rolling her eyes and snarling at me the whole time unbeknownst to everyone in the room. Forget her! I had bigger fish to fry.

Once I got in the bathroom, I began pacing back and forth with my hands on top of my head.

How...

HOW!?

How the hell did he find us at the park that late at night? White men don't live in that area for him to know our whereabouts. We got to the park fresh out the hospital! Jarell nor I didn't tell anyone about our favorite spot at the park.

What the ...

It had to be some sort of combination of my mom and Laurie because what the hell would someone like Nathan want Jarell for?! He didn't have any ties to him, and I doubt he would stage an entire abduction over some petty high school shit he was far removed from. Why would Jarell even know someone like that to the point where he'd get kidnapped by him?

Okay. Here was something more rational and made a bit more sense. Maybe Nathan wasn't in charge of the whole abduction and was just hired as a hitman. What if Sir Shotgun was the one who hired Nathan because Sir Shotgun was related to Marcus or Martell? Maybe Nathan was friends with Sir Shotgun, and once Nathan found out about what Jarell did to either Marcus or Martell (because Laurie told him), Nathan told Sir Shotgun, and then they organized the whole thing.

I sat on the toilet, trying to get myself not to throw up from confusing myself.

I had to get the hell outta dodge. I would talk with Momma later. I had to tell Jarell ASAP. If he would answer his goddamn phone!

Chapter Twenty-Two

Point of View: Jarell Hendricks

Double tapping the sleep button on the side of my phone after Siri announced that Jade was calling me yet again, I put the phone in my sweatpants pocket, hoping this was her last call of the morning.

"Kylah, you ready to go?" I called out, standing up and moving out of my room after I had finished tying my shoe.

"Almost!"

"Hurry up! You're gonna be late for school, and then you're gonna make me late for the bus to therapy." I made it out to the living room and leaned against the wall, crossing my arms to wait. Walking her to school was something I looked forward to, but the shit was becoming a lot because Kylah did everything imaginable to exhaust a nigga. From talking nonstop to bouncing off furniture and the walls, to wanting to play something with me… lowkey? Ma was gonna have to get lil' sis evaluated.

"Okay, Relly!"

"Did you eat your breakfast?" I asked.

"No!" she shouted back.

I huffed and went to the pantry of limited snacks and pulled out a Strawberry PopTart for her after feeling around for its smooth wrapper and bumpy top, indicating the sprinkles. I hated when Ma left for work and didn't have anything already made for her for whatever reason. At least she never failed to give her a bath the night before with Kylah's school clothes out and ready so that I wouldn't have to deal with that nightmare. Either way, Ma was excited to be at work earlier so that she could work more hours instead of going in an hour later after making sure Kylah got on the bus safely… even though she was supposed to be taking her on the days I went to therapy. Whatever. Again. She always thought about herself.

Shortly after I grabbed her PopTart, Kylah galloped out of her room, her hyper self panting with her backpack rattling with markers and crayons.

"Rough time getting dressed this morning again?" I asked.

"A little," she wheezed.

"Here," I said, giving her my hand that held a napkin I picked up for her PopTart. "Put my hand on your face. You need to calm down before we go."

She did as she was told as I wiped the sweat I knew was there off her forehead and threw it in the trash.

"Take your breakfast and put it in your bag. Hurry up so you can help me down the stairs so we can go." I pushed the pastries her way and she quickly snatched them, throwing them in her bag.

"I'm ready, Relly! Can we play I Spy when we walk?"

"Nah. We're gonna work on walking without games today. Let's go."

Kylah took my hand, helped me down the porch steps, and off we went, taking the fifteen-minute walk to Western Ave Elementary. This time, Kylah rambled on and on about different things, but the topic for today was favorite foods. She shared her love of apples and oranges, and how much she hated the fruit cups they gave at lunch time. All I could do was laugh, sharing the same sentiments. When there was a lull in the conversation, about halfway to school, I changed the direction of the discussion.

"Kay Kay," I called out, tickling her fat little neck with a finger and pinched her chunky cheeks.

She squealed and giggled. "Yeah, Relly?"

"School been going okay? How are your friends? They've been treating you nice?" I questioned, double pressing the sleep button on my phone again as it buzzed against my leg.

"Yup! Relly, I even made friends with a couple big kids! Some fifth graders. They come to our class to read to us, and they come to help us learn in class. Then we get our own big kid to read more stories. I get the same girl! Her name is Deja."

"Oh, that's cool they give you a kid mentor at school. You like Deja?" I asked.

"Yes! She reads all the cool books to me," she bragged.

"I bet. What about your other kindergarten friends?"

"I like them too, like LaTasha, Armani, and Tyshawn."

"I'm glad school is going good for you and that you have good friends, Kylah. I got a question though. Has anyone asked you about your dad since I been walking you to school?" I asked, holding her hand as she led me down the sidewalk.

"No," she answered, her head dipped low since her voice didn't inflect the way it usually did when she looked up towards me to speak.

"What's wrong?"

"Nothing."

Damn, here we go with her keeping shit away from me.

"Kylah, please tell me what's on your mind. Why the sad voice?"

"I wanna know my Daddy, Relly," she pouted. "Where is he?"

A long pause grew between us before I sighed and looked towards the sky. The last thing Kylah needed was to be left hanging about something like this. Whatever her kindergarten friends were saying about her not having a dad, whoever they were because it wasn't like we had a bunch of two-parent homes around here, had her moping like I wouldn't have thought.

"Kylah, let me tell you something. Big brother Relly is gonna teach you your first big girl life lesson. You think you can handle it?"

"Yeah! Because I'm a big girl now!" She jumped up.

"Okay." I chuckled. "Here goes."

Ruffling her soft, curly hair, I stopped walking and kneeled to her level, holding her small shoulders. I prayed I looked into her eyes right now.

"Sometimes, there are reasons why we don't know someone. There are also reasons why we don't get to meet a certain person, okay? Sometimes it's for safety. Sometimes it's to protect others. With your dad, Kylah, it's to keep you safe. Understand me?"

"Yes, Relly."

"I know you'll always want to know who he is and where he is, and I know you gon' keep asking when you get older. Maybe Ma will someday find a way to tell you more about him. But I need you to understand that many, many people don't have daddies. Including some of your friends. Those people are still normal. I don't have a daddy either and look. You still love me, right?"

"Mmm hmm," she responded.

"Yeah. I know. You show me how much you love me every day." I nod. "And I love you too, Kay Kay. You're smart. Bright. Energetic. Funny. Probably very pretty too. And you know just how to bother your big brother the way no one else can," I said and tickled her belly the way I always did to make her laugh, and she did with a squeal. "You are all those special things whether you have a daddy or not. Remember that. Because your big brother Relly never got to see the special things in himself."

"Why not?" she asked. "Is it because you don't have a daddy either?"

I smiled. "Nah. That's a big girl lesson for another day. We can only do one big girl lesson at a time."

"Awww man," she whined playfully.

"One more thing. I want you to know your big brother Relly will always protect you no matter what. I can do some things daddies can do, too. I know it's not the same, but it's the next best thing. So, from now on, I'm going to tell you every day just how smart, funny, energetic, nice, and pretty you are because it's important you know this early. No matter what other people will try to say about you," I said, gripping her shoulders a little tighter, wishing I could manually instill this lesson in her brain and know that she gets it. To know that she will never question any of it.

"Really, Relly?" she responded. "I'm special?"

"No doubt," I said. "Now let's get you to school."

~ ~ ~

"How did your homework go, Jarell?" Trisha asked as I made my ass familiar with the couch at the therapy office again.

"S'cool." I took off my backpack, pulled my journaling papers out, and got settled. "The whole activity doesn't change the way I feel about Ma, though to be honest," I admitted.

"Okay, and what about your reflection regarding the situation at your ex-girlfriend's apartment?"

"That was cool, too."

"Alright, then. You ready to share with me both items? Start with the situation at your ex-girlfriend's place."

"A'ight. I mean… with that whole thing, I guess I should've told Jade the truth. Tell her not to leave me alone with Laurie because I don't trust her. Or I coulda told Jade to take Laurie with her to wherever she was going. That way, it wouldn't have been an opportunity for things to get as far as it did. I coulda been more proactive for sure because I had a feeling in my gut that things were about to go left."

"Very good." She jotted in her notepad. "Is there anything else you would like to share about that situation?"

"Mmm… nah. That was it."

"Okay. That was excellent reflection on your part. I love your comment about proactiveness and trusting your instincts. When you're proactive, you have more power over yourself and your decision making. We have instincts and gut feelings for a reason, and we should listen to them. Moving forward, I'd like you to practice recognizing and naming the feeling in your belly that you get when something doesn't seem right. It's a hard skill to master because sometimes, we don't listen to it, and then we kinda let things slide, which leads to conflict. Even I'm working on that. I don't want you to go beyond that initial practice with that, though. Just focus on recognizing and naming it for now," Trisha explained.

"A'ight. That don't sound too hard." I nodded. "And it makes a lot of sense."

"Awesome. I don't have any other feedback, other than I'm proud of the work you've done, and that I'd like you to do that same type of reflection each time a negative situation happens you're involved with. We will talk about your mom after what we have planned today. Is that fine?"

I nodded.

"Alright. Are you ready to move on, or would you like to continue discussing your reflection a little more?"

"Nah, we can move on. Thanks for helping me with that, Trisha."

"You're welcome. Okay. For today's theme, that situation is a perfect lead into discussing control and power."

"Okay..." I spoke.

"With that Laurie situation, do you understand that whole thing had everything to do with personal control? How you controlled your actions, how you controlled your emotions, how you controlled your words?"

"Yeah, I realize that now, especially when I was journaling."

"Great! So now, let's talk about what you do when you have a lack of control. In your eyes, what happens for you when you feel like you don't have control or when you feel powerless? Can you describe your actions when you feel like you've run out of options or when you have limited ability to change or control the outcome of a situation?"

"Mmm." I pondered. "I mean... I try to deal with the situation the best way I can. Sometimes I try to talk to the people who are involved, but it's rare I say anything because people don't listen to me anyway. It's just like Ma. Every time I express anything that's in disagreement with something she's in control of, it's a conflict or there's so much pushback that the shit ain't even worth it."

"But you do know that advocating for yourself leaves a record, right? You can always say that you've tried to express your concern, but if you don't, they'll never know how you feel."

"Yeah, but what does that actually do except make the next person feel guilty after the fact? It doesn't the change the action that could've been avoided in the first place," I countered.

"Interesting," Trisha said, writing notes down. "I have a request. Do you mind telling me more about what happened with your mother's ex-boyfriend after her time at the hospital? This is a situation where you felt powerless and without control, right? A situation you felt your mother could've avoided or made a better decision after you expressed your concern about him that she did not listen to. I am assuming you didn't have much control after his surprise visit, right?"

"Yup. You right."

"Okay. Tell me what happened when you left from the hospital. And then, we can talk more about control."

Chicago, Illinois – March 2010

After the winter storm, Nathan kept his promise.

He took us to this fancy hotel in downtown Chicago with all the skyscrapers, and he paid for a room for both Mommy and me. I ain't never been around such nice stuff! It's a two-bedroom suite with so many cool things. The flat screen TV is the best! It has all the cartoons and movies I had ever wanted to watch for a lifetime. The swimming pool downstairs has a jacuzzi, a basketball hoop, and a slide. Even our hotel room has a hot tub jacuzzi and huge glass showers! The mini kitchen comes with cool silverware, sparkling glass plates, and glass cups.

We even have room service where you can just get on the phone, order what you want, and they deliver it to us! That's my favorite part!

Did I mention we also don't have to clean a single thing? We have ladies come up to our room every morning, asking us if we need cleaning. For some stupid reason, Mommy always makes me continue doing chores, like washing some of the dishes we mess up when we order room service so that the ladies don't have to clean it all up. She says that even though Nathan had paid for us to stay there for a little while, I can't get too spoiled or what she calls "beside myself."

Oh yeah! Don't even get me started on the beds.

They're big and plush. I can't help myself, but every morning, I jump on it like it's a trampoline. Sometimes, I try to do backflips on and off the bed as a trick. Mommy just laughs at me while telling me to be careful, and Nathan watches as he sits next to Mommy super close to her, either shaking his head or just staring at me. I don't know what either of those two looks mean, but it doesn't give me a good feeling. It's almost like he can't wait for me to disappear to school or somewhere else so that he could have Mommy all to himself.

Nathan is ... okay, I guess. Many days, I overhear him make Mommy a ton of promises like, "I'll buy you whatever you want, just tell me. I'll give you the world because I love you." Or, "I promise I will take care of you as long as you let me. I'll buy you a house, a car, jewelry, and all the clothes. Just let me take you to California." He even says things like, "You are the most beautiful woman in the world. I want you to have my kids. How could anyone let you get into a situation like this?"

*And Mommy eats it up. She adores him because he's been treating her with kindness and showering her with everything he tells her he's gonna get. I just wanna know where he gets the money from, but it don't matter because I'm getting everything I need. Kinda. It's not everything I **want**.*

No matter what though, Mommy deserves it, and I do appreciate Nathan for making her the happiest that I've ever seen her because it makes it even easier for me to deal with her. But... there's just something that doesn't sit right with me.

I don't know. I just get bad vibes all around from him.

Even though he's doing so many good things for us, he just rubs me the wrong way, and I don't know why. What he offers to us like having food and warmth, is so much better than the way we lived before. Plus, he took us to the mall to shop after Mommy was released from the hospital and bought us some dope clothes.

I can't wait to go to school to show off my outfits. I'm gonna show them who was the real broke ones out here in these streets. Just the thought of me bursting their bubble and shutting them down made my day!

But Mommy's eyes are filtered. She can't see what I see because I ain't that attached to this Nathan dude. Some of these promises seem like ... too good to be true. Especially because he never makes **me** *none of these promises.*

Maybe it's meant to be like that. Maybe he wants a life with Mommy without me. I pray Mommy doesn't regret having me. Especially since she's spent so much time leaving me all alone in the motel and on the streets.

Right now, it is Friday evening, and Mommy and I are at the pool while Nathan is upstairs handling what he calls "business" on his computer. Sometimes he disappears like that and calls it business. Sometimes even? He flies out to different cities on the airplane and comes back days later to check on us and gives Mommy gifts from all the other places he's been. But this time, he's just in the hotel room. I don't care what he does. I'm glad I can have my mom to myself right now. Because spending a lot of time with her had been so rare for the last few months, and I want to hold on to it before it goes away again.

I've already jumped in the pool a million times, backflipped off the diving board and all of that until I'm tired and snuggle up with Mommy on the pool chairs next to the jacuzzi. We just lay together in silence until she sits up and looks down at me with a question in her eyes. I give her one back, hoping nothing is wrong.

"Jarell, I want you to be honest with Mommy. What do you think? Nathan's a wonderful guy, right?" Mommy asks.

"Why do you ask?"

"Just want to know. You know he's upstairs planning out our move to California, right? He plans on moving us out there on Sunday. Maybe even tomorrow."

"Huh? Wait. So, we're leaving Chicago? Forever?"

"I think so, baby. I think it's for the best. I know you won't be able to say bye to your friends at school, though. Or your teachers, so I feel bad about that."

"I don't like them anyway," I snarl. "Not like the school and friends when we lived in the Wells."

"Okay, well good. Then it won't hurt you as much. That's why I'm asking you about what you think about Nathan, especially since the hospital visit. I thought a lot about what you said. I should make sure that you're comfortable. So, I want you to tell me what you think."

My heart warms. Mommy did think about what I said. I'm so glad, and I take advantage of considering what I think about him in a way I can say with words. Words she can understand.

We sit for a while, but she's on edge, anticipating my answer. I don't make her wait any longer as open my mouth, hoping I've formed my thoughts enough to use my words right.

"He's alright. He's getting us a lot of stuff which is good. It's better than being homeless. But there's something about him, Mommy. I don't think he likes me," I say without looking at her.

She stiffens up. "Really? Why do you think that, baby? He always talks about how he's excited to have something like a son to look after."

"For real?" I say with wide eyes. I feel a tingle in my chest. I've always wanted a father. Always.

"Yes, baby. He says he enjoys being around you, that you're the son he's never had. Why do you feel like he doesn't like you?"

Ehhh. Dang. Now, I don't even want to say anything else negative anymore. Or tell her my truth because maybe I'm wrong about my instinct. It's just that he looks annoyed with me when we're alone together. When he takes me out shopping and tells me to pick out what I want, and when I do and try to share my excitement about it, he's so... standoffish.

It's even like that when he takes me to school in the mornings. Sometimes, I tell him about all the bad things I experience at school to get advice, but he tells me he's not in the mood to have a conversation. And then he lights a cigarette and smokes all throughout the drive to school. He doesn't want to listen to anything I talk about, and he's not interested in anything that has to do with me.

But then, there are times where he shows signs that he cares. I remember the time when he took me and Mommy to the movies one Friday, and I saw a new movie poster that I got super excited about and begged Mommy to see later. He just laughed, and then he ended up taking me to the movie the next day, and it was the time of my life. He had bought me a supersize popcorn with soda, and it was just the two of us. He felt like a father that day.

So, I don't know. I don't know if my thoughts are true enough to tell. At last, I answer Mommy's question.

"I don't know. Maybe I'm just thinking too much about it," I say and shrug my shoulders.

"I think you are too. I think he's great for us. The way he treats me, the way he takes care of us, and his willingness to be a father figure... I think this is God's answer to what we've been hoping and praying for, Jarell," she said.

I don't want to, but I nod in agreement. I'm just not sold on the guy, but I weigh inside my head... experience more homelessness, or live life like a rich kid? Plus, no matter what I tell Mommy about Nathan, she will come up with some excuse that will try to make me think different about him. It's a losing battle. I also don't want to leave Chicago. But... could moving with him be that bad? Especially if he's anything like how he is right now?

"I guess we can go Mommy."

"Really?" she squealed.

"Yeah. I just want you to be happy," I say.

"Thank you, baby. You're always looking out for your Mommy. You know how much this means to me," she says and kisses my forehead.

"Of course, Mom. I think it will be okay."

And this day is probably the last I'll see of Chicago and its fancy hotel. On to California. The place where everyone apparently loves.

~ ~ ~

"So, don't you see it even more now? Ma wouldn't have given a damn about what I had to say because he was getting her everything she ever wanted! She was all in; she wasn't going nowhere. What control did I have? None."

Scribbles and scratches on paper as usual, before she drew out a long, exhausted sigh.

"Jarell, I just want you to know your feelings are valid. You have every right to feel betrayed, neglected, and have a mistrust for her. I want to start by saying that. But here is also what I'd like you to consider. The more you allow me inside the specifics of this situation, the more I realize how complex it is. Sometimes when you're in a situation, the person who has hurt you the most doesn't have control, either. So, I'd like to ask you this one more time. Do you truly believe your mother had complete control and power to not leave that hospital without Nathan, knowing what she was being offered?"

I threw my hands in the air. "Hell yeah! She gonna sell out the safety of her kid for some material shit? She could've told him to leave the hospital and we could've figured something else out together. Why do you keep asking me questions like you tryna take her side? She was the prostitute. She was the one who left me in the motel rooms alone every night without food. She was the one who could've gotten a better job! She coulda made so many decisions that didn't need to result in this. Stop asking me dumb ass questions!" I yelled.

"You're right. She's not innocent. However, I'll be very honest with you and tell you right now that based on your perspective and recount of this situation, your mother wasn't a prostitute by choice," she responded with a bit of a hard edge.

"You always have a choice. Ain't that what you told me? All this shit coulda been avoided." I shrugged, digging my heels in. "Since we're talking about control, what's so different about this situation that she couldn't control what the fuck she did that led to my eventual abuse, huh?"

She didn't answer right away. Instead, she shifted in her seat, seeming to have leaned further back in her chair.

"Jarell, do you know anything about human trafficking?" Trisha asked.

"No, why?" I shrugged. "So?"

"I noticed you have a new iPhone when you walked in this morning. I'm glad. Do you have Siri and speak screen set up, yet?"

"Yeah, Ma set it up when she gave it to me on my birthday," I replied. "Don't know how she got her hands on that kinda money once again, but whatever. She tryna make up for kicking me out the other day with being nice and shit. Why do you ask?"

"Ask Siri right now to tell you what human trafficking is. Then, we'll go to the full article on reader mode. Let Siri read the full article to you through Speak Screen. When she gets done, I want you to tell me how the events of you and your mother's life match up with Siri's explanation. I think it'll help you understand why I've made some of the perspective-taking comments I've been making."

"Bet. Hey Siri," I called. The phone dinged in response. "What is human trafficking?"

"Here's what I found."

When Siri finished explaining, I blinked as silence filled the room. Wait. Huh? *What the fuck did I just hear?* Nah. She needed to tell me more based off that tidbit. A repeat. Something!

"Hey Siri…"

Beep, Beep

"What is… sex slavery?"

"Here's what I found."

At first, Siri didn't read the article out loud the way she did for human trafficking. But when Trisha hit reader mode and then had Siri read the full article out to me, my lungs collapsed.

What the hell did I just learn? My dry mouth dropped to say something in reaction when Siri was finished, but… nothing. No air, no nothing. I blinked several times, now wishing I would've remained ignorant.

"Trisha… d-does this happen a lot? Is human trafficking that common?"

"Yes. It's an international concern, but California is the state in our country that has such a widespread issue. It's one of the biggest human rights violations to ever exist other than genocide and the slave trade. The African slave trade."

Wait. Wasn't slavery over? I was always taught in Social Studies classes at school that it was! Teachers told me and everybody else that the world outlawed slavery and shipping humans, and it doesn't exist anymore. So, all this selling human like cargo was still going on all over the world this whole time, and no one said anything? No one teaches about this in school. Why?

"I… my … Trisha… based on everything Siri said… are you telling me that me and my mom … you're not telling me what I think you tryna tell me… are you?"

Trisha didn't acknowledge my question. She just left me on silent.

"It's time to share the other half of your homework," she said, adopting a different tone. The kind of heaviness you hear at a funeral or when you hear someone share bad news. "I wanted you to list everything you believe is your mother's fault that you felt has destroyed you. Then list whether you believe the choices she made were in her control. After that, we will begin discussing the compassion and patience piece, now that you know what the circumstances were. We'll begin to define compassion a little bit, today. Finally, we will do some mindfulness to wrap things up."

I grabbed the Braille paper folded in my backpack with my answers on it and delivered Trisha a long, long stare her direction as I ripped the paper in half, and then in half again… and then in half twice more.

I wasn't finna share that shit with the new information I had. I needed to start over.

Chapter Twenty-Three

Point of View: Jade Williams

Enough was enough.

School was gonna have to be on the back burner this morning. Jarell had no idea what the hell he was doing ignoring all my calls. Yeah, I understood he had this amazing ability to drive anyone into his brain's oblivion without remorse, blinking, or thinking twice. _Congratulations Jarell, your silent treatment is unmatched._ But this was not the time for all that. I didn't have time for his fucking shenanigans or him being in his feelings right now. I didn't know how much longer I had to be safe for this primary reason: Laurie knew where my new apartment was. Enough said.

She couldn't be trusted ever again. Who knew what she was telling Nathan now that we have fallen out, and who knew what she _actually_ knew about the kidnapping?

Of course, I weighed my options of what next steps I could take. Calling the police on both Laurie and her uncle was priority, and it was the first thing I was gonna do until I got a mysterious message Easter evening when I got home. Then again Monday morning. And then again, last night. At this point, the last thing I wanted to do was send text messages or call anyone anymore because I didn't know who was watching or if my shit got tapped or hacked somehow. This one message in particular had me going:

> **_Unknown_**_: Don't do anything stupid, like calling or going to the police. We're watching. Remember. We know who your momma is and where you live._

"

So, fuck that. I wasn't about to mess around with calling the police. Instead, I drove straight to Jarell's house before Kylah went to school. If he wasn't gonna answer my calls or my messages, I was gonna have to force the situation, and I was prepared for his backlash. Because one thing about Jarell? When he wanted his distance, he didn't play around about it.

When I arrived, I paced up the walkway and banged on their screen door.

"Jarell, it's me! Please open up!" I called out, and once he opened it, I rushed inside the house with no hesitation, bumping him out of the way.

"Why you storming up in here like you own the spot? What's the problem?" Jarell called out with a scowl and shut the door behind him.

"I will tell you after we take Kylah to school," I said. "Please. It's important, and you've been ignoring my calls."

He shook his head. "Okay, I see it's urgent and all, but you ain't in the clear right now for everything that happened at your place last week."

My mouth dropped, clutching my chest. "Really, Jarell? Laurie ruined your birthday. Not me."

"And you let her to do it, Jade. Why would you even put me in a situation to hurt that girl when I already got pending battery charges? I ain't ready to even deal with you right now because I got a lot on my mind. I'ma call you later," Jarell said and pushed the door back open and motioned for me to leave. I was about to open up my mouth in protest as the tears burned the back of my eyes, but it was interrupted by delight.

"Jade!!!"

Kylah appeared in the hallway and dropped her backpack, sprinting towards me like a cheetah chasing prey. Thank God for this girl. Seriously. She always saved the day. Kneeling to her level, I caught her strong embrace as she knocked me on my butt.

I looked up to give Jarell an "ah ha" smirk he obviously wouldn't see, but it was priceless to watch his hand clutch his forehead in frustration with Kylah and her innocent unawareness of conflict.

"Hi, my favorite honey bun!" I cooed, kissing her chubby cheek.

"I missed you! Where have you been? We have to finish playing Barbies!" she whined.

"I've been aro—"

"Kylah, let's go. You'll talk to Jade later," Jarell interrupted. "I gotta get you to school."

Standing up, I panicked. Did he not understand!? This was the worst possible time for Jarell to dismiss me.

"We can take my car so that it's quicker today," I offered with a smile. "That way, Kylah will have more time to be with her friends in the morning. How does that sound?"

"Ooh, yay!! Relly, can we drive this time? I wanna ride with Jade! Please?" Kylah begged, jumping up and down in front of him.

He turned his lip. "No. We're walking like we always do. Get your bag you dropped in the hallway and let's get outta here. You'll see Jade another time," Jarell said to her, but murdered me with his gaze and burrowed brows.

"Are you gonna be that petty?" I retorted. The one time I thought he was actually learning something and growing in therapy, now I had to take it back. Childish wasn't even the word for how he was acting right now.

"Relly…" Kylah stomped. A tantrum was on the horizon as she twisted and jerked. "Come on please? Why not? Why can't I go with Jade? Rellyyyyy!!!"

"I said no! Stop whining like a two-year-old and let's go," Jarell ordered. "You too old to be acting like this. Get up!"

"No! You're not my dad! You're just a stupid brother. I'm riding with Jade!" she screamed and cuddled up to my legs. I closed my eyes and put a hand on my head. This was going south too fast.

"What did you just say to me?" Jarell whispered with a fore-boding threat.

"Honeybun, do what he says, alright?" I whispered back to her because Jarell gave her a glare she winced at, prompting her to hide behind me. But that didn't stop Jarell from coming over and yanking her with aggression after he ordered her to come forth, but not in a way that hurt her either since she didn't cry or yelp out. His hand wrapped around her forearm to keep her still.

"Kylah, I don't know who you think you are, but don't talk to me like that again. I been the real nice big brother Relly, but I'm not one to play with. You feel me?" Jarell snarled with a stiff finger of his free hand in her direction.

"Mmm hmm." She nodded in fear as tears wet her face.

"I don't care if I can't see, and I don't care if I'm not your dad. Your dad ain't here. As your 'stupid' brother, I'm responsible for you because Ma's at work. So, guess what? You're gonna do what I tell you to do. What if I called you stupid? You would be crying right now. Ain't that right?"

"Yes," she cried.

"Get outside. And if you think you gone come home and tell Ma I yelled at you, she ain't gone do nothing about it after I tell her what you said, either. What you gotta say now?"

"Nothing," she murmured.

"That's what I thought. Say bye to Jade."

"Bye Jade," she whispered with a sullen wave.

Kylah moped out of the front door without a single peep, leaving Jarell and I together alone for a moment.

"Jarell..." I started, stunned at him even getting mad at his sister like this. Never saw him in that light.

"Jade, I'm serious. I'm not in the mood to hear anything from you right now," he interjected the second Kylah made it out the door.

"I'm here for a reason, alright! Kylah was the only way I could get you to listen!" I shouted, yet Jarell remained unconcerned. "I'm not safe, Jarell. And you aren't either."

"What are you talking about?" He shook his head with both hands out in question.

"Look... it's about the kidnapping. I think I found one of the guys who had us in the basement."

Jarell froze, his only movement blinking and the wrinkles of his frown disappeared, a look of anticipation taking its place.

"Who?" he asked, his voice now hoarse.

I cleared my throat. "It's a lengthy story, so I will tell you after you take Kylah to school. I'll be on your porch waiting when you get back. Since you won't let me give y'all a ride."

Before I allowed him to respond, I walked out the door and sat on the porch, crossing both my legs and my arms with an attitude. A long fifteen seconds passed by before Jarell followed me outside, closed the door, and locked the house with his key.

"Come on," he directed, looking down towards me. "You're walking with us."

With a deep breath, a huge part of me wanted to be petty right back and say no, but the situation was too serious, and I had already messed up his birthday. The least I could do was be the bigger person.

Chapter Twenty-Four

Point of View: Jade Williams

This was one awkward vibe. Only thing pleasant about this whole walk was the clear skies and beaming sun with a little bit of wind to alleviate the heat. Everything else was miserable. The tension between Jarell and I was thick, and Kylah, who could talk anyone's head off, had her lip poked out the entire way. After dropping her off as she went inside the school without much of a farewell, the silence remained as we retraced our steps back home. I was thankful that for once, I wasn't the one who broke the pressure to speak because I just didn't know where Jarell's head was at right now.

"A'ight, Jade. Hear me out. I'm sorry for being rude, okay? I feel like I apologize to you for being that way more often than not, but look. You ain't innocent in this. You got one chance to tell me what you know about the whole kidnapping thing. I ain't willing to talk much about anything else or hear your apology about your little friend Laurie," Jarell said with his hands stuffed in his old jeans pocket as we walked down Slauson.

Well. He wasn't about to be granted that wish. I wasn't about to take the fall or the brunt of her crap, so before I got to the meat of what I wanted to discuss today, this Laurie situation needed to be cleared up so that he could let this petty ass grudge go.

"Listen. I'm sorry about what happened on your birthday whether you wanna hear it or not. I just wanted y'all to hash things out, and I went about it the wrong way. Laurie and I's friendship is over. We can talk about that whole situation later since I got more pressing shit to talk about, but she was wrong as hell, and I ended it the second you left the house," I responded.

"Yeah... just like you 'ended' the relationship with me, yet you're... never mind," Jarell started, and ceased by clenching his teeth and looking towards the traffic as his jaw flared.

I rolled my eyes. Fuck it. If he didn't accept the apology, oh well. We had bigger fish to fry here, and we needed to A: be on one accord, and B: be a team. We didn't need to be at odds with the crap we were about to face together. Again.

"Speaking of Laurie, Jarell, one of the guys who kidnapped us is her uncle."

The words spilled out like loose stool, and honestly, I would rather have it that way instead of stuttering and stammering in fear of his reaction. A second of silence lingered before Jarell stopped walking, damn near stumbled, and looked my way with the kind of scorn I never want to see directed at me again from him.

"What? And you brought her over to your place and put me in a position where I almost threw her off the balcony? If you don't wanna be cut off right now where we stand Jade, you better start explaining. How do you know this? Tell me the whole thing," Jarell demanded, squinting. "You knew, huh? You had to know something about this all along. I swear to God, Jade... if you don't tell the truth..."

As my eyes ballooned and shifted around the area, watching people gaze our way as Jarell yelled at me, I grabbed his wrist and dragged him to a small little alley. "Lower your voice! You got people looking at us!" I whispered.

"I don't care 'bout none of these people! Tell me the truth!" he screamed.

"I am telling the truth! I didn't know, Jarell, relax! You would've known everything had you answered your phone!" I exclaimed.

He crossed his arms and stood a little taller with his chin up. "What did Laurie tell you?"

"She didn't tell me anything! This is how I figured it out." With a sigh, I gave him a full run down on everything that happened at the house on Easter. "Believe me. I only connected the dots because I recognized his eyes from the cut-out holes in his mask from that day. Jarell, I swear to God, I never knew who he was or that he was even related to her. Besides, I would have never brought her to my place if I knew. I'd like to be safe, too!"

Jarell exhaled and swiped a hand down his face. "You gotta tell me more because this is ridiculous. Why would someone like her uncle want anything to do with me or you when he has no connection with either of us? You think he'd snatch us up over me beating up Laurie's boyfriend? She had to have lied on me for him to be this involved. What does he look like, Jade? Be specific."

"I got the same questions you have! I don't know what she told him, but it's clear she told him everything that went down at school between you and Martell. As far as what he looks like? He has some scary ass, blue eyes. Like, they're almost wintery. I can't even describe how intense they are. Only person's eyes I've seen close to being that intense is Kylah's, but she's much more beautiful."

"Okay, what else other than the eyes?" Jarell's voice wavered, which I didn't expect.

"Um, he's huge. Bulky. I can't tell if he's like... big boned, muscular, or fat. He has like brownish blondish kind of hair with this ugly comb over and he's real scruffy in the face. Long nose. He's intimidating. If you could see, I'd show you a picture I managed to snap of him."

The more and more I described him, the literal life drained out of Jarell's body as he stiffened and clammed up, staring at some arbitrary point on the ground. I stood watching, waiting for him to react or move, but he didn't. I was about to open my mouth to ask him what was wrong, but he finally showed some sign of life by drawing out a long groan.

"Awww no... no, no, no. Fuck!" he hissed with his hands on his hips and head dipped.

"Jarell? You okay?" I asked, becoming a little concerned that he might pass out. "Jarell, what!? Tell me!"

"Jade… what's that man's name? If you know… please tell me," he whispered. Only his mouth moved.

"Laurie's mom said his name was Nathan. It's her brother."

Jarell then closed his eyes in confirmed disappointment.

"What, Jarell? Say something!"

"Jade… that's my ma's ex. Are you telling me that we ran away five years ago, and now he found us because of your mothafuckin' friend?" he roared as I cringed.

Never in my life did I think my heart could sink to the ground the way mine just did. I tried to shake my head to even make sense of his allegation, but nothing worked. I even attempted taking myself back to the details Jarell had given me when he told me all about Nathan and his cruelties a few weeks ago and just couldn't make the connection. How the hell could that even be possible!? Wasn't he on the run from the police? There was no way… Laurie's uncle… Jarell's abuser… no way!

"Woah, woah, woah. Wait. What!? That's your mom's ex-boyfriend? The one who…" He nodded before I could finish. "How do you know?" I squawked.

"What's the last name?" Jarell inquired.

"Well, Laurie's mom's name is Stephanie Kaminsky, but her maiden last name is Schmidt."

He made a scruff sound in his throat.

"Yeah. That's his fuckin' ass. Oh my God. I can't believe this shit," Jarell uttered and stopped walking as he gripped his forehead with a hand. I couldn't even breathe, so whatever Jarell was feeling right now had to be unimaginable. This shit was more than a coincidence and more than weird.

"Jarell…" my voice wavered as Jarell turned his back. "I don't even know what to say. I had no idea about any of this! Please believe me. I would never set you up like that with Laurie if I knew. I know how much your history with that man is serious and everything he's done to you and your mom. You weren't able to recognize his voice at all when we were in the basement?"

"He never said anything!" Jarell whipped around to yell at me. "Of course, I woulda picked it up!"

As I thought back to that day, again, the guy allowed everyone else to do the dirty work as he watched. Unfazed. Was he the one to set up the whole thing? I still had so many questions. So many things weren't adding up.

"What do you think he wants? I mean, for all of them to say that they were about to get payback for all the things you had done at school fighting people, I don't know understand how and why he's even involved. Unless he's using them as a decoy or something," I pondered.

"I don't know what that man is up to, Jade. I'm confused as to how he just shows up here without being caught by the feds already. We fled miles and miles away from where we used to stay, and he just so happens to be related to your best friend?"

He pressed his lips thin and held his hips with both hands, gazing towards the ground before he continued speaking. "That mothafucka operates in weird ways. He probably wants my mom." Then, he gasped. "Aww shit! What if he knows where Kylah is!?" He paused. Then, paced up and down the alley as he clutched at his head again.

Okay, okay, okay. Think Jade! Come on. What can you do to diffuse this situation? My eyes roamed around, thinking of ways to get Jarell to simmer down as he mumbled and grumbled to himself. I was gonna have to keep the news about the text messages to myself. There was no way he was in the headspace to deal with that, too.

With a level head, I spoke. "I think you're thinking too deep into this. First of all, I don't even think he knows your mom got pregnant since he left after that whole incident, and you both fled. Second, I don't think he has any idea of where your mom and sister are. Maybe that's why they had us in that basement. To get the information out of us. I don't know!"

Jarell just stood, looking towards me with narrow eyes and a partially opened mouth.

"You gonna be that naïve? Those bitch ass niggas found us in an isolated area of the park after leaving a hospital and threw us into trucks! What makes you think he won't find my sister or my mom?"

So much for being optimistic…

"True… we gotta call the police Jarell! Now!" I pulled out my phone. Forget about those text messages!

"No!" Jarell shouted. "Don't do that. I don't trust them, and they ain't even do what we needed them to do the last time we called! They dropped that whole case, talking about some 'they can't find him.' That's why he's out here all willy nilly and shit. Please, don't do that. Let's figure out our own plan."

"Jarell, fuck that! They can always reopen a case. That bastard needs the death penalty. What do you mean not to call the police? I gave them descriptions and everything of what I saw that night. He matches the profile," I tried reasoning. "He doesn't need to be on the streets any longer than right now."

"Jade, I get all that, but that's not the only reason why I don't want you to call."

"Why else would you let him off the hook?" I frowned, my face scrunching up.

"It don't matter. Let me handle it. You did what you had to do to find out who did this to us and now let me take the rest. I can't let him get to my Ma or my sister."

He tried to walk by me to end the conversation, but with a strong arm, I stopped him dead in his tracks by the chest and pushed him back to where he was without mercy.

"Jarell what? Based on what you told me, that man is no joke. And obviously he has people working for him all over the place, so they'll murder you before he ever does. Hell, they might be watching us right now! Jarell, you cannot go into that situation alone. I won't let you put your life on the line like that," I pleaded, throwing my hands in the air.

"Jade, you know what this means to me. I've been waiting for this moment, and you know all the damage he's done. Shit, you even said it yourself! How you wanna find him and kill him, and that's after learning just snippets of his bullshit. So, imagine how I feel?" he snapped.

"But Jarell, you're blind. How are you ever gonna find or know where he is?"

"If you take me over to your friend's house, we won't have this problem." He shrugged.

"He was only over there for Easter. Who knows where he is now? Again, Jarell. Even if you're nose to nose with him for the first time, *you're blind.* I know you hate to hear that, but it's reality, and your other senses will only get you so far. I know I've underestimated you before, but this is next level shit. That guy ain't no high school fluff you been dealing with," I reminded him.

"I don't care what he is. I can't be this helpless ass coward I used to be with him. I want him to try that shit he used to do on me now. I dare him," Jarell said with tight lips and closed fists.

I sighed, putting both hands on his chest. "That sounds cool and all, and I want nothing more for you to put him out. I want that kind of revenge for you, too. But listen. Putting him in jail is the best thing to do. And that way, all his other hitmen will follow." I smacked my lips and huffed. "What the fuck! What kinda dude is this that he got four people to do his dirty work for him like that? I ain't never seen no shit like this in my life. I mean, you see it on TV, but it hits different when it's right in your face."

"Nathan always been a criminal, Jade. I just realized in therapy that he's a trafficker," he confessed.

See... this man was no joke.

"You're making my point, Jarell. That's why you shouldn't go in this by yourself. Like I said, we're probably being watched right now!"

"I don't care. Here's what you need to know. Kylah ain't going to school tomorrow at least, so I'll need your help with that. All the other mess with Nathan, I need to figure out on my own."

"Jarell," I whined in protest.

"End of discussion, Jade!" he replied and walked by me to head to the main street. This time, I didn't stop him as the tears welled in my eyes. "In the meantime, send me that picture you took of him. Let's go so we can figure this thing out about where Kylah's gonna go."

Jarell walked away and took a left down the sidewalk, leaving me by myself in the alleyway for a moment. Letting out a huge exhale in defeat, I wiped my eyes dry with the back of my hand and moved out of the alleyway when my vision was clear. By that time, Jarell was already a block ahead of me, pacing towards his mom's house.

Yeah. There was no stopping him. At all. He had his eyes on the prize; and if I was him? My eyes would be on it, too. Couldn't lie.

But he had to be stopped no matter what, and I couldn't stop him with just me alone.

There was one more way… the only way I could save him. I just had to play my cards and my words right. The last thing I needed was for Jarell to end up dead.

Chapter Twenty-Five

Point of View: Jarell Hendricks

Trigger Warning – Physical Abuse

What was sleep?

Because I ain't have none of it since last night.

All I did was sit at my window and let the dry, spring breeze float through the room as I calculated every step in my head of what I was gonna do to that fuckin' bastard when I got my hands on him. I was breathless through the dreams as I cracked my knuckles and pounded my fists into the pillow so I wouldn't scare anyone in the house by punching holes in the wall.

The rest of the night? I got down and did push-ups. Like old times at the wee hours of the morning while I visualized the worst way I could put Nathan six feet under until the heat of the sun's rays beamed through the window and onto my back.

Unbeknownst to Ma, Jade and I agreed to keep Kylah out of school today for her safety until we could figure out next steps together long term. Since Jade was unwilling to stay home from school to watch her while I went to therapy, we both agreed Kylah would go over to Alise's house this morning until Jade got out of school to bring her back home. I ain't know Alise that well, and I wasn't feeling taking her over to a stranger's house, but I trusted Jade. She wouldn't put Kylah in harm's way. It just meant I had to figure out which route to take to deal with this. Before it was too late.

Today, I didn't sit in my favorite velvet couch during therapy. I sat at the round table in the middle of the room this time. My right foot tapped endlessly, and my knee shook nonstop, too. I couldn't even imagine what I looked like right now to Trisha. No doubt it was bloodshot eyes with dark bags underneath, and scruffy looking since I didn't do too much grooming before I left.

"Jarell..." Trisha called out.

No answer. I just bit the inside of my cheek, contemplating on whether I should even reveal Nathan's return to her. The less people who knew, the better.

"Jarell, are you able work with me today?" she questioned with caution.

Nothing. My foot tapped louder.

"I know our session together last time was hard. We should take the time to process some of that information today. I didn't want you to find out the cruelties behind your mother's life and decisions in that way. I just needed you to understand some of my questioning and have some background information about a serious, serious crime and situation that many young women find themselves in. I am not saying that your mother—"

"It ain't that, Trisha," I whispered.

"So then... what's wrong?" she asked with a voice so soft, I visualized a cloud.

"Nothing. S'cool. Let's just get today over with, please," I uttered with the tips of each finger on both hands meeting each other in the middle.

"Well, I would like to know a few things before we do that. First, you're not sitting on the couch. Second, you look like you're holding yourself together by a hair. Is everything okay? Please. Whatever it is, let's talk about it," Trisha coaxed.

I smacked my lips. "What you got planned in that notebook today?" I asked.

"We were going to continue talking about compassion and patience, and then of course unpacking human trafficking a little bit, but... we can table that. I just need to know how you're doing and if you're alright."

I sighed, shaking my head. "No, I'm not okay. He's back... he's here."

"What? What are you talking about? Who's here, Jarell?"

"Nathan. My ma's ex."

She went stone silent on me. She was just as stuck as I was because the stillness gave me no other clues.

"How do you know this?" she interrogated.

"It don't matter. He's around," I said.

"Then you need to call the police. Do you know where he is right now? Where he's staying? Here, why don't you call them right now-"

"I ain't calling nobody," I interrupted and hit her with a sinister glare in her direction.

She froze. "Jarell... this isn't something to play with. You cannot fool around with people in the trafficking business. They're like... kingpins and drug lords without the drugs. Or maybe with them, too. I don't know."

"I told you, Trisha. I ain't gone say it again. I ain't callin' nobody."

"You can't be serious. Why would you want someone like him roaming freely on the streets? When did you find this out?"

"Yesterday, but it don't matter because I'm gonna handle it."

"Oh... oh no you don't!" Whatever jewelry she was wearing rattled against each other, signaling a fervent head shake. "Don't do what I think you're trying to do. Don't try to take matters in your own hands, Jarell. You've worked so hard in therapy with me. It's extremely dangerous for you, and it puts you and me in legal liability."

"It puts you in nothing, so stop making shit up because you want me to call the police. I ain't calling them. I don't even trust them! They let that bitch ass nigga go the first time after they knew even just half the shit he did to me and my Ma. My fucking ex-girlfriend found the mothafucka before the police did!" I shouted.

"I'll call them myself if I have to. You shouldn't do this to yourself. You're on the right path, and I'd hate for you to regress and ruin your life by trying to get rev—"

"You have no idea what that man has fucking put me through, alright?" I boomed, shaking the walls. She gasped and a thump hit the back of her chair. "Fuck, Trisha... you don't get it. You don't!"

"You're right," she quickly surrendered. "I will never get it. I can only empathize and help you grow, but I can't do that if you're in jail, okay? Here. Why don't you help me understand where you're coming from? Let's dig a little deeper. What is it that you want to handle with Nathan? What are you seeking from him? What exactly did he do to you that you want to get even for?"

I paused as my throat closed again and my spirit almost ran out of my body to some place safe. To some place where any memory or any part of him didn't exist. Any recollection of time spent with him was degrading and it would re-traumatize me again.

I can't believe I just let all that abusive shit he did to me happen. I didn't fight back to protect myself at all with him, like I was a weak link. I just let it fucking happen, and I hate myself for it. How could I call myself a man or call myself in charge of protecting others like Ma or my sister when I let someone violate my own body on so many occasions? I ain't a man by any means. I wasn't deserving to be labeled as such.

I sighed with a hand on top of my head. Fuck. If I didn't tell Trisha everything Nathan put me through, she wouldn't ever get it. I rocked my head back and forth, contemplating as she just sat there and waited for my response.

I was about to say no, that I wasn't telling her shit, but I stopped myself. I had never confided in someone about *anything* the way I had done with Trisha. From the moment I heard her voice call my name on the very first day of therapy and I saw what I thought was her presence in front of me, she just felt like a grandmother I never had, but had always wanted. Just so she could listen and hear me the way no one else would. And care for me.

Because that's what Grannies do, right? She even responded to every one of my issues in the way I expect a granny would. Thoughtful. Wise. She was a great listener.

Trisha was different.

"I... I don't want to tell you anything," I tore from myself, "but I'ma tell you so you can understand why I have to do this for myself and where I'm coming from, Trisha. I need you to understand. I do."

"Alright, alright. I'm listening. I'll stop talking now," Trisha conceded.

~ ~ ~

April 2011 – Red Bluff, California

It's a warm, sunny April day. I'm off the bus in good spirits because it was a decent day at school. Plus, it's my favorite day of the week. Thursday. Because tomorrow is Friday. And a special day.

I walk across the green, plush grass to head home in the beautiful sunset. This place is so country and different from Chicago.

And not in a good way, even though it's all nice looking. The reality is that it's been a nightmare living here. More than that.

We've been here for over a year now, and I still can't get used to it. I have to run across a corn field to get to my bus stop in the morning and run the same one back. We live right off a county highway in this country ass place as semi-truck drivers rattle the trees and grass, and sometimes our house as they pass by. There are almost no Black people and a few Mexicans here and there.

It's why I don't have many friends... I just go to school and come home.

I'd rather have it that way. These kids always make stupid comments about me, and the teachers do nothing about it. I keep my anger inside and just dance about it when I get home because I promised Mommy I wouldn't fight anymore. Especially here. These White kids can't fight for all the shit they talk, and I'm too skilled for them to defend themselves. With all those factors, my consequences for fighting are always way worse. I learned that the hard way when I knocked someone unconscious at lunch with one punch for calling me a stupid porch monkey because I had to repeat 6th grade for all the school that I missed when we were homeless. Got suspended for three days. Then I had to get a beating from Nathan about it, too. For each day I was suspended.

Yeah. It gets down like that.

It wasn't always this way. When we first got here, he treated us the same way he did when we were in Chicago. Maybe for like a couple weeks. But then I had noticed a lot of changes as time went on. He asked Mommy to do certain work and things around the house, and the more time went on, the more he asked her to do.

On the weekends, sometimes, she disappeared out to a little shed next to the house and stayed there for hours while Nathan watched over me inside. When it had first started, I always wanted to look out the window to see what she was doing or if she'd appear, but Nathan made it very clear from jump that I have to stay away from the front of the house when she's there. When Mommy returned, she was always exhausted. I was so tempted to ask her about it when we had those slivers of seconds alone in the house when Nathan was away, but I found myself wanting to talk about other things and bond the way we used to rather than talk about what she did in a shed.

Eventually, Mommy became his worker. Including yard work. At first, I was out of doing any work for him for the most part, but then he started forcing me to do stuff within weeks of our stay. If it isn't done to his liking, he yells at us. Except the yelling turned into punching and abusing Mommy. I tried to fight him one day for it... the first day he swung on her and blacked her eye. She laid on the ground crying as I squared up with him, but instead of fighting, he pulled out a gun and the cold metal touched me right in the middle of the forehead.

I peed myself that day.

The threat was very clear, too. **"You soft bitch. I will spill your guts the way you just soiled yourself. Don't you ever try to fight me again."** *And that was the last time I ever sought to cross him.*

It doesn't help that he's huge. Six foot five huge with fiery, yet icy eyes. So, when he hurt Mommy, he hurt her, and I can't do anything about it. The one thing to make myself feel better is dance, even when he started beating me too along with Mommy's beatings around the time I turned twelve. Now, I do anything I can to avoid any trouble with him, even though it isn't our fault that trouble comes our way. Fault means something different to Nathan than how we define it. If it upset him, then we did something wrong.

As the bus drives away, I jog across the field and slow down once I reach the house. All of me is hoping Nathan isn't home. That maybe he's still at work so Mommy and I can catch a break. Just last night, Nathan slapped her for not having his dinner ready in time when he got home, so I'm trying to hurry up and help her with what she needs before he comes. I swear, I'm counting the days when we can run away.

I walk in the door and sure enough, Mommy is cleaning up the living room. It looks spotless so far, yet she's wiping tiny little specs of dust away.

"Sup, Mom," I call out with a smile as I walk in the door.

"Hey baby. You're in a good mood. Good to see." She looks in better spirits today too, minus the fact that she wears a small scar across her face from Nathan. I ignore it. "Nathan has some chores he said he wants you to do. It's not much, and it's posted on the refrigerator. Make sure you finish that before you do your homework, okay?"

"I don't have homework," I say.

"Alright. Make sure that your backpack is empty without homework then before you do anything else. Because you know he's going to check your bag."

"I know. Do you need help in here before I start?" I ask.

"Umm," she says and then looks down at her watch. "No, I'm pretty on track to finishing up on time. He'll be here in about an hour, so hurry."

I put my backpack in my room and then move to the kitchen to see his note. It says that he wants all dishes to be washed, dried, and put away. Alright. Easy enough.

I clean the dishes and everything, thinking about what I want to do when I'm done. I think I'll start with my origami pieces today since today isn't a TV day. Yup. Nathan has limited my TV time. I have so many pieces I want to display, but I know Nathan won't let me. So, I just store them elsewhere.

I finish the dishes, and I've already started origami in my room with the door closed when Nathan walks in the house from wherever he was at. There isn't much commotion like usual with the two of them, so it must be a good day all around for everyone. I hope it continues.

Minutes pass by, and I'm deep into a piece I'm working on when suddenly, yelling back and forth bleeds through the walls until it grows louder and louder to where I can't even concentrate on some difficult folds on my paper.

"You pieces of shit never do what the fuck I ask you to do!"

"Nathan, please. It's something so small that I can handle right n—"

"Shut up!"

POP! I close my eyes and sigh as I get up and turn on my speakers to put on music. The more screaming Mommy does, the louder I turn the speakers up. I take a deep breath as I stand in the middle of my room and move with the music. I swear, the time goes so much faster this way, even though my world slows down as I hit every step, every move.

I'm in a groove and vibing when heavy thumps turn into pounding footsteps coming in my direction until my room door bursts open with Nathan wavering in the walkway, almost falling over with a bottle of beer in one hand and something else in the other. Fumbling, I take my remote control and turn off the speakers.

"Yes, sir? What do you need?" I say with a raised eyebrow.

"Don't you 'Yes, sir,' me," he snarls and then punches me dead in the chest with all his might. Knocks the wind out of me to the point where I fly back onto the bed and clutch onto my chest and cough to breathe. "I love how you and your stupid ass mom always act like you've done nothing wrong."

I blink. I have no idea what he's talking about, but I'm afraid I'll be punished worse for admitting that. Because I look down and realize he has his brown belt in his other hand. I swallow.

"First, you didn't wash all the dishes like I asked you to. There's a shot glass on my nightstand in the bedroom that should've been washed. Second, this music you keep blasting! What, you think that's gonna save you from not hearing the ass whipping your mother often deserves?" He steps closer to me with lips that disappear and a vicious glare. My skin drops several degrees. I cower and move to the corner of my bed, putting my hands up so he won't hurt me.

"Look at you. Already scared and I haven't even touched you. Get down here," he says with a tight mouth after setting his beer bottle down. With one hand, he tugs my shirt and tosses me from the bed as my knees strike the ground. Then, he stands over me. "I know your birthday is tomorrow, and I tried to give you less chores so that you can enjoy your night and enjoy your day tomorrow, but it looks like you can't do anything simple."

I rush to scramble beneath my bed, trembling and whimpering, but he grabs my leg and drags me back, carpet burning my arm.

With nowhere left to go, I duck and cover in a fetal position and endure his ruthless wrath. I grit my teeth and hold my breath to get through it without crying. If I cry? It gets worse.

"You're hiding? Be a man!" he threatens and pulls me by the shirt to lift me up, ripping it half. Then, he wears me out until I fall to my stomach. I try to crawl away with the little strength I have, but I can't. He just... keeps... going...

My silence breaks.

"Nathan! Nathan! That's enough! He's screaming, now. Please, just stop!" Mommy comes running in, a knife in her hand, but he pushes her little body down to the ground before she can take a stab at him. Shortly after, his gun comes out of his waistband, and he points it at her.

"Shut up!" he shouts and strikes me again. "Put that knife down." She drops it in an instant. "I told this boy to stop crying! Be a man! Be the grown man you've always thought you were you little shit!" Nathan screeches, and the world moves in slow motion as I take on more of his fury. Over and over and over until it gets so bad, I open my mouth to scream, but nothing comes out.

"Nathan! Stop!" Mommy cries, reaching out to me on her knees "You're gonna kill him. We're sorry. Don't kill my baby. Please. That's my baby, and you're hurting him. You're hurting him bad..."

When he strikes again, I shriek louder than the last.

"Nathan! You're gonna kill my baby... please... please, I swear I'll do anything. Tell me what you need me to do. I'll do it. Please..."

Surprisingly, her frantic pleading gets him to stop.

"My baby," she sobs and attempts to scuttle to see if I'm alright, but Nathan stops her.

"Get over here," Nathan growls and grabs Mommy by her pony-tail and hauls her to the next room. He shuts the door and all I hear is her wailing. I close my eyes and just lay on the floor panting as every part of my body is on fire, along with my throat. Letting my head fall back again, I try and cancel that out by allowing my brain float to a different place. But I can't. Maybe if I had just looked in all the rooms, this wouldn't have happened... I'm so stupid. This is my fault. I should've known better. I should've known...

~ ~ ~

It's the next day. Time for me to get ready for school, but I am just out of it. I think about going back to bed since I stayed up scrubbing my own blood away from the carpet last night after Nathan had come back for something else and told me I had to, but I know that'll warrant a beating if I don't go to school.

266

After I brush my teeth and shower with care since the water stung my wounds, I shuffle through my closet for something to wear. On any other day, I'll wear some nice polo shirt and jeans, a long-sleeved button up, or some long-sleeved graphic cartoon shirts. And for my birthday, I always attempt to look extra nice. But I'm not feeling it. Don't even give a fuck that it's my birthday. That might be my activity later. Burn all these clothes Nathan bought me.

I gaze at the last thing at the end of my closet. It's the big black hoodie Gregory gave me during the blizzard last year. I grab it and smell it. I snuggle with it. I remember what he told me when he gave it to me – "Keep it on. It'll protect your head, ears, and nose." Hell... maybe it'll protect other things, too.

I put on a white t-shirt first and throw the hoodie on. It's still big, but I've must've grown a lot because it doesn't drag on the floor anymore. I put on some jeans underneath and take a long look in the mirror. My eyes are demon red with huge bags underneath, and my lips seem to be in a permanent frown.

I look away and throw the hood over my head. Now, I feel secure and shielded. My body is protected. Just how I want it to be. I'm never taking this hoody off again.

I limp out of my room, and crackling bacon and bubbling eggs cooking fill the air. When I walk into the kitchen, Mommy is standing at the stove. Out of the corner of her eye, she sees movement, and then turns toward me.

"Hey honey," she calls out with a smile, but it disappears when she sees the way I look and what I'm wearing. She swallows and gives me a concerned gaze. I look away. "Oh, baby. I know what happened yesterday is hurting. I know it is. Please try not to let him ruin your big day. I know it's hard, but I'm not letting him ruin my Mommy moment on my son's birthday."

The guilt in her eyes crushes me, but I try not to let it show. I just sit at the table, without words.

"We are going to get out of this soon, okay? We don't deserve this kind of life," she whispers to me. Then, she puts the plate of food in front of me. My stomach flips, and I almost gag. So, I push it away.

"Jarell, you have to eat. I don't like how you haven't been eating. When's the last time you ate a real meal?"

I shrug.

"See? That's not good. You're getting too skinny. I made all this for your birthday. Can't believe I have a thirteen-year-old. You're growing up on Mommy. And I want to take you out later today sweetie, okay? I don't care what he says," she says and reaches out to touch my back. As soon as her hand meets my body, I flinch, jerking away from her. Hard. I clutch onto the arms of my hoody with such tight fists, my knuckles almost go white while my body shivers. I try to blink them away, but the tears come in a downpour. Like rain.

Her eyebrows wrinkle as she stares at me with wide eyes. "Woah. Jarell? I barely even touched you." She reaches out and touches me again, and I jerk away just as violent, almost tipping over in my chair.

"Jarell..." Ma starts, but I interject.

"I'm not hungry."

I rise from the table and rush to the front door without my backpack before she can say anything else.

I hear her running after me when I get to the front door, and as soon as I do, I sprint down the steps and run onto green plush field as she calls my name out. I do not know where I'm running to. I just sprint, and sprint, and sprint. I do not stop. I do not feel tired. I run until I reach a cornfield. And I even sprinted through that. I keep running and running and running, hoping I run off the cliff of earth. Hoping I can fall into an abyss of darkness so that I could never... ever... ever...

~ ~ ~

"Jarell?" Trisha calls out to me as I enter reality again. "Jarell, are you okay?"

I can't continue. I just let out a rugged cry, pulling my shirt to my eyes and soaked it. At the same time, a mode of fury nestled in my chest until I stood and began punching the air, the wind of my aimless blows crashing against the office walls.

"Do you understand what the fuck I wanna do to him, Trisha? He beat me over a fuckin' shot glass. I don't wanna put that mothafucka in jail! I wanna get what's due to me! What's owed to me! That's what I fuckin' want, and I finally get the chance!" I slapped my chest and screamed to the top of my lungs as the tears squirted out of control. "This is what he did to me! Every single scar!"

I ripped my shirt in two with bare hands and stood like a display. A showcase of what Nathan put there from his belts. His whips. His beer bottles. His cords. His sticks. His bricks. His fists. His hands. His feet. His shoes. His furniture. His everything!

"Jarell..." Her voice trembled. The intensity of her compassion grew within the space as she still sat down watching me with intent.

"Trisha, not only did he do what you see... after he beat me that day before my birthday? He came to my room that night." I sniffed, rubbing at my eyes. "He came every... fucking... night since that day and violated me in ways I don't wanna remember, and Ma never even knew. He never stopped until the day he threw bleach in my face and blinded me before planting that seed called Kylah in my mom. Which means he did it for months."

I paused, sniffing again before continuing.

"The day he blinded me, he kicked me so hard that I have permanent issues with fertility now for the rest of my life because I had to get surgery. I can't even reproduce, Trisha. The most basic human shit. He took everything from me."

As I stood and the words heaved out between sobs, I pulled up my shirt up to my eyes again.

"What if we never escaped? He probably would've eventually..." I swallowed. I didn't wanna say the "R" word. I didn't wanna see, just to not be able to unsee, what he had done to my mom... done to me.

"I just don't understand. Why did he target Ma, Trisha? Why did he want *her*?" I whispered. "Why *her*? A foster child with no family or no one to protect her. Why wasn't it someone else so that I wouldn't have been dragged into that shit just to be…"

Everything that had brewed in my chest began to crack as I buckled and fell to my knees and wept.

"I… I'm trying to understand. Why didn't any of the schools call somebody to help me? Isn't that mandatory? I wore that same fuckin' dirty ass oversized hoody every goddamn day for years. I thought that maybe if I smelled bad enough, looked dirty enough, someone would come save me. Did they just ignore me? It's like I didn't exist. I was invisible. Then I get here to LA after us running away to try and start over my freshman year, but when I got to the school, people started making all kinds of lies and assumptions about me. They say the worst shit like I'm not even human. I'm a crackhead. A homeless hobo. A dirty bum. A demon. A killer. Talking about my clothes and my eyes. Telling me I need to kill myself. Telling me I don't deserve to be alive."

I heaved inward.

"Trisha, I swear to you, I will never admit this anywhere else, but Crenshaw broke me. Nathan was one thing but adding the nightmare of being at school on top of it all… they tore me down so much. I didn't do anything to them, Trisha. I just wanna know… why did *everyone* fail me and my family? And now Nathan's just back like nothing ever happened? What do I do?"

Then, something inside of me exploded like a missile. For a long time, I sobbed in an egg position, hugging myself with my forehead on the floor out loud like I was in the middle of an empty, endless flat field where sound didn't exist. A cry I never knew I had within. I thought it had all come out with Jade when I shared a small part of my story to her, but nah. These cries were primal, ferocious, unrestrained, and *infinite*. Boundless. Unlimited.

The intense crying went on for minutes and minutes and minutes until my voice went hoarse.

It remained quiet around me until I stopped wailing and hyperventilated and hiccupped instead. It was at that moment where Trisha sniffed.

"Jarell…" she called out. Her voice wavered. "Come on…try and get up."

For the next few moments, Trisha encouraged me to stand and sit down on the couch. There was nothing I'd been through harder than lifting myself up in this moment. My body weighed a ton, and I was convinced I'd never walk again. When I couldn't rise up, I punched the ground, but with Trisha's help and her strength to lift me, I made it to the couch. Then, she sat next to me and pulled me to her chest in a strong embrace and wept with me as she rocked me back and forth for a while until she was in a place to talk.

"Thank you for feeling safe and comfortable enough to grieve in this space. I felt every single part of it, and don't you dare apologize for it. You needed this. I am so, so sorry about what happened to you, Jarell. God, it breaks my heart," she sobbed. "You never deserved that, and this was never your fault. I need you to believe that. Please tell me you believe that."

I shook my head against her chest. *No. I didn't believe it.*

"Jarell… this is fully that man's doing. I don't know what else to say to ease your heart. You are not a demon. You are not a killer. You are not a homeless hobo. You are not a crackhead. You are so far from those things."

I continued sobbing like a baby as she spoke after a stretched bout of silence.

"Do you… do you remember our conversation and activity when I asked you to write what you have and what you lost?" she asked.

I nodded.

"Let me tell you what you have that you never wrote. You have a *future*. A bright one. A future you can now fully control. You are unique. Talented. You are not broken. You are wicked smart. What you can take away from this is your ability to survive. Your unique ability to navigate the world around you and understand the world for what it truly is. Your ability to give to others the way you give to your little sister that you love. And you wanna know what? You may think you can't have kids at all, but there's still hope there." Another long pause ensued. "I-I'd like to ask you a few questions, if you don't mind?"

I nodded, wiping my eyes with the back of my hand.

"Now that I know your full story, we have a ton to unpack and a ton to work through. We may not even unpack it all in the weeks we have remaining. If you can process and answer these questions, great. If you're not in a space to think or process, that's great, too. We can do it later. Just let me know."

I nodded and whispered, "Go ahead and ask."

"I'll start with this. Now that you've shared, all of this is on the line, and you're deep into the grieving process, how do you think you want to move forward? Where do you see next steps for yourself and your future after today?"

I sniveled, trying to take it all in.

"I don't know," I hiccupped. "I just... I want to start everything over. I want to move away where no one knows me and be alone and live my life the way I wanna live it and just... I don't know. I don't know how or where I'm gonna go. I don't have anybody. I don't know if I'm ready, either. But I do know I don't want to keep living like this and being reminded of everything by staying with Ma and Kylah. I do wanna work through this pain I feel on my own and in peace. But I don't wanna leave my sister behind. I'm just scared, Trisha. I'm scared as hell about all of this... him being back... I just..." I stammered.

"Understandable, Jarell. I know it's hard to articulate. But starting over is also doable with the right support and the right financial situation," Trisha said.

"I don't have support. I don't have money, either."

"Well, some of the financial pieces can be taken care of if you apply for disability through the government. Talk to your mom about this. You may have your mother's emotional support, too, if she's able to give it, but you have to be willing to start the conversation with her to help you transition to being more independent. Would you be willing to talk to her about moving out on your own?"

"Yeah, but... I don't know. I don't know how I'm gonna do this by myself, Trish. I've been independent in a lot of ways, but it's different when you gotta pay your own bills or take care of your own spot," I said.

"I understand. My advice is that you talk to your mother, and you two can plan the best course of action."

"It's not the time to do that. I can't talk to her about this yet because the last time I tried, she put me out on the street. And now, we gotta deal with dude being back." I shook my head.

"Here's a tip. When you start the conversation, lead with forgiveness in your heart if you're able. Lead with empathy and compassion, the skills we've been working on. You now know your mother's situation deeper than you ever have known, thanks to you opening up in this space here. Start by acknowledging those pieces, but also center your emotions and be honest with how you're still feeling about everything you've both been through. Please, do this *before* you insist on moving out. Again. Know your needs. You're nineteen, and for you, it's time to start your life. A new life, and your mother may understand that. You can write your own future because you have control now. Remember when we discussed control?" Trisha asked.

I nodded.

"Yeah. You have control, dear. Way more than you think. Continue to think about these things. You can leave your mom's house when you're ready and when you have the proper financial and emotional support. Your sister will still be there. She can even visit you. I'm just giving you opportunity to think about your options because you do have them. But before all of this, you have to put that monster in jail, first. You cannot ruin your future by seeking the kind of revenge you're thinking of."

"Trisha..." I attempted to object, but I was just too exhausted.

"Listen to me, Jarell. Please. The first step to healing and closure with Nathan is wrapping him up with the law. Please don't mess around. He could hurt your mother. Your sister. Your ex-girlfriend. You cannot leave him on the streets like this. He is a danger to everyone, and his trafficking crimes obviously run deep across state lines. There is probably another family he's got in bondage right now that are just like you and your mother. Don't wait on this any longer." Trisha encouraged.

"I hear you." I sniffed. "Can I stay here for a little while longer?" I asked. "I don't wanna leave here yet. Please."

"Today, I can accommodate for that. My client after you has canceled their appointment." She hugged me tighter and I melted in tears in her arms again. "Take as much time as you need."

Chapter Twenty-Six

Point of View: Jade Williams

I never thought I'd be driving up this cul-de-sac again in Ladera Heights, but here I was on this lovely, sunny Friday after school, jeopardizing a nice day to try, once again, to make amends with Janet Robinson. I never canceled our "appointment" the way I wanted to last week, which I was thankful for. This visit was desperate, and unfortunately, I needed her.

When I pulled up to the house, I checked out the street and next door's driveway for any unusual cars or people I didn't recognize. A heightened sense of my surroundings nowadays was paramount. I didn't even like being outdoors or in public anymore because I felt so exposed. So vulnerable. Like I was gonna get kidnapped again.

I damn near sprinted to the front of the house and used the spare key to let myself inside. Today, Janet wasn't in the living room sipping on wine or reading some fashion magazine. But a faint smell of seasoned grilled chicken lingered in the air, which led me to the next part of the house.

"That must be you, Jade!" she called out before I stepped into the kitchen and dining area.

"And you're right," I replied the second I appeared in her line of sight.

"Figured."

She didn't provide me with any additional acknowledgement after that. She just moved past me to put an empty plate from lunch or whatever into the sink and clear the kitchen counter. Had me standing there looking all types of crazy.

To lessen the tension in the air, I moved deeper into the kitchen and sat at the breakfast bar, hoping to get her to even pause and give me her attention.

"So…" I started, looking around, cutting into the awkward energy. "You know why I'm here. I don't know where to start other than to apologize for how things went the last time we spoke here."

"Mmm hmm," she turned towards me and responded with puckered lips, leaning against the counter. "You apologized on Easter, so is there anything new you have to add?"

"I just want us to get along, Ma. The way things used to be, but with new boundaries," I confessed.

She blinked like I had misspoke or something. "Boundaries?"

"Yeah. Boundaries. You don't have any excuses not to follow them either like me 'living under your roof, so I have to play by your rules' anymore. I'm eighteen with my own crib and my own gig. You support me for nothing emotionally, mentally, financially, none of it so you can't say you won't respect my boundaries because of any of that either. I'm only here because I care about having a long term, healthy relationship with you. Other than that? I would have no need for you. So, you willing to hear me out or what?" I asked with my arms stretched out.

Momma stared at me for a long time, sucking the inside of her cheek like she was trying to think of some slick comeback, but she rolled her eyes as I watched her come up empty.

"Fine. What are your so-called boundaries, Jade?" she uttered.

"Hear me loud and clear. If you can't respect these boundaries, we cannot, and I mean *cannot*, continue having this mother-daughter relationship you want, alright?"

"Girl just tell me these damn 'boundaries' and stop talking to me like I'm your little child!" she shouted.

"Fine. Boundary number one. You don't get to control who I date or who I have sex with. That's none of your business. You can comment all you want about it, but you're not gonna try and control it by harassing me or harassing whoever I'm with. Boundary number two. You don't get to verbally abuse me. That's over with. Your job raising me is finished, so you getting to say whatever you want, whenever you want, however you want to me without a clap back isn't gonna fly. I will not respect you if you don't respect me, and that's on period. And boundary number three. You will never threaten or put your hands on me again. I make my own money and pay my own bills. You literally own nothing of mine, and that includes my body. Keep your hands to yourself. There. Are we clear on this?"

The entire time I listed these boundaries, she huffed, puffed, rolled her eyes, smacked her lips, and shook her head. The whole nine. Did she even hear any of it? Mainly, the bigger theme – *I'm grown as hell?* What was with her?

"Are you done?" she asked with hiked brows.

"Yeah, I am. Are we clear on it?" I repeated.

"The only thing I'm clear on is that you don't want to be held accountable for your bad choices that I raised you not to make. You're just calling it boundaries." She shrugged.

Bad choices? I chuckled in my throat. Something was wrong with her. She needed to be in therapy just as much as Jarell did. That little crutch she held about her past was getting old. An excuse. Who cares she got knocked up young and ditched by some thug? She made that choice to open her legs, so she needed to also suffer the inevitable that came with being a parent – something as simple as their child having their own life.

"Momma, why can't you just accept the fact that I'm grown up, now? Did you think you were gonna control me all my life? I mean dang, I don't know what it's like as a mom, but ... did you ever anticipate that one day, I'd grow up?" I asked.

I don't know what the hell Janet was thinking about. What if I never had Corey to help raise me? What kind of person would I be? Did he provide the balance in my life, or did I just know better?

"I've already explained myself to you, Jade. I'm not gonna repeat myself," she replied and pulled out her phone, scrolling through it.

"I get it. You don't want me to make the same mistakes that you did. Cool. Understandable. But you're taking this way too far. I've messed with no one anywhere near the caliber of my daddy. At all. Ever. Why can't you see that I'm already established? At eighteen? Why you so hellbent on focusing on what could go wrong rather than giving me props for everything already going right? That you've had your hand in?"

Smacking her lips and throwing her phone down, she stood up and spoke with a harsh edge.

"Jade, you have to understand that all this dance mess can end with a bum lowlife and a pregnancy! What gig and money you gon' make with a baby in ya belly that the nigga won't look after? You're not going to college. I didn't and have never pressed you about that. I even let you go to the high school of your choice with Laurie. And hell, if I hadn't been riding your ass all the time, you'd probably be a high school dropout because you rely so much on dancing!"

I smacked my lips and tried to protest, but she stopped me with a firm hand up.

"You don't understand that your body changes after a baby and some folks will replace your ass so quick during your pregnancy and maternity leave that you get forgotten about. Then you're confused when you return. Especially in an industry like dance. You think Alise won't do that to you because she's tryna get her bag with all her new changes at the studio? Then what? Your problem is that you trust that bitch too much. Don't you understand me?" she asked with her arms out.

I looked away with crossed arms as she continued.

"I had to be hard on you about something! If I was gonna accept you not going to college, then I had to make sure you had decent high school grades, set you up to where you get to a decent bag, and make sure you were hooking up with a decent man! AGAIN. Mind, Money, and Man. Because if you get knocked up without a decent man with money, where were you gonna get it without depending on me? I ain't tryna take care of no thirty-year-old down the line and her child!"

I shook my head. If I was born a boy, would there be the same level of fuckery? Instead of breaking her neck trying to prevent me from getting pregnant, hell, why not teach me how to be safe if I was gonna engage in it? Why not talk to me about my options for birth control?

I only knew about the pill, condoms, and abortion as pregnancy prevention. Abortions were in moments of desperation, not prevention. I had knowledge of these three options because of health class, not Momma. I've heard of others in passing like the shot and the ring but was scarce on the details of how they worked. I mean, I could've looked it up, but there were too many resources to even sift through to find out what was actually true. Seeking out information directly from Momma was a death sentence, even if I was asking about it to be well-informed. Even if it was to have safe sex with Mike, the guy she literally broke her back for me to be with.

Damn, man. There was no way I should've been scared to have sex because of my own mom and what she'd think. Jarell's lack of fertility was what made me so comfortable to go forward with the act other than my feelings for him, and that right there was the problem.

I wish I could tell her these things. So many other things too, but Hell would freeze over before she'd be willing to hear it. Maybe if we can get our relationship salvaged back together, and I can see that she would actually follow the restrictions I've set, I could have a truthful discussion about things moms and daughters talk about one day.

"Look Momma. I get where you coming from. I do. But listen. These boundaries still stand. You have to trust that you've raised the woman you wanted me to become, even if I do make mistakes. Alright? You can't protect me from everything. I'm not gonna get pregnant. I'm not even seeing anyone. I just want to live my life free from your scrutiny. Please. I want us to repair and grow, but I can't do it if we're gonna continue operating like this," I pleaded.

For a long time, the silence expanded between us with my eyes begging her to just agree as she looked me up and down, but her eyes showing that she was also truly considering it.

"Please," I whispered.

Licking her lips, she closed her eyes and nodded after an exhale.

"Fine, Jade Anastasia. I don't have anything else to add or say."

Letting out a huge breath out in relief, I held my hands on top of my head.

"Thank you. Thank you for finally just hearing me out. I don't want us to keep arguing and going back and forth. To be honest, and Corey reminded me of this, but you all I got as family. I can't have us in a toxic situation, Momma. For real. So, I hope you're genuine about this," I said.

She stopped moving and looked me dead in the face before speaking. "I'm gonna try to the best of my ability. I won't be perfect, but I'll try."

Wow! This couldn't be the Janet I grew to know.

"I'll take that." I nodded.

Now, both of us sat in a weird stillness, looking around at everything except for each other. Momma was smart enough to play it off after about ten seconds when she pulled out her phone again and pretended to be looking at something important or interesting. I couldn't blame her. I mean, it wasn't like we were about to be buddy-buddy and catch up like old time friends. I said what I had to say, and now, in her eyes, there was no real need to stay.

"I'ma..." I thrust my thumb towards the living room, "I'ma head out. Before I go though, I have a question for you."

"What is it now?" she mumbled.

"Do you know anything about Ms. Stephanie's brother, Nathan?" I asked.

She looked up from her phone with her eyes but didn't shift anything else on her body.

"Mmm, not really. All I know is that he's some transient dude who can't stay in one spot long enough for anyone to keep up with him. Don't talk to him much. Only met him twice. Why?"

Twice. Wow. So, she knew him before Easter. All this time. *Alright, Jade. Here we go. Play your cards right.*

"Okay." I took a deep exhale. "This is gonna sound real crazy, but... I'm in trouble with him. Like, to the point where I feel threatened," I confessed.

Now, I had her undivided attention. Dropping her phone, she frowned and leaned forward, her elbows resting on the counter.

"Wait a second. What?" she asked with a scrunched face.

Stick to the story you crafted, Jade. Nothing more, nothing less.

"Well, here's the deal. Long story, but I'ma make it short. So, Laurie and I kinda got this little falling out thing going on. We got into a real bad argument a couple weeks ago, and it's been brewing until we got into a fight at my apartment the last Sunday. Like, a fist fight, and I ended the friendship when it was all over."

Momma laughed out loud.

"Wait, wait, wait. You and Laurie? Fighting? For what? You gotta tell me the long version because this already don't make sense." Momma frowned.

"It's because I told her I don't like her boyfriend Martell because he almost raped her at a party when she was drunk a while back. So, we've been arguing about that, and it kinda reached a boiling point last week."

Momma pursed her lips and shook her head.

"You girls let some boy come between y'all? For real?"

"Momma, let me get to the point, okay?"

She rolled her eyes. "Go on."

"Alright, so after the fight, she tried to call the police on me, but Alise was there and witnessed it. Laurie was the one to swing first, so she kinda gave that idea up and stormed out the house." Perking up, I whipped my phone from my pocket. "Here's where it gets crazy. So, the other day, I started getting these weird text messages from unknown numbers saying things like this."

I pulled up the screenshotted messages with threats and handed it to her. She scrolled through each one with a frown.

"What the hell... this is insane," she whispered. "This is from Laurie? I don't believe it. Where does Stephanie's brother come in?"

I licked my lips and nodded.

"Good question. You know me, and you know I know Laurie too well. Her sending threats like this just didn't seem like something she'd do, even if we're falling out. Like, she ain't even built like that, and you know that too," I began as she nodded in agreement.

"So, Easter hits, and when I came to the house to talk to you, Laurie answered the door at first, and had a little chip on her shoulder. But after I talked to you and I went outside to get some air and then came back in, her uncle answered the door after. He was real chippy and mean to me. Like he knew some things. It low-key had me shook."

I shivered just thinking about his eyes. He had the kind of look you'd have nightmares about, and I wouldn't be surprised if Jarell still did at this point. That man was different than any other person I'd ever met. His vibe and energy screamed hostile... and ruthlessness.

"Hmm, now that you explain this, there was a bit of tension between you two when Stephanie introduced you to him," Momma pondered with her index on her chin.

"See... I know. If you even picked it up, I know it's him, Momma. He's the one sending me threats, and he gotta get dealt with. Who do you know that can stop him? I don't want to go to the police right now, especially since I'm so involved with this other case."

She paused and put a hand up.

"Hold it. I ain't done. I just don't understand why a grown ass man who is barely around the city would be doing this over two teenage girls fighting about some boy. Uh uh. I ain't Boo Boo the Fool, Jade. This is bigger than you're letting on. You telling me the full truth?" Her eyes bucked.

I swallowed. What do I say now!?

"Yeah, Ma! I am! If there's anything extra to it, I don't know about it. All I know is that I got these messages and he's the one that was acting funny towards me other than Laurie. I can't think of anyone else who would send something like this because it ain't like I got a bunch of beef with anybody else," I countered.

She cut me a glare through eyes that were nearly slits. "I just find it hard to believe he'd even get involved with a bunch of petty ass female drama by trying to hurt you or threaten you about calling the police. How bad did you beat the girl up?"

"Well..." I sighed. "I mean... I had her by the shirt and almost threw her off the balcony. From the seventh floor."

Her eyes widened.

"Are you serious right now, Jade? Over a boy?"

"I know, Ma!" I yelled, and then dropped my shoulders once she gave me a look for raising my voice. I then looked away before I kept speaking. "I know. I know I messed up. But this got me scared, and I need your help. Any strings you can pull to get him to stop? Without me having to call the police? Maybe you can call them?"

She huffed.

"I'll see what I can do, but I ain't making no promises because all of this sounds absolutely absurd. You saying you want independence from me but asking me to save you from your own mistakes at the same time, which is senseless. So let this be the one and only mistake you'll make that you'll need me to save you from now on. I'll take your word for it that it's Steph's brother, and I'll think about next steps."

Again, my shoulders relaxed, and my muscles melted into Jell-O. Thank goodness!

"Thanks, Momma. Can you keep me posted?"

"Yes. I will."

"Cool. Well… that was it. I ain't gone keep you. I'ma head out and get ready for the studio. I'll also hit you up about graduation details, too," I said as I walked towards the front door.

"I'll be looking forward to it."

With that, I walked out the door, feeling like a winner. I just prayed she didn't find out anything that would make her flip the script. I just needed her to get Nathan's ass off the streets and fast.

Chapter Twenty-Seven

Point of View: Jarell Hendricks

Exhausted ain't even the word.

To keep it a buck, I ain't even know if I had the energy to sustain a desire for revenge after my session with Trisha the other day.

The only real plan I had in my head was if he and I were together all alone in an open space one on one. This scenario was unlikely to happen, but if it did, I already knew how it was all gonna go down; I could taste that blood right on the tip of my tongue. But for real. What was up dude's sleeve, anyway? He could've hurt me already if he wanted to... so what was making him drag this out?

So much shit was going on in my head, but now that he was around, making sure he hadn't gotten to Ma or Kylah yet was of utmost importance. He could have at it with me, but them? That was a different story and it had me shitting bricks.

Like every day, it was my quality time with Kylah, walking her to school on this Monday morning. Keeping her out of school to go to Alise's house was no longer an option. It would not only require me to explain the reasoning, but it would also make Kylah uncomfortable. Dumping someone else's kid on someone I barely even knew who had no clue of the situation wasn't cool. So, she had to go to school until I figured out how I was gonna tell Ma about everything.

The helpful thing Jade did do with this whole situation was sending me that picture she took of him at Laurie's place over Easter, and I had a plan to get the information I was seeking from it.

Like normal, Kylah was her cheerful self, yapping away this time about this new Disney movie Zootopia and how she got to watch it with her classmates at school earlier this week. I was half in and half out of the conversation until I just couldn't take it anymore. I was about to not only catch her off guard, but I was also about to fuck up her mood in a way that would likely mute her for much of the day at school. Which might've been a blessing for the teachers, lowkey.

"Relly, are you listening? Who would be your favorite character?" she asked, tugging onto my arm, begging for my attention.

Blinking out of meditation, I smacked my lips and looked down to her.

"Kylah, I know we're talking about Disney, but I need you to do something for me on my phone," I said, whipping it out of my old, rugged jeans pocket.

"Okay!" she exclaimed, all outta breath.

"Bet, calm down. Just gimme a second. Hey Siri," I called out.

Beep... Beep...

"Open messages from Jade."

"Here are some recent messages from Jade..."

"Ooh, is Jade coming to be with us?" she asked.

"Not today," I replied. "Stop walking for a second."

I stopped as Siri pulled up Jade's text messages.

"Here, I want you to press this picture Jade sent me," I said and handed her the phone. "And when it opens, I want you to tell me if you've ever seen this person before."

"Okay," she said, and silence followed for a little while.

"Did you open it?" I asked.

"Yes." Suddenly, her voice was as loud as a mouse's squeak.

"A'ight, so what was the next part I told you to do? Have you ever seen this person before?" I asked with a firm edge, reaching my hand out for her to return the phone.

"Umm…" she uttered, and then gave it back.

"Kylah don't play me. Tell the truth. Did you or did you not see this guy before?"

"Well…" she started as her foot moseyed around on the ground. The same way I do when I get nervous, feel anxious, or when shit gets awkward. "If I tell you, would you tell Mommy?"

"I'm your big brother. Of course, I'm not gonna tell. You trust me, don't you?"

"Mmm hmm."

"Okay, so then tell me the truth. Please."

"I see him before. He waits for me after school before I get on the bus," she revealed.

My heart fell to the pavement as my throat closed up. Fuck… fuck… FUCK!

Okay, okay, okay. Keep it calm, Rell. Keep it real cool. Breathe. Breeeeaaathhheee… just breathe. In your nose… out your mouth. You can't scream or yell. You'll scare her. Just keep it smooth. Play it off…. Wait! Don't speak yet. Take another deep breath. Breathe…

"When was this? When was the last time you saw him?" I whispered.

"I don't remember."

"Was it like… recent? Like, yesterday or sometime last week? Please, try to remember," I pleaded.

"No."

"No what?"

"Not yesterday."

"Then when was it, Kylah?" I asked, my voice raising.

"I don't remember, Relly," she whined.

"A'ight, listen. If you ever see this guy again outside, you need to run back into the school and tell your teacher, okay? I can't believe you were outside talking to strangers, and when I asked you about it before, you didn't tell me!" I couldn't help but yell as my arms flailed in the air.

"But he's not a stranger, Relly! He said he was my Daddy, and that he wanted to spend time with me," she cried.

I closed my eyes as my heart stopped again. If it stopped one more time, that might be it for me. It took everything inside not to squirm, explode, ball my fists, fidget, or anything else that showed my obvious discomfort. I couldn't believe this shit.

"And you believed him?" I asked.

"Yes," she squeaked.

"He's not your father or your dad, Kylah. He's dangerous, and I need you believe me when I say that you need to tell your teacher if you ever see him again. I can't even believe they got five-year-olds talking to people outside the school community without supervision and shit. Sick of these fucking schools. Let's go," I grumbled, held out my hand for Kylah to take and proceeded to walk her to school in silence.

She wouldn't dare say another word either because I even felt on my own heat leaving my body and roasting the bubble around us. Words didn't get exchanged until we reached the school.

"Kylah, I'm dead ass serious. Don't you play with me. If you see him at all today, run back into the building and tell someone. Don't stick around and say anything to him. Do you understand me?"

"Yes."

"Nah, like… do you understand!?"

"Yes, Relly!"

"A'ight. I'll pick you up after school, so I'll be back at two-thirty sharp. Maybe even a little earlier if I finish taking care of what I need to do today."

Without any other exchange, she walked into school, and I tilted my head back, trying to keep the anxiety at bay. What the fuck was I gonna do?

I sighed and collected myself. I'ma have to do some last-minute communication out because this shit was ridiculous, and yet, I was ready to rip anything and anyone apart with bare hands.

How the hell did he find my sister!?

I damn near ran back home and whipped out some paper, my stylus, pen, and as fast as I could within a couple hours, penned a letter to Jade. Something she could keep forever because I was at the point of no return. We were gonna have to run away and relocate or hide far, far away from here. Especially if I wasn't gonna kill him outright and get rid of him forever.

Shit!

I couldn't even think. Didn't have much time to, so I just poured out what was on my heart to her. After a couple hours of writing, I filled two pages to the end with my last words before I rushed out the door to Crenshaw to deliver it. This had to be a sprint to that school because a nigga was running out of time before all this mess caught up to me. Because he could've been meeting Kylah as recently as last week for all I knew and would be planning to meet up with her today.

~ ~ ~

I didn't expect to find myself at Ma's job hours later. At all. I had never been to La Quinta on the edge of Inglewood before and had no idea of how to even get here, but with the help of the bus app, my OrCam glasses, GPS, a few good Samaritans, and Siri, I managed to arrive around one p.m., just an hour and a half before Kylah was gonna be released from school.

After I jogged to Crenshaw High to deliver Jade's letter to the front office before hopping on the nearest bus that would lead me there, my mind raced about how I was gonna break the news to Ma about Nathan's surprise return. I ping ponged from one decision to another. It was either wait until Ma got home from work to tell her, take Kylah to a safe place after she was finished with school and then call Ma to tell her, or last, get to Ma right away, tell her, and then get the hell outta the city as soon as we could after pulling Kylah outta school.

So now, here I was to do the final option, standing in line at the front counter and doing everything I could to stay calm, grounded, and focused before I could speak to someone about

Ma's whereabouts in the building. I had already traded my OrCam glasses with regular sunglasses to conceal my eyes and identity while waiting, finding any excuse to do something before I released nervous energy out to anyone who was around me.

Now, I didn't feel another person's body heat ahead, signaling that I was next to be served.

"Can I help you?" A lady with a super light voice called out, and I moved towards it, still trying to maintain my composure.

"Hi." I cleared my throat. "My name is Jarell. Jarell Hendricks, Rachel Hendricks' son. My mom is scheduled to work here until about six or seven tonight. Do you know where she is or when she has a break?"

The stiff, professional air between us lifted and lightened after my introduction.

"Oh hey, Jarell! It's finally nice to meet you. Your mom and I are pretty cool, and she talks about you and your sister a lot. Always going on about how proud she is of both of you. But I know your mom by Radiya and not Rachel, so I hope we're talking about the same person," she said with a hint of suspicion.

"Yeah, that's the same person. Sometimes she just goes by Rachel. Do you know where she is? I need to talk to her about something. It's an emergency," I responded, adjusting my sunglasses.

"Is everything okay?"

"Yeah, everything's cool. I just need to know where she is."

"I haven't seen her since a couple hours ago. The last I saw, she got into a black truck with someone I've never seen around here before," she said.

"What?" My heart pummeled through the skin of my chest. "Do you remember what the guy looked like?" My eyes swelled.

"Um… he was Black. Tall. Dreadlocks. She seemed friendly with the guy. Like she knew him."

Huh? A Black dude with dreads? Shit... I hope she wasn't getting into the business of prostitution again. Some of those connections in my head were already starting to happen – like how she was able to afford this new iPhone she bought me?

"Did she get in the truck at the front? The back outside?" I interrogated.

"It was the back. We were both outside taking a morning break. Try checking the back again," the clerk said. "She's been back there smoking cigarettes on her breaks lately, and she's due for her next break for lunch, so she may have come back already, and I just didn't see."

"A'ight, bet. Thanks. Which way is it to the back from here?" I asked.

"Oh sure! Just head on past those doors, take a right, and then the door as at the end of the hall," she said.

"Okay, my bad, but I actually can't see. I'm blind, so if you just lead me to the doors you're talking about, I can find the rest of the way," I confessed.

She gasped.

"Oh my goodness! I'm so rude for that! You don't even look it, and your mom never told me," she said with remorse as she moved from around the counter.

"Yeah, don't worry 'bout it. If I take these sunglasses off, it'll make a lot of sense," I said. "I'm following you."

No other words were exchanged as I followed her footsteps to the door as if she herself was in a rush.

"We're here. Are you sure you don't want me to walk you to the exit?" she asked.

"Nah, I got it from here. Thank you," I said with a nod.

"Okay. Let me know if you need anything else. I can't keep the door propped open, so you'll have to go around to the front again if you want to reach the concierge."

I nodded again, just wanting her to be gone already. "Cool. Thank you."

She walked away, and I maneuvered to the back door. Feeling my way around, I found the knob and opened it, the sun rushing to my face.

I looked left and right, searching for cigarette smells. This moment was the first time I would appreciate her smoking since it would make it easy to locate her, but there was nothing.

Dang, man. Maybe she went back to work in the rooms and would be out here soon. Instead of waiting in the lobby, I sat down on the steps back here and proceeded to run myself ragged with thoughts about her ex, his motives, and my next move. Until quiet footsteps through the hot breeze interrupted my thoughts enough for me to daze out. Just to see if I was hearing things that weren't there.

But then, the safety clicked on a gun. Before I could protect or brace myself, that window of decision closed in an instant.

"Get your mothafuckin' ass in the truck, nigga. Now!" the ambiguous person growled into my ear, startling the hell outta me as the cool, heavy metal of a gun thrust against the back of my neck, pushing my head forward.

What the...!?

"Damn," I hissed and stiffened. Resisting for a second, a few thoughts flashed through my mind. Are there surveillance cameras back here? Should I fuck this nigga up right here and throw him off guard the way I knew I could? Was he with more than one person? Who was around right now? Should I yell or scream to alert people walking or drivers who might be around the way? Damn, it man... I ain't have time to think!

"Nigga, get a fucking move on! I ain't playing with yo' ass. Gimme your phone and get yo' goofy ass in the truck before I put a bullet in you in front of your momma, mothafucka!"

Oh, this must be that dread head nigga 'ol girl in the front was talking about. Damn, this nigga got Ma? Were they together? Was he one of those hitmen from the first time Jade and I got kidnapped? I didn't recognize his voice from the last time, but that ain't mean it couldn't be the case. Now I had one choice and one choice only.

With a tight grip, whoever this dude was took me by the tricep and yanked me up real close to him and kept his gun at my waist. This man must've had a silencer or something because it was still broad daylight out here. He wasn't gonna shoot me, but I ain't wanna make no assumptions, either. Niggas was crazy these days, and I had no idea who else was around.

After I gave up my phone, he tossed it on the concrete somewhere and pushed me as I stumbled over my own feet before he opened what I think was a truck door and threw me inside. As soon as I was in, familiar whimpering, groans, and sniffles met my welcome in a blubbering mess. Like English was trying to come out, but it was super muffled.

"Ma!" I whispered. "What the hell is going on?"

Her crying continued without an answer. Instead, some slight shuffling in the front of the truck occupied the pocket of silence before a deep, rugged voice rang out directly in front of me.

"Did I tell you to speak, Jarell?" The voice was so memorable, so triggering that I gagged. And then gagged again to the point where the contents of my stomach filled my mouth.

"You always had such a bad habit of speaking out of turn, but I'm about to shut that down. You say one more word, and I'll off your punk ass like I've been wanting to do since you were fucking eleven years old. If stupid ass people would've done their jobs like I asked them to a few weeks ago back in Fresno, you'd already be dead. But it looks like I gotta do it myself... which might be better anyway."

I swallowed the contents of my mouth, but it came right back up. Again and again.

"And if you throw up in my truck, I will put a fucking bullet in your forehead right now!" he bellowed.

I should just rush his ass and crash this damn car if he pulls away, I thought, but the moment the thought was complete, the heaviness of another firearm met my nose, and then my skull. Damn. More than one person.

"Don't you even think about doing shit, mothafucka! I see it all in your eyes," the guy who wasn't Ma's ex and had dragged me to the truck seethed. The cool metal created a dent in my forehead as he pressed harder, causing Ma to cry even louder.

"Shut up, bitch!" another unrecognizable voice yelled.

Her hushed screams came to a stop as my worst nightmare in the front seat chuckled in his throat.

"Glad you set them straight. Knew I could count on y'all," he said to his apparent hitman. "But Jarell, you made it easy for us. Didn't have to try and find where you'd be, and you came right over to your mom's job. For what?" the scumbag asked.

In response, he laughed at my silence.

"Well alright, folks!" he yelled out with grandiose enthusiasm. "Sit back and enjoy the ride. We're about to pick up my precious daughter from school. Well actually, my lovely girlfriend back there who ran away will pick up *our* daughter, and then we're going to take a nice little ride up north where we used to stay. Have a little family reunion, shall we?"

Goddamnit! *Not Red Bluff.* My head fell back, and the tears seared the corners of my eyes, but they abstained. But damn that pressure behind the eyes was real.

At some point, I had another choice to make. Be willfully killed in front of my sister and Ma and traumatize them forever being in the presence of my dead body, be killed tryna fight back, or just succumb to his plan and pick my battle later. I knew what I wanted to do. But with these guns pointed at my head? The last thing I needed was for the bullet to hit me, travel, and then strike Ma in the midst.

I squeezed my eyes shut.

Fuck!! A nigga did NOT plan for this shit to happen.

I don't know what to do!

Chapter Twenty-Eight

Point of View: Jade Williams

Only two weeks left. Two weeks. That's it, and then I walk across the stage and leave this dumb ass school for good. My mind was so preoccupied with Nathan, Jarell, my mom, and just being on edge all the time that the measly six weeks I was so worried about flew by like the speed of light.

However, the more I sat around here watching some of the Sophomores rise into the new Junior D-Block class, and the current Juniors ready to take the place of us Seniors for the throne, the more my mind pondered on Jarell's mom and her lawsuit against the school. Because other than the tight security and school resource officers patrolling the Junior and Senior wings while making some of them clean up graffiti in the hallways, these fools were preparing for a shift and change in D-Block "leadership." As if there was no lawsuit or community unrest about everything that had transpired this year.

It was fascinating, yet at the same time, disheartening.

Although I spent most of my days loving this school and all the shenanigans we got into, the memories came flooding of the many crazy times on D-Block hall as I sat dazed in Trigonometry.

We pickpocketed money outright from people we didn't deem worthy of walking through our hall. Especially if they looked weak.

We jumped anyone who dared to talk back or stand up to us.

We ribbed anyone who wasn't wearing any of the latest styles or fashion... or if their hair was wack.

We poured baby oil on certain parts of the hallways and watched people fall to their demise and laughed our asses off if they got injured.

We threw Freshmen in garbage cans if they graced our hallway.

We threatened teachers who gave us bad grades or if they dared to call the principals on us. Especially if we were athletes.

We brought weed to school. Pills to school. Booze to school in water bottles.

We were a fucking nightmare.

My stomach churned. We did and said horrible stuff to people, but somehow, I was the only one to walk out of that group changed. Jarell had made my tables turn and turned me upside down that day in late August earlier this school year. The day I learned he was the most bullied person of our Senior class, and I hadn't even known him. He had bumped Martell in the hallway by accident, and Martell told him to commit suicide.

Crazy because it wasn't the first time someone on D-Block publicly invited a non-member to end their own life, and I wasn't fazed all those other times when the invitation was extended, either.

But on that late August day? It was a little millisecond ... right after Martell spilled the insult from his lips that Jarell displayed his pain. A raw emotion lodged deep in his blind eyes. A look so poignant, my heart almost stopped. Then, like he knew his eyes showed way too much, he made it disappear. But it was too late; I had already seen it. And it shook my ass to the core.

I will never, ever forget that day or that look in Jarell's eyes.

Now? I found it hella disappointing that not a single member of D-Block who are Seniors, at least from what I could see, didn't feel remorse or moved at all by the pain they inflicted on others at any point of their time here. How were they gonna function in the real world without shitting on and bullying everybody else as a high?

And then the victims of our bullshit.

I was sure so many of them wanted to see every penny snatched from this school as a result from Jarell's mom's lawsuit, if they even knew about it. And possibly would want to have its doors closed forever. I wouldn't be surprised if many of their parents co-signed to be a part of this lawsuit. I just prayed they didn't because I ain't want nobody coming for my throat and my money, claiming that I bullied their kid or because I was guilty by association.

BRRRIIINNNNGGGG!!!!

The bell for sixth period jolted me out of my full-on daze, prompting me to rise and scurry out the classroom. First one out. Again, I ain't know why I was rushing because I wasn't heading to my final class for the day. Instead, I had an appointment in the office, which I dread more than going to the class in which I had almost drowned. Literally talking to anyone at this school had me irritated.

I slithered and twisted past bodies from the upper classmen to the lower classmen as I made my way to the main office and sat in the waiting area early until the secretary told me it was okay to go into my guidance counselor Mr. Dyan's office.

When I walked inside, his tall, slender body sat behind the desk as the light above him made his bald brown head look like a bowling ball. So much so, I almost chuckled at it.

"Good afternoon, Jade! Good to see you again. Have a seat." He motioned with his hand towards an empty seat in front of me, and I took the invitation and slouched back. His fingers clickity clacked across the keyboard of his computer with narrow eyes to see the details of whatever was showing on the screen before he perked up and gave me a smile with all teeth.

"Alright! I was just reviewing your fourth quarter grades and teacher comments. It's looking like you got yourself caught up on all your schoolwork that you missed, Jade," he said. "Grades are in for those missing assignments, and it looks like the results have risen you to a passing status. I thought I was going to have to meet with you a lot longer than we need to come up with a plan of how you are going to pass and develop some alternative suggestions to help you towards degree status, but you're on track to graduation. Congratulations!"

"Thanks, Dr. Dyan," I said with a wry smile.

"What's with the long face? Aren't you excited?" He smiled big with his hands out in question.

"Of course, I am. I can't wait to get up outta here," I mumbled, shifting my eyes away from him and his cheesy ass grin.

I'ma be real, I never did like dude. He was always tryna make it seem like he was better than all the other people who looked like us around here. Always preaching about pulling up our pants, pulling down our shirts, or that words like 'finna' are slave mentality language. To him, somebody was always gonna work at McDonald's for the rest of their lives if they didn't go to these stupid ass, meaningless classes like Calculus. Nobody liked this cornball or his mixed kids he was always bragging about with their ivy league statuses.

"So that means you're celebrating by going to prom this weekend, right?" he asked.

"Nah. I'm not going." I shrugged.

"Why not? Not the Miss Queen Bee Jade Williams, right? You lived for this moment!" He sat back with curious eyes, yet a kind of devilish smirk that radiated some message I didn't quite understand.

"I'm just choosing not to. It's that simple," I replied.

"Well... suit yourself, I guess. The important part is getting across that graduation finish line. Don't you see what happens when you get rid of these no-good thugs and crooks in the hallways and focus on your goals and your schoolwork? You see success. I always had faith in you, Jade and felt like you were so much better than who you hung around. I'm glad you came to your senses and stopped being someone you weren't. You can leave people like that behind and let them fail on their own. Either dead on the street or in prison, because that's their only two options. Not some rapper or the NBA."

I took long mug with my eyes from his head to where I could see him, as he sat at his desk. I smacked my lips and gave him a long side eyed glare before grabbing my backpack to stand up. He had some nerve...

"Bye, Mr. Dyan," I said and proceeded towards the door, but stopped just as I was about to turn the knob. "You wanna know something?"

"What don't I already know, Jade?" he asked, intertwining his fingers.

"Whether or not I made the grades to graduate this year, I still woulda been just as successful without a high school diploma. I make more bag than you ever will with your fake, plastic surgery wife and your uppity kids. Folks that look like you and me make it every day without this shitty school system with people like you running it. Whether they wanna be a rapper, NBA player, or not."

Without giving him a chance to respond with that blank ass face, I walked out of his office, hopefully, for the very last time. Aggravated, I walked past the front office counter, ready to finish up my day when the secretary called out my name.

"Jade! Slow down! Come back, please."

I whirled around, tilting my head all the way back and throwing my hands in the air. "Hugh. What is it now?"

"I got a letter this morning from... Jarell Hendricks, I believe? I think he was a former student here. He asked me to deliver it to you," she said, holding out a white envelope towards me.

Baffled, I frowned and walked towards the front desk. She had some nerve referring to him as a former student. As if he wasn't supposed to be in school right now and walking across the stage in two weeks. As if this school didn't force him to drop out.

"Huh? A letter to me? From Jarell?" I squinted.

"Yes." She nodded with wide eyes.

"Are you sure?" I asked.

"I'm positive, Jade. He came here around ten or eleven o'clock and told me to deliver it to you. He didn't say much after that. He just walked out and left," she replied as I took the envelope from her.

Immediately, without opening it, I swiped my hand across the middle of the envelope and felt the raised bumps of Braille. Hmm...

"Well… okay. Thanks, Ms. Brand," I said, still reluctant before walking out of the office.

Alright, this was throwing me off. Why was Jarell writing me a letter in a language I wouldn't be able to understand? Why couldn't he just text me? He had an iPhone now, and he could've used Siri to send me a message. Even if it was a long one. Why didn't he just do that?

As I strolled down the hall, not in any rush to go to Gym, I pulled the letter from its cover and opened it. Nothing but a white paper with raised dots going down the entire page. There was very little white space without Braille writing.

Wow!

What the hell was this about!?

He had a lot to say, but now, the shit was scaring me.

I had no idea what to even do. Who was supposed to translate this thing? Did he do this on purpose to leave me to figure this out? I couldn't talk to his Special Education teacher, Ms. Jenson. I didn't want her reading this and knowing anything about Jarell's business or his whereabouts, but she was literally all that I had. Maybe she had a community of individuals who knew Braille and could connect me with another educator somewhere who had no ties to Jarell who could read this for me. I mean, because how else would I do it?

Without another moment of second guessing and planning, I walked straight to Ms. Jenson's office, hoping she was there and not working with another student. I mean, I couldn't see why she wouldn't be in her office; when Jarell was here, he was her whole life. The woman barely left his side, so now that he was gone, who else could she possibly follow around?

Sure enough, when I went in, though, she was in a meeting with five other adults I had never seen in our building before. Fuck. I couldn't just barge in with my emergency, but I wasn't leaving until I could talk to her. I ain't care what she was doing because something just didn't sit right with me about any of this.

I sat outside her door in the hallway until it looked like her meeting wrapped up. Immediately, I stood and walked in her room as her colleagues mingled with one another, conversations about business completely absent from the space.

"Jade! Hey... long time no talk. What's up? You need something?" Ms. Jenson asked with a big grin. So ironic. Because she hated my ass not too long ago. Not until she saw that Jarell and I had a thing.

"Yeah, I do. Do you know anyone other than yourself who could translate a letter in Braille for me? I need to know. Like, as soon as possible."

"Is everything okay? Is this about Jarell?" Ms. Jenson questioned, her smile fading away as she scanned me from head to toe.

"Yes, it's about Jarell, but I can't give you details, and I can't have you read this letter either. I need someone who doesn't know him to read it," I said.

"Well, it's your lucky day because all of us in here in our meeting work with either the deaf, hard of hearing, or the visually impaired. Susan over there is the Braille language teacher over at Hamilton, and then Patricia is the other Braille language teacher at Lincoln. I'm sure they can help you with whatever you need." She pointed.

I probably folded inwards by the time I let out that huge gust of air stuck in my belly and chest in relief.

"Thanks, Ms. Jenson. I'll ask them."

"Okay. Keep me posted if everything is alright. I miss Jarell, and I wish the best for him."

Nodding, I skirted around Ms. Jenson and introduced myself to one of the Braille language teachers, Patricia, and gave her a full run down of the help I needed. She explained she would need to sit down in a private space somewhere in this school building to read the letter, as her hands would need to touch it and since it was meant to be confidential. I knew just the place.

The school courtyard.

Nobody ever went there, surprisingly. Maybe because it was too out in the open for folks to do horrible shit in which they wouldn't be able to get away with. Which was why the whole fight with Jarell and Martell a couple months ago in the same area got broken up before it could get too deadly.

I led Patricia to the courtyard after giving Ms. Jenson my gratitude and farewell. She and I set up shop on a bench with a mini table as I handed the letter over to her.

"So, Patricia. Thanks for translating this for me, but whatever is in this letter cannot be shared. I'm serious. I don't want anyone getting into trouble," I warned again.

"I'm fully aware of confidentiality, Jade," she said with a tinge of annoyance.

"I'm just making sure. Thanks again for doing this because you don't have to."

"No problem," she said as she unfolded the letter, put it on the table, and put both hands across the Braille writing. "Here we go!"

Dear Jade,

I pray these aren't my last words you, but I wanted to write you this letter in case they are. Bad news. I found out Nathan been talking to Kylah at her school outside this morning. We're all in deep trouble at this point, Jade, and I know he's gonna show up real soon. I might die in the process, but I'm okay with that. In case these are my last words, I want to tell you a few things.

I'll first start by saying that therapy has been life changing for me. I've only been in for about three weeks, but those sessions have made me think about my life in ways I never have before. It's opened my eyes to the deepest, darkest corners of me and brought them to light so I can begin to process and work through them instead of hiding it all. I'm not close to healing yet, but I am proud to say I don't regret going to therapy at all. Thank you for being the one to push me.

Honestly? I need to thank you for a whole lot more. I'm happy I opened up my heart just a little bit to let you in, and I'm even happier you opened your heart to allow me to see the real you. All that other image shit you were trying to uphold and all that... that part of you I don't even see anymore. Barely remember. I see someone who cares. Who loves. Who is loyal. Who will go to bat for the people close to you. I appreciate that about you, Jade, and I am indebted to you. For saving my life in more ways than jumping in a pool. I need you to know that there is no one else in the world right now who has my heart the way you do.

But this is what I also need you to know. If I make it out alive with this Nathan shit, I'm asking for this simple request. I ask that we separate. No being lovers, no being in a relationship, a couple, friends or associates. Nothing.

I know this sounds harsh. You might still think I'm hung up on everything that happened on my birthday, but I'm not. If I make it out alive, Jade, I plan to move away to start my life over. I want to leave everything behind just to focus on me. I need to take this new journey alone. Honestly? I hope we don't see each other at all. Maybe for some years. Maybe even for some decades. I just need time. I can't keep facing you while being a version of myself I hate and a version of myself you don't deserve. You deserve love from me when I am able to give it.

I gotta come to terms with the past. I need to find forgiveness not only for myself, but for my Ma. I don't even know how I'm gonna pull this off, but I still got so many areas where I need to address my demons and grow. I pray you find these things, too. And I pray you get better friends because I'd hate to see you again just to be around trash ass people you hang with, and then the next thing I know, I'm backsliding into a space I don't want to be.

I hope to get my GED one day. That I get to be in the workforce and not living under Ma, using her as a crutch and for money. I want to be independent and happy. You're probably wondering who I would talk to or be with on this new path, but I plan to get a guide dog to help with healing. I'll be fine.

I want to finish up by saying that we've been through a lot in such a short time, and you will always have a special place in my heart. But this is what I need. I finally realize that the best thing you ever did for me was to break up with me. It was the best thing for you, too.

Please don't come to my mom's house looking for me or to even fol-low up after this letter. Like I said. If I make it out of this alive, I will be long gone, as much as it hurts me to leave my sister behind. If you'd like, keep in touch with Kylah, especially if Nathan doesn't take them away. Please. She loves you, and she needs someone that is some sort of extension of me, because she's going to be lost with-out me here.

Anyway. Thank you for everything, Jade. This shit hurts to write, but it's time for me to love me a little more. At least for a little while. Actually, a long while.

Until we meet again,

Jarell Hendricks

Before Patricia even finished, I was already bawling. This was absolute horrible news. Nathan found Kylah? How!?

"This sounds pretty serious," Patricia whispered with a sol-emn look.

"I know. Thank you for reading," I said and reached my hand out for her to give up the letter, which she did without hesitation.

"Well… I will leave you be to process this. Good luck, Jade. And good luck to that fella, Jarell, too."

I wiped at my eyes with a nod. "Thanks."

When she gathered her belongings and walked away, I texted Momma immediately. Did she do what she was supposed to do and handle Nathan like I asked her to? Because I mean shit, if she did, Jarell may not be in as much trouble as the both of us might think.

With the jitters, I waited for her reply, and when the buzz came, the dreaded two letter word appeared.

A plain old, "No."

With no other words before or after. No context. No explana-tion. No nothing.

I buried my head in my hands, cried some more, and grappled with so many different options and routes I could go with this. I could call the police. I could hurry up and take Jarell and his family back to Corey's spot for safety. I could try and confront Nathan myself and beg him to leave Jarell and his family alone with a prayer that he wouldn't hurt me again in the process. But most of all, I couldn't help but continue to ask…

Why were Jarell and I kidnapped in the first place? Why did Nathan just stand there when we were trapped in that warehouse basement as four other guys had their way with us, but he just acted like he was there for the show? Why didn't he just reveal himself and hurt Jarell when he had the chance? I was just so lost, but with everything unfolding the way it was now? This had become exponentially more dangerous.

After a moment of staring at Momma's response, I just broke down.

None of this was gonna end well. And for some reason, I got a queasy feeling… a deep, deep sick feeling in my gut that I was already too late. Something in the wind told me I would never see Jarell or his family again.

Chapter Twenty-Nine

Point of View: Jarell Hendricks

This ride had an uncanny familiarity. Roped wrists. Cramped in a trunk. Hella bumps and potholes along the way.

But this time, it hit different.

Ma and I's bondage in the trunk with the backdrop of Kylah's mindless, innocent giggling and laughter in the front seat while Nathan cooed and played with her on an iPad was a level of disrespect and mind fuckery I had never experienced in my life. It had Ma's eyes flooding like river overbanks as the tears dropped onto my shoulder and me sitting with a rage so tangible in my chest, I could've had a heart attack. I told Kylah to run into the school to tell someone if she saw him again. But Ma and I had an unspoken agreement. We wouldn't scare Kylah by letting out any peep of distress back here. We were on the same page with that.

The ride to Red Bluff lasted just as long as the ride to Fresno. When we came to a complete stop, whoever the driver was put the shift into park and sighed a breath of relief and exhaustion.

"Okay, my sweet baby girl," Nathan said as soft as a feather. "We're home. I know that was a long ride, but you did such a good job. We're gonna go inside and you can take a nap, play the iPad, or watch TV in my room, okay? Then we'll go out for ice cream."

"Yay!" she exclaimed.

"Alright. Let's go."

"Will Mommy and Relly be coming with us? Relly told me not to talk to you. So will he come, too?"

"He told you not to talk to me?" Nathan asked as I clenched my fists. If I could whoop Kylah's ass, I would.

"Well…" her voice drifted as if she felt like she had done something wrong.

"Don't listen to your stupid brother. I am your father. I proved that to you. Weren't you happy to see your mother and I together when we picked you up from school?" he asked her.

"Yeah!" she cried with joy.

"I knew you would. Let's go on in, okay? I'll get you tucked in Daddy's big plush bed, and you can watch TV or play on the iPad for a little while, and then I'll come get you to head out. What's your favorite ice cream?" Nathan asked.

"Chocolate! With sprinkles." I could just hear the beam in her voice.

The innocent little voice that was about to be defiled. Just the thought of what Nathan would do to her in that bedroom led the tears to flow immediately. I bit down on my lip as hard as I could to prevent a tearful gasp to be heard, which made my body shake. I was only consoled by Ma leaning her head against my shoulder.

When Kylah's little voice no longer squealed and had faded off in the distance as she yapped away at her dad, the trunk door flew open, and multiple guys hemmed Ma and I up and out the back, dragging us towards what I believed to be our old spot in Red Bluff. It definitely smelled and sounded like it, anyway. Country ass air with the stench of manure drifting with the wind as we were situated right off a county highway further up ahead.

As they hauled us away, to be real, I ain't even resist. My body flopped around like a fish as I let them manhandle us. I wasn't finna give them any kind of energy, knowing it needed to be saved for Nathan and Nathan only if, somehow, we could get it in on one on one. Fighting these bitch ass niggas wasn't even worth it. Not at the expense of dying in front of Ma. With the way she was screaming and wailing, my body in dead form would end her. Kylah didn't need us both gone.

Our final destination wasn't the main house, where I expected us to go. Instead, we went to a little shed on the same property. The same one Nathan forbade me to go as a kid when Ma would come and go here sometimes, and I never knew why. As an older teenager, I could make my guesses as to what and why she had gone in there, but I ain't wanna think about it now.

Ma didn't resist too much either as her cries remained stifled with something either covering her mouth or face. Once we were secured and tied up to our chairs, Nathan came and made his way back into the picture with inaudible words exchanging between him and his men before Nathan said to someone, "You stay. I need you here for this."

Multiple shoes stomped across the cement and out the door before the shed went quiet.

"So..." Nathan's footsteps crept closer between us as Ma whimpered and sniffed. "We meet again, Rachel. Or is that... *Radiya*, right? Why'd you hide your identity from me for all these years?" Nathan asked with this fake affliction in his voice that made me want to rip from this chair.

A bunch of mumbles and stifled words from Ma tried to come out until a tearing sound ripped through her muffled communication, and then, clear English came through.

"Nathan... why...?" Ma sobbed. "What is it that you want? I just want you to leave us alone so that my family can be safe."

"*Your* family, huh? I don't care what you want. You lied to me! You had the child we've always wanted together, and you had the nerve to fucking run away and hide from me!? You had the nerve to think I wouldn't find out, wouldn't want to meet her, and you're talking to me about *family*?"

Then, a blow. A slapping sound that echoed off the walls, leading veins to bulge from my arms. I twisted, writhed, and jerked to escape from this goddamn chair, but I just ended up nearly flipping over, much to the amusement of his stupid ass hitman. The lucky one to stick around.

"Where do you think you're going, you dumb bastard? Who do you think you're about to try and save?" Nathan growled.

His feet rushed to me almost as fast as his voice whipped from my mom towards me when suddenly, my chest caved in as my back slammed against the backrest of the chair. My mouth dropped open, almost involuntarily, to get air, but it didn't come until after Ma's scream shattered the silence.

"Stop punching on my son!" she screeched.

Nathan chuckled out loud as soon as my lungs opened wide enough to take in air, but it seemed like my airway closed again. This scum of the earth hit me hard as hell... I just prayed I wouldn't have a heart attack or that my already fragile ribs, that he broke some years ago, didn't collapse or break again.

"That'll make him sit still for a little while," he mumbled. "That punk can save himself."

"Nathan, please. You don't have to treat him this way..." Ma begged. "You never did have to treat him the way you have. He's done nothing wrong..."

"Fuck him! He's the reason why we could never be what we could've been!" he yelled. "But you know? Now that I've found you, we can start brand new, baby. You ... me... our daughter... the way it always was supposed to be. Or should I kill you for lying and then take my daughter with me?"

I bit my lip, still struggling to breathe, clenching my stomach to let the pain pass as Ma continued crying her words out.

"I can't go with you. Please don't make me go. There is nothing left for us, Nathan. You betrayed me. You abused me, manipulated me, and you raped me for Kylah to even be here. Yes. At first, I wanted a family with you because I thought you were a good man. Someone who would take care of us and love us, and be a true family man and help me in a crisis, take my son in and..."

"Take *your* son in? Somebody else's kid?" he roared, causing even me to flinch. "I don't care! I gave you the family and the kid you said you wanted, and now you want to switch things up by trying to leave me and leave our home?"

Ma said nothing.

"You know, Radiya, you caused a lot of trouble for yourself. You know that, right? Because the way everything ended up didn't need to happen the way it did. Had you gotten rid of your piece of shit son and let his bastard ass stay with his dead father's side of the family or put him in the foster system in Chicago, you could've started fresh with me. We could've lived lavish and happily ever after in Los Angeles. That was the plan. But no. You wanted to keep him. I wouldn't have had to punish you by making you a worker and punish you by making you watch me torture Jarell. We would be the happy family you wanted. But no. You decided to keep him. You decided your own fate and his fate too!"

Ha. This... *this* was why I was mistreated and abused by him? Because he didn't want to take me in, take care of someone else's child, and wanted to start his own family on a fresh slate? Nah. What a fuckin' liar. He was a *trafficker.* His agenda would've been carried out regardless. I ain't believe none of this shit he was jackin' right now.

"I just don't understand how this happened... I don't get how you found us. How you found both of my babies... how you found my real name..." Ma whined.

"You can thank your best friend Lynette and her son for all of this," he declared.

Wait a minute... Lynette...

"How the hell does he know Lynette?" I whispered out loud to nobody in particular as a sharp pain sent a lightning bolt to my chest again.

"Look, you stupid crock of shit. Stop talking out of turn! If you have questions, then ask Lynette's son right across from you," Nathan barked. "Don't you ever address me!"

I choked to death on my own spit. Lynette's son... *ALEX!?* Alex Washington? My best friend from the Wells projects who stood by my side through literally everything growing up along with Rob and Jonathan, who were now dead from a fucking shoot out, leaving me without any genuine friends? My homie for life? Was he the dread head nigga Ma got in the car with during one of her breaks at work?

"Alex?" I asked in utter disbelief. "Is that you and is that true?"

"It's him, Jarell," Ma confirmed. "I just have no idea how him and Nathan even met, and most of all, how the hell he or his mom knew I was even out here in California to tell Nathan where we were at."

"What a nice little family and friend reunion, ain't it, Jarell?" Nathan laughed like this was his favorite sitcom.

"Are you serious, mothafucka!?" I bellowed. My temperature spiked to a thousand degrees as more veins popped out from my neck this time.

"Alex, I can't believe you would do this. How could you set me up and betray us…" Ma wept, simultaneous as my outburst. "When I saw you show up to my job today, I trusted you. I was so excited to see that you were still alive, even though I was wondering how you found me. Your mom was like a sister to me… how could you?" she sobbed while a short distance away, Nathan still cackled like a hyena.

A stupid smug in Alex's voice arose in response. A non-response. "I had a job to do with a whole lot of stacks a nigga needed. Sorry."

My blood seared everything in me. Alex. Alex Washington. The boy who was at my side every day, every night like we were blood. Walked to school together, beat people up who bullied us together, who made sure we had every class together in elementary school, played with action figures together, hooped together… survived together, fought and made up like siblings together, argued over girls together. I just couldn't… This was way worse than hearing Nathan's true intentions for hating me the way he did.

It had always been this way. I was the common denominator of just not being wanted, being in the way, feeling like I was the burden on someone else for simply existing, or being loathed for being me. I don't think I could ever get used to the feeling of being seen like trash to so many people. But this shit right here with Alex? One of the only niggas who actually did value me and care about me?

I couldn't take this.

"You bitch ass nigga!" I exploded and spat towards Alex. "You gave this abusive mothafucka information about my ma because you wanted some paper? Nigga, fuck you!" I busted into sobs. "We were brothers since diapers, spent our last days surviving cross-fire. I cried for days because I thought I'd never see you again, and this is what you do?!"

"Save the speech, bruh. A nigga had to do what he had to do." The shrug was there, yet his voice held an undercurrent of something else that wasn't as insensitive or apathetic. Couldn't put my finger on it.

"I can't believe you," I wept. "We was boys, man. What did we do? What did we ever do to you? How did you even know we were here?"

This time, Alex went mute as his footsteps fell back against the wall before Nathan interjected.

"Ahh, cut the sad ass sob story. Let's get to the point and off this fucker the way it should've been done a few weeks ago. I'm sick of dragging this out."

Sending a dirty glare his direction, I spat towards him, too.

"Nah, you shut the fuck up! Let me out this chair and fight me!"

"Jarell please don't do this... please. I don't want him to hurt you, baby," Ma whined, but no one paid her any mind. Instead, Nathan drowned her out.

"Oh... pretty bold, aren't you? You talk back... and then you spit at me? Listen. You're not making it out of this basement alive no matter what. So, you get two wishes. I'll grant them, and then it's over for you. Those amateur fucks should've done what they were supposed to do to get rid of you back in Fresno. Then, you wouldn't be sitting here. But don't worry. They're no longer around, either." He snickered a sinister one. "So, as I said. Two wishes. If I don't like the wish, you lose it. Be wise."

"Answer these questions. How the hell did you find us here in LA, and what Alex gotta do with this? How do you know him?" I asked. "Tell me why you didn't just kill me when you had the opportunity in that basement a few weeks ago. Just tell me the truth, *Nathan!*" I screamed.

"Hmph..." Nathan reacted, the smirk all over his voice. "First question, I'll answer. Second question, I won't. Third question, nope. Fourth question, sure."

"Whatever, dog. Just 'fess up," I said.

"Before your buddy Alex even got involved and gave me the inside scoop about your mother's whereabouts, I had already had tabs on you to know you were in Los Angeles and that Radiya was alive. See, my sweet niece Laurie, who just so happens to be your girlfriend Jade's best buddy, told me all about you when I came to visit my sister out in Ladera Heights one day. She had come home from school upset that Jade had almost drowned in a pool in gym class and shared with the family that it was her boyfriend Jarell's fault. Knowing me, I thought, *Jarell, huh? Name sounds familiar. Tell me more about Jarell.*"

My fists clenched behind me. I knew... something in my gut told me to throw that dumb ass bitch off Jade's balcony...

"And boy did she spill those beans!" Nathan continued. "She told us, meaning my sister Stephanie, Laurie's dad, and me, all about you getting into a relationship with Jade, how nobody likes you, and all the crappy things you did to her friends, like beating them up. She even shared photos of you and Jade that had circulated around the school when Jade tried to lie and say she didn't have a thing for you.

"After she shared such vital information, she kept going. She told us that both of you were sent to the hospital after the pool drama, and she was heading there to visit Jade. But instead of letting her go on her own, I volunteered to drop her off so that I knew where you both were. As I did that, I thought:

'Hmm... maybe I can find the kids and the family members of the kids you fucked over, set up something, and have them get rid of

your ass once and for all. That way, there would be no criminal or murder trace to me for a little change in their pockets while I have someone find your mom.'

Did my research after Laurie gave me her friends' contact to set that up and had them follow Jade from the hospital all the way up until both of you went to the park. You know the rest of the story after that. But somehow, those fucking idiots let you in that basement with an ankle tracker that I still don't know why you had on. So, there's your answer. One request left."

He sighed and paced back and forth, his shoes echoing off the cement.

Surprisingly, I thought I'd be upset. Thought I'd might cry halfway through his soliloquy. Thought I'd get even more pissed or angry or whatever. But he simply confirmed what I already suspected.

Puckering my lips with a slow nod, I spoke.

"You know what, Nathan? I been waiting for this day. Play fair for once in your life. Put the guns down, take me outta this chair, and fight me. Fight me one on one."

Nathan laughed.

"Fight a little punk like you? I think you'd rather be shot in the head instead like I planned. It would be much less painful. Actually, painless."

"You scared? Is that what it is? What, you threatened by me?" I raised a brow.

"Threatened? By you? Ha! Trying to attack my ego. Oldest tactic in the book. Blah, blah," he mocked.

"If I win, you pack your shit and get outta here. You leave my mom, my sister, and me alone. If I lose, you can kill me like you been wanting to do. You can have whatever life you wanna have with my mom and sister. So, what's it gone be?" I offered.

He laughed some more.

"You think it's that easy? That I'll just 'pack my shit and go?' You're dumber than I thought. And you're betting quite a lot on yourself. It'll be like old times where I beat the crap out of you for fun. It's nostalgia for me."

"Bet," I said. "Let me out, then."

"No. I've already enjoyed my years having my way with you." He scoffed. "Sorry. All your wishes are gone."

"Aye, just fight him," Alex interjected.

"What did you just say?" Nathan whispered.

"I said, just fight him." Alex stood his ground. "If an ass whooping is what the nigga wants on his last day here, I'd say give it to him. Give him his last request he wants today. Let his ass die in pain a little bit before we give him one to the skull," he explained.

My stomach turned. How could someone like him say some shit like that? About someone he used to love? The room went quiet, the only sounds being Ma's light weeping and begging Alex not to do this.

"You know kid?" Nathan said, his voice directed away from me, so I assumed he was mentioning Alex. "I wish you were around, more. You speak my language. Untie him. Not like the blind bitch can do much."

"You got it," Alex said as his footsteps clacked towards and then behind me.

The scratchy rope against my wrists and my ankles loosened until I was free.

"I suggest you kiss Radiya goodbye because this is it for you. I'm not holding back, Jarell," Nathan said.

"When have you ever held back?" I asked while taking him up on that offer. Honestly? I was confident in my ability to fight for sure, but I just didn't know how I was gonna hold up with this dude. But I couldn't psych myself out. I knew how to handle myself if everything went according to plan.

After I gave Ma a final kiss, the room went silent except for Ma's cries, as I stepped away from her and zeroed in on my other senses on this battlefield.

I kept my breath shallow so I could hear Nathan's footsteps across the cement floor to always gauge his location. Those same footsteps that echoed in the hallway when he'd approach my door every night. Those steps had never changed. Ugh. But it made my temperature rise as the memories rushed back to me. I couldn't wait to pound him.

"You gonna make a move or what?" I cajoled.

No response. He just circled around me, sizing me up.

"You ain't ever had no problem diving right in and beating my ass before. What's with the wait? You scared now that you got a grown man in front of you, and not an eleven or twelve-year-old huh? Bust a move," I barked. "Or do you only beat little kids and women? Or are you only bold enough to touch lil' boys' dicks?"

Broke him. He rushed towards me with pure aggression. He was gonna try and football tackle me, so once he was within my bubble, before he could grab me, I braced myself, putting my weight behind my legs and swung a mighty one with my dominant left as it crashed into his cheekbone.

My knuckles split apart as his feet staggered back before his hands slapped the floor with a loud SPLAT! Hell yeah, that bitch fell on his ass no doubt. It only took one. This was my opportunity! I scurried in his direction to pin him to the ground and thrash him, but just as I moved in, his foot slammed into my knee, causing me to buckle and fall forward.

"Fuck," I hissed, gritting my teeth.

Damn, I knew better than to rush him head on. I should've approached him towards the side, but I got too excited. And it was even more unfortunate that I couldn't get up quick enough because he delivered a mighty one to the nose, knocking me straight to my back that I couldn't anticipate because I couldn't see. My face went gushing.

"Oh my God! Jarell!" Ma screeched. "Help! Somebody! Somebody help!"

"Now what? You thought that little haymaker was gonna put me out?" Nathan shouted and then punted me right in the ribs again, causing me to coil inward.

Fuck! He was as strong as I remembered. But I was smarter. I wasn't finna go out this easy, although without a doubt, my ribs were broken again. Don't matter. This pain wasn't shit to me. Low-key? It was a benefit he got me down first. It was a perfect way to think he had the advantage when I could put him right back on the defense.

The second he got on top of me and attempted to rain conscious ending blows down on me, I blocked a couple before I lifted and enclosed my arms around his body beneath his armpits, pulling him towards my chest. Now his arms had nowhere to swing. Then, with my leg, I trapped his left foot, pushed his dominant arm down, and flipped him over.

Jiujitsu sweep. Or should I say a real nigga sweep.

Within fifteen seconds, I was in the driver's seat on top. My head was now against his chest and as I nestled between his legs. My arms sprawled out and locked his arms down, again, leaving him with the inability to punch even as he attempted to deliver body blows from below. To punish him, I headbutted him right in the gut.

"You asshole!" Nathan grunted out, and somehow, went full hulk mode and beasted me right out of that lock hold, causing me to fall back. In no time, he was right on top of me again.

"You little piece of shit. This is over. I'm not about to play this game with you. Say a prayer because this ends here," he growled, the stench of his breath spraying over me.

"Jarell, he's pulling out his gun, get up! Get away from him! Nathan don't! Please! Don't shoot! Oh my God, please don't shoot my son Nathan! Ahhh!!!" Ma shrieked.

Before I could even take my next breath or even try to move from beneath him, a single, loud shot rang out.

Then, the world went still.

Chapter Thirty

***Point of View*:** Jade Williams

I refused. I refused to accept my last day of interacting with the guy I loved to be telling me that his abuser had returned to town. I refused to accept that his final words to me were that Nathan had found his sister, triggering an immediate escape situation.

I couldn't live with that on my heart. I just could not NOT see Jarell again. I barely even had a decent picture of him. The only ones I had were on Christmas Day where he opened presents, plus the ones folks took of us hugging and being together around the school to prove I was cheating on my ex, Mike Harrison. But all those photos were either low quality or low lighting. There weren't any other tangible memories of the true him that I could cherish of his handsome face without sunglasses or his hood up. I just had his origami masterpiece of me that I kept with some of my other most prized possessions, like expensive jewelry Corey gifted me as a young girl.

If only there was a photo when he showed that twinkle in his eyes which held his jest, sarcastic humor, flirting, and hints of sexual teasing towards me. The personality, a treasure, he exclusively granted to me other than to his family during his time in LA. When I worked to break all those barriers he erected over his heart and saw him for who he was? He was special. Is special. Intelligent. Sensitive. Thoughtful. Affectionate. And an empath.

I couldn't imagine harboring so much pain and anger that the real you can't even show.

I refused for Jarell to be fragment of my memory, washed up by new memories that would come in my life as I get older because we never saw each other again. I loved him. What could be done to save him safely? That didn't include endangering myself and others? But most importantly…

Why did my own momma let me down? She had one job! And now I had to think of plan C, D, and E.

Calling the police was still a huge "Hell NO." The fact that I had gotten a brand-new phone with a brand-new number, yet I had still gotten those weird text messages, I wasn't gonna take my chances. Corey was another option too, but putting him at risk wasn't right, either.

There was no one I could trust. At all. No friends. No confidants. No nothing. In some ways, I was just like Jarell in that regard.

The only place I felt like I could turn to was the dance studio. The one thing I could control. Something that brought true joy.

When I made it to Hip Hop Emporium, it was empty. Lights off, like it had closed up shop for the night. Good. I touched nothing. Instead, I turned on some dark R&B on the speakers. Partynextdoor and Sonder vibes.

And I just danced. Danced. Danced. And danced away. My soul left my body to enter the world of movement and flow. On another planet. In another dimension. No concept of time. No concept of day or night. No thoughts. No nothing. I barely heard the music. Just an intimate date with dance. The only love that hadn't let me down a single time ever in my life.

I went until my body was too sore to move. It wasn't until a voice rang out that I was brought back to semi-consciousness.

"Damn girl, I ain't seen you dance with that much passion since… I don't know. Since ever. You been working hard on your stuff, huh?" Alise smiled, holding her hands to her hips.

I just huffed and puffed, trying to calm down as I stared at her.

"So… you gon' answer me or what?" Alise asked beaming with all thirty-two. "What's the special occasion that you went so hard for? You ain't have nobody to impress up in here today, so what's up? I'm glad I got it all on camera, though. You mind if I post some of it? It was just too dope not to."

My chest heaved and heaved, then fluttered until my eyes became wet. I hadn't heard a single word she said.

"Jade?" Alise called out, her smile faltering just as quickly as my tears came.

That was it. The moment she called my name was when the inside of my body was the tropical storm and my eyes were the product, raining down on the studio's floor.

I turned away, putting my fists to my eyes to stop myself.

"Jade… please tell me what's wrong," Alise said after rushing over to me.

The last thing I wanted to hear from her was that Jarell's problems were not my own. That breaking up with him was still the best thing ever, and that I needed to focus on myself. I would've nodded my head and moved on about a year ago but now? I couldn't. I was stuck.

I simply collapsed in her arms, and we both fell to the floor against the studio mirrors, and I just laid on her lap and soaked her leggings as she ran her fingers through my pixie cut with one hand and caressed my back with the other.

Alise could forget about an explanation. Not about Jarell. Not about this situation, and definitely not how going through all of this has stripped me of everything. How the hell did I get in the middle of this shit? Seemed like everything went downhill since meeting Jarell, but I wouldn't dare blame him. Guess this was more of a reason to start new after graduation. Set new goals, make new friends, and adopt my *own* values.

The only thing that made my stomach twist about this was the *privilege*. I could do all those things with no questions asked and without many problems. It wasn't like that for Jarell or his family.

They couldn't just start over. They couldn't set new goals. They couldn't have a new outlook on life. Their past haunted them everywhere they went.

And that was what worried me. How could I walk out of this situation involving Jarell with certain advantages while he and his family still gripped onto the shorter end of the stick?

It wasn't fair.

"Jade… you're scaring me, girl. Wassup?" Alise asked after what seemed like about an hour straight of her consoling me.

"It's nothing, Lise. I can't talk about it, but I'm finna go to my momma crib right quick. I'ma catch you later," I said, rising up from the floor and her lap as quick as I could.

"Your mom?" Her eyes expanded. "You sure about this? I thought you ain't mess with her? Won't she make whatever your problem is worse?" she asked, her eyes following my every move as she still sat on the ground.

"Probably, but I gotta do this. I'ma talk to you later," I said and turned on my heels to pay my egg donor a visit. I had to go down swinging for Jarell… even if it meant telling Janet the truth. Even if it meant extracting the why behind her misstep.

~ ~ ~

This time, I wasn't going to Janet Robinson's place without support. I've learned my lesson. With the raggedy bones I had to pick with her? There was definitely going to be a need for mediation. Dad was coming along with me today. It was in Janet's best interest because at this point? Beating her ass was a real option.

Before I drove out to her place, I gave Dad a call. Didn't even fill him in on the situation, but instead, had asked for him to play facilitator because I had to talk to Ma about something that was likely gonna be heated. He didn't ask many questions, either. Good. He was probably under the assumption that this was my first attempt talking to her since the last time he and I met. I'd rather have it that way.

We took Dad's SUV in pure silence to her spot, which wasn't far from where he stayed. Her car was right in the driveway, and that made the nervous energy grow in my stomach more than before. I hadn't rehearsed lines or much less rehearse my thoughts and how I was gonna approach her. I was literally going off the strength of my emotions.

"You ready?" Corey asked with concern and giving me a onceover the second his truck was parked.

I didn't even answer him. I just got outta the car and paced up the lawn before finding her spare key where she leaves it. Letting myself in, my eyes scanned the lower living room and office area that she camped out in at this time of the night, but she wasn't there. When I heard a few dishes bang and clang towards the back of the house, I zeroed in towards my target just as Corey walked inside.

"Jade, slow down," Corey called out, but I had already disappeared to where I needed to be. And there she was, this time, taking out dishes to start making food.

"You're back," Janet said, giving me a fleeting glance as I stormed into the kitchen. "Using that spare key to your advantage, aren't you? Almost feels like you're living here again. You might as well keep it."

Janet hadn't even looked up again once she saw my appearance because she was oblivious to Dad shuffling inside.

"Momma, what the fuck? Why did you just leave me hanging like that?! I asked you to figure things out about Nathan, and you're just gonna tell me no and leave me out to dry? I can't depend on you for nothing, I swear to God!"

"Woah, woah Jade! Watch your mouth!" Corey bellowed, shoving me slightly in the back from behind.

"Oh, and you bring Corey along with that potty mouth of yours, I see? You thought he was gonna come and protect you? I'm not bothered by your little outburst, Jade. Go somewhere." Janet shrugged and waved me off.

Corey stepped forward and closed the gap between Janet and me with a frown and traded glances with us both, trying to understand what the fuss was about. All I cared about was getting to Janet, but his big body ass blocked me from being able to see her, much less get to her.

"Momma, or should I say Janet, you kill me. What's wrong with you? Why can't you ever be there for me when I need you the most? I literally told you how dangerous Nathan was, and you can't even do a favor. I don't know what to do with you anymore. I want you to be a mom I can depend on so bad, but time and time again, you show me who you are. I can't deal with it," I said, the tears bursting out like a hose.

Corey moved out the way just in time for me to see her reaction, but still remained in the middle of us. Her smirk and flat eyes held something that suggested she knew something I didn't, which prompted my fists to ball. I was milliseconds away from jumping over Corey.

"Jade, I am not gonna try and put someone in jail for threats that I don't even know he actually made. What you told me were speculations. I talked to Stephanie about the situation, and she said she has absolutely no clue what I was talking about, and that Nathan wouldn't do such a thing," Momma shot back.

Every muscle in my face tightened as my arms shot out from the sides. "Why would you go talk to her? You know she's gonna defend her brother, and she ain't got nothin' to do with this! That's common fucking sense! Why is it that you never take my word for anything? Why is that I have to bend over backwards for you to do anything for me? I told you I was in danger, and you're brushing it off like it's no big deal! You saw the text messages yourself!" I screamed.

"Jade!" Corey shouted.

"Nah, nah, it's okay, Corey," Janet said with her hands out in front of her, signaling for him to simmer down. "To answer your question? It's because I know you're lying, Jade Anastasia."

The way that calmly slipped from her lips with the straightest face in comparison to my explosion forced me to pause. Corey stood nearby with a slight frown, quietly coaxing her for more information through his eyes.

"Let me tell you something, Jade." She pointed a rigid finger at me. "I told you from the beginning that I wasn't Boo Boo the Fool. You thought I wouldn't be smart enough to ask Laurie about the fight you had with her? You think I'm that stupid?"

My heart spiked to my throat. I swallowed as my brows burrowed, feeling salty as hell.

"Yeah. Look at you. That man didn't do a damn thing, and because I know you have a petty streak about you, you're trying to drag me into doing something because of your falling out with Laurie. I know everything that happened at your apartment, but I'ma give you the opportunity to come clean. You either tell me the truth right now, or we end this here, and then your ungrateful ass can be outta here for good."

"Janet, chill. You know you don't want Jade out for good. Jade…" Corey declared in a near whisper. "Tell me what's going on. I'm confused."

"Corey, this girl told me she was in danger with some man who happens to be her best friend's uncle. Jade and her friend have some sort of petty beef, and she tried to say her friend's uncle has been sending her threats. And she asked me to send him to jail, Corey. It's ridiculous. Jade is full of shit, and I'm not going to enable her," Momma said with twisted lips and a deadpan look.

Corey turned to me and shook his head. "Did you lie to your momma about something like this? If you did, it ain't cool. This ain't something to lie about."

Janet continued her lecture. "Let me handle this, Corey. Jade, I am beyond disappointed that you had the nerve to come up in my house, demand all these boundaries and a desire for us to start fresh, and the first thing that comes out of your mouth afterwards is a lie. How can I even trust you? How can you even come up in here and accuse me of being a terrible mother when you can't even get your own shit together? So, you know what? Let me hear it. By that look on your face, you know good and well you're caught. Tell me what happened at your apartment, Jade Anastasia. And if it's anything less than the truth, I promise you, we gon' have a bigger problem than this."

Fuck. With an open hand, I clutched onto my forehead, desperate to figure out what my next move was gonna be. I didn't and wouldn't wanna be deterred so easily. At the end of the day? This was Janet Robinson. She was as manipulative as they come. I didn't care what Corey had to say.

"What did Laurie tell you, first? Then, I'll confirm if it's true," I countered with my arms crossed. "She lies just like anyone else."

Janet waved her finger. "Aht, aht. That's not how this works. You tell me the truth, and I will confirm. I'm calling the shots here. You don't get to come up in here and tell lies, and then expect me to be on the defense. Try again."

Damn.

I didn't have much of an option, did I? I was backed all the way to a corner. Guess it didn't matter what I said at this point. Regardless, I was in deep shit with her, and there may have been no coming back. Instead of feigning defeat, I stood a little taller with my shoulders back and sported an indifference Ma changed her body language to.

"Fine." I shrugged. "I didn't lie about much. The only thing I lied about was the person who put their hands on Laurie. I wasn't the one to do it. Everything that happened at the apartment happened. Instead, it was Jarell that did it because Laurie swung and busted his lip because she doesn't like him the same way you don't. Jarell retaliated, and honestly, she deserved it for picking with him. Everything else I told you is true. Nathan sent those messages to me. I know he did! Or it had to be someone who works for him. He was actually one of the people who almost got Jarell, and I killed in this case I confronted you about. I'm too scared to call the police because I feel like someone's gonna come for my neck for snitching," I explained. "I'm not lying about that!"

"Oh, give me a break." Janet huffed, her eyes glued to the ceiling.

"I'm not lying! I'm serious! Nathan was one of the men who—"

"I don't care!" she screamed to the top of her lungs, rattling a glass sitting in front of her on the breakfast counter. "You lied. I knew this was all about Jarell, and you think you played me. I ain't no damn fool, Jade!"

"Janet, please. Chill o—"

"Shut up, Corey. I don't need your fucking mediation," Janet griped and then pushed him out of her way to make eye contact with me. "Jade? We are through. I don't care about Jarell's history with Stephanie's brother. If that man wanted to do something to you or me, he would've done it already, and you're sticking your nose in business you have no stake in. This is what I'm talking about. You would rather throw me under the bus and into harm's way by trying to 'get rid of Nathan' because you are so clouded by that boy. I don't get it. So, you know what? You can shove those boundaries you came with up your ass because I'm not dealing with you anymore. If Jarell is what you want? Then go get him. Have at it, Jade. I'm done," she said, swiping a hand under her chin.

"Oh my God!" I roared, rising to storm her, but Corey dashed and stood in front of me before I could. "You don't even realize that I was tryna get you to do the right thing! I don't even wanna tell you this, but Nathan is an abuser, Momma! He isn't what you think he is! That whole family isn't, so I don't know why you trust them and kiss their ass more than you trust me! I lied to you about Jarell's involvement because I knew you'd do this. I was scared to tell you anything related to him, and it's so ridiculous that I have to tell you all his business for you to even try and understand."

"Jade, calm down. Take a deep breath." Corey tried by placing soft hands on my shoulders, but I snatched away.

"No, Dad. Janet wants the truth, so I'll tell her the truth. And I'm sure after this, she'll feel so stupid for being damn near forty and acting like she's twelve. So let me talk. A few years ago, Jarell's mom and Stephanie's brother were involved with each other somehow, and he was a complete wreck over their lives. Nathan assaulted Jarell's mom daily and even raped her. Any time his mom didn't do want he wanted her to do, Nathan used Jarell as a punishment, and one of those punishments was throwing bleach in his face that ended up blinding him for the rest of his life. His mom tried calling the authorities, but he skipped town to avoid arrest. After he skipped town, Jarell and his mom ran away. They ran away here to Los Angeles for the last five years, and now, they just found out that Nathan's back. *That's* why I wanted you to put him away. You hate Jarell so much for no reason, yet the whole time, he's suffered from child abuse, sexual assault by Nathan, and bullying at school because he doesn't have the nicest clothes and he's poor due to them leaving that situation with zero money. And guess what, Janet? You were the straw to break Jarell's back."

"Me?" she asked incredulously, pointing a finger at her chest.

"Yes, *you*! Why? Because of your childish antics at the hospital, you pushed him to a suicide attempt."

When she heard that, the color left her body. I gave her a long glare, a sarcastic smile, and a nod in return.

"Yeeeeahhh. Yup. Jarell and his mom sat and waited for me by my bedside to wake up after that drowning incident when you weren't there yet to make sure I was okay and wasn't alone. After you barged in, cussed him and his mom out, and threw everything you had at him as your personal thank you, he broke into tears right after security removed you because he couldn't handle one more person mistreating him."

Silence overtook the room.

"When you left, his mom tore his clothes trying to stop him from attempting to kill himself, and we had to call for help. He got admitted to the psych ward that night and became an in-patient on strict suicide monitoring. *That's* your legacy. *That's* who you are. You should feel stupid. You should be ashamed that you made an eighteen-year-old survivor of child and sexual abuse try and off himself because you have no morals or empathy for anyone other than yourself. You suck as a human, and since I'm speaking my truth, I'll just go on and say that I just straight up don't like you. I've tried to make things right, but until you get yourself in order, *I'm the one that's done.* You have nothing to be done with me about because all I'm doing is living the life I want to live, and not how *you* want me to live. Now. The truth is out. Do you have anything else to say to me or for yourself?"

Nothing. Janet just stared at me without emotion, except her eyes glistened… and then puddled. That was the only sign I had that she felt at least something. Dad, on the other hand, stood nearby just as stunned and speechless.

"No? Nothing to say? Great." I clapped. "Didn't think you would. Here's your fucking spare key," I said and slammed it down on the counter. "I have all the shit I need outta this house anyway. Goodbye, Janet. Dad? Good luck with her. I'm not coming back here. Ever. This is it for real. Don't even think about suggesting we work things out because it ain't happening. If she wants to work it out, she needs to come to me. I won't be a petty bitch like her and not listen, but she better be sincere. I'm out. I'ma go take a walk. Peace. I said what I had to say."

No one stopped me. No one said a word. No one moved. Except for me, right on out the front door as I paced down the road to the nearest coffee shop so I could take an Uber home. Because I ain't wanna hear Corey's peacemaking ass either.

Nothing felt better than the pressure of maintaining a relationship with Janet being released from my shoulders. I didn't feel obligated to. I was on offense, and if she wanted to make amends, it was going to be on her. I was sick of this unspoken rule of deference that younger folks or a child had to be the one to make things right with their parents. She was the toxic one. She needed to do it on her own and come to terms with her own issues. I ain't have nothing to do with that.

I smiled as I secured the Uber ride on my app. Nothing felt better than this, even though the whole conversation was nasty. It was everything I had ever wanted to get off my chest. I was ready to move forward. On to graduation this weekend… and hopefully, without Janet Robinson being there.

Chapter Thirty-One

Point of View: Jarell Hendricks

POW!!

A single shot reverberated off the shed walls and stopped when the world went still. My chest wouldn't move. It wouldn't heave, take air, nothing. It was stuck. My hands shook harder than someone dying of hypothermia as thick fluid ran down the side of my neck. The presence of a dark cloud seemed to hover over me when, suddenly, a huge, almost boulder like weight fell right on top of my body, cutting off the very little oxygen supply I had. All life around me dimmed, moved in slow motion, and all sound I managed to hear came through muffled, blubbery, and echoey. Like I was underwater.

"Oh my God… Oh my God… Kylah! How did she get in here? Get your hands off her. Kylah baby, put that down sweetie, okay? Put that gun down. Mama never taught you to handle dangerous things like that," Ma begged while soon after, Kylah's hysterical crying overtook the twilight zone.

"Did I do something wrong, Mommy?" she sobbed. "Did I hurt Daddy and Relly? Ahhh! Daddy's bleeding, Mommy!"

"I hear you baby, but… I need you to put that gun down. How'd you get it?"

"He gave it to me, Mommy," Kylah wept. "He helped me shoot it."

"Okay. Thank you for telling me. Give that gun back to him. Right now. Okay? Listen to Mommy, sweetie," Ma pleaded. "Good girl. Now come over here. What happened? Tell Mommy what happened. Why are you down here? Come to me, please. Don't look over there."

"Daddy took long for ice cream, and I came to see Daddy. You were screaming Mommy, and I got scared. When I came, Daddy try to hurt Relly bad. But Mommy, Daddy's hurt, and so is Relly! Did I do something bad?" Kylah cried.

"Alex, why the fuck would you do this? She could've killed Jarell!" Ma thundered.

"I wasn't gonna let that happen, Auntie. I'm a marksman, and I wasn't gonna let Rell go out like this. You heard the girl. She came in because she wanted to know what was taking him so long, and dude was about to shoot Rell. I had to let her do it because ain't no system finna take a five-year-old to jail with her fingerprints on the trigger. I ain't tryna have none of us go to the pen for murder," Alex tried explaining.

"I don't give a fuck! She don't need to be seeing all this blood!" Ma yelled.

"Here. I'll untie you, and you take her," Alex's deep voice rang out as his feet shuffled and busted into action. My chest still felt like the world sat on it. "I'll check on Rell after I let you out, too."

"No! I will check on my son. I don't trust you to do anything right now regarding him!"

More scuffling and shuffling took place as I struggled to maneuver out from under this boulder. Soon after, the heaviness seemed to get a little lighter, and it felt like I was on the verge of being able to breathe again. When it was completely removed, I took a huge heave in, but it was too much at once. A coughing attack was the result.

"Jarell, baby. You okay? Please tell me you're alright." Ma's light voice soothed me as she touched all over my body, checking for anything life threatening.

"I don't know. I think so," I replied, and then squeezed my abs to lift myself up with her help. "W-What happened?" I asked.

"Nathan was about to shoot you, but Kylah shot him with Alex's help after she ran in here to see her damn dad. She could've killed you both!" Ma exclaimed.

I shook my head and blinked, trying to clear my head, push through the pain, and understand everything.

"Wait, what? How did she get the gun? How did she not get hurt from the blowback? Why couldn't he shoot dude himself?" I questioned after a bout of coughing.

"That's what I'm tryna say! He's a fucking coward for making a five-year-old do that. He's been trying to explain himself, but honestly, I ain't tryna hear it. He can come and try explaining it to you, but I don't trust his ass. I'ma get Kylah taken care of. You be careful with him."

With that, Ma got up and her little footsteps paced outta here like she ain't been manhandled at all today. I squeezed my abs tight again to lift myself to sit up straight, but I couldn't as my chest caved, and I fell right onto my back again.

I grunted and turned over to my stomach to try and lift myself by the arms and knees instead of relying on my midsection, but it was more like I was writhing and rolling around rather than try- ing to rise up.

"Let me help you," a deep, familiar voice called out. Alex.

He reached out to touch my arm, and I went ice stiff. I wanted to beat the fuck outta him just as bad as I wanted to put Nathan six feet under. How dare this nigga put my sister in this situation? I would never have put a little girl in that kind of position. Bitch ass nigga.

So… I took advantage of his help to lift me up. That was all I needed before I gathered enough energy to fuck his ass up. Once he lifted me to my feet, I pushed him in the chest as hard as I could. His feet stumbled back like he had tripped over something. Prob- ably over Nathan's dead body.

"Nigga fuck you! Not only did you have me and my momma out here in danger 'cause of some snake shit, but you made my sister shoot and kill? Take this ass whoopin' bro, real talk!" I shouted, wavering on my feet. I didn't care if I couldn't walk anymore. Didn't care if I was on my last leg. He was 'bout to get his one way or another.

"Damn, nigga! I understand how you feel, but it's not what it seems or looks like," Alex stammered, trying to backtrack and calm me down. The moment his hands laid on me, I slapped them away and swung at him, clipping him right in the temple.

"Don't fuckin' touch me! I don't wanna hear shit!" I heaved, doubled over as I clutched onto my side in pain. That swing almost put me back to my knees again.

"I know I deserve everything you giving me right now, but I just need you to hear me out, a'ight?" Alex shouted at me to the point where I felt his spit.

"No, I'ma fuck you up!" I screamed, still limping and trying to charge at him. I swung a mighty right hook without even thinking twice, but he dodged it. Sucka was just as fast as he used to be as he grabbed my shoulders, slammed me against a wall, and pinned me there.

"Jarell! I'm not letting you fight me, man. Calm down! I ain't ever seen you like this before, bro. Full of rage and shit. You were always the calm one back in the day. Wassup with this? I barely even recognize you," Alex nearly whispered.

"The fuck you mean 'wassup?' You made my sister shoot that gun. You kidnapped all of us. Sold us out! I should rip you apart where you stand, bitch ass nigga! I swear to God. Let me go!"

"Watch your mouth, bruh. Listen to me. This was a setup, yes. But a set up for me to get rid of that Nathan mothafucka, alright? It's not what it seems, so just chill and hear me. Please," Alex pleaded.

"Shut up! I'ma beat the shit outta you fair and square," I seethed, cracking my knuckles.

He took a step back when it became too much to keep me pinned against the wall.

"Rell, for real, bro! I'm not fighting you. You're hurt, and it wouldn't even be a fair fight. Please! I had to use y'all to get rid of that bitch. Can you just hear me out man? I'm for real, I have the answers you're looking for, but if you riled up like this, I can't. Sit yo' ass down man, real talk."

With my fists balled and the tears burning at my eyes, his plead was enough to stop the smoke from coming out of all openings of my face as I stumbled back against the wall for its support. Doubling over, I grabbed my side and clutched onto my chest again.

"See look. How the hell was you gon' fight me in this condition? Are you okay?" Alex asked with genuine concern, but I just wasn't having it. I slapped his hand away that he offered to help when it touched my shoulder.

"You got five minutes. Start talking. And if it ain't worth hearing, we fighting no matter what," I said, huffing and puffing.

"A'ight. Cool. Five minutes is all I need. I'll start from the beginning. I know you probably don't even remember this, but a long time ago... that day where we got sprayed on the courts where Rob and Jonathan died? The last day we saw each other before getting kicked out the Wells was the same day I told you I had joined a gang. You remember that?"

I did, but I wouldn't give him the satisfaction. Instead, I death glared his way without a word.

"Well anyway, a nigga got in so deep and swept up with that mess, I somehow went from being a part of a petty gang with my cousin to getting wrapped up in underground organized crime pushing real weight. Not that petty ass corner weed shit. I'm talkin' pushing major weight. Can't tell you who I roll with, but I'm on my boss's radar because of the paper I rake in. To him, I'm some young rising star. Fresh new blood," Alex expounded.

"Get to the point, nigga!" I shouted. I didn't have time for story time because I just didn't give a shit. I wanted the truth!

"I'm getting there! Just chill, a'ight? The gag is that my boss man is tight with Nathan as partners. My folks push drugs, and Nathan's folks push women for truck drivers travelin' the country.

Him and his network rake in a lot of money, and we get our supply of women through him, and he gets his supply of drugs to give to his clients through us. This partnership thing been working real well. But on the low? My boss wants the whole shebang of Chicago. He wants the trafficking business and the drug business to himself so that he can make a whole lot more money and take over the Midwest. To him, Nathan is in the way. You know what that means, right? My boss wants him dead."

I blinked. *Damn.*

"Now here's where I come in and how I got involved with your situation. Not too long ago, my boss hit me up and told me to meet up at HQ because he had something to discuss with me and that it was important. I head over there, and my boss and Nathan are sittin' together drinkin' like they lifelong homies and shit. I get settled, and Nathan shares that he needed a favor from me in exchange for some major paper. Nathan goes on to tell me that he knows my mom Lynette, and he had been seeing her best friend Rachel since they met at some bar one night before we got kicked out the Wells. Apparently, Nathan and your mom hit it off on the low around eight years ago, and y'all had moved with him out to Cali for a couple years."

Hmph. *Hit it off,* huh? I'd like to hear from Ma about how that happened...

"But he said Rachel had run away with her son Jarell and he'd like to get in touch with her again because he thinks she might have his kid. He believed she was either back in Chicago or hiding out in Cali somewhere. Now, as he's telling me all this, in my head, I'm like, *I don't know no Rachel... I only know a Radiya close to my moms*, but I ain't say nothing because I already knew he was talking about your mom because he mentioned your name. I wanted to hear how much paper he was talking and the terms of the agreement before I opened my mouth to tell him he had the wrong name. And that's when my boss hopped in to shake shit up," Alex explained.

"What'd he say?" I asked.

"Well, he told Nathan that before he gave specifics about this favor he needed from me and the price tag, my boss's whole organization would have to get a cut of the money as a reward, too. My boss wasn't finna have Nathan coming up on our turf tryna take his guys for the sake of small favors. So, Nathan was like, *'Cool. Understandable.'* And that's when he gave me the rundown of who I needed to find and what we were gonna do once they were found for 100k total. 50k to me, 50k to my boss's org. That 'they' was Auntie Radiya, your little sister, and *you*."

I shook my head.

"After Nathan left, here's what ended up being my final terms from my boss: Go to California. Do what Nathan tells me to do but get in close. Kill Nathan, take his money, I get my split from Nathan's agreed terms, and then the rest goes to the business. When I come back home, I move rank and become his right-hand man for some real money since we would take charge of Nathan's network and I would make bank, bro. I mean, life changing money, Rell. Or, if mission fails, my family is threatened and so am I. He ain't give specifics about that threat, but I've seen the outcomes of those who don't fulfill his orders. So, I did what I had to do. I only had one week to figure out everything."

"Alex…" I sighed.

"Jarell, man. I was sick to my fucking stomach knowing that my mission was to link up with Nathan to get rid of you, man. Now that I handled him, I'ma be a real hero because that idiot let his guard down. I got in real close after I hacked into the system and did a background check on ya mom. I found out where she lived, where she worked. I caught a plane right up here and just followed her around and figured out where your little sister goes to school, and all of that within a week. I had to make him trust me, first, Rell. I couldn't give him any clues that I was on y'all side, so I had to say and do some fucked up shit to make it believable. I wasn't gonna let him destroy you or my Auntie. I wouldn't be able to live with myself. Y'all were like family, man. More like family than our actual family who wouldn't take us in after we got put out the Well's. So that's what happened. I'm telling you the honest to God truth."

Woah. This shit was way bigger than me. I couldn't even wrap my head around it. I still had hella questions. But the only thing I got out of what he told me was his excitement to continue Nathan's business. To go home and take over what Nathan had left behind. That was the shit that killed me.

"So... after all of this... you're gonna take over Nathan's trafficking business? After knowing what it did to my mom... and me, too?" I whispered. "He raped my mom in front of me, Alex."

"Man..." he wavered.

"This is where you're at in life now?" I asked, the tears finally puddling.

"Jarell..."

"If you do, Alex... I don't know. Every part of dude's business ruined our lives. You don't even know the half..." I said as my voice shook.

He let out a huge exhale as his hand slapped his forehead and swiped down the rest of his face.

"I can't answer that, a'ight? I just can't believe he did all that. Made Auntie one of his hoes, raped her, and abused the hell outta you. All because she wouldn't give you up to the foster system. That's some crude shit, man. Is... is he the reason you can't see?" Alex asked.

Still guarded, even though those mechanisms were starting to come down and crumble on the inside, I nodded.

"Threw bleach in my face," I mumbled.

He sighed... nearly in a growl.

"You sick fuck!" he yelled, and then his foot slammed into Nathan's body on the ground. "Rell, you ain't gotta worry about this mothafucka no more. He got a bullet right to the forehead."

I gritted my teeth.

"Yeah... and you made my sister do it. What's the reason? It better be a good one too, otherwise we can still squad up, real talk.

I don't appreciate you tryna save your own fuckin' ass. That shit ain't cool. So, get to talkin', nigga."

"Listen, man. I'm the one that saved all y'all. I ain't tryna go to prison for doing the right thing for us both. Dog… if you knew the type of man I am now? If you knew how I roll out in these streets, you would know I'm ruthless and I don't give a flying fuck about anybody. I care about making money, and I care about taking care of my momma after all the shit we've been through growing up. I could've left all three of you hanging, but I had your sister pull that trigger because they ain't gonna send a five-year-old to prison for self-defense. You're injured. Auntie is hurt. Your sister is not. We can walk scot free from this, especially if we train her to tell the police that her dad was hurting y'all. That makes sense, don't it?" Alex suggested.

I still wasn't buying or hearing it. I smacked my lips and stood up straight. I prayed I looked into his soul right now because what I was about to say was the ultimatum.

"Look, bro. I'ma tell you the only way you're gonna make up for all this if you have any fuckin' shred of morals. Give us that 50k you were gonna get rewarded. I need it to move out and get my own spot, and Ma needs it to support herself and my sister."

"Man…" he trailed off.

"Shut up and listen. I can tell you've already made up your mind. Like you said. You care about nothing else but money. You're gonna go back to Chicago, move up rank with whatever dirty, foul shit you're doing with your life now, and make way more money than this 50k anyway. If you're gonna make money from a business that ruins so many people's lives… including ours, then you owe us that, man. Plus, for having my sister kill her own dad, and for even turning us into him. Give us that, and we can forget this shit ever happened. Forget we ever ran into each other," I suggested.

He scoffed… damn near gasped.

"Rell… you for real wanna pretend like we ain't ever run into each other? After all these years? No matter what's going on right now dawg… I missed yo' ass too, bro. I really did, and I'm man enough to admit that. Watching Rob and Jon die still haunts me, fam. You were my only real friend. A brother to me… the only one left. It's really gon' be like that?" Alex asked with a shaky voice. Like a lump was in his throat.

"Hell yeah, nigga. If you're gonna associate yourself with something as low as running a trafficking business, I don't want any part of you. Ever again in my life." I blinked with firm resolve. "You're dead to me, nigga. Just like our other two friends."

The shed went quiet. For a while. I stood still, and so did he.

"Fine," Alex finally said. "I guess… I guess giving you the money is the least I can do, and we can forget about everything. But, just remember this, Rell. I know your heart, and you know mine. Better than anybody's. When you're ready? You can call me. I'll leave my number with your mom."

I scoffed.

"I won't need that shit. Get outta here."

"Hmm. Wow. Stubborn ass. Some shit don't ever change." He tried sounding nonchalant, but there was a heaviness to his voice I just couldn't ignore. "I'll pack the money with your mom. I'll give y'all a lift back to LA. I'ma cut dude's shirt off and burn it so that your fingerprints aren't on his body. Then, we'll just leave dude here to rot until the feds find him."

I wouldn't dare show him his little showcase of regret affected me in the slightest. All I had to say to this nigga after that was:

"Bet. Let's go."

Chapter Thirty-Two

Point of View: Jade Williams

Today was graduation, and I barely wanted to be here. What was even more embarrassing was that half the people I expected to be sitting out on the gym floor with a cap and gown weren't even here. There was something like five-hundred kids in our graduating class, and probably a little over half of our class appeared to be walking across the stage.

From D-Block? The only notable folks graduating were Mike, Erica, Laurie, and Arianna. No Marcus, no Martell, no Tazz, and many others. Martell surprised me for sure because he had to have passing grades in order to be on the basketball team at school, but he must've failed English or something fourth quarter. That had to be the case because you had to have four full credits of English to graduate, and he had been on the team all four years.

Karma for his ass. But for everyone else not here, it was a total indicator of our school culture. Oh well. I'm just glad I passed and was about to be outta here and onto my future as a celebrity dancer full time. No more cheerleading, no more immature shenanigans, and no more popularity contests. Good riddance, Crenshaw!

The people who showed up today for me was Corey, Alise, and surprisingly, two of my dancers at the studio, Brielle and Tiffany, who tagged along with Alise. Janet wasn't one of them, and nothing made me happier to not see her. I didn't know if I could stomach her kee-keeing and haha-ing with Laurie's family like a fake ass valley girl while she would likely show disdain for Corey and me after what happened the other day.

As I sat in my designated spot in the gymnasium and scanned the crowd, navy blue and gold balloons were everywhere as various family members continued to file inside even as the graduating class had already taken our chairs as they scrambled for the best remaining seats possible. A small part of me died inside watching a family with a mom, dad, and siblings waving at their graduating son, but I smiled it away. I had the people I needed in my life right now who needed to be there, even if it wasn't a nuclear family. It was enough for me at the moment, and I had the opportunity to allow new, better people in my life once I walked across the stage. If I wanted to, I could forget about everyone here at Crenshaw now. That thought alone brought me comfort.

I just wished Jarell was here with me.

He was supposed to be graduating. He was supposed to be the happiest he had ever felt in his life after accomplishing something so major after everything he's been through. Especially when he was so close to completing his graduation requirements. A quarter away from passing. God. He was robbed of so many milestones.

I shook my head and the sentiments about this away. I had to make sure I had a positive day myself.

I sighed and scanned the graduates for Laurie. She sat next to Arianna with all smiles, like nothing much had bothered her about Martell not being there. That was a shocker, considering how she was always on his tip. I had expected her to be inward and moping about him. Good for her.

But that still didn't erase the feeling in my gut about her running her fucking mouth to her uncle about Jarell and me. She definitely coulda caught a fade or two, but on the real? I just let it go. I didn't want anything to do with that family at all, and even engaging with any of them would just drag it out longer than it needed to be. But most of all, it would put me at even more of a risk with Nathan. She was gon' get hers. Just wait for it.

Now that everyone was filed in, the ceremony could begin. The keynote speaker was boring as hell. Only person who was lit was the valedictorian, who everyone liked, including D-Block. He was one of the rare people in the school who was excluded from our hallway antics because he was just cool with everybody, but just wasn't about that D-Block life. And then, after what seemed like hours, the names got called to receive diplomas. Good because I was damn near knocked until I got my name called. Corey, Alise, Brielle, and Tiffany all cheered loudly for me in the stands. I smiled and shook my head at their crazy selves.

And that's when it hit me.

I was graduating with a diploma in my hand, and it was the end of this chapter in my life. It seemed like it took forever to get to this point, but it was here, and I was done with school forever.

Wow.

Ya girl was an adult now. Like, for real.

After I sat back down and stared in awe at my certificate, the rest of the ceremony flew by, and before we knew it, everyone was throwing their graduation caps in the air. I ain't care about throwing shit. I wanted to be the first one out.

As the graduates filed out of the gym, I found a spot close by the exit door so I was visible enough for my folks to locate me. Once they did, my dance family were the first to shower me with hugs.

"Congratulations, baby girl!" Corey smiled, the last one to greet me with a bouquet of flowers in hand just before someone tapped him from behind and asked for an autograph. I giggled. I always seemed to forget that he was an ex-NBA player. After he quickly signed the man's shirt, he turned to give his undivided attention to me again. "Come here! Give ya old man a hug."

Cheesing, I stepped to Corey and allowed him to wrap me up and rock me back and forth. I could've broken down. There was no way I could express how grateful I was to Corey and the support he had given me throughout my life. He was the definition of a real man.

"I'm so proud of you, Jade. I know everything going on with your mother has been stressful, but you still did it. You graduated. You are amazing, and I'm excited to watch you grow into the woman I always knew you could be," Corey said, grasping onto my cheeks and looking into my eyes.

"Aww. Thanks, Dad." I smiled. "Have you heard from Janet at all?"

"Nah. After you left the house once you were finished laying it on the line for her, she kinda stormed off to her room and slammed the door shut, and that's when I took my cue to leave. You were right though. If she wants to make things right, she's gonna have to do some reflection and then come to you. I promise I won't come in between the middle of that. I didn't realize how deep the wedge has divided you both. But you know, I'ma always tell you to give her a chance. She's the only mom you have," Corey elaborated.

"Yeah. You know I'll listen to her. I'm not like her, but she's gotta grow up." I shrugged, cradling the flowers in my arms.

"I'm already knowing," Corey said, and got tapped by someone else, wanting to take some photos. He sighed and rolled his eyes where they couldn't see, but I sure did. I laughed. "Excuse me, Jade."

"Dad, go on ahead. I got my dance fam here. You go and be famous." I waved with a chuckle.

With a grateful look, Corey obliged his fans as I turned to the ladies who had given me a couple of cute teddy bears and cards. We chopped it up about my graduation dinner this evening and how we couldn't wait for some bomb ass food when the conversation was stymied by one of the girls' observation across the way.

"What's wrong with her over there? Ain't you supposed to be happy at graduation?" Alise whispered to Brielle with a slight head tilt to bring attention to who she was talking about.

We all followed Alise's signal and landed on Laurie's mom Stephanie, whose face was flushed and bloodshot red as tears popped from her face. Her husband tried to hide and console her, but Stephanie went nuts. I couldn't hear what she was trying to say because she was so hysterical, but the rest of Laurie's family was able to corner her and get her to settle down somewhat.

"Yeah, I don't know what's up with that," Brielle responded, watching the scene. "Somebody always got some drama. Can we all just be happy?"

"Nah, I heard from one of them that someone in their family died. Something like that lady's brother or something," Tiffany said.

"Which lady?" I asked with a frown.

"The lady who's crying."

Woah, woah, wait. Nathan died?

"Uh uh, hold up. Who did you hear that from?" I asked with wide eyes.

"I don't know who they are, but one of her family members said it when we were walking out the gym as ol' dude tried to push her to a place away from everyone," Tiffany replied.

My mouth dropped as I turned my head back to the scene ahead, and Stephanie's husband was having a real hard time trying to get her under control. Even worse, Laurie was making her way out of the gym to meet the family, but another family member intercepted her and directed her away from the commotion. Once they were in a safe area, the family member whispered something Laurie gasped at.

"Something's wrong with Uncle Nathan!?" she blurted out.

"Shhh!!" Her family member attempted to silence Laurie, and instead of keeping her there, they both went outside of the school.

My hand covered over my mouth. Goodness. If this was true that Nathan died…

What did Jarell do to him… if he did anything at all? Was he okay? Was Kylah and his mom okay? Gotdamnit, now I didn't wanna be here anymore. I walked across the stage, got my shit, and now it was time to go.

Go to Jarell's house.

I don't give a single damn about what Jarell said in that letter. Now that Nathan was gone, I felt a lot safer now to go without feeling like a surveillance camera burned my ass the entire time. I just prayed they'd be home, but first, I needed some context and as much information as I could gather.

"I'ma be right back y'all," I said to my group.

Whipping out my phone, I rushed to a corner of the hallway away from the chaos and searched up Nathan Schmidt on Google. The first headline popped up on my screen that nearly made my mouth drop so low, a beehive could probably live in it.

HEADLINE: *Nathan Schmidt, 52, found dead of gunshot wound in Red Bluff vacation home*

When I opened the full article and read through how he was found dead with the suspects at large and a whole bounty out for his killers for up to $250k, I nearly peed. How did that happen? Who shot him? Jarell couldn't have. Was it his mom? Goodness.

I kept reading the article further for more detail, and even more was uncovered. Two additional individuals were also found dead a couple days ago and were thought to be linked to Nathan's death and potentially, also linked to an abduction case involving two teens. Fuck! *That was Jarell and me!* Not only that, but Marcus was the primary suspect in the deaths of those two individuals as his mugshot sat right in the middle of the article.

Shit!

What the hell was going on!? I couldn't even wrap my head around it, but obviously, all of these crimes were connected to Nathan somehow. I just didn't have all the pieces to the puzzle, and probably never would.

My stomach bubbled. I had to check up on Jarell and his family. ASAP. This was a lot. The last thing I wanted was for any of Jarell's family to be in jail because of a dirty scumbag like Nathan who deserved to be six feet under for all his filthy deeds.

Nah.

I had to drop everything and go.

This was way too serious to be playing around.

~ ~ ~

I sped as fast as I could, weaving in and out of traffic to West Fifty-Sixth Street and ended up making it to Jarell's house within ten minutes. I had barely given any of my folks who showed up to graduation for me a farewell, letting them know I had an emergency, but my graduation dinner was still on for seven tonight. Thankfully, no one made a big deal about it and let me go on my way, including Corey.

When I arrived, a huge gust of relief whooshed over me as Jarell sat on his porch step, playing with a piece of origami in his lap. The relief was so intense, tears formed. My first instinct was to rush and tackle him with a hug, but ... self-control. Self-control.

When that initial feeling passed, now, my chest fluttered like a butterfly. How the hell was I supposed to approach him? I wasn't gonna just drive away, but Jarell also wasn't the type to be bluffin' on his own word. He said didn't wanna see me again for a while; he was dead ass serious. Sometimes, I hated he was so consistent, and I was the rule breaker.

Swallowing and adjusting the front of my pixie cut curls, I slipped a heel out of my car and just sat there. Should I tip toe to him so that I wouldn't be detected or deterred by my own noise? I sighed. *Girl. Suck it up. How many times have you confronted Jarell when he hated your guts, and you withstood the storm of his will to push you away and get rid of you?* And yet, I was still here. I couldn't stop being persistent now.

With pep talk after pep talk, I slid out the car, shut the door, and walked up his mom's entry way. As I got closer, my heels clicked and clacked towards him. He paused and frowned as his eyes left his origami piece and followed my feet.

"Hey. It's just me," I said just above a whisper when I got within three feet of him.

His frown got deeper. "Jade? What are you doing here? I thought I told you not to —"

I threw my hands up. "I know. I know. Hear me out. Please. I know. I know what you said, but I just couldn't end things like this. I read about what happened on the news about Nathan being found dead after being shot. Are you okay? What happened? Is your mom and Kylah alright? Please loop me in, Jarell. What happened with Nathan?"

"Who?" Jarell frowned.

I threw a hand on my hip and shifted my weight, shooting daggers at him with a glare. Was he for real? Did he get drugged or something?

"Um, seriously? Don't fuckin' play with me. I came by here to make sure you were alright. Nathan got shot, and there's a bounty out for the killer. And then there's more shit coming out about other people who were killed in connection to Nathan's death or our kidnapping, and even crazier? Marcus is in jail now for being the primary suspect of their deaths. What the hell is going on?" I exclaimed, throwing my arms in the air. "Were you involved at all? Please tell me everything is alright with you, Jarell. I can't have you in jail or in prison. Please tell me."

"Jade, I don't know nothing about what Marcus did, and ... I don't know what you're talking about regarding this Nathan guy either. I don't even know who dude is," Jarell said with a flat tone, but he gave me a look of distress in his eyes that told another story. When that sign lingered for a while, an eerie talent Jarell was able to execute when it came to how he could send clear messages through eye emotes, I caught on in an instant.

As much as I hated not being able to pry and get information, I nodded with a confirmation he couldn't see.

"M'kay," I simply responded. "My bad."

The moment those words left my mouth, the look in Jarell's eyes disappeared. Damn it. I was dying to know what happened, but I guess I'd just have to settle for non-closure. More information may come out in the news, or... later when Jarell wasn't so personally affected by it. Whatever it was, it had to be very, very serious. I just hoped everything would be alright...

"So, like I said," Jarell leaned back against the porch step on his elbows like I had never brought this news up. "I thought I told you not to come here anymore, Jade. I meant that. I didn't just say it for shits and giggles, and I didn't take all that time to write my thoughts to you just to be straight up disregarded."

I blinked, then huffed. Wow. The brash edginess of his delivery despite his body language saying otherwise rubbed me completely wrong, but the times where he exuded and expressed full-on warmth made up for everything. It was what kept me coming back. What made me feel so attached.

"I honestly don't care. I needed to make sure you were okay," I countered with a slight shrug.

Both of his brows shot up and his lip poked out with a sardonic nod.

"A'ight, bet. Cool. You're saying you don't give a shit about what I said, how I feel, my reasoning, my goals, my healing… just as long as you get what you want, right?" Jarell asked without his voice raising a single time. His eyes were now halfway closed as he looked towards me, this time, with ambiguity and an absence of irritation.

Huh? I couldn't read him right now. Was he being sarcastic? It was almost like he was teasing me, but I wasn't sure. Either way, anxiety rose in my chest at the thought of him getting the wrong impression about my intentions. I rushed to sit down next to him to remove the power dynamic of standing above him. I hurried to explain.

"No, Jarell. Listen. It's not what you think. I know I'm coming off like this indifferent, smug bitch, but it's not that. Let me just me real. I care about you so much that this shit hurts, alright? Ninety percent of this visit was to make sure you were okay after hearing the news, and the other ten percent is …"

I faltered, and Jarell raised just one brow this time.

"What's the other ten?" he asked with this almost sultry affect. What the fuck was going on with him? He was throwing me for a loop.

"I mean… it's just that…" I leaned my head and I rocked from side to side. "You know why, Jarell. Stop playing with me. You dropping that letter on me and trying to leave me like this… or attempting to ghost me without any sort of closure felt like a bigger heartbreak than anything Mike had ever done. I know I'm the one who broke up with you, and I know I can't give up on my dreams to juggle everything that is us, but… damn I feel so lost. I never wanted to break up, but knew it was the right thing to do, but that doesn't change how I feel about you. I've given my all to you, Jarell, and I —"

Before I could say another word, Jarell's gritty hands went to my plump cheeks and pulled my face forward to press his lips against mine. My eyes ballooned and for a second, I almost pulled back, but when he pressed into me further, I moaned with no inhibition as the world around me collapsed, falling right into his love. I closed my eyes, parted my lips, and he followed suit to welcome some slight tongue action from me, and we went at it right on his porch until things started to feel out of control.

My skin bubbled the further and deeper in, damn near ready to claw at each other's clothes to eliminate them before Jarell stiffened up as if an epiphany slapped him. Then, he pulled away, panting.

"Damn girl… listen… I… we… um… I uh…fuck… my bad…" he stuttered and struggled to regain his composure as he whispered against my moist lips.

I sighed and dipped my head in disappointment. He took that opportunity to take a couple of scoots away from me.

"Fuck," he uttered and turned his head, barring me from whatever emotion he displayed as he stuffed his hands in his pockets. "That was uncalled for. Especially after everything I said about us separating. Damn. My fault."

I let out a throaty chuckle. "Jarell. Stop hiding. I thought we were past that. You know you wanted this. You know I wanted it, too," I replied, caressing the side of his face with the back of my hand. He snuggled into it the way he always used to. "You just tend to show it. I guess you were right. On your birthday. That we can't hide how we feel. Remember saying that?"

A phantom smirk played at his lips, but his eyes held the jest he tried to keep in check. I couldn't help but laugh and push his arm ever so slightly before he spoke.

"I know. It's too hard. This is a prime example of why I need this time away from you. I need this time to become someone you can truly love, and not this bullshit version of me. You're in love with the wrong me, Jade, and I hate it. Give me some space to figure things out, okay? A lot happened in therapy for me, and I just need the time to be alone and grow. I can't have romance complicating this shit. You know our chemistry is too strong to not act on it. We can't even call ourselves being friends."

"But... I don't want to leave you all on your own," I pouted. "I don't want you to leave at all!"

"You know this isn't about you, and more about what's important for me right now," he explained. "I'm not gonna be by myself. I'm gonna get a guide dog and everything, but Jade... please..."

"I know," I interrupted. "I know, Jarell. I'm just selfish and... I love you. Even as a friend. I'm so happy I came to see that you're in one piece and that everything is okay. I hope one day we can sit down, and you can tell me how therapy has helped you. I'm excited to see the new and improved you once you're comfortable. I just..."

I sniffed as the waterworks burned at my eyes.

"I'm proud of you, Jarell. I am. I know we haven't known each other super long or anything, but it feels like you've been in my life forever."

"Jade don't flatter me. I haven't done much yet." He turned his head away.

With a gentle hand, I reached out and grabbed him by the chin, turning his head towards me again. His eyes softened and looked towards me without any barrier clouding his emotions. I shed a few more tears at the fear, hesitation, and doubt swirling in there.

"I'm serious. I'm proud, Jarell. You're still standing, and you're moving towards a better you. Do you understand how many people would have given up? After everything you've been through?"

Blinking, Jarell tried turning his head away again and shifted his eyes towards the street, but I wouldn't let him. I kept my hand firm on his chin and turned it back to me. This time, I initiated the contact as our lips became one again. Fireworks popped at my core the deeper Jarell and I kissed as his grip on either my face or clothes got more and more intense.

"Hey! Since when did you think it was okay to be tonguing down somebody at my house, Jarell Hendricks? Your sister is down the hall… she don't need to be coming outside and seeing that." Rachel's familiar voice rung out.

With a low groan, Jarell's head reluctantly leaned away as he rolled his eyes. I had no shame or embarrassment being caught as I snuck in another peck.

"See, this is why I need to move the fuck out," Jarell mumbled under his breath against my lips, leading me to a giggle in response. "My bad, Ma," Jarell corrected and adjusted his clothes.

"Sho' don't look like you wanna apologize. I ain't never see you doing *anything* like this before," she replied with her short arms crossed, leaning up against house and eyeballing us both.

Jarell smirked, and although he couldn't see it, I gave him a deliberate gaze with a smile, too. He and I both were probably on the same page, knowing what went down in his bedroom some time back when his mom and sister were sleeping in the wee hours of the night when I snuck in through his window during a thunderstorm. An experience neither of us would ever forget.

"It don't matter," Jarell said and rose up from the porch. "Can you give us a second?"

"I guess." She shrugged. "Just be mindful of who's in the house back there before you decide to do adult actions, alright? Y'all ain't at the point of needing condoms, are y'all?" Ms. Rachel asked with her neck jutted out. "We get 'em free at the hotel store."

"What? Nah, get outta here with that," Jarell grimaced, and I bit my lip to stifle a laugh.

"Damn, no need to be rude. I'm just checkin'," she mumbled and walked away. "The way y'all tonguing each other down, y'all sho' act like it."

Jarell waved her off. When she made it clear inside the house, closing the screen door but leaving the entrance door open to keep an eye on us, Jarell turned back to me with a huge deep breath.

"Jade, you already know what it is. As sweet as this is, and as much as I want you to stay, I gotta end this here, and I gotta stick to my word. Don't know when I'll see you again, but just give me time, a'ight? Hopefully, we'll link up down the line, and I'll be in a better place. Keep in contact with Kylah though, for sure. She's gonna need someone like you so here's my mom's number," Jarell expressed, licking his lips. Jesus I could've melted. All of this drama and trauma had me forever forgetting how fuckin' fine Jarell was to me.

"I can do that," I managed to respond without slipping out what I was thinking as I entered his mom's number in my phone, although I already had it from when she called for his birthday. "I actually would love that."

"Good. I know she would too. But a'ight, tell me this. Since this is how we're parting ways, is this the closure you needed?" he asked with a grin.

With a deep breath, I stood up with a smile, too, wiping the dust from my graduation dress.

"Yeah. It is. I feel much better knowing you're alive and safe. I can actually accept that we're moving on for a while. It'll be hard for me, but I know it's for the better. And it's for you."

"Bet," he said, and then a stretched pause followed before he squinted and licked his lips, practically undressing me with his eyes. He needed to stop that. "You know I wish I could see you. Can't express how much I still long for that. I know you look great today with those heels on. It must've been graduation."

I smiled. "Yeah, it is. How'd you know?"

"Because I don't think you'd smell this amazing if it wasn't. That's why I couldn't help but kiss you. Congratulations. I know you happy. Com'ere. Gimme a hug," he whispered with his arms stretched out.

With no hesitation, I wrapped my arms around his midsection and pulled him in for a long embrace, managing to keep my emotions together in the process. He smelled so earthy and just ugh… let me get outta here before I never leave.

"I guess… I guess this is it," I pouted with my lip poked out as I pulled away.

"Yeah. Let's not drag this out longer than it needs to be. Later, Jade. By the way?"

"Yeah?" I perked up.

"I love you, too, Jade. Okay? Just wait on me."

He gave me one last toothless smile before moving past me and inside. When Jarell closed the door behind him for good, my head fell back with more tears burning at the corners. Well… I guess I should be happy that he said "later" instead of "goodbye."

I suppose today was the end of so many chapters for me and the mark of new beginnings. End of my high school chapter. End of the road of being a narcissistic, petty bitch who lived for drama and clout, end of the relationship with my mother for good, and end of Jarell and I… for now, as we prepared for a bright future ahead. My future with dance as a Youth Choreographer, future with making new friends, my future with developing an even closer relationship with my stepfather, and finally, a test of my ability to deal with major heartbreak. Because this right here was no happy ever after. This shit hurt more than anything I could've ever imagined.

But here's the thing…

There was always gonna be room in my heart for Jarell no matter what.

Whether it was a romantic partner, a lifelong friend, or even, dare I say it, just a golden memory. And that was only if we had never seen each other again. I doubted it though. Because he finally told me that he loved me too. *And I knew he meant that shit.*

Chapter Thirty-Three

Point of View: *Jarell Hendricks*

THREE WEEKS LATER

Laying on my back in my twin sized bed, I "stared" at the ceiling above as my mind ran ragged. I been doing this a whole lot more than usual lately, and that says a lot because I sit around and think a lot anyway. Ever since that whole showdown in Red Bluff, everyone in the house seemed to be in a reflective state with this unnerving silence weighing the air. It was almost like no one wanted to say anything to each other or interact to trigger anyone. We only talked if we had to. What Ma had said when she came on the porch after busting me and Jade making out was the most I had heard from her mouth in one sitting for the last few weeks.

Most of all? Kylah wasn't herself.

Everything that went down matured her in a way Ma and I had always wanted to avoid. Just another unspoken agreement between us with the way we communicated and raised her. By far, Kylah was much more innocent than I ever was, but that shit was gone now by one pull of a trigger. Ma had to keep reassuring her that she had done nothing wrong, but that wasn't gonna change the things we couldn't take back.

Over the last couple weeks, when I was able to go back to therapy again, I spilled everything that had happened to Trisha, and a part of me felt like she was gonna scold me for seeking revenge in the first place instead of calling the police like she wanted me to, but she didn't even go there. She was just happy I was okay and told me she was proud of me. Even said she was glad he was gone.

For some reason, just those simple words meant the world to me. It made me trust her more than at any point of time I confided in her in this journey.

Now that the dust had settled, I couldn't help but think about Alex.

Man. Alex.

He had followed through with giving up those fifty thousand dollars to make up for everything, which was cool and all, but that money ain't mean shit to me. I ain't see dude in years, he still was like a sworn brother, as mad as I was with him. I ain't want him involved in any of the shit he was doing. But what could I do? He got himself caught up in this life the moment he joined that gang as a lil' bit. There was nothing I could do to fix that. I had to be okay with not being able to control others' actions and try to find the patience and the good in 'em. A therapy skill.

I was just glad he did the right thing for the wrong reasons, and it led to Nathan being out of the picture so none of us would live in fear anymore. But, I had a feeling this case was gonna catch up to him.

Because it caught up to us.

What seemed to be a free kill, it wasn't that simple. Even though we hadn't done a single thing wrong, all this shit didn't stop the investigation from knocking at our doorstep. Authorities connected the dots and figured out that Nathan was associated to our family due to Ma's attempt to lock his ass up the first-time years ago for domestic violence and child abuse.

So, with that, Ma and I started as primary suspects due to suspicious behavior and items at her job at the hotel. This included truck skid marks in the back of the hotel, which matched up with the stolen SUV's Jade and I were abducted in.

See, we woulda been super in the clear, but because Alex's dumb ass took my iPhone when he tagged us at Ma's job and threw it on the ground, it was evidence that we may have been involved with Nathan's death somehow. I had to tell them that someone attempted to mug me but failed. It wasn't like they could ask me who I thought it was or if I could give a description of the potential "mugger" … I couldn't see! It was the only time I was grateful for the disability.

Authorities weren't that deterred though. They even interviewed the employees at Ma's hotel, and her coworkers shared with them that Ma had never returned to work after her break. Instead, she had been reported as an employee who left work without permission. With those two pieces of evidence, plus the cameras in the back of the hotel being taken out and destroyed, they weren't giving up on their relentless questioning of us about Nathan. However, neither of our fingerprints were on the destroyed cameras and none of our fingerprints matched any item in Nathan's home that would suggest our appearance there. Good thing Alex was smart enough to burn Nathan's shirt because I woulda been screwed. My hands were all over that thing.

All Ma and I could tell them was that we were never with Nathan or in Red Bluff at all. I ain't even know what kinda specific questions they asked Ma, but all I knew was that whatever she told them, it got them off our case.

To be honest? All this shit was chaotic. They were gonna be at Alex's door real soon. Because his prints may have been on my phone, which was still seized, and his fingerprints may have been on the cameras outside the hotel, too.

Either way, after all the questioning and multiple undercover detectives at our doorstep day in and day out about where we were that day and what we did, we had authorities off our ass. *For now.* It woulda all been fucked up had I succumbed to Jade's loud ass questioning on the porch, but thank God I ain't get nailed for that. It had been a couple days since they've been around.

The thing was, though?

I shoulda been clicking my heels at Nathan being gone, but my stomach and heart remained hollow. It was the revenge I sought. Desired. Begged for. I tasted his blood on the tip of my tongue. I just didn't get myself sometimes.

I let out a huge exhale as I still laid flat in the bed. When was I gonna tell Ma about all the shit I been thinking and had already spoke with Jade about in my letter and with Trisha in therapy? Because everything on my heart went way beyond just this situation with Nathan. I had been working up the courage to let her know what's been on my mind ever since I confessed to Trisha that leaving her and Kylah was something I needed to do for my own healing. What would Ma think if I told her I wanted to leave the family?

"Approach your mother with forgiveness and compassion," Trisha had said.

But she never explained to me how to do that, and I had to be the one to break the ice in this house. I couldn't take another day of us pretending like everything that had happened at the shed in Red Bluff was some awkward secret. I was just gonna have to wing this and wherever the conversation took us? That's where it was gonna end up as I tried to incorporate Trisha's advice.

Rolling out of bed, I stood and stretched long, far, and wide with a loud yawn before shivering and getting the stiffness out of my body and neck. On any other normal day, Ma would call out from the living room and tell me to shut up with all that noise as a joke, but nothing came. I smacked my lips. Where the hell was she at?

Trekking out of my room and in the living area, I followed the reek of cigarettes. Damn, she been knockin' em back lately but whatever. I didn't complain because I understood it. So instead, I let my presence speak for itself as I stood in the middle of the doorjamb.

"Can I help you?" Ma asked without much emotion.

"Can I come sit next to you?" She nodded without affect, and I ambled on over. "How you feelin'?" I sat next to her on the sullied couch that probably had multiple owners before it came to be with us here.

"I'm alright. Just still wrapping my head around everything over the last nine months," she said, blowing out a steady stream that mixed with the stench of beer.

Damn. Not only was Ma picking up the smoking habit, but the drinking, too? Wow. This was a first, and yet, I wasn't havin' it. If I was gonna move out, I wanted Kylah in a situation that was healthy and safe. She ain't need to be with a drunken, smokin' ass mom who couldn't handle herself.

Kylah needed to be as far away from bullshit as possible. She was already suffering from PTSD, which stands for post-traumatic stress disorder. Something I learned in therapy the other day and realized that I had, too. Since everything went down with her dad, I would have to come to Kylah's room to sleep with her at night some days because she wouldn't stop crying about it. The only reason I could deal with it was because her cries were so similar to mine after Nathan would leave my room at night after assaulting me, so there was no way I could ignore her. She would snuggle up to me and fall right asleep, knowing that her big brother protected her.

But now? Ma would have to figure out how she was going to soothe Kylah at night and to come clean to her in an age-appropriate way and stop smoking and drinking to avoid that reality like a mother was supposed to do. I was adopting too many parent roles, and sometimes, it felt like Ma was taking advantage of it.

"I got a few things I wanna talk to you about, Ma. I know everybody here been kinda going through the motions for the last few weeks, but I think it's time to start coming back to reality and start talking about some real things," I said as I leaned my head on her shoulder.

I didn't care about the bar smell clinging to her clothes. Even though I was grown, everything that has happened with the two of us drove a serious wedge between us. Ma and I were inseparable when we lived in Chicago.

"Oh wow. I haven't felt you lean on me like this since you were eleven or twelve-years-old. When you were my sweet baby boy. What's going on with you?" she asked as her arm wrapped around me and pulled me closer to snuggle.

"Well, can I start with just some questions about certain things? You won't dismiss me or anything, right?" I asked without giving her my eyes.

"Hmph." She chuckled in her throat and took a puff of the cancer stick. "No. I've learned my lessons about doing that to you. So, what's up?"

"What happened with the school lawsuit? You only said somethin' about it once, but I've never seen you go to an appointment or anything with a lawyer. Everything good with that?"

"Um… well… things were going well at first. But now that I've gotten that twenty-five thousand from the fifty thousand we split, I kinda feel like we don't need to go through the stress." Her shoulder that I rested on shrugged.

I frowned and lifted from her body with a frown.

"You saying you only did the lawsuit to get money?" I asked.

Not only did her body tense up, but so did the air between us.

"Oh! No, it's not that. It's that we've been going through so much. I don't want to put us through the ringer with a legal battle when no one is truly going to be held accountable for all the things they put you through. All they gon' do is give us money. We already have that now. I wanted justice in a whole different way. The principal did resign, so that's justice in some way. A little bit. I just want people to see you as a human. And to see you for the special person you are. I'm sorry if that came off as just wanting the lawsuit for money," Ma explained.

"S'cool. You made it more clear, so thank you." I smiled and rested my head back on her shoulder.

"Good. Speaking of legal stuff, I paid your fines for the whole Martell situation. Thank God, they reduced it to just a misdemeanor and not a felony," she revealed, fanning herself.

Yeah, that whole court situation about fighting at school was for the birds. Thank goodness Ma did file a lawsuit against the school because that was probably the only reason why I wasn't doing a year in the slammer for the way I messed Martell up a couple months ago. That, and the judge's knowledge that I was going to therapy on a consistent basis with a log record to show for it.

"How much was it?" I inquired.

"Fifteen hundred."

"Oh, that's not that bad. I think the max was ten thousand."

"Yeah, so I'm glad it got reduced. Now, we won't have to worry about any of that anymore," Ma said.

"True," I said as she leaned forward to reach for her beer on the table in front of us, the pee-smelling liquid tickling my nose. This wasn't good. I hoped it was her first beer and not the fourth or fifth. "You know Ma?"

"Yeah?"

"I think you should try going to therapy yourself," I suggested. "It's helped me. I think you'd benefit from it, too. I know you're kinda avoiding it to stay strong for us, but you ain't gotta hide nothing anymore. Nathan's gone. I'm grown now, and you should want to be your best self for Kylah. It's still early with her, so you can start fresh."

She swayed her head back and forth.

"You know? I thought about it, but I just don't think I'm ready to face all the horrible things that have happened. It's not about staying strong for you all. It's about being scared."

Hmm. Straight honesty, no sugarcoat. I could respect that.

"I get it. I was scared, too. But once you get into it, it becomes something you wished you would've done a lot sooner. Trust me."

"Hmm. I'll think about it," Ma said.

"Well... here's something me and my therapist kinda been talkin' about, and I'm gonna need your help with it."

"What is it, sweetie?" she asked.

"Well..." I faltered.

"Everything okay?" Ma panicked.

"Yeah, everything cool. I just... I think I'm ready to move out and live on my own, Ma," I asserted.

Immediately, Ma grumbled.

"Um... what?"

"Yeah, Ma. I think it's time for me to move out and get my own spot," I confessed.

A long pause followed as her shoulder stiffened up against the side of my temple.

"You're... thinking about leaving here?" she stuttered.

"It's more than just thinking about it at this point. I'm serious," I said.

Before saying anything else, she straightened up, causing my head to fall to the wayside and forced me to sit up straight, too.

"Jarell... are you even ready for something like that? I mean, I know you're grown up now. You're nineteen, so I should've expected this would come sooner or later, but how are you going to support yourself? You don't even have a job lined up, nor have you talked to me much about your plans after high school. You didn't get your diploma, so there won't be too many opportunities out there for you," Ma said.

"I get what you sayin' and all, but I gotta branch out on my own someday, somehow. You know me. I'm independent, and I been walking these streets and navigating the world both blind and with sight for a while now without anybody's help. I figured stuff out on my own because I had to, so taking care of myself ain't new to me. I'm sure I'll figure out the whole job thing later, but in the meantime, I could apply for disability. I shoulda did that last year when I turned eighteen," I said.

She groaned with reluctance.

"Yeah, but I just didn't think you needed to apply for it yet because you're living here. But I suppose since you're thinking of leaving and going on your own, I guess it would be time to look into that, huh?"

"Yeah. Don't tell me you put it off because you ain't want me to leave or somethin'…"

"Well… I mean…" she fumbled, her hands resting on her lap beside me as one of her fingers brushed against my thigh.

"You can't protect me forever, and I been without protection when I was much younger so…"

"I know. I just… Jarell… it's hard. With everything that has happened to you and everything that I've allowed to happen… even with kicking you out after mentioning what Nathan had done to me… I just …"

"Ma. I get it, but there's nothing you can do that'll change my mind. I need this for me. Please. I just need you to help me out," I begged. "Help me find a spot and help me move in there. I've never asked you for much of anything my entire life. But this right here is important to me."

My eyes softened. She puffed and took a swig.

"I want to help. I do, but… I just don't want you to be alone while you've had such serious thoughts of harming yourself. I don't want you to turn up dead by suicide," Ma admitted, her voice how shaking.

Damn, she was still stuck on that? I wasn't convinced. Her high pitch told me everything.

"Nah. Ma, what's holding you back from letting me go? Can you be real with me instead of skating around it?" I blinked.

Another long pause before a deep exhale as her head leaned back.

"I'm just… I don't know. I'm not ready to let you go because… well for a lot of reasons, Jarell. The main one being your health and safety."

"I haven't had thoughts of suicide for a while now," I said.

"Define a while."

Damn…

"About three weeks."

"Hell naw, Jarell. Three weeks? That's not enough time to believe you wouldn't do it. I can't have you out here doing anything self-destructive when I don't have my eye on you and when your sister isn't around to stop you," she objected as she flew to stand up.

"Ma, I understand! But look. Therapy has been helping me with that. I promise. I'm not gonna hurt myself. I just need to be on my own. I don't know what else to say or what else to do to make you understand that it's the best thing for me. Like I said. I'm not one to beg. When you say no, I usually just back down, but I ain't backing away from nothing this time. Especially this. I need you to help me for once."

She grumbled, but I wasn't gonna let that deter me.

"I just… I understand everything that happened to us since we got kicked out the Wells was rough. I realized most of it ain't your fault, and I'ma be honest. I resented you a lot for everything, but I'm learning to forgive and move on. I just need you to be a mother to me, Ma. I want you to be a mom to me the way you are to Kylah, alright? Please," I whispered. "Please help me."

She left me in the quiet and verbal dark for a while as she put out the remaining cigarette in her ashtray and pulled out another cigarette. I frowned and tried so hard to not shake my head. A glass thump hit the small round coffee table in front of us. The way its echo bounced off the table indicated its emptiness. Man… I had to get through to her, now! Before she got too messed up to even engage.

"Please, Ma."

"I guess you're right, Jarell," she finally spoke. "I mean, you're technically an adult, and I can't argue. I gotta let you fly your wings at some point, right? With my support."

"Fasho," I agreed.

"I'm hearing you. As much as I may not agree, I'll help you. I'll help you with the apartment and with applying for disability. But I got more to say before you leave this living room," she started with a heavy voice.

"What, now? What I do?" I said full of dread.

"Nothing. I just wanna say that I'm proud of you, Jarell. You are a survivor in every way. Your path to healing and watching how therapy has changed you in even little ways has been inspiring for me. I know I haven't said it, but it's true. I will always be proud of you, okay? I've never met anyone as strong as you. I love you, Jarell."

Man... I wasn't no pussy ass nigga, but moms was finna make a nigga tear up for real.

"Ma... save the flatter..." I mumbled and turned my head away with one corner of my mouth lifted upward.

"Don't give me that. Come give Mommy a hug. Remember when you used to call me Mommy?"

I groaned and threw my head back with a smirk. She laughed out loud.

"How could I forget? You always used to cramp my style with that shi- I mean stuff."

With a swift swing, she smacked the top of my head as I laughed and playfully ducked away.

"Stop cussing. Anyway. I miss those days so much. Seriously. If you're gonna be moving out, I want my hugs again," she said through a smile.

"Alright, alright," I moped and stood up. "Fine."

With a huge embrace, Ma wrapped her arms around my midsection and squeezed the life out of me as her head rested on my chest. Short self.

"Dang, Ma! You gon' kill me!" I chuckled.

"I'm so proud of you, baby. I can't say it enough."

My cheeks heated. "Thanks, Ma. It ain't nothing."

"Yes it is. It is something. You don't understand how strong and how special you are. My baby is growing up! I can't take it."

"I been grown, Ma. This ain't new. Let me go," I said, still grinning. She was doing way too much now.

"You're handsome. You're getting so tall. I still feel like you're growing. I hope you and Jade get back together one day," Ma said.

I nearly stumbled.

"How you know we even broke up?" I asked, taking a step back and looking down towards her with a raised eyebrow.

"Don't worry 'bout alla dat. Just know Mama knows."

"Yeah, whatever. Since you helpin' me now, I'ma go start taking things down in my room and clearing out stuff I won't need," I replied after giving her pursed lips.

"Whatever you gotta do to make yourself feel good about starting this journey." She sighed. "You can tell Kylah whenever you're ready. No pressure."

"A'ight. Thanks, Ma. I appreciate this."

"No problem, baby."

I walked towards my room counting my wins and blessings. There was so much more I coulda talked to Ma about. I could've apologized for resenting and blaming her for everything that had happened. I could've talked about how I still felt some hesitation trusting her, because it was my truth. I hadn't forgiven and forgotten, yet. I could've talked about our past life and allowed for us to come to terms with some things together.

But I didn't.

I'ma save it for later. We had the rest of our lives to do that. This right here though? This was icing on the cake. I had finally gotten what I wanted and what I deserved. The first major thing in my life. It was almost overwhelming.

Taking advantage and now that this support felt solidified, I sat down in my room and wrote down a few important things to myself to keep, reflect on, and use as long-term goals as I start this path on my own.

Promise #1: Grow to love yourself. Unconditionally.

Promise #2: Don't be afraid to be vulnerable with yourself and others.

Promise #3: Connect with Jade again when your heart is open and ready. She may or may not be available, or may not even be around, but you won't live in regret if you tried her again.

I smiled, folded my paper, and put it in an envelope to not be opened again for another few years and began taking down my origami from the ceilings. Ma was probably dancing on the inside, since she would now have her own room to be in instead of sleeping on the couch every day. She would even have a place to put her clothes!

Shit. A nigga was just grateful that I had another chance at life. Another chance at starting over. And another chance at figuring out what love is, its different forms, and what it can be.

I laughed to myself. Man... there had to be a God out there. I wasn't supposed to make it out none of the shit thrown my way in my life.

I wasn't supposed to be alive.

I had the worst life and the worst past. I didn't think anybody could suffer any more than I did. But I was still standing. I've learned I have so much fight in me. And I was ready. For healing. Growth. Peace. Just ready for a new me and a brand-new future. That I could control.

Like my therapist said.

Meet the Author

Author Janee' Thompson writes realistic Young Adult and New Adult novels that capture the unique experiences of young Black men and women taking it day by day through their own personal struggles. While many popular novels for Black teens and new adults focus on racial tension and navigating racial oppression through a youthful perspective, Janee' intentionally creates masterpieces that de-sensationalizes racial trauma and focuses solely on characters' individuality amid their Blackness. This is what makes Janee' a unique writer within these genres — experiences of anti-Black oppression rear its ugly head every day. We shouldn't be subjected to read about it for entertainment. We are more than our oppression.

Janee's why and passion for writing lies in building empathy and seeing her imaginative characters go through transformation and personal growth. Although her writing is strictly for entertainment for ages fifteen and older, she does tackle serious issues such as friendship, bullying, sex and sexuality, mental health, homophobia, falling in love, and family dynamics within the Black culture in hopes that the reader will grow with the characters, too.

Janee' grew up in Southeastern Wisconsin and she is a K-8 educator. She has a Bachelor's degree in Elementary Education with a minor in English, and a certificate in Creative Writing. She also has a Master's degree in K-12 Educational Leadership and Policy Analysis. She has won several career and community awards such as the Early Career Educator Award, City-County Humanitarian Award, International Literacy Association 30 under 30 recipient, and is a PEOPLE Program Scholar.

In her personal life, she has a handsome husband, and she loves shopping, singing, playing basketball, and of course, writing. She is a staunch advocate for children's success, racial equity, and any and everything Black.

No Ordinary Vengeance Soundtrack

Eyes On Us - Amber Olivier

Trauma - H.E.R. ft. Cordae

Gettin' Too Heavy - 3LW

Girl Like Me - Jazmine Sullivan ft. H.E.R.

Let 'Em Go - Allure

Lovely - Billie Eilish & Khalid

My Future - Billie Eilish

Release Me - Blaque

This Way - Khalid ft. H.E.R.

Real Upgrade - Tink

Bad Blood - NAO

Demonz - Juice WRLD ft. Brent Faiyaz

Bitter - LAYA

Nothing Burns Like the Cold - Snoh Aalegra

Worse - Snoh Aalegra

Gravity - Brent Faiyaz ft. Tyler the Creator

Pick Up Your Feelings - Jazmine Sullivan

10k Hours - Jhene' Aiko ft. Nas

So Done - Alicia Keys ft. Khalid